Sleeping Waters Awake

A Western Colorado Story

Sleeping Waters Awake

A Western Colorado Story

Chamaine Ready

This book was made possible by years of tender loving care on the part of my parents. Sleeping Waters Awake was born from a genuine love for others and a desire to search the truth, because truth matters. I am forever grateful to have been raised by caring people who were brave enough to share a story that they themselves did not live, simply because the lives of the people involved have significance. Even in death, these lives carry eternal value. It is a rare thing to find those who tell stories simply because the characters within them have something to contribute to the rest of the world.

Mom and Dad, you are in fact, beautifully rare.

Many others took part in this journey of justice and for them I am also grateful.

You know who you are:

Thad, Rhonda, Blake, Jennifer, Courtney, Leah, Melissa,

just to name a few.

To my children and grandchildren, I am grateful for your patience and understanding. This was a process that took time; time that I wanted to spend with you. However, this book is for you. You must never lose sight of the truth that people matter. When you engage in the stories of others, you are connecting with others and sharing in their importance.

Finally, this story is dedicated to women and children everywhere who are victims of crime. This is only one story in an ocean of injustices against women and children.

Their lives matter.

My Place

It's here.
The place I stand.
This peaceful place, in a peaceful land.
A silent space of waters blue,
With ripples soft and breezes few.
No thoughts of darkness from the past,
No cares for tomorrow's questions asked.
All that's here has calmed my way,
Reflecting colors of light, just for this day.
Forever I long to be here still,
I'd stay forever, in forever's will.
If I could carry it with me, all my life,
Holding it dear through all the strife;
But then where would I go?
Where would be my escape?
When new trials call,
When my will, I must shape?
There is another place I know,
Just like this one.
And when it's time, there I'll go.
But for now, this place holds me still
To ponder the raindrops, with wonder fulfilled.
How many raindrops will it take for me?
Falling on me, in me, for peace, this peace I need.

Betsy Kendall, 1975

Chapter 1

It was late into the morning of August 23, 1975, nearing the noon hour, and the sky was already fired up hot. Five-year-old Tristan was content to be wearing nothing more than a tee-shirt and his white little boy briefs. Had his mother been there, he certainly would have been dressed. He wondered where she was, his mother. It was very much unlike her to be nowhere in sight. Earlier, in the wee hours of the morning, he had looked for her. He checked the kitchen first, which is where he often found her. He then circled back into the bathroom, peeked into the big bedroom, finally landing in the small living room, calling her name, expecting her to chase him down with her sweet welcoming grin. She didn't. He thought of the nightmare he had, which seemed like so long ago. He didn't know for sure if it had really been a nightmare. He only remembered crying and stammering back to bed in a stupor when she wasn't in her bed. The whimpering was fresh in his mind. That certainly had happened.

Trey looked for her too. He was only two years of age, but if his big brother did it, so would he. He followed the big family dog, Bear, around the house and throughout the yard. Certainly, Bear would know where she was. Her intelligent nose had never failed them before. Trey had no reason to think of how unusual it was that the back door was already open when they aimlessly walked through the kitchen and into the back yard. He nestled his tiny little bum into the dirt to sit with Bear, as she took a break to rest herself beneath a row of drooping sunflower

1

stalks. Trey looked up into the midst of the sunflowers sagging down close to the ground, and he reached for the withering leaves, picking at the petals that had lost their luster. Some petals broke free and floated to the ground. He didn't question why. At his young age, he had no reason to think of such things. Tristan noticed. He watched intently as the petals fell slowly to the earth. His mother had planted those flowers. She had cut a few and gently placed them in a vase on the kitchen table. Thinking of those pale-yellow petals and the fingers that had so carefully handled them, made Tristan's stomach hurt. He thought it was because he was hungry, which he was. But somehow, he sensed that there was more to it than that.

By mid-afternoon, Trey had freed himself of his dirty tee-shirt and it lay lonely in the back yard tussled in a sandy mess. Tristan had managed to rummage throughout the kitchen trying to find something to eat. He and Trey certainly needed to eat. He had seen his mother do this many times before. The refrigerator had a couple of tomatoes in the bottom drawer. He didn't like tomatoes. The loaf of bread would do. *Bu...but, where's the...the peanut butter? I...I can't find the peanut butter. Mamma.... mamma, where... I... I need the peanut butter.* He gave up on the peanut butter sandwiches when his search in the refrigerator could not produce the peanut butter. When Trey came toddling into the kitchen, Tristan had muscled a chair up to the counter. *Cereal. Mamma gets...gets the cereal from up...up here.*

Trey looked lost. Why was mother not making them put on clean clothes? Where was breakfast? "Where Mamma go?" Both of his tiny hands were in the air, palms to the sky. Tristan looked to him with sad disappointment. "D...D...Don't...don't know, Trey. C'mon. C'mon" He climbed back down to the floor, but only after grabbing the box of Cornflakes close to his side. He took Trey by the hand, clinging the box even tighter with his elbow. "Sh...sh...she'll be back. Real soon. Ya...Ya. Soon."

2

Time passed the day away and she didn't come soon. She didn't come at all. Tristan now was the lost one. He hardly spoke, even when Trey cried because the cereal, he had eaten no longer fueled him. They both made attempts to entertain themselves in the front yard. Trey whined for something more to eat. Tristan shuffled into the house and back onto the counter again. *The...the cookies. Where.... where are the...the cookies?* He remembered that she had put foil over the top of the tray the night before. He had watched her do it. Climbing back onto the counter, he carefully crawled on all fours until he saw it- the shiny gray cover, with light dancing off its wrinkled surface. Of course, she had hid them in the corner next to the refrigerator, where they wouldn't be able to see.

Climbing down slowly, Tristan was quite thoughtful of his care package. Placing it on the table, he tore off the foil. Trey had been at his heels the whole time and stood wide eyed in anticipation. There were at least eight cookies staring up at him. That would certainly do the trick for now. He looked around the kitchen, expecting their mother to come around the corner and playfully warn him that he could have only one. Tristan expected this too, but something made him dreadfully afraid that this may never happen again. He grabbed a handful of cookies, handing several over to Trey. He wanted to sit in the middle of the kitchen floor and sob, but he couldn't. Trey looked at him with the hopeful trust of a lost kitten in the arms of a sweet child. Tristan's chest hurt now (not just his stomach). As he led his pint-sized brother back outside to the sagging sunflowers, he glanced around the living room one more time.

Where...where are you Mamma? Where are...are you?

Chapter 2

Sweaty tension made its way down Karla's chest, seeping down into the awkward strides that released her anxious thoughts. She walked with a purpose. As she approached the metal framed glass door, she stopped to breathe. *She's found something. That's why she called. Certainly, she's found something.*

Once inside the office building, Karla leaned her elbows onto the sterile white surface of the counter. "I have an appointment. My name's Karla Galletti." She politely smiled while fidgeting with a lost paperclip on the counter. The receptionist smiled back and made a quick call. "Just have a seat. She'll be right out." Karla didn't hesitate to settle into the waiting area with a woman's health magazine as a distraction. The date of February 2012 in the top right corner indicated it was a few years old. *They should toss these when they're more than a year old. Everything in here's already outdated. Guess it doesn't matter, just passing the time anyway.*

Just about the time she finished an article on the health benefits of garlic, her appointment came calling. Karla didn't say much. Instead, she let her eyes of anticipation do the talking. The law intern that Karla had met in college was less transparent with her well-manicured posture. The pretty young woman with the business suit and promising future smiled quick and short then hesitated before speaking. "Ok. I have to be honest, this isn't going to be easy. The information you gave me isn't matching up with anything I find. I need more to go on, Karla. I've done a few wide scale searches and came up with some local names. But

4

none match anything you've given me. I've found names that could possibly match, but then the ages don't. Are you sure she lived in this county? You have to get me more, Karla, I'm sorry. I just don't have enough. Work on him some more, and maybe give it more time. These things can be delicate, and timing is everything."

"More time? I'm twenty-three years old. How much time does he need?"

"Just hang in there and keep trying to get him to open up. He's got to, eventually, right?"

"You don't know my Pop. My birth certificate, that should be everything you need, shouldn't it?"

"Well, yes, it should. But something's not right. Karla, I can't match up your birth certificate with what's in the system. It's not a county issued certificate. Here's what I got. Keep it. You should have one that's legit, anyway. I can't explain why they don't match or why the name isn't the same. That's not typical, or even reasonable. I need more information to move forward. I really am sorry. But, don't give up."

Easy for you to say.

Pushing out into the city sidewalk streets, Karla shook her head in confusion. *Damn it Pop! What is this? Why aren't they the same? For God's sake, Pop!* Winding her way around the corner to meet the bus, she mentally made plans for lunch. *Something with garlic.* The distant sound of an acoustic guitar grabbed her ear and she turned to meet it. Her breathing relaxed, and she stood listening to the raw street music with both admiration and envy. She watched closely as the musician's fingertips tapped gently away at the strings. *I could do that.* She smiled at the thought of how she had been able to master those last few chords she had learned. She dug into her purse, pulled out a five-dollar bill, and tossed it into the empty guitar case. "Thank you," she whispered to the young but well-worn face nodding back. Forgetting the heat and her thoughts, she loaded into the public bus full of body heat, alcohol, and cheap perfume, humming away the silence of those sitting blankly around her. No one noticed her. She was comfortable with that.

Lunch time came quickly. Karla's mood was light as she prepared the meal. Grabbing a bag of fresh garlic and a vine of tomatoes, she set to work. She completely submerged herself into the task. Humming a song, she had woken up to set the rhythm and pace of chopping and stirring. She had settled on a spicy tomato sauce that would cover the handmade pizza dough. It wouldn't be just any ordinary pizza. Her pizza crusts were thin and delicate, and she always painted them lightly with olive oil before baking. Once she topped the whole thing with feta cheese, it would certainly be a delight that her Pop would notice. He loved food.

As she finished the last touches of arranging the table settings, she heard the thumping of her father's heavy footsteps coming down the hardwood staircase outside the front door. The sound became louder as he approached the entrance to their two-story flat. Pulling the pizza from the oven, she straightened her posture while sliding it, a colorful array of reds, different hues of greens, and sprinkling of white, onto the table. She tilted her head slightly and grinned. *The lead chef from the college would be so proud!*

Ramone flew through the threshold of the room with a boisterous sigh, tossing his briefcase onto the bench near the door. "Hello, Princess! Oh, damn, you got lunch all ready. Good. I'm starving." He sat down, barely looking in her direction, and immediately started loading his plate, while unloading his plan. Without wasting any breath, he rambled. "So, you're planning on coming in today, right? We got a new client, and I'd like you there for the interview."

"Well, I...."

6

"So, you'll be there? It's a cold case, of sorts. Solved, supposedly. The client doesn't think so, though. Wants us to review and see what I can come up with to help him get what is needed, so he can move forward with legal proceedings for some kind of release or exoneration. We'll see what he's got, and if it's worth even moving forward. You'll need to set up and have the audio ready before he gets here."

Karla was picking at her food by this time, biting the inside of her lip between bites. "Well, ok. I was planning on finishing that song I started. And I need to stop by Angelo's. The manager said she'd take a look at my resume then give me a call. I know it's not the chef position I really want, but they are known for working people up into the kitchen team from the floor."

"I still don't know why you even applied. For God's sake, Karla, you have a job." He sprinkled red pepper onto his half-eaten slice of pizza.

Hesitating, she chose not to argue. "And, oh, while I was downtown, I saw this guitarist, down on 34th Avenue? He was playing something using the same chords that I just got down to a 'T'! I wanna add to the bridge of...you know...the song. You should hear it. I could play what I've got done so far. Later. You know, when we're done."

"Sure. Why were you on 34th this morning?"

"I had that meeting. You remember, with my friend from school? Remember? The one who ended up going to law school? The one...helping me...look for...Mom?"

Ramone stiffened up. Without looking up or slowing down his consumption of her masterpiece, he bit out sharply "You still on that kick? I told you, it's a waste of time. She doesn't want to be found. And I still have never been able to figure out how you got to be friends with this girl, anyway. You aren't interested in law at all."

7

Funny. He thinks I have friends.

Karla swallowed away her disappointment. Silence settled the space unnoticed. Silence that stayed around for several minutes. Finally, Ramone looked up. "Besides, we have work to do. Real work. This man, his name's Trey. He's a professor at the University, and his father was convicted of murder decades ago, when he was just a little tike. He's convinced he's innocent. Said he's inherited boxes of information to go through from his brother, and I certainly can't do it all by myself." Ramone checked his watch and pushed himself away from the table, with his fourth slice of half eaten pizza still on his plate. Karla had barely touched hers.

"It's time to get going. There's still a lot to be done. You wanna just bring that with you?" He nodded to her plate then stood up, quickly heading to the door.

"What about the leftovers? We can't just leave them out, Pop. I gotta clean up."

"Get them wrapped then." He turned to grab his briefcase and flew out of the door. As she wrapped what was left of lunch, she listened to his footsteps clumping up the stairs. Sighing slowly, her mind began to race with the thought of working another case. Her job of being the sidekick at a small private investigation practice wasn't her idea of a fulfilling career. She had gone to culinary school against his strongly vocalized wishes and had even entertained the idea of studying music theory. That never happened; although she had managed to buy herself a guitar and a keyboard. Unfortunately, she rarely played them away from the comfort of her bedroom. *Why the hell did he even give me piano lessons if he never wanted me to really play?*

Karla sat back down in her chair, with her elbows pressing into the table and her forehead resting in her hands. She fiddled with her short silky blonde hair, which was pulled back into a ponytail. Smoothing the surface of her hair, she rested the tips of her fingers onto the back of her neck. Her eyes scanned the room and settled on the front door, as she breathed away the tears that were attempting to escape.

Chapter 3

"1520 Parkerson Avenue. Yes, sir. It's a two-story brick building, we're upstairs. I'm looking forward to meeting you too." Karla hung up the phone and continued sorting the files in front of her.

"Was that Trey?" Ramone turned into the small waiting room bouncing with typical energy. One would think that a man of his relatively large build would move a little slower. His bushy white head of hair was a bit ruffled from having his hand pressed against his head as he worked.

"He said he pulled it up on his phone but wanted to make sure he had the right place."

"That means he's on his way. Did you get that set up for me? And, also, could you look something up for me before he gets here?"

Karla stared at him with a file in her hand. "Didn't you want me to get these put away first?"

"You're not done with that yet? There's this website. Trey and his late brother put together this site. I want you to have it up on your laptop so I can reference as we talk. Just bring in your laptop when you got it open."

Karla stacked her work into a corner near the coffee pot. She sat at her laptop and looked behind her. He was already gone. "Pop! Pop, what's the site?" She hoped he was in earshot. He wasn't. Getting up again, she made her way into his office. "Pop, what's the site?" He was bent over his own computer, which was much older and less user friendly than hers.

"This damn thing keeps freezing on me."

"You need a new one. Just shut it down. It probably just needs cleaned up. You have it on a schedule, right?" He didn't answer. She let it go. "So, what's this site? You didn't give me the site."

"Oh. Here." He wrote the website onto a sticky note and she quickly took it, without waiting to see if his computer was back up and running.

Once back at her own workstation, she quickly logged on and found bakersontruth.com, just in time to hear the door squeak open. Trey was younger than she had expected. Although, she wasn't sure what she had expected. She had conjured up the image of the stereotypical professor, with the grey comb over hairdo, the glasses and a book in hand. Trey was in his late thirties to early forties, with a full head of well-groomed hair, and his smile spoke of authenticity, not the pretension sometimes predictable with a title of "professor". He was, well, normal. So much for stereotypes.

Standing up quickly, Karla greeted him with a genuine smile of her own. "Hello! I spoke to you on the phone." She reached out her hand "I'm Karla. Very nice to meet you."

"It's good to meet you as well."

"Let me tell the old man that you're here." She stepped away into an adjoining doorway, taking her laptop along.

Within seconds Ramone appeared, holding out his hand with an exuberant grin. "Good morning to you, sir! Come on back. Let's talk."

Trey simply nodded, seeming a bit anxious while scanning the space around him as they entered Ramone's office. The two men sat in century aged wooden chairs at a table that was losing its shine and riddled with stains. "I can bring in coffee. Just made a new pot," Karla declared proudly. With Trey's smile of approval, Karla didn't waste time, "Do you take anything in it?" Trey declined and thanked her as she disappeared into the other room.

Ramone clicked to a particular page of the bakersontruth.com website in front of him, as Trey quietly waited. When Karla snuck in a cup of coffee for each of them, Trey whispered, "Thank you", then leaned forward to see what Ramone was reading. Ramone sipped a quick drink. "There's a hell of a lotta information here. How long you been working on this?"

"All of my adult life, really. My brother, Tristan, he did a great deal of the research, and built the website, so he pretty much headed up the charge. I first started looking into this when I was a teenager."

"Do you mind me asking how your brother died?"

"Not at all. It was an auto accident. Motorcycle. It's been hard. We were very close, he was a great brother. A great person."

Karla sat across the table ready to take notes. She sat still, feeling compassion, as she watched Trey's demeanor change. He leaned back and shifted in his chair and took a drink of coffee. Ramone broke the thoughtful mood. "So you said that since your brother passed you've taken over all of this. Have you updated the site with anything new?"

"No. But it needs to be. I have found that some of the information may not be as accurate as I thought, or just needs verifying. Tristan got much of what's in there from interviews, and I'm finding that some of it hasn't been validated. Don't get me wrong, most of it can be, but I want it all to be supported well."

12

"Of course. So, what's your overall agenda?"

"To determine his innocence, of course. We can't go for another trial, he already had two. But there are other legal actions that can be taken. I need solid evidence. Even though he was convicted on nothing more than circumstantial evidence, circumstantial evidence won't get his conviction another look."

"Yes, I've brushed over the evidence, and you're right. The evidence against him was weak. Circumstantial at best."

Karla listened. Not just to his words. Trey fidgeted with his coffee cup and leaned back again into his seat. Then fidgeted more.

"Tell me about your father." Ramone's open -ended questions were intentional.

"He's a complicated man, that's for certain."

"Complicated? How so?" This time Ramone leaned back.

"Well, for starters, he's highly intelligent, and that can be misinterpreted. Sometimes its mind blowing. Intriguing and misleading all at the same time. He's often seen as arrogant. Throws his intelligence around. Makes people uncomfortable. You have to know him to understand him. Really know him. He's just not an easy man to figure out. His character was put in question in both trials. It seemed there was a great deal of character bias affecting the perception of the facts. The character bias, I get. It was well deserved. The distortion of the facts, that's another thing altogether."

"So, in other words, he didn't make much of an impression with people. Huh?"

"That's an understatement."

13

"So, even your perception of him is limited, right? He's been in prison for nearly 40 years." Ramone pressed.

"Oh, of course. Yes, my frame of reference is limited. But we write letters. Lots of letters. And I visit regularly, have my whole life. His letters are priceless. Full of so much. I mean, vividly detailed and an endless stream of information. He's meticulous about anything technical. I get lost in his five-page descriptions of the makings of a camera, when all I asked him to tell me was what he liked to use best. I mean, I like it. I do. I just don't always know where he's going with it all."

"Does he answer your questions? Do you have any doubts at all that he killed anyone? I mean, you say he's innocent, but you obviously have many questions, or you wouldn't be here. Does he have answers for you?"

"Sometimes. He can ramble about things that I don't need to know, but, yes, he seems to talk straight much of the time. Oh, he's not been a saint. That's for certain. Admits that himself. I mean he said right off the bat when being questioned that he was headed in the wrong direction, doing things that would eventually land him in jail. He was open about his illegal conduct. I know there were things he was involved in that were shady. He wasn't nice to people at all. He was a terrible husband. He knows all that, admitted the error of his ways. But he didn't kill anyone. The evidence just doesn't say so. A lot of evidence was kept out of the trial. And the headlines, well, they only printed what made him seem guilty. You compare what he said back then to his version of what happened, to all the letters he's written, to what he's saying now. Nothing's changed. His story is consistent. He has an impeccable track record in prison. Nothing I've come up with says he's a murderer. The evidence against his conviction, in favor of innocence, only gets stronger as time goes on, and the prosecution's case only gets weaker the more I dig."

There was a sense of awkwardness in the room as Trey spoke. Though both men were unaware of it, Karla paid attention to such things. Feelings of conflict and frustration were all too familiar. *Stop and breathe, Pop. You're missing it.* Even at 64 years of age, Ramone hadn't begun to lose his mental clarity. He had graduated from the police academy with top honors and successfully worked his way up the ladder of law enforcement success. When he retired, he had no choice but to open a private investigative practice, just to keep from getting bored. He was all about the chase. The chase for information and truth. For Justice. Even for those who may not appear to deserve it.

I know you're no stranger to conflict, Pop. Stop listening with your head all the time, will you?

Ramone spoke frankly, "What exactly are you wanting from me?"

"Well, objectivity, I guess. And someone I can trust. Yes, that's it, someone I can trust. Time is ticking, you know. I feel like I'm running out of time. He's running out of time."

Karla spoke up, almost startling them both. "How long has he been in again?"

"Getting close to 40 years." He shook his head in disbelief. "A lifetime, really."

"You've visited him often?"

"Oh, absolutely. Every year, all my life. The whole family. We all go. I usually go up to Colorado to see my grandparents as often as I can, and we stop to see him while we're up there."

Ramone was content to move forward. "Well, just looking at what you have put together, I see holes in the prosecutor's case. It could come up empty, but I'd be happy to help you out the best I can."

I knew you would, Pop. I knew you would.

The two men held out their hands to bestow the universal symbol of trust. Ramone smiled. "Besides, I've got an old friend who lives up in that area. You probably don't remember him, Princess, but you used to climb all over him like a jungle gym." He let out a short chuckle, then went on. "He'll be a help to us with all the locals. Bill's been there since 1978, and probably remembers the case. You said the second trial wasn't until '81?" The quick pause wasn't enough for Trey to answer. "He retired from the police department up there. I remember when he took the job, he said that things were a bit of a mess. But Bill, well, he stayed out of all the politics. Kept his nose outta business that he knew nothing about. It'll be nice to see him again. I think the last time he came down here for a visit, you couldn't've been more than eight." He wrapped his arm around Karla's shoulders as if she were still eight years old. She laughed it off as if this sort of thing happened often.

Trey relaxed, and his smile spoke volumes; but his eyes spoke of something slightly different. There seemed to be a longing of sorts. Karla watched him with wonder. So many questions she didn't dare to ask. But what she sensed for certain was his relief that there was someone out there who had a similar need to question what is at the surface and go deeper. Trey finally spoke up to clarify what Karla sensed he was feeling. "You know, the 1970's were a crazy time for so many people. But for me, they were my beginning, my welcome into this world. The earliest years of my life. I just wish I could remember them. If only I could remember more."

If only.

Immediately after Trey's departure Ramone sat down at his table, the room illuminated simply by the light of an old, slightly functional computer screen. Karla stood in the doorway and watched, then was surprised to feel the buzz of the cell phone in her pocket. She walked into the other room to answer it, hoping it was a call back from the restaurant. Her face lit up when the head chef on the other end of the call asked if she could come in for an interview. *The chef? I thought they were just looking for wait staff?* She agreed to a time and place and rushed back into Ramone's office to share the good news. As she rushed in, she expected Ramone to look up and see her anticipation. He didn't. Walking over to his side, she glanced to see what he was reading. *I guess it can wait until later.*

Ramone's eyes were scanning photographed images of an old article, looking ragged and torn with age. He studied the black and white picture of a house neatly situated on the page in simple journalistic fashion. Karla brought her face in closer to glance at the article from over his shoulder. It was a small house, with a large window in the front and a carport to the side, barely visible, deep alongside the back yard. A house typical of many in the 1970's. It was nestled on the quiet neighborhood street of Ouray Avenue, in the ever-enlarging family friendly city of Grand Junction, Colorado. This single-family structure was the home in which Mr. and Mrs. Curtis Bakerson had once resided with their two small boys, Tristan and Trey.

As Ramone studied the magazine article more intensely, he turned to the next page. "Looks like a beautiful place, don't you think?"

"Sure." Karla wasn't looking at the picturesque scene of the Gunnison River flowing silently on the page to the left. She was distracted by other black and white photographs on the opposite page. Photographs that depicted poses of picture perfection, smiles and all.

Beautiful indeed.

Karla hesitated and brought her mind to where Ramone's eyes had settled.

"So. What's up with all of this?" She pointed to the full-page photo he was studying.

"That's the crime scene."

"Oh." The photos took on new meaning.

Karla thought back to an American history class that she had taken. A section on mid-western United States discussed the two rivers of that area, and the role they played in Ute Indian culture. The merging of the Grand and Gunnison Rivers were the backbone to a lasting settlement of the area. Without these rivers, life wouldn't have been sustainable in this desert valley wrapped loosely in mountain terrain.

Ramone stretched his arms to the ceiling. "So, you should start packing. I'll get us a flight out as soon as possible. Maybe this week, if I can."

"That soon?"

"Well, I already called Bill. He knows we're coming."

"I knew you already had your mind made up. Why did you wait to tell me?"

"Well, yes, I was interested the minute I looked at his website. But I had to meet him to be certain. Maybe he'd change his mind after meeting us. You never know."

"Who would turn you away?" She smirked. "After all, you're so damn charming." She tried to hide the subtle indignation creeping in.

He grinned back, taking her teasing as a sign of father-daughter affection. "Besides, I had to give Bill a call no matter what. I needed his insight, a case this old could be a pain in the ass to find information about. Wanted to make sure we weren't walking into something we couldn't handle. He's pretty excited to see you, anyway. Damn, he's been trying to get me to come up for years. It'll be a nice trip. Why wouldn't we go right away? No reason not to."

No, Pop. Guess not. I'll just call that restaurant back. No sense in even trying to get the job now.

Chapter 4

Ruth Bakerson closed her eyes, letting droplets of the morning light seep through her eyelids. *Home. So, this is home.* She stood in the backyard of her family's new house, laying out the landscape of the grass as it met up with the dirt patches lining the fence line. A breeze slid past her cheekbone as she opened her eyes to see Curtis lug a weighted cardboard box into the house with a heavy grunt. She walked over to his aide, "You alright? Should I go grab some help?" Heading toward the back door of the house Ruth looked around for someone to assist.

Young Tristan followed behind at the edge of Ruth's heels. He began to whine, tugging on her skirt, and Ruth turned to gobble him up into her arms with a slight grunt of her own. *You sure are getting too big for this these days.* Taking the camera from off her shoulder and hanging it around the top of the gate that led into the carport, she secured Tristan onto her back for a ride. The screen door clinked behind her as she politely bellowed into the kitchen, "Hey, where is everybody? Curtis is about to drop the box of books, I don't know...." She nearly ran right into Edward, Curtis' friend from their church, as he hurried passed her. Curtis' frustrated voice behind her caught her off guard. "I've got it. I'm fine." Edward winced a smile at her to ease the tension.

Ruth kissed Tristan's forehead after placing him to the floor. She instinctively turned around to rush back outside to retrieve little Trey. He hadn't been walking for long, and his tiny legs skirted awkwardly

20

behind their dog Bear, in the grass, who was leisurely strolling the yard. She paused to watch Trey settle himself in a patch of dirt, scooting his bottom into a comfortable spot to dig with his hands. *A garden. That's a good place for a garden.* It was a small and cozy yard. She imagined shrubs along the side of the house, and with the enclosed fencing, it would be ideal for a growing family. She glanced back over to the narrow section of dirt along the back fence line, bare and dry. *That's the place. Nothing elaborate, just a few flowers. Sunflowers, maybe.*

The clumsy St. Bernard roamed the property as if she had owned this space for years. Smiling into the sky, Ruth rustled Tristan's hair, who had followed her back outdoors. *Thank you, God. For my family. For the piano practices and choir meetings, trips to the mountains, walks along the riverbanks. Thank you for this yard, the garden I will plant. The dog. Everything.*

Ruth's thoughts were interrupted with Tristan running the perimeter of the yard, the grass under his skinny little legs. She chased him down, with Bear taking the lead. Swooping the child up from his armpits she twirled in circles watching his feet dangle in the crisp fall air. She heard male voices bellowing in laughter from the open kitchen window and plopped Tristan to the ground onto his bottom. Tristan tried to get up, but the twirling resumed in his inner ear, and he couldn't maintain a steady stance. Ruth giggled as she scooped up Trey from his perch in the dirt, to retreat into the house and get back to the work at hand. Tristan attempted to gain his balance and followed with an unsteady gait, close behind. Once inside the doorway, she slid Trey to the floor to watch both boys hustle their behinds into their new bedroom where their toys awaited them.

Ruth greeted two men standing near the Frigidaire talking lightheartedly with Curtis. "Hello! Hi Edward! Thank you for stopping by to help out." Her smile was infectious. "What have you brought in for me to unpack?" She peered into a large box on the floor.

21

Edward introduced Ruth to a man that she had yet to formally meet. "This is Grant, my cousin. I've been trying to get him to come to church. Thought if he met some folks who went there, he'd be more interested."

She smiled again. "So, you put him to work? That doesn't seem all that motivating. But, we do appreciate it. Thanks so much for coming over and helping."

Curtis watched intently as Grant nodded an inappropriate grin in her direction. Curtis' pleasant demeanor hardened, and he glanced past Ruth to the door. "Well, we do have a great deal of work to do, so we should get back to it. Shouldn't you be tending to the boys?" His voice was stark and demanding. This time Ruth's smile was forced. "Yes. I'll go check on them."

When Ruth came into the hallway, Tristan was peeking into the master bedroom with wonder. She directed both of them to follow her into the kitchen to help her unload a box of crude unmatched set of dinnerware. *Ok, even if they only watch, I'll be happy.* Just as she got to work, she glanced over to see Tristan dart in front of Curtis at the very moment that he collapsed a crate onto the kitchen table full of breakables. "For heaven's sakes Ruth, will you please make sure you're watching out for him? He's going to cause an accident." Curtis was polite, but the harshness of his voice was clear. *Alright, change in plans.* "C'mon boys, I'll do this later." She scooted them back to the bedroom, "Let's just play in here with your toys." She ruffled Trey's hair and kneeled down to dump a box of blocks and cars onto the floor in a heap.

Oh dear, I think I left my camera outside. "Listen you two, stay right here and play. Ok?" Ruth scurried down the hall to make her way back through the house. Still looking behind her, she failed to see in front of her and accidentally bumped into Curtis. He was visibly rushed with another heavy box in his arms. He shot her a stern look of disapproval and resumed his mission with increased intensity. Ruth followed him into their new bedroom to try and ease the tension. Curtis dropped the box to the floor with an unsteady and solid thud. He leaned over to the side to stretch his throbbing back.

"Do you want me to help you unload it?" Ruth sensed his aggravation.

"No. I got it. Just go back to whatever you were doing. Which was apparently not paying attention."

"I'm sorry. I just didn't see..."

"Stop making excuses and pay better attention. That's all."

"Well, here, let me..." Ruth reached down to begin opening the box, and he slapped her hand away. "I said you don't have to help me!"

She backed away a step, keeping her eyes fixed on his. "Ok. I'm sorry."

Curtis darted around Ruth, stopping just briefly enough to shove her out of the way with the palm of his hand. "Just stop playing around and get your own work done and let me do mine. Please." She perceived his tone exactly as he had intended: demeaning.

Ruth stood still for a few seconds to gain her sense of dignity, then made her way into the hallway. She peeked back into the children's bedroom once more to assure that they were both entertaining themselves. They were.

Once outside, Ruth grabbed her camera and stopped long enough to glance upwards and watch the clouds hovering close in the distance. *Those could dump any time.* She looked to the truckload of wooden furniture and Curtis' model airplane equipment parked in the carport. She yelled toward the house, hoping Curtis could hear through the open window "It's going to rain! You all should get out here and get these things inside as quickly as possible!" Ruth knew that if Curtis hadn't put away all of his equipment before the storm, she'd be the one to hear about it. As it turned out, he was in earshot. He peeked through the screen door. "That doesn't look so good."

Fall thunderstorms in the valley were a spectacle to the senses. As was typical, the storm on this day began in a dribble, sputtering the ground lightly. A gushing downpour accompanied by a majestic show of lightning could follow by nightfall. Knowing this, they all hurried their tasks along. Curtis found the rainy weather an inconvenience, but Ruth found it comforting. In spite of that, she knew they needed to get everything in, as not to not ruin what few possessions they had. Curtis had recently begun a new job, which would help a great deal financially. But they certainly didn't want to have to replace anything. Ruth knew deep down that if anything were to get damaged, it wouldn't be her things that would get replaced.

Curtis' new job was timely. Ruth was thrilled when it turned out that an old high school mentor of Curtis' had a home across the street. This man was no longer judging high school science talent, but instead had taken over a growing electronics company in need of good leadership, and now they needed a good pilot. Curtis was in fact a good pilot. Tri-Star manufacturing was in the midst of re-inventing itself, and the industry was on a forward roll that was soon to boom in ways that only wise investors could predict.

Curtis brushed past Ruth in the kitchen on his way out to the carport. She watched him as he passed, attempting to judge his countenance. Once Curtis had slipped through the door, Ruth felt confident to lift herself onto the counter to sort the top shelves, not realizing that Tristan had made his way into the kitchen. As she stood high on the counter with Tristan looking up at her in envy, Curtis bolted into the kitchen and halted, "What are you doing? Where's Trey?" He was clearly angry. Tristan froze, quiet and still.

24

"I'm putting these things away." It was difficult for Ruth to hold back her own escalating agitation. She did, nonetheless.

"Well, get down. Tristan's going to think it's ok to climb onto things. Where's Trey?"

"Trey's in the boy's room playing."

"We have a ladder in the shed that you can use. Worry about that later though and mind the children."

Suddenly, they were both distracted by a woman's panicked voice echoing in through the front screen door. They glanced at each other in confusion. The voice sounded distraught and full of fear. Ruth jumped from her perch and followed Curtis out the front door and into the drizzling rain. She warned Tristan to stay inside. "Go back to your room and stay with your brother." she commanded. He complied without question.

A young woman of about twenty-five, wearing cut off shorts and jogging barefoot down the street was yelling frantically. "Damn it Andrew! Andrew!....Blair!....C'mon boys! Where the hell...." She stopped short when she saw Ruth standing in her front yard and jogged over to her. "Have you seen two little boys? I ....I can't...."

Ruth immediately understood the problem. "What age? What were they wearing?"

"Andrew's about....." She was interrupted by Grant, who had emerged from the house following the sound of the mayhem. He swiftly made his way into the street to meet her. "Jesus, Betsy! What the hell?! What the hell is wrong with you? Can't you keep an eye on them for five minutes?!"

Betsy's eyes began to tear up and she shook her head in an attempt to defend herself. "I was! They were just…they were playing, and then I just, oh, fuck you, asshole! I was watchin' them. All I did was…."

Grant rushed past Betsy, toward her house across the street, as he called over his shoulder. "Never mind, let's just find them." Betsy stopped for a second to look at Ruth for help. Her chest heaved in and out, clearly in distress. Ruth walked over to her. "Don't worry, we'll find them. Kids wander off. It'll be ok." Ruth turned around to Curtis who was standing in the yard, baffled at the whole scene. She was prompted to make sure her own children were safe. "Would you check on the boys and make sure they stay in their room?"

Ruth stood in the street looking up and down in both directions to gain some clarity as to where to look. She caught sight of Bear, who was sniffing around the garbage can in her driveway. "Bear girl, how'd you get out?" *That's it!* Ruth sprinted passed the dog through the gate and into the back yard. Her chest sank in relief. She yelled as loud as she could, back into the direction of the street. "I found them! Here they are!" Ruth watched in sympathy as Betsy bolted toward her, splashing her bare feet on the asphalt, with tears streaming down her cheeks to match the droplets of rain dripping from her hair. Betsy stopped at the open gate and closed her eyes, breathing in deeply as soon as she saw her two boys, who were throwing rocks over the back fence into the alley. "Holy shit! Thank you so much. That scared the shit outta me!" Ruth held her breath hoping her children hadn't come anywhere near to hear this poor choice of language.

"You're damn lucky, girl! What's it gonna take for you to pay attention, for Christ's sake!" Grant was making his way into the carport, shaking his head at Betsy, as if she were a child.

"Shut the hell up! I was! What're you doing here, anyway?"

26

"Helping some friends of my cousin's move. Just get your kids and go home. Let these folks get back to settling in."

Ruth didn't know her, but she immediately felt sorry for her. "She's ok. I'm sorry they were able to sneak over here without any of us noticing." She glanced over to Grant, who immediately changed his accusatory tone, trying suddenly to appear supportive. "I guess we all should've known that they had walked over here. Here, I'll help you get them home."

Ruth caught him glancing her way, as she called Bear to come back into the yard, swinging the gate wide enough for all of them to get through. Betsy followed her lead, ignoring Grant's presence, turning to Ruth as they walked across the wet grass. "No. I'm sorry. All I did was just change my clothes, and when I came out, they were gone. Thanks for your help."

Ruth put her hand out to Betsy for a more formal greeting. "By the way, I'm Ruth. My husband, the one in the carport, is Curtis." *So much for asking him to check in on the boys.*

"I'm Betsy." She grimaced half a smile calling out to the two boys who were unaware of the panic they had caused. "Alright, you two! Get your little butts back to the house! You scared the shit outta me! Who said you could leave? You're gonna get you're butts tanned leavin' the house like that!" The two boys turned wide-eyed, realizing the trouble they were in. Ruth's spirit lit up at the realization that these two boys seemed to be right around the same age as Tristan and Trey.

Grant followed close behind them, unaware of the fact that Edward and Curtis were already back to work. Ruth sensed Grant behind her. She couldn't decide if this made her feel uncomfortable or flattered. He was, after all, an attractive man. She avoided the conflicting sense of his presence by turning her attention to Betsy's young boys. Intrigued by

27

the way they were dressed, or more accurately the lack of clothes, she felt inclined to invite Betsy to stay, in order to be helpful. *I'm sure I've got some things that would fit. Would it be rude to ask?*

Andrew, looking near the same age as Tristan, grabbed his brother's hand in retreat, wearing nothing but his white brief underpants, which by this time, were soaking wet. The rain had moistened the ground to a soft grime, which stuck in between his toes. Blair, in much the same manner, was dripping from head to toe. His cloth diaper was hanging nearly to his knees, as he jumped into a small slimy puddle. Ruth nearly laughed out loud, barely containing her amusement. *I hope that's just rain dripping from that diaper.* She smiled at Betsy as the boys heeded their mother's command, sliding their feet across the grass to clear away the muck they had managed to find along the fence line.

Grant, Ruth, and Betsy, with her children in hand, made their way toward the protection of the Bakerson's carport. Edward met them at the back doorway, annoyed to find Grant wasting time with the women. "Hey, the kids are fine. Let's get done what we came here to do." Grant shrugged his shoulders, "Sorry, ladies, I guess these nitwits can't unload a truck without me." He winked at Ruth, and then nodded to Betsy. "Make sure you get them some clothes on. Jeremiah will have you a good one, if he sees them out here in this rain like this."

Betsy rolled her eyes and turned to pick up Blair onto her hip. "They're fine. It's just a warm rain. Why don't you just mind your own damn business?"

Ruth tempered the tension she clearly sensed between them. "You know, I have some clothes that would fit them both perfectly. Would you like to bring them in to meet my boys? I know they would love to have someone to play with right now."

Betsy seemed delighted at the invitation. "That'd be great! I know, they look a mess, don't they? I just hadn't gotten them dressed yet."

"It's no bother. You can just bring the things back over another time."

"Oh, sure!" Betsy followed Ruth into the kitchen, and then into the boy's bedroom, where Tristan and Trey sat on the floor playing contentedly, having missed the whole dramatic event. They did, however, take special notice of the two unfamiliar boys in the doorway the minute they appeared.

Ruth immediately went to a box in the corner of the room to retrieve some dry clothes, while simultaneously introducing the strange wee ones who were anxiously standing in their underwear, beaming with anticipation. "Boys, this is Andrew and Blair. Say Hello. They're our new neighbors. C'mon, say hi. Don't be shy now. They've come over to play." Trey jumped up to meet them with a jiggle in his step. Tristan sat and watched them enter the room, eyeing Andrew as he took a seat next to him, who had noticed the train cars scattered on the floor. Ruth glanced over to Betsy, passing her a stack of folded clothes. "Would you and your children like a snack or some juice? I could also get some coffee brewing. It would only take a few minutes." She looked down to Tristan who was silent and still, in awe of the idea. He stared anxiously at Andrew, who was now grinning ear to ear at Tristan (while energetically bouncing up and down as he kneeled on the floor). Betsy took the clothes, then made her way to the bottom bunk of the boys' bunk bed. "You've got so much unpacked already and put away even. Shit the beds are even made! You got a lot done! Holy shit, girl!"

Ruth was slightly taken back and smiled an awkward grin as she looked around the room to see if her children had noticed the foul language. Fortunately, Trey, Andrew, and Blair hadn't even looked up from their giggling as they dug into the toy box. Tristan was standing close by looking at Betsy with a strange but curious stance. Ruth smiled at him, motioning a hand gesture to the toy box, giving him the permission to join the others. She looked to Betsy, who still held clothes in hand. "Oh, you're welcome to use the bathroom, just one door over, if you'd like to dress them in there." Ruth somehow wasn't surprised to watch Betsy stroll over to her boys and strip them naked right then and there, dressing them haphazardly as they attempted to play. She chuckled quietly as Tristan eyed the whole thing.

Once the children were somewhat occupied, Ruth was inclined to invite Betsy into the kitchen to make coffee and prepare snacks for the children. "Oh, I know I have a jar of peanut butter around here somewhere. I'm so sorry for the mess. I've just been putting things away as I go, but I haven't yet finished in here."

Betsy looked around, a bit taken back by the apology. Aside from an open box on the kitchen table and two empty boxes snuggled into a corner, one neatly stacked inside the other, the kitchen was bare.

"Here, I knew I must have put it in here, you know, in the cupboard near the fridge. My mother always said, food near food, dishes near dishes, makes for cooking efficiency." She shrugged her shoulders in jest and emitted a single chuckle. Betsy's smile in return was polite but confused.

Ruth didn't waste any time gathering the bread and paper plates, having peanut butter sandwiches made within minutes. Betsy stood watching in wonder, as Ruth sliced the sandwiches into perfect little triangles, and stacked them neatly on the plate. "Would you like to take these to the children? I'll be right in with the coffee and juice." As Betsy turned toward the doorway, Ruth spoke up again. "So, how do you know Grant?" She glanced around and through the doorway to the carport, making sure the men were occupied outside.

"Oh, just went to school together. Not that we're real close or anything. Just have a few friends in common, that's all. He knows my ex-husband, well soon to be ex-husband, anyway. How'd you guys become friends?"

"We just met him today. His cousin goes to our church. We sure appreciate their helping us. He didn't have to stop by. Seems a nice thing to do."

Betsy didn't bother to glance around to see if anyone was in earshot. "Well, you can bet there was something in it for him. Hmm." She laughed. "His cousin's into church? Who would've thought?" She shrugged her shoulders.

"Why do you say that?" Ruth was curious.

"Oh, nothing, really. Grant may be a cop, but he doesn't strike me as the churchy kind. Don't be thinking that cops are perfect angels just 'cause they've been given a badge."

"He seems nice enough."

"Oh, he is. He's really nice, if you wear a skirt. I mean, it's not like he does anything malicious or anything. I mean, he's law abiding and all. Just don't let that polite demeanor fool you." With that, Betsy strolled back into the boy's room to pass out sandwiches to the children.

When Ruth carefully shuffled back into the bedroom carrying a tray of paper cups half filled with juice, Betsy was sitting cross legged on the floor helping Blair and Trey keep a block tower stable to avoid tipping. "Careful, the big ones on the bottom. Like this, wait. Don't put that one on yet." She looked up to greet Ruth, shaking her head.

"Do you ever get tired of being ignored?"

31

"Always," Ruth laughed, "But, I must say, the boys are fairly good about minding me. Most of the time. Of course, not always." She paused. "Coffee's not quite ready yet. Here's some juice. But they have to sit. I normally don't allow snacks outside of the kitchen. But, if we sit with them, it should be fine." She closed the door and laid a blanket down for them to sit on.

Betsy followed, guiding her children to the blanket and taking the cups from the tray. "I bet they mind your husband. These boys worship their father. They do anything he says. I don't know why. It's not like he's around much."

"That's probably why. They hear us all the time. A father's voice can be novel sometimes."

"I guess that could be it. It's not fair, though. It's ok for him to just up and leave whenever he wants. He's even got a new girlfriend, my girlfriend by the way. Or she could be an old one by now, who knows. Leaves all the time, but he's the fun parent."

"Oh." Ruth stopped short, unsure how to respond. "Your husband has a girlfriend? I'm confused, one's a friend of yours as well? Oh, I'm so sorry. Are you trying to work things out?"

"Sure. If that's what it's called. We break up all the time, but yeah, I guess. I mean, I know I'm no saint. We had agreed to explore and be open minded. I just didn't think he'd go after my best friend." There was a silent pause. *Be open minded? What does that even mean?*

"Shit. It doesn't matter anyway. He'll come back. He always does. Hell, I don't know if I'll let 'I'm though."

Those words again.

Tristan looked to Ruth wide-eyed and cautious. This time Trey heard it too and he snickered in response. Tristan nodded his head back and forth at Trey in quiet reprimand.

"They're so cute! Look at 'em! You have adorable kids."

Kneeling on the floor, Tristan hesitated to join the stranger playing with his toys. With his hands on his bended knees, he sat still. Andrew, on the other hand, leaned in slightly toward Tristan with a grin, pushing the train engine in his hand toward Tristan in anticipation of a grin back.

As Tristan sensed that the two women were watching them, he looked to Ruth for security. "It's alright, dear, just play." She looked to Betsy, hoping she understood. "He's a little shy."

Betsy laughed out loud with raw compassion. "Andrew will bring him out of his shell!"

Within minutes, Ruth forgot about the boxes and the chores needing to be done. She sat content to be chatting and laughing, connecting in a way that only women in need of friendship can. Ruth relaxed even more as she learned more about Betsy. "So, are you able to be at home with your children most of the time, or do you work somewhere?"

"Oh, of course I'm home a lot. But, yeah, I work some. I'm a waitress. Right now I'm at the bowling alley just up the road. It's not bad work, you know. My best friend, well, I guess she's not my best friend anymore..." Betsy rolled her eyes in disgust. "...well, stupid little bitch. Anyway, she helped me get some work on the side, just doing a few things here and there. I don't make a lot, but with Jeremiah's help, I do ok. He does help. At least financially, anyway. He runs trucks. It's good work. Works for his family. They have their own business, building shit and stuff like that. Everyone in his family owns a business of some sort. I think they must got a lot of clout and money and shit in this town. At least that's what it seems like."

33

By this time Ruth was no longer personally taken back by the foul words. However, she continued to take a deep breath, watching her boys cautiously with each crude word.

"So, Grant I know, but there were a couple other guys outside, which one is yours?"

"The tall one. With the 'flat top' cut. He likes things neat and orderly, including his hair."

Betsy laughed loudly, which made Ruth smile a genuine smile of adoration.

"So, what about you guys? What's yer man do? You guys get it on much?" Betsy raised her eyebrows with a sly grin.

Ruth wasn't accustomed to talking about such personal things, so she ignored the latter question. "My husband is a pilot. He just acquired a new job a few months ago. They do some sort of electronic work. I really don't know much about it."

"Yeah? What about you?"

"Oh, I stay home with the kids. I have worked, but this new job of his should be enough for us. I used to work at the Daily Sentinel, and we've just started a new photography business together. I'm looking forward to building that. Curtis is quite the photographer, and I'm picking it up, too. It gets us out into all sorts of beautiful country together. I really enjoy it."

"That sounds fun! I like getting out, too. I get crazy all by myself. My friend and I, not the bitch, another friend, we love to go dancing. I'm big into music and going places. And I write a bit. Nothing fancy, you know. It's more just for fun."

"Writing is a wonderful hobby. I'm interested in music, too. I play piano. How nice that we both like music. I play at my church, and sing, too. Curtis sings in a men's quartet. You should come with us this next Sunday."

"I'm not so sure I'm into the whole church thing. I mean, my friend Derek, he's into church some. I was having some problems awhile back, and he had me go stay with some nuns. My ex-best friend, you know, the one, well, she dispatches for the city, and she always said it would be good for me to go to church more often. I mean the nuns, good women, and really kind and everything. But, I don't know about that whole not having sex thing. Damn, those women gotta be saints."

"I don't think you would have to stop having sex with your husband if you went to church," Ruth giggled, a bit embarrassed.

"Oh, no sweetie, not just with my husband. Besides he's not getting any from me any time soon! C'mon, women don't just have sex with their husbands anymore! Break away, sweetie, there's a whole world of opportunities for us women out there!"

Maybe that's why you're having marriage trouble. Ruth needed to change the subject. "You said you like to write? What kinds of things, like stories or poems?"

"Poems, mostly. I write about my feelings and life and shit. It's supposed to be healthy for your psyche. You should really try it. It's so freeing! Like you're putting all of you out there in the open for the gods of life to see!"

"I don't know that I want any gods of life seeing my thoughts," Ruth jested, trying to keep things light, "But, I do write sometimes, mostly about what I read. I love to read."

35

"Oh! I've got a great book! Derek just gave it to me. I haven't had a chance to read it yet. But I bet you'd love it! It sounds like you're a spiritual person, right? I'll bring it by sometime. I can't remember the name of it right now."

"Sure, bring it on over. I'll take a look at it." Ruth politely complied, doubting that she'd actually read anything that may include 'the gods' or 'breaking away'. *But, do tell me more about you.* "So, I'd like to read some of your writing if you'd be alright with that."

"Oh, hell, of course! I don't know too many people who has cared much. But, sure, I can let you read some." Betsy straightened her back slightly, sitting a little bit taller at the thought.

It certainly didn't feel like two hours had passed, and Ruth realized the time only because her boys were showing signs of hunger. Trey, being run down beyond his limit, was curled up against Ruth's chest sucking his two middle fingers. Tristan looked over to Ruth from behind his wooden structure and grinned. Ruth caught Betsy from the corner of her eye watching their boys play. *I like her.* Reluctantly, she suggested an end to their time together, keeping her from her duties. "I would love to do this again. It was so nice to get to know you. I should get back to all of the unpacking, though. There's just so much to do. Am I alright to stop over sometime?"

"Yeah! You bet! Just pop on over, I can tell the boys get along great!"

Yes, they do. And it seems, so do we.

Later that night, after dusk had settled around the house and Ruth had prepared her boys for bedtime, she curled up into the sofa and leaned back with a contented sigh. Curtis sat down beside her and pecked a kiss onto her cheek. Then, without much delay, stood back up again.

Ruth leaned up to him, "You should sit for a while. It's been a busy day."

"Oh, I'm fine, dear. I have a few things in the shed that still need a good cleaning. Did you finish with the kitchen and the bedrooms?"

"Fairly close. I visited with our new neighbor some. It's a shame how I came to meet her, with her losing track of her children and everything, but...."

"Hmmm. I wondered what had happened to you. I almost have everything done outside and, in the shed,, but need to finish some cleaning."

"She seems quite nice."

By this time, he had already turned his back to her and was walking into the kitchen to head out of the back door.

"She's really quite delightful!" Ruth raised her voice so that he could still hear her. "And did you know? Her children? They are the same age as Tristan and Trey. It couldn't be more perfect!" Her excitement rose as she elaborated, and by this time she was nearly yelling. Curtis halted his path in the opposite direction and turned around, peeking back into the living room.

"Have you seen Bear? She's not still outside, is she?"

Ruth lowered her voice, as well as her enthusiasm. "Yes, I brought her in right after dinner. I think she's in the bathroom. I found her there later this afternoon. She's taken a liking to the bathtub."

"The bathtub?"

"Maybe it's the coolness of the porcelain, I suppose."

Curtis resumed his stride out to the side carport with a head nod at the humor of a dog in a bathtub. Ruth would have enjoyed the humor as well, had she not just been side barred by the dog.

She turned to peek through the window out into the shadows of the street. Rain dropped lightly onto the asphalt in a rhythm that gave her a sense of stillness. The streetlights were few, but just enough to allow dim reflections to bounce from the wet surface. She could see the dark outline of the large building at the end of the street. It looked out of place among the rows of houses all around it. Ruth imagined a day when she would be able to teach her boys to ride bikes in the graveled parking lot. She had no plans to leave this neighborhood until her boys were well grown. That's how it is done in her world. You settled down and stayed there. You built roots. You built foundations.

Ruth's attention was diverted by a car which pulled up in front of Betsy's home. She watched as Betsy greeted a man intimately at her door. *Is that her husband? Of course not, he wouldn't be knocking at the door.* She watched Betsy kiss him, barely visible across the street, through the rain and dark shadows. *So, this is what it means to 'break away'. Seems merely broken.*

Chapter 5

After wiping down the countertop with a damp cloth, Ruth stretched a layer of clear Saran Wrap over the plate of freshly baked cookies. Working methodically, she smoothed the surface with a smile of pride. Her pace quickened, rushing out to the carport to dump the garbage, as the boys would be waking up soon. Taking in the overnight rain that had left behind the smell of wet foliage and muddy gravel, she shook away the morning chill. Glancing across the street Ruth saw Betsy in her doorway chatting frivolously with a man poised confidently on the step. Betsy waved to her, and Ruth gladly waved back.

Ruth started to head into the house but turned as she heard a car turn sharply into Betsy's driveway and screech to a stop. Another man emerged, slamming the car door behind him. Ruth could hear the squabble as it brewed. *This must be her soon to be ex-husband.* He was angry and loud, "What the hell is this, Betsy?! I'm not even gone a day, and you're already movin' on? Jesus, you're a tramp!"

"Get over yourself, asshole, he's just a friend! And who the hell'r you callin' me a tramp? Look in the mirror!"

The other man slowly backed away from Betsy in an attempt to casually go to his car. Jeremiah gave the man an angry nod. "What'r you afraid of? I'm just pickin' up some shit of mine. She's all yours. I don't give a shit anymore. She's crazy as a cyclone, anyway. Have at 'er. Just stay the hell away from my house and my boys. This place still belongs to me!" Jeremiah pushed his way into the house, as Betsy awkwardly stepped down to the grass. At that point, Ruth watched Betsy walk the dazed man to his car, her body language speaking of apologetic embarrassment. The man drove off, leaving Betsy standing in the grass. Ruth felt the inclination to go straight over there to console her. Instead, she snuck into the house, hoping that Betsy hadn't noticed her watching. *This is none of my business. Maybe I should wait to go over there. Or I could be a distraction. I bet she could use a distraction.*

Back in the house, as she reached for the box of oatmeal, she heard a light, barely audible patter behind her. Turning, she caught Tristan looking up at her beckoning for the morning ritual of tickling hugs. "C'mon little guy, I'll get you!" She chased him with giggles into the children's bedroom, and he rolled onto the mattress. Trey lay on the bed, kicking the wall with his fingers in his mouth.

Trey chuckled, and she wrapped her arms around the both of them, welcoming them to the morning. "Alright, you two. Up and at 'em. We've got things to do today." Trey crawled onto her lap, and she rested her chin on the top of his head.

"Wh...Where's Daddy?" Tristan asked, climbing from the mattress and heading toward the door. "He's at work, Darling." Tristan stood in the doorway, as if he was processing what that meant. In all reality, Ruth didn't know what that meant. She knew next to nothing about Curtis' new job, other than it involved flying. Of course it did, that's what Curtis did. He loved to fly.

Ruth grinned in recollection of the first time Curtis set up his electronic airplanes out in the parking lot of their previous apartment. The grown-up toys were quite intriguing and not really for the children. The model airplane hobby was not so much fun and games, as it was an engineer's tool for tinkering. To Curtis it was serious engineering, the way he often rebuilt the devices to suit his own preferences. However, Ruth remembered how the airplanes had put the boys in a trance to watch Curtis maneuver them in the air. Tristan's eyes had widened in bug eyed curiosity as if his father had held magical powers, while he watched the planes glide through the space above them. Curtis was just as entranced, like a child in his own world. That's how she viewed them.

Tristan didn't ponder his father's absence long, and in a matter of seconds was asking about breakfast. Ruth carried Trey on her hip and led them into the kitchen for oatmeal and raisins. From his perch on the kitchen chair, Tristan saw the plate on the counter wrapped in plastic. "Can... can I...I have ...cookies, please?" He slowly and politely asked. With the word 'cookies', Trey's eyes lit up. She sat down in the chair between them. "When we're all done with breakfast, we're going to get dressed to go see our new neighbor, Mrs. Betsy. You remember her, with Andrew and Blair? Remember?" This time, Tristan's eyes lit up as he bit his lip. "So, I...I can have one?"

"We get cookies when we go to see Mrs. Betsy and her boys. But we have to ask. When you give something to someone, it belongs to them. So, we have to ask. Alright?"

He nodded and Trey nodded too, watching and copying his brother. Ruth glanced up to the clock on the wall. *Good. It's been over an hour. Surely he'll be gone when we go over there.*

As they crossed the street, Ruth noticed Jeremiah's car still parked in the driveway. She took in a deep breath, worried about the unannounced visit. *Maybe we should turn around and go back home. That was a tense moment that I saw. We may be intruding into her personal matters. Maybe it'll be a good thing. Maybe she needs me to interrupt.* She couldn't quite sort out why Betsy's love life kept invading her thoughts. Betsy was a pretty girl, so the thought of her having to ward off suitors wasn't too surprising. *She's still married, though.* Not to mention, she wasn't exactly warding them off.

There was a spunky spirit about Betsy. She was less refined than Ruth's more mature acquaintances from church. Although different than what she was used to, she found Betsy to be somewhat refreshing. Even Betsy's appearance intrigued Ruth. She didn't seem to need much time prepping her look, having natural brown curls that lay casually around her face and onto her shoulders. Ruth, on the other hand, liked the predictability of rolling her hair in plastic curlers at night. She didn't curl excessively, just slightly on the ends of her straight and fairly short strands. Occasionally she might change it up a bit and pull it back away from her face. She typically pulled her hair back only when she needed to keep it out of her face.

Trey tripped clumsily over his own feet as Ruth hurried him along across the street. *It'll be alright. It could prove to be helpful.* "Wha we go, mamma?" She neared the concrete step leading into the home, with Tristan at her side, Trey clinging to her hip and the plate of cookies in her hand. She took in a slow and strong breath of the morning air and let it out just as slowly. *I sure hope this is alright.*

Before she had a chance to knock on the door, it swung open. Andrew stood before them grinning ear to ear. "Mommy! Mommy! Hurry!" He jumped up and down squealing with energy only a child is allowed to display.

"Oh my God! Look who's already up and shining this morning!" Betsy beamed as she opened the door. *So, it is alright. She's happy to see us.* Tristan hid behind Ruth's leg and peeked up at her for reassurance. Ruth smiled, "I brought cookies. I presume your young ones like cookies?" Betsy laughed, "Oh, God, they love food of any kind. C'mon- let's have breakfast!"

42

They walked inside a home laid out much the same as the Bakerson home. It was a small, two-bedroom place, with a kitchen just off of the living room. One would have thought Betsy's home to be much smaller than Ruth's, but it was merely the clutter and debris that made it only appear smaller.

As they entered the kitchen, Ruth smiled at Blair. He was kneeling at the kitchen table on a silver metal chair, scooping Rice Crispies into his mouth. Milk dribbled down his chin as he barely chewed, looking inquisitively at the visitors. He grinned when he saw Trey, letting loose of a surge of milk and little gold chunks onto his chin. "Oh, for God's sakes, my little monster, let me clean you up." Betsy pushed her nose into Blair's tiny snout and kissed him with it, like a seal kisses her pup. She reached to the nearby counter to grab a cloth and then wiped his face, streaking it more than cleaning it.

A cat strolled across the stove investigating the scene. Betsy walked to the refrigerator. "You guys want milk to go with those cookies?" Ruth obliged with a nod. "You can't have cookies without milk." She placed Tristan onto an open chair, and stood behind him for comfort, placing her hand on his shoulder. Ruth scanned the kitchen and wondered where Betsy might produce clean drinking ware. It appeared that every dish she owned might be dirty. But Ruth was misguided. Betsy opened a cupboard to reveal precisely three plastic cups inside. *I hope they're clean.*

Despite the messy living conditions, Ruth anticipated staying for a bit. They all waded through the rubble to Andrew and Blair's bedroom. She initially held onto Trey, not sure of what mischief he might find if he was left to crawl to his own demise. He was squirmy, not wanting to be held back from exploration. He saw, he whined, he squirmed, and finally, Ruth gave up and he was put down to conquer.

As they turned into the hallway, Jeremiah emerged from the master bedroom. He was in the midst of putting on a shirt, partially exposing

43

his hairy chest. He stopped short when he saw them approaching. "What the hell? Were you gonna tell me we had company? It's bad enough that I gotta show up here first thing in the morning to find some strange man leaving the house, now you got friends coming over without me knowing?"

"Oh, just shut the hell up, will you? I live here, not you anymore, remember? You're the one who left. I can have who the hell I want over." Betsy motioned to Ruth to follow. "Just ignore him. He just came by to pack up some of his shit. He's not staying."

Jeremiah brushed passed them, fluffing his messy head of hair with his well worked hands. Ruth turned to watch him grab a denim jacket from a broken coat rack leaning against the wall. He mumbled something through bearded lips as he closed the door behind him. Betsy was already digging in a dresser for clothes to put on Blair when Ruth entered the room. "He's gone I hope?" Betsy didn't look up in an attempt to brush the tears away from her face before Ruth could see them.

"Yes. He left. Are you alright?"

"I'm always ok." She blinked away the truth with a short pause. "My friend Suzanne is stopping by soon. I'm sorry to be so distracted. She's taking the boys tonight."

"Oh, am I interrupt…."

"Oh, God no! I don't have to leave 'til later. We got all day. She just wants to hang out before I go."

"Going anywhere fun? Will you be gone all night? She must be a good friend to keep your children for you. I don't know the last time I've left my boys overnight. I'm not sure that I ever have."

"She's a doll. That's what she is. A beautiful and kind doll-face. I don't know what I'd do without her."

44

How very nice. Ruth sat on the edge of a twin mattress nestled in a wooden bunk bed, wondering if she was imposing and feeling out of place. That feeling was quickly distracted by a knock at the door.

"Be right back!" Betsy jumped into action and disappeared through the doorway. She reappeared within seconds with a young girl of about four years of age, holding loosely to Betsy's fingertips. Her mother trailed behind.

"This beautiful angel is Tiffany. Sweetie, say hello to Ruth."
Tiffany blinked, looking curiously around the room and then to Ruth. "These your kids?"

"Yes, dear, they are. This is Tristan and Trey. I'm Ruth and it's very nice to meet you, dear." Ruth looked up to Suzanne, who was leaning against the doorway, with pride in her tone, "Don't let her pretty face and pig tails fool you. She can hold her own with all these boys. Just watch."

Betsy made the formal introduction. "This is my new neighbor, Ruth, Ruth Bakerson, the one I told you about. Ruth, this is my friend Suzanne, Suzanne Denison."

Ruth was flattered. *She talked about me?* "Hello." It was all she could muster up.

"They play together all the time. She's quite the social butterfly, she is." Suzanne made herself at home on the floor, crossing her legs underneath a pleated maxi skirt. Her halter top bared the glow of her smooth feminine shoulders.

By this time Tiffany was already leading the group of reluctant boys in search for sidewalk chalk located at the bottom of the toy box. Tiffany had decided they were all going outside to play. Suzanne looked to Ruth with warm welcoming eyes. "You planning to stay for lunch? I make a mean grilled cheese." She looked to Betsy assuming she had permission to take responsibility for lunch plans. "You have cheese, right?"

"I think so, let's go look." Betsy led the women out to the kitchen. Ruth tagged behind, glancing back into the bedroom to get a comforting eye on the children before leaving them all to play on their own for a few minutes. "Do you mind if I use the restroom first? I can find my way into the kitchen."

"Of course. It's right there." Betsy pointed Ruth in the right direction.

While opening the bathroom door, Ruth could hear Betsy and Suzanne dive right into heavy conversation as they headed into the kitchen. Making her way to the kitchen, Ruth hesitated in the doorway, concerned that she may walk in on something that wasn't intended for her ears.

"C'mon, Bets', it's not that big of a deal. I mean, I know Jennifer's getting in over her head an' all. But the move could be good for her. Maybe it will change things." Suzanne's voice wasn't as convincing as her words.

"There's no way in hell moving to Aspen with Pete will be good for her."

"But it's out in the country, outside of town. She says it's beautiful and secluded. She says Pete will take good care of her."

"And you believe that? Oh, God, girl. I know you know better. That last run I did to Montrose almost went south. Derek says that Pete's walking into a war zone up there. Derek says the feds are all over that place."

"The feds are only after the big shots. Pete's not that big. He's keeping it under the radar. Jennifer's my sister, Bets' and I have no choice but to trust what she says. She's going, with my permission or not. And

46

besides, Derek's crew should just stay the hell out of all this. They're barking up the wrong tree and will never get what they're looking for. Are you thinking of hookin' back up with them? Bets', you know that's stupid. Just stick to earnin' your keep waitin' tables. It's just too risky and you know that."

"Well, I trust Derek. I've known him for so long and besides, Derek's not gettin' involved, but he seems to think it would be fine, if I wanna. But, I'm not sure I wanna. He says that Pete's the one in over his head. And Jennifer's just stupid if she's gonna…"

Betsy's voice trailed to a slow stop, as Ruth slowly entered the kitchen. Betsy recovered the awkwardness with flare, "Hey, girl! You're just in time to cut these sandwiches up. You should see this, Suz', she's an artist she is. Perfect little triangles all stacked in a pattern and everything. C'mon, show 'er." Ruth was relieved to have a job to do, and proud to be bragged on. Suzanne winked to Ruth with a kind smile, settling Ruth's insecurities.

After enjoying a few minutes of meaningless chatter and a simple picnic on the floor of Andrew and Blair's bedroom, Ruth excused herself to take the boys home to be put down for a nap. She gathered up her two tired eyed little boys, while balancing the plate of leftover cookies. "I'll just leave these on your counter in the kitchen, if that's alright. You're welcome to have what's left."

"That's cool. I can bring your plate back tomorrow then?"

"Yes. Any time." *Please do. Tomorrow.*

Ruth walked much slower heading back across the street, with the weight of Trey's body wrapped around her. When the boys were snug in their nap time routine, she finally snuggled herself into the living room sofa for a break of her own. She glanced through the window to Betsy's house before opening her Bible.

47

Ruth's reading was distracted a few times, but only to ponder the words on the page. This was particularly true when a passage of words in the book of St. John spoke to her about a story Ruth knew as "The Woman at the Well". She imagined the scene of the story as Jesus spoke to this woman with compassion, about the many men in her life. It happened at a water well. And it was at this water well, that, as the story goes, this woman was given a new life and new perspective. *"….whoever drinks of the water that I shall give… will never thirst…."* Ruth couldn't help but turn her gaze once again through the window to the house across the street. She closed her eyes in silent prayer, then reopened them to look around her own living space.

The end tables were set and polished at the exact angle of the sofa. The TV shined from the far end of the room. Even the windows gleamed through the freshly washed curtains. After some thoughtful contemplation, Ruth sat back in the sofa refreshed. Order. Her home was becoming well in order.

Chapter 6

Streams of smoke circled through the air of Betsy's bedroom, not having a place to dissipate. Turned with her back to the source of the smoke, Betsy's sleepy eyes fixated on the wall across the room. Bradley sat up, exposing his bare chest from under Betsy's faded bed sheet. Light from the morning daybreak tried to poke in, but the curtains kept the sunshine at bay. Bradley's solid stature shifted and hovered over Betsy's body flirtatiously as he strummed his fingers lightly across her backside, gliding his hand up to her shoulders. Betsy tried to contain the repulsive shiver that emerged, as she slowly turned to face him. "You know I have to be somewhere soon. I got to head out in about thirty minutes. You parked up the road like I said, right?"

Bradley inhaled another drag from his cigarette, "Yeah. I'm not an idiot. I thought we'd be able to go another round. You know, it may be a few weeks before I come back."

A few weeks too soon. She grinned at him, teasing him, hiding her true disdain for him.

"Well, you know, I got shit to do." *Thank God.*

He shrugged, grabbing his shirt from the floor. "Suit yourself."

49

After getting dressed, Bradley looked at his watch and realized that he had shit to do as well. "Well, I gotta go anyway. I just moved into that house up at my grandparent's place, and still gotta a load of boxed up shit I stuck in a closet and forgot about."

"Oh, yes, up where that no-good cousin of yours lives. I bet you two have a ball out there."

"What are you insinuating?"

"I know what goes on out there. I got my hands in a few things too, ya know."

"Not this shit, you don't." He winked.

"Oh, really? Care to share?"

"Nope. Not today. It's out of your league, anyway baby." He grabbed a small bag of marijuana from the desktop and shoved it in his jacket pocket. "This shit, it ain't nothin'. It may be the best shit this towns got to offer, maybe. But there's more happening these days. This is petty cash shit."

"I don't think the old man who grows it out there thinks it's petty cash. I hear he vacations at sunny beaches anytime he wants. But whatever you say." Betsy lit up her own cigarette and blew smoke into the air, just barely above his head. "Besides, you guys are all full of shit. I'd rather not wallow in your kind of shit, anyway."

Bradley laughed his way to the door. Betsy didn't bother to follow. She heard the front door click his departure and welcomed the silence that followed with a few more puffs of inhaled relief.

The time on the alarm clock at the other side of the room called Betsy into action. She knew she had to hurry if she was going to pick up a paycheck from work before meeting Derek at the restaurant for breakfast. Throwing her purse in through the open window of the station wagon parked in her carport, Betsy hummed a quiet tune.

Within minutes the car was pulling into the parking lot of the nearby bowling establishment, and buzzing mental distractions kept Betsy from noticing the flashing lights in the rearview mirror. With one leg peeking out from the open car door, she noticed the young, slender police officer walking toward the car. "Shit! Are you kiddin' me?" She protested in his direction. Leaving the door open, Betsy sat back in exasperation. "What'd I do? I just pulled in. I know I didn't do nothin'. You can't nail me for nothin', if I didn't do anything."

The officer smiled nervously. "Good afternoon, Ma'am. I'm Officer Randy Endergard, how you doing this morning? I'm just lettin' you know about your taillight, Ma'am. Can I see your driver's license, please?"

My taillight? It's fine. What the hell? Betsy was both annoyed and confused. "I'm in a bit of a hurry. Just picking up my pay." She pointed to the door of the building before digging through the purse in her lap. He took her license, glanced at it, and then leaned down low to hand it back. When she leaned forward to take it, Officer Endergard moved in close to whisper something to her, which caused her to pull back uncomfortably. He spoke softly. "I'm just letting you know to watch your back, Ma'am. You're being tailed. I'm not sure why, but rumor has it that you're a target, and I just wanted to warn you." His tone was genuine. The officer stepped away and nodded before returning to his squad car, still flashing its lights.

Pushing aside this unusual encounter (subconsciously passing it off as some sort of joke triggered by a jealous lover), Betsy walked shamelessly through the double doors. Within a flash she was back out again, rushing to her car with an envelope in one hand. Her aloof way of dealing with such things was more of a coping mechanism than ignorance.

51

Betsy tried to hide her anticipation, looking in the rearview mirror, she primped her hair one last time before heading out onto the highway leading to the center of town. The small bobby pins held her hair secure away from her face, but the ends flowed onto her shoulders in complete freedom. *I hope Trevor is with him.*

Once Betsy rolled to a stop, she noticed Derek's car parked in a nearby space. With a combination of relief and excitement she saw Trevor climbing from the passenger's seat. Exiting from the car, Betsy stood to wave at them. "Looks like I'm right on time."

"Hello, beautiful." Trevor's voice was gentle, relaxing her shoulders and lighting up her eyes.

"I'm glad you could join us." Betsy pecked a light kiss to his cheek, taking in the feeling of his hand touching the small of her back.

Derek spoke matter with a matter of fact tone. "Alright, girl. You hungry?"

"Well, always." She shot a shy glance in Trevor's direction.

Derek kept his mind on matters at hand as they entered the restaurant and settled into a booth. "You sure you're ok with all of this? I can tell them you'd rather not."

"I know Dwaine. I'm not worried. You, on the other hand, worry far too much. It's not like I've never done this before."

"I know. But this is a bigger deal. There's more at stake these days, with this new group you're mixin' with now. They have insiders all over the place, and I'm not directly in the mix anymore, so I can't intervene if you need me to. Just remember what I said, Dwaine's new contact is quite the sweet talker. Don't let him take too much time. Just get in, then get out. You know, like ol' times. You ok?"

"Of course I'm ok. Would you just chill out? Holy shit, you need more sleep. So, who's this new guy with all the goods these days?"

"You're making a drop for a man they call the 'The General'. Some out 'a towner who's wanting to set up shop here and make his mark around these parts."

Betsy laughed out loud. "What? The General? Really? I know him! He's not so bad. Damn, this will be a breeze. He likes me."

"He likes everyone with a pretty face."

"Oh, c'mon, you make him seem so pathetic. I kinda like him back. He's charming."

"You need a lesson in charm my dear lady. He's deceitful." Trevor warned.

"Well, I already know that, but I still like 'im. I didn't know Dwaine was working with The General these days. Dwaine tells me everything, and he never mentioned that. How long has this been going on?"

"Don't ask so many questions, girl. And make sure you don't call Dwaine by name. You're not supposed to know his name."

"You act like I don't know anything, Derek. Well, as charming as The General is, he'd be a hell of a lot cooler if he didn't run with that sleazy sidekick of his. Who the hell hired him down there at PD anyway? Sorry excuse for a cop if there ever was one. As long as that tall dark and handsome prince charming continues to hold hands with that dirt bag, he'll never get a seat with the City Council. You think he's got a chance?"

Trevor took Betsy's rants more seriously. "Don't even consider it. There's no way this town will put an outsider from Chicago on the city council seat. He's doesn't know who runs things in this town, does he?"

"Well, I'd be in his court. This city needs new blood in the mix."

53

The conversation was halted as Derek noticed a city patrol car pull into an alley adjacent to the restaurant. "We should order and get on with things." He pulled a menu over to scan it.

"Why do you bother looking? You know what's on it," Betsy teased. Derek scolded her with his eyes from over the top of the menu.

Even my own brother doesn't harass me like you do. She rolled her eyes and smiled over to Trevor in jest. The remainder of their breakfast time was spent in idle talk ranging from how the boys were faring to work related gossip down at the Sheriff's department. Derek never hid his lack of enthusiasm over the Sheriff's Department having to share a building with the city Police Department. His allegiance was clearly with the county Sheriff and it showed every time he spoke of work. "Well, something just isn't on the level, that's all I know. They don't seem to be screening new recruits too carefully these days."

Trevor nodded. "Yeah, well, with the chief bringing in his own teams, why would he care to put too much into the local rookies signing on."

Betsy liked this sort of talk. It made her feel as if she was a part of something important. "You guys like the new chief? There's a lot of shit being thrown around about him. You think it's all true?"

Derek cut her off before she could get started. "Don't mind yourself with the likes of him. Let us do that."

When she opened her mouth to instigate more, he quickly interjected, "We should get going. You all done with that? C'mon, girl, no wonder you're so thin, you've hardly eaten half of it."

Trevor refuted the observation. "She's perfect. Quit giving her such a hard time for heaven's sake."

"Just lookin' out for her, that's all."

Her eyes twinkled at them both as Betsy scooted from the booth and sauntered between them to the door. She stood at the entrance feeling grateful for them as Derck paid the waitress at the register, knowing she was well cared for. Once outside and glancing up at the sky, she used her hand to shield her eyes from the bright sunlight. "Well, I guess it's off to charm The General! Wish me well." Trevor leaned to her for an embrace and whispered, "I'll call later." She batted her droopy eyes into his with a language that he clearly understood, then she turned to stroll down the sidewalk of the city's quaint downtown business district.

Being the oldest area of the city, the street was lined with two story brick buildings, close together with an occasional lot hosting newly remodeled motels and service stations. As larger chain corporations had begun to make a dent in the city, only those higher end businesses were moving out near the college across town, along the area of North Avenue. The North Avenue district was becoming the economic beat of the city, gaining more attention from city officials, leaving the downtown area the ability to maintain its small-town atmosphere.

Betsy made her way into a little pub and found a bar stool near the back of the room, where she waited to be approached. In a moment a well-dressed, distinguished looking man snuck up behind her. He leaned over her shoulder, gently touching her cheekbone with his curly beard. Tall, dark, and handsome for certain, he seemed far too young to be leaning solidly onto his polished wooden cane. She hadn't ever asked anyone why he was called The General, and certainly never asked about his real name. He sat down beside her and placed his hand over hers. "Let me buy you a drink, gorgeous."

"It's not even noon yet," She giggled.

"No one as beautiful as you comes into my bar without getting a drink."

Betsy's smile flattered him. "Well, if you insist."

One Jack Daniels and coke and fifteen minutes later, Betsy realized she needed to move on. He touched her hand again. "Let Dwaine know that I've got more comin' next week. He knows how to reach me." *I thought we weren't supposed to use names? That must mean he trusts me. Or he's testing me.* The General winked Betsy on her way, as he handed her a rolled-up copy of the local Penny Pincher newspaper. She tucked it under her armpit, suddenly feeling an unexpected twinge of anxiety in the pit of her stomach.

Relieved to be back outside, Betsy took in the daylight as it soaked into her skin. Glancing ahead, she noticed a man she knew, but very much disliked. *The General must need him for something. I can't imagine someone as nice as The General being so tight with such a sleazy dirt bag.* Betsy avoided the man's cold stare by searching the parking lot across the street for Derek's car, which was camouflaged by several trucks and a row of shrubs. *Fucking dirt bag. Doesn't deserve a badge.*

Skipping with a bit of a jog to get across the street, Betsy quickly made her way to Derek's open window, leaning in to reveal the package. Her momentum was high. "That was easy as pie."

"Well. Then I trust you've got this all under control from here. When you get to Montrose, give me a call from that phone booth on 3rd Street. Don't try using another one, just to be on the safe side."

"I've got it. Besides, this isn't even your deal. Don't know why you even care."

"Just watching out for you, that's all."

"Oh, and while I'm there, I was thinkin' I could go see Dwaine's show. Maybe I could find someone else to take the boys and Suz' could go with me."

"C'mon, girl, you think that's a good idea? Is Suzanne legit? I mean, I worry about her, and that sister of hers. Dwaine seems to think that she's crossin' some codes. And Pete's in a world of trouble and doesn't even know it. Is that girl oblivious to what's going on around her?"

"I'm just talking about going to see Dwaine's gig. I love his shows. Kill two birds with one stone, that's all. Might as well enjoy the trip. Trevor, you know I got this, right?"

Trevor leaned toward the window to face her as close as he could without overpowering Derek's space. "Of course I do. Don't let him rattle you. He's just being a big brother. I'll be over before you leave anyway." He looked to Derek as he settled back in his side of the car and asked, "You good with that?"

"Sure. Let'r do what she wants," Derek shrugged.

"C'mon, man. She's not a kid anymore."

"You weren't the one who had to haul her ass out to the Whitewater Nuns to keep her alive."

Betsy rolled her eyes. "Dammit Derek, that was years ago. I was messed up then. I'm not that person anymore. For God's sake give me a break."

"It's by God's sake that you're still alive, Betsy. But, ok. By the way, you got groceries in the house?"

"Yes. I got food. My new neighbor brought some things over yesterday. She's a doll. You'd like her."

"Well, I'm sure she's a good girl, like you. No doubt if you say so. How 'bout you get yourself on home, and make sure to take good care of that. Get it packed up right away so the boys don't find it. Oh, and keep the creeps away. I hear you're entertaining again. They're talkin'

57

all over the place, even down at the fire house the fire hounds are spreading crap. You don't need that kind of reputation from guys like that. Ok?"

Betsy pushed away the inclination to tell Derek about the strange warning given to her earlier by Officer Endergard. Instead, she flirted with a giggle. "Yes, sir. Consider it done." She humored them with a flick of her four fingers in the air and spun around leaving them with nothing but her backside to admire. As she walked away, her face softened into a thoughtful gaze. *For God's sake does everybody talk about me? At least I know I can count on Trevor. He's so nice.*

Chapter 7

Sunlight engulfed the pavement and peered through the windows of the small Cafe Caravan, which was a café' by day, party tavern by night. Despite being conveniently located at the end of two busy cross streets, it was nearly empty on a Thursday afternoon, especially since the lunch rush had fizzled out. Betsy's voice rose above the few scattered patrons, as she chatted aimlessly with the lack of awareness that she was in a public domain. Suzanne sat in the booth across from Betsy, listening while watching through the big picture window as people passed by. Her fingers subconsciously combed through little Tiffany's hair.

Andrew sat on his knees munching away at a plate of french-fries, watching his mother with Blair in her lap, rocking him back and forth in rhythm with her voice. Blair appeared tired, but Betsy's movement kept him from being able to snuggle into her. Tiffany's eyes were glued to Betsy's every word, with the look of anticipation of what might fly out. As usual Betsy didn't notice. "Oh, for the love of God, Suz' I will go with you if you don't want to go alone. I know you think it's no big deal, but you really should get up there to see her. I'm serious, Suz', this is your sister, and you know you should step in. The shit Pete's got her int…" Betsy shook her head in frustration as she paused. "Jennifer just needs someone to get up there and bring 'er home."

Suzanne took in a deep breath to break the tension. "Jennifer's an independent soul Bets'. I've tried to talk to her. For God's sake, she's in love." Suzanne rolled her eyes. "He's not so bad, really, it's just that it's easy money. And she says they're just going to get ahead a bit. Jennifer trusts Pete, and just wants him to be able to get his business up and running. She's not gonna listen to me, you know. She never has. Not when he's wooing her and promising her the world. And besides, they're married now, so what can anyone do now? You remember what that's like, right? To be in love?"

Betsy stopped and looked out of the window for a few seconds, chewing on the inside of her lip. She turned back to Suzanne, with a sly grin. "Well, actually I do."

Suzanne looked at her with curiosity.

Betsy brought the tone back to the topic of Jennifer. "And, even though I do, I'm still trying to be rational about things."

"What're you talking about? You're in the middle of a separation. You thinking you still love him and gonna let him come home?"

"Oh, hell no! I'm not talking about Jeremiah, I'm talking about Trevor."

"Which one's Trevor? Is he that fireman?"

"No. That was a dead end. He's the Sheriff Deputy I've been seeing, remember? I thought I mentioned him to you."

"I vaguely do, I guess."

"God, he's so sweet! Like honey! Pure golden honey!" She tossed herself back into the vinyl cushion simply beside herself.

Suzanne grinned softly. "You really like him, don't you?"

Betsy started to respond but hesitated as she looked up.

The air in the room immediately changed when the door jingled open and a mass of boots clamored inside. Keys clinked and holstered hips jostled as a group of uniformed officers sat into a nearby booth farther down the row of windows. Betsy tried to hide her insecurities as they came near.

"Quit dawdling, Rookie. I'm hungry." Bradley sent a wink in Betsy's direction as the crew of officers casually strolled by them. Betsy ignored him by glancing out of the window, and then quickly leaned closer into Suzanne. "Do you know the young guy in the front?"

Suzanne pulled the straw from her lips after taking a sip of her soda. "Nope. Must be new. Looks like he barely got out of high school. Poor guy. I wouldn't want to be stuck with those two. You're not thinking...."

"Oh, God, hell no. Didn't you hear me? I'm Trevor's girl now. It's the real thing, you know."

"Is he married?"

"Why would you ask that?"

"Because most of them are."

"Oh, shut up, it's not like I go looking for them. I never know until after the fact."

"Well then, is he?"

"Ok, fine. So, this time I knew from the start. But, just stop it, it's not like that."

"So, you're not really his girl. His wife holds that title, don't you think?"

"I said knock it off. It's not like that. There are circumstances you don't know about."

"Alright, fine. I'll stop. Just don't want you getting hurt."

A quick moment of silence rested between them, and a smile from Betsy cut away the conflict that had attempted to surface.

Suzanne's voice lightened back to the rookie police officer. "So, why the interest in the new guy, then?"

Betsy shrugged. "I don't know. He just pulled me over the other day outside of work, that's all. I didn't get a ticket or nothin'. It was just kinda weird. I think he said his name was Randy, or something."

"Did he hit on you? I hear there's some cops around town hittin' on girls. I even heard they were doing bribes. You know, trade-offs instead of tickets. If you know what I mean."

"No, not that. Just wondered who he was. That's all. Really? Trade-offs? Shit, some of these guys have no conscience at all. God, I hate assholes."

The women sat quiet for a several seconds as Betsy busied herself wiping Blair's messy face. The group of officers' jovial background noise was loud, almost as if they were deliberately making their presence known.

Betsy could hear Travis, Bradley's cousin, snapping a sharp command toward the waitress. Betsy leaned in again to Suzanne and whispered, "You know, if I could get away with it, I'd smack the shit out of him. I can barely tolerate Bradley. Travis is worse." She coughed out a slight chuckle.

Suzanne was careful to whisper back, "Well, at least you don't have to live around the block from him. Between Travis and that asshole excuse of a cop running tight with the General, I can't even walk down the street without getting sick to my stomach. I mean, you'd think I'd feel safe with two cops in the neighborhood. Not in this town. Not with them."

"I always told you that you should move. I mean, I know, you got some shitty neighbors. But, I think you're wrong, some. I did a job with the General recently, and he was really respectful. I wish people would learn the difference between the hard stuff and just the light stuff. He's not running the dangerous shit. I mean, really, it's not right, you know. Decent hard-working people getting picked up for little petty shit, and the big shots, the one's doing the major shit. They get nothin', nothin' but filthy rich. It ain't right. The big shots, the ones' runnin' the hard stuff, them, I'd have a problem with. This guy's actually pretty cool, and his game isn't hurtin' no one. It's the high dollar shit that's the real problem these days."

"God, you're so trusting of anyone who sweet talks you, Betsy. The guy's using you to sell drugs, and that dirty excuse of a cop friend is helping him. What difference does it make what kind of drugs they are? And I gotta live on the same block as all three of these jokers. Don't act like any of them are the good guys."

"Well, all I know is that you can't live life thinking everyone is bad. I mean, I guess Travis wouldn't be so bad if he weren't hangin' with 'you know who' these days. Does Travis ever even say hello to you? Shit, we've known 'im for years."

"Why would I care?"

"I guess you're right. He just acts so smug whenever I run into him. Like he's better than me. So, anyway, I wonder who this new guy is. And I don't know the other guy, either. Do you?"

"No. Seems like there's a lot of new blue signing on these days."

"The other guy's kinda cute."

"He needs a haircut. For a cop, he sure doesn't look like one. Besides, aren't you in love?"

"I just said he was kinda cute. Since when do you like a clean cut, anyway? Your man's got all sorts of hair."

"Ya, but he's not a cop."

The waitress stopped by their table to check on them with a weary smile. "You ladies need anything?"

"No, we're good. But, thanks." Betsy knew the waitress and couldn't let her curiosity pass. "Hey, do you know who the new guys are?" She pointed inconspicuously behind her with her head.

"I know Randy. His last name is Endergard, I think."

"Yeah, that's 'is name."

"He's a local. Lives out in Whitewater with his folks still, helping on the family's ranch. Good folks. Why? You lookin' to break him in?"

"For God's sake, you too? Dammit, will you all quit giving me shit."

Suzanne grinned sarcastically, teasing. "Yeah. She's in love, after all."

The waitress looked to Betsy in sincere interest, tilting her head a bit to hear more.

Suzanne continued to tease. "With a married man, no less."

"Oh, girl. You'd be better off with the young rookie. I'm not hearing any more of this."

She left them to go and tend to the demands of the other table, with a snicker under her breath. The two women heard laughter from the table behind them, and Betsy looked to Suzanne, who was facing in their

64

direction, to see what the commotion was about. "She didn't say anything to them, did she?"

"No. It didn't seem like it. I think they were laughing at her for some reason, as she walked away. Don't make a fuss, we got one of 'em coming our way."

"Is it the young rookie?"

"No. The cute one with the hair," Suzanne smiled.

Colin was also new to the police department but was no beginner when it came to winning the adoration of women. He approached their table with confidence.

"Hello ladies. I just wanted to let you know that I have noticed you have very well-behaved children. I'm sorry for any disruption we may have caused you." He smiled loosely. "We certainly wouldn't want to keep you from enjoying your lunch. We haven't done that, have we? Sometimes we get to joking around, and it can be a little loud."

Suzanne smiled sweetly. "We're fine. But, thank you for asking."

Betsy nodded in agreement and added, "These little guys - and gal," she winked at Tiffany, "are the best kids ever. So, of course they're well-behaved." Andrew giggled, snuggling up close to his mother, while Blair seemed oblivious that he was being talked about.

"Well, you ladies have a nice day," Colin nodded, grinning at everyone at the table, then walking in the direction of the bathrooms.

"He seems nice enough." Betsy concluded with a shrug of her shoulders.

"Shshsh…" Suzanne warned, as the other officers all stood to their feet and shuffled by, one at a time. Betsy could feel the silent mockery as Bradley and Travis passed by their table. Once they were far enough

65

away, she whispered, just in case they were still in earshot, "Travis acts like he doesn't even know us. God, he's sleeping with the tramp who used to be my best friend. And at the same time she's with Jeremiah. We all used to be friends. He could at least say 'Hi'."

"Betsy, why would that matter? You two aren't friends anymore, and who cares who he's with. I'm sure he doesn't care about you sleeping with Bradley. I mean, I think it's stupid, you don't even like him."

"That's different. It's work. And he doesn't even know anything about what's going on with that. I swear that whole building is a mess of gossip. At the PD side anyway. I wonder what other dispatchers he's sleeping with."

"That doesn't matter. Why do you care? The point is, he doesn't care about anything we do, so you shouldn't give him a single thought. Like I said, it doesn't matter. We were never really that good of friends with him anyway. It's all history."

Because it apparently isn't history. Betsy didn't have the heart to tell Suzanne about what Officer Randy had said when he pulled her over. *It has to be Travis or Bradley, who else could it be that would harass her like that?* She didn't want to worry Suzanne. She had enough to worry about with Jennifer. As it turned out, Betsy didn't trust everyone, no matter whom she slept wit

Chapter 8

Andrew's eyes followed Betsy's movements in a curious daze from the hallway, as she buzzed from her bedroom to the bathroom, and then back again, changing clothes several times. Betsy was in high speed preparing for the night ahead. The blouse she had hand washed lay over the heating vent in the bathroom. *Dammit! I hope this gets dry in time.*

Standing in front of the small metal framed mirror in the bathroom, Betsy poked large ringlet earrings into her earlobes. She stood stationary staring at herself in the vague reflection. The glass was spotty, streaked with faded remnants of evaporated moisture. Betsy stood motionless as her eyes spit firecrackers of life off of the glass. Her back teeth gnawed the inside of her cheek to subdue the confusion that she saw in her reflection. *I shouldn't go. I should stay with Suzanne and be strong for her. She needs me to be strong. This is selfish.*

Betsy's eyes softened, as she blinked away tears. It had only been a little over a month since Jennifer's death. The accidental overdose didn't take anyone by surprise. But it was a loss, nonetheless. Jennifer was gone, and certainly Suzanne needed her to be supportive. *Maybe I should just stay in at her house. But then, she wasn't your sister, after all. She was hers. Maybe she just wants to be alone. Shit, I don't know. I want her to go. We can get someone for the kids. I know we can.*

67

Betsy strutted her anxiety into the kitchen clonking the floor with thick platform boots, which elevated her thin stature quite unnaturally. Her miniskirt lay loosely around her nonexistent hips, only exaggerating the fact that she didn't eat enough. She calmed her mixed emotions by humming a hymn that she had learned from Ruth, while at the same time tossing several mini boxes of animal cookies into a paper bag. The boxes were made to look like circus train cars, filled with creatures marketed to childlike imaginations. Betsy couldn't help but be disappointed. *These don't look like circus animals. Just cheap mass-produced vanilla wafers formed into shapes that are supposed to look like an animal of some sort. If I made animal cookies, they'd be much more realistic with colors and candy beads for eyes. And they'd be bigger. Elephants are big after all.*

Andrew continued to follow her with anticipation, as his mother prepared for his overnight trip to Tiffany's. Not Suzanne's house. Andrew always let everyone know that it was Tiffany's house. Betsy seemed to read his mind, as he stood close watching her.

"You're excited, aren't you? Just do what you're told and stay outta trouble. Aunt Suzi's not feeling well, and don't go messin' up her house an' all. Ok? I heard about you and Tiff' gettin' into the bathroom cupboards last time. Hair rollers aren't Martians, little one."

"But we're just going to Mars to fight 'em! Tiff' says Martians are green, and da curlers are green."

Betsy chuckled under her breath, not finding a motherly way to respond.

Andrew jabbered away about the spaceship they used to "...chase 'em down and kill 'em..." while she made one last trip into the bathroom. He stopped talking to stare at her in admiration. Betsy applied several additional strokes of lipstick and smacked her lips together with a "Pop!" She looked down to Andrew and smiled, which made him put his head down and run away, as if he was ashamed that he had been caught watching her. Betsy chased him down the hall teasing him with his laughter nearly echoing off the walls. Grabbing her plastic gold purse and Blair from off of the floor, all in one swoop, Betsy trudged them all out of the house in a flash.

As they drove past Ruth's house, Betsy glanced across the street and felt a sudden rush of sympathy. The Bakerson house looked quiet. Too quiet. The sun had just started its descent into the horizon, and shadows began to emerge where light just recently glowed. Ruth had turned on the porch light, which meant she was already preparing the boys for bed. *I wish you were going out instead of climbing into an empty bed alone.* Her pity turned to resentment towards the husband who left Ruth at home to be with another woman. *It's just not fair. You deserve to be happy.*

Betsy had tried to see things through Ruth's eyes. Ruth had said many times that she was happy. Betsy didn't believe her. It was no secret to either of them that Curtis had not been faithful. Betsy preferred to handle such things with an attitude of entitlement rather than forgiveness. "What's good for the gander, is good for the goose." She would say. Ruth would laugh it off, but it wasn't a real laugh. And Betsy knew this.

The night began in the usual way, with Betsy showing up at Suzanne's apartment, typically waiting for Suzanne to apply the streaks of glittery eye shadow to her eyelids. This night, however, Suzanne had opted out of their typical night on the town. She had volunteered to babysit instead, against all protest that Betsy could muster up.

When Betsy arrived on Suzanne's doorstep, her thoughts of Ruth's looming loneliness were replaced with Suzanne's loss, her own guilt of going out to have fun without her, and even more guilt from having Suzanne offer to babysit, and then letting her. She handled her mixed emotions in her typical way. She pretended they didn't exist. Little

Tiffany answered the door with a bounce in her voice, "Mommy, Their here! Hi Andrew…." Tiffany pulled the door wide to let them in, immediately leading the boys into her room. Betsy sighed, fighting away the guilt, "Are you sure you want to watch the kids? We could get someone still. I don't feel right leaving you here with them."

"Just stop, will you? I want to. I just feel like I want to spend more time with Tiff' these days. You know? It's like losing Jennifer has really made me rethink shit. Life is precious, and for God's sakes go live it. You go and have yourself a great time. You're not changing your plans on my account! God, you've been waiting all your life for a man who really gives a shit. So, git already."

Betsy bit her lip, looking carefully into Suzanne's eyes. "But my original plans included you. I wanted us to go, all of us. You sure you won't change your mind?"

Suzanne shook her head with a clear "No."

Betsy sighed again. "You sure? It's not too late to call 'im and have him meet us somewhere else, or I could just tell him I'm not coming. He'd understand. I really don't feel right about leaving the boys with you. I just want to be there for you and…."

Suzanne smiled sweetly letting Betsy know that she was absolutely sure. "Please. I want life to be normal. This is my new normal. Tiff' loves having the boys here. It's a breath of fresh air watching them play together. It makes me feel like things are ok, and it's all ok. I mean it. Go. If you keep arguing I'm just gonna get pissed off, and nobody wants that, right?"

Betsy reached around Suzanne and squeezed her hard, as if she didn't want to let go. "I love you, Suz'. I'm so sorry. I want to do whatever you need me to do."

70

"Then git the hell outta here. That's what I need. No pity, nothing different. Just normal. Ok already? Now, before I get mad." She grinned in a way that put Betsy at ease.

Betsy's worries about Suzanne faded due to the distractions in her mind and anticipation that she just couldn't control. She parked her car along the side of the road at the end of a vacant piece of property and waited. It was a big lot, big enough to be a schoolyard park, but instead, it was riddled with nothing but weeds and dirt. She turned her headlights off and sat restless, waiting impatiently.

In the distance she could see Trevor's shadow strolling along a dry dusty trail. Frequent foot traffic was common between the road and the newly developed housing complex that lined the outer edge of the property. Eagerly, she opened the car door and waved to him. He waved back with a lit cigarette that sparked trails of smoke into the air, barely visible.

Betsy stood against the door frame watching his approach. As soon as he was within reach, she left her perch to reach for him. He planted a passionate kiss on her, as she squeezed his hand in hers. Releasing her, he moved around to the passenger side of the car and climbed in. With a slight huffing of breath, he leaned into her for another embrace before she could get situated for the drive. This time the kiss was longer, and he ruffled her hair with his fingers. Sitting back in his seat, he breathed in again. "So, you said you had a surprise?"

"Patience, my love. Patience." Betsy lit a cigarette and took in a long draw.

"Well, if you insist. How's Suzanne holding up?"

"I think she's doing really well. I mean, as well as she can be."

"Has she said much about it? Whether or not Pete's got a case or not?"

"No. She's not sayin' much at all about the details. Suz' is still grieving ya know? What's anybody gonna do anyway? If they say the overdose was accidental, how's anyone gonna prove otherwise? Pete's just wasting his time. And money. The lawsuit won't go anywhere. He's stupid to even try. Nobody sues the law and wins. Not around these parts especially."

"I guess it depends on what he's got. What he knows and all. If he has any proof of foul play."

"Well, I don't think it matters as this point. I just hope Suz' is alright. She acts like she's got it all together, but it's hard to tell. God, she's such a rock. If only I could be that strong."

"But you are. You really are." He grinned at her compassionately. Betsy smiled as she blew smoke out through the opened window. "Maybe we should talk about this later. I really don't want to think about any of it right now. It's just too much. Anyway, she told me to go live and enjoy life. So, I should, right? So? Shall we?" Betsy put her hand to the gearshift on the steering wheel and grinned a positive change into the atmosphere, pulling the car out into the street.

Betsy's change in demeanor caused Trevor to switch gears as well. "So, since Suz' isn't comin' with us, does that mean plans have changed? We can still go there. I'm up for that, still. I just didn't know, since it's just the two of us…"

"I said patience. You'll see." Betsy shot him a flirtatious grin and turned her eyes to the road.

The drive through town and across the Colorado River leading southward to the outskirts of the city was quiet. It was a scattered community of family homes, two grocery stores, several churches, and only three gas stations. One lonely tavern sat nestled next to a country diner, leaving residents of this area few social options without driving across the river and into town.

Betsy and Trevor drove all the way through this Orchard Mesa landscape along the only highway that connected the city's borders with neighboring southwestern towns. It was a mere fifteen minutes from the heart of the city, so it didn't really matter that its neighborhood amenities were scarce. Soon, they had left the scattered lights of suburbia and merged into the darkness of rural isolation. Betsy tapped her fingers in rhythm to the radio's beat on Trevor's knee as she drove, looking in his direction every few seconds. They topped a small hill, leading them into a vast open array of desert hills and irrigated ranch lands. This stretch of desolate highway was better known as the ghost-like town of Whitewater.

The highway split the Whitewater community into two sides. On one side, a simple blink would delete the town's historical motel equipped with an old store and gas station. On the other side sat a few adjoining streets, with rows of single-family homes, and in their midst was a one room post office. The surrounding array of land was home to generational homesteads, many still in operation, while others were only etched in history.

In its prime, this community was considered a boom town. The motel was a refuge for travelers, and the grocery store once served locals and travelers alike. Although the motel was still open for business, it served very few patrons, mostly with a weekly or monthly rental fee. The grocery store now served as a community meeting place. There was also an old school building set slightly off the highway, which was visible from the road, if one knew to watch for it. It too housed the occasional church or town meeting. This old building sparked memories Betsy couldn't help but to share, "You know, I used to go to church there. I can't believe they called it a church."

73

"You mean that hokey group of hippies that gather out here using all sorts of drugs to get them all spiritual and such? Bunch of nut jobs is what they are. Please tell me you weren't one of them?"

"What 'ya mean? They're not all hippies. You'd be surprised who goes there. I mean, ya, there are some wanderers and drifters that make their way in. But I could tell on some people. People who you wouldn't expect, you know."

"Well, why don't you?" Then he paused. "You don't still go, do you?"

"No, silly. And yes, I could tell you, but not tonight." She grinned.

"I bet you have some great stories. It got pretty crazy, right?"

"Got? You mean gets. It's still crazy out here. At least that's what I've been told. I hear they've got quite a following. It's all weird, there's all kinds of shit that they take to get in the mood of things. I guess it's all about awakening your spiritual self. With a little help, of course. I get it, all the getting close to nature and all. I mean, I get the Mary Jane shit. It's not so bad, right? It's just marijuana."

"I think it's a cult, that's what I think. And I hear that weed isn't all they use."

"Well, no, you're right. They use the harder stuff, too. It's not a cult like everyone thinks. But, because of all the hard drugs they use, is why I quit going. I'm not into the hard shit."

"Do you know much about where they get their stuff?"

"Only the crops. This old guy grows a huge crop up near the top of the mountain. Suzanne says there's other shit going on somewhere around here. But I don't want to talk shop tonight."

"So, what are we doing?"

74

"You'll see." Betsy glanced over to him with eyes that twinkled like the stars. Trevor looked back at her with admiration. The moment was starkly interrupted with an unexpected distraction. A small four door car recklessly sped past them and spun into a graveled turnout into a cloud of dust, just past a row of small farmhouses. Trevor's trained responses kicked into gear. "Pull over, there are flashing lights coming up behind us." Betsy slowed down to stop onto the side of the road, as they watched city patrol lights whizzing by them in a high-speed chase.

"Turn off your lights and pull up a bit. I wanna see what's going on." Trevor nodded with a respectful but commanding voice. Betsy inched the car forward along the roadside, just enough for them to see an officer pull up behind the derailed car, which had stalled out from its sudden stop in an attempt to gain control. Betsy leaned into the windshield and squinted. "I know that guy. The cop. Well, just met 'im once."

"Yeah. Me too. He lives out here. Just joined the department not too long ago. Don't know him well, though. His name's Randy. A young rookie."

"Yeah. I know him personally, just know of him, sort of. You know, like I said, met 'im once." She wanted to say more, but it didn't feel like the right time to bring up Officer Endergard's warning.

"Jesus, what the hell?" Trevor watched a man emerge from the dust of the stalled vehicle, walking with an unsteady gait to meet Officer Endergard. The man was staggering toward the lights of the patrol car as Randy stood tall with his hand on his gun, calling out rehearsed commands. Trevor and Betsy couldn't quite hear everything that was being said (even with their windows down); but Trevor recognized the reckless driver. Travis was visibly laughing, not adhering to Officer Randy's commands. Randy then began to move toward Travis casually, taking his hand away from his side, relaxing his stance.

75

"Is that who I think it is?" Betsy questioned, somewhat confused.

"Yep. It is. That son-of-a bitch. We probably shouldn't stick around. I don't want them to know it's us that's gawking."

"Certainly they already seen us, don't you think?"

"Oh, Randy hasn't noticed yet. He hasn't even turned around. And, Jesus, Travis is too drunk to notice anything right now." He paused to peer closer out his open window.

"He's got people with him. Looks like a male in the passenger side and a couple of women in the back. Wonder who it is?"

"They might notice we're here. I bet it's Bradley. And probably a couple of those slutty dispatch girls. You know Bradley is moving out here? Him and Travis have family out here, don't they?"

"Yeah. Grandparents, I think. Ya, they're gonna notice us. The women are looking back this way. C'mon, pull out. Let's move on. I've seen enough."

Betsy crept the car out onto the highway and quickly picked up speed to pass the whole event by, hoping that they weren't recognized. She knew that if Bradley were in that car, he'd surely recognize her station wagon. Looking in her rear-view mirror as they passed, she couldn't tell if they had been noticed. Betsy drove on in silence for a few minutes. Trevor broke the stillness, "I'll find out what it was all about when I get to work. Don't worry, nobody noticed us."

"What if they did?"

"Not a big deal. It'll be everywhere by tomorrow, even the news. I mean, if I'd been in my car, I'd of caught it on the radio anyway. I can't see that anything's going to happen with it. Travis is a favorite of the Chief. It'll come to nothing, I can bet on that."

Betsy's anxiety dissipated with each reassuring word that he spoke. She smiled to him as she turned off of the highway, onto the winding road of Lands End, driving them past large plots of ranch land scattered with cattle, which were hidden in the vast darkness. Only a few homes were visible, seen as shadows, randomly scattered on either side of the road, sleeping quietly for the night. Her mind settled back into her own thoughts, and she quickly set her sights on the road ahead, and the night ahead. The distraction was easily averted.

As the car climbed along the twists and turns, the air cooled. The landscape began to morph into the mountain habitat of a higher elevation. Betsy stretched her head out of the car window to allow the breeze to flip her hair up and into the fresh air as they drove.

Within a few minutes the asphalt changed into the thud of dirt and gravel. It made the way a bit bumpier, but Betsy didn't seem to notice. She quickly turned and swayed the car as if following a familiar maze. Trevor watched her in amusement. Although he knew exactly where she was taking them, he embraced it as a spontaneous adventure. When they reached a pull-off that overlooked the massive valley below, Betsy halted the car to a quick and reckless stop.

The view of the valley below was breathtaking. In the crisp night, the two love birds could hear their own breathing as they exited the dusty car and took it all in. Betsy had quickly pounced from her side of the car, scampering over the top of the hood, in order to stand near Trevor. She lifted her arms to the black sky with a careless stretch. Trevor watched Betsy's foolishness with a chuckle, and then looked into the open sky to meet the stars for himself. Betsy, with her hands on her hips, turned in the direction of the city lights, which twinkled far into the distance. "It's beautiful, isn't it?"

Trevor glanced down at the city, then over to Betsy. "Yes. Quite beautiful."

The city lights blinked their energy in all directions, as if they were playing a song of sorts. Betsy felt this. "If a city could sing, what do you think it would say?"

The night was quiet as she thoughtfully gazed forward. "I bet this one would have a lot to say. Don't you think?"

Trevor stood still, simply gazing at her, not sure how to answer.

Peace captivated them as they stood high above the city on a dirt road very few travelers dared to take. The stillness was just too much for Betsy to take.

"C'mon! Jump in! We're going camping!" Her sudden burst of energy startled him, and he twitched a little in surprise. "Ok. Do we have what we need?"

"It's all in the back, my love. I grabbed some stuff at the last minute. I hurried so I wouldn't be late. Don't worry, all we need is a sleeping bag and a little food for the night." Betsy chuckled. "I've been camping before, I know how to do this. Just relax." Trevor closed the passenger side door just in time, as Betsy flung the gearshift into drive and spun the car back onto the dirt road. His hand searched for something to clutch, as Betsy reached her head and shoulders out of the window with only one hand on the steering wheel. Before he could say anything, she had tucked her one free knee up under her body to lift herself up off of her seat and awkwardly lean out into the air. She pulled her head up to the heavens as far as she could stretch and began to squeal out of control like a wolf howling to the moon. "Woo, hooo! Whoooo Ya!" Betsy's free arm was waving wildly out of control with her face reaching up to the sky, as she bellowed for all of darkness to hear her.

"Holy Jesus, Mother of God, girl, don't kill us!" Trevor laughed nervously.

With heavy breathing, she slid back inside with a thump and squirmed into place to regain some control. Betsy looked over to Trevor with a silly nod, who was speechless, his eyes wide in exhilaration. Fiddling carelessly with the radio, she attempted to get a signal from a local radio station, as she steered the car in its solo race up the steep curves of the road, bouncing along the washboard surface.

Trevor shook his head finally able to speak. "You're not going to get a signal up here."

"Oh, shit, just fuck it! We can sing instead!" She began a rough rendition of a one hit wonder she was quite fond of, while tapping her fingertips to the dashboard to try and find the beat. "C'mon, I know you know it!"

Through muffled laughs, he managed to follow Betsy's lead and pick up where she was in the song. The two of them made of mess of it, as they were off key and loud, but the attempt was genuine. It was everything they both could do to keep up with the lyrics in sync, but they sang on, repeating what they knew, until they reached their destination.

When Betsy slowed the car to a stop under the moonlit night, the trees above them rustled the surface of the hood of the car, giving them a sense of solitude. The night took over, and Trevor could contain his passion no longer. He reached for her, pulling her face into his.

"Shouldn't we get into the back, where the sleeping bag is?" she whispered, as he caressed her neck with his rough skin.

"No." It was the only response he could exhale, as he carefully sank her down onto the bench seat.

Chapter 9

Hazy beams of dust streams filtered into the concrete storage unit through the large open doorway, settling light onto boxes stacked neatly along the wall. Karla sat on the floor, with one leg tucked under her and the other stretched around an open cardboard box. Sweat rolled down her back, causing her tee-shirt to stick lightly to her skin. She wiped her forehead to keep the salty wetness away from her eyes.

A whiff of hot air sifted past her and rustled the pile of photographs laying in her lap. "Have you seen these, Pop?" Her eyes were fixed on the black and white image of a young woman in her early twenties who peeked back at her with deep dark eyes. When she didn't get a response, she glanced up and scanned the small room. "Pop?" Her voice echoed off the walls.

Ramone strolled in casually making small talk with Bill, who had just arrived.

"Oh, there you are, Pop. Hi, Bill. You remember me, don't you?" Karla stood up to put her hand out to shake his, and he reached around her for a hug instead. She smiled briefly to hide her embarrassment because no matter how hard Karla tried, she hadn't remembered him.

"Of course I do! And damn! You look just like your mother!"

Ramone shot him a glare, which confused Bill and Karla alike.

"You knew my mother?" Karla's heart rate shot up in seconds. *I don't look like her at all. She was so pretty. He knew her?*

Bill looked to Ramone uncomfortably for signs of help with how to answer.

Ramone came to the rescue as expected, "We don't have time for personal talk right now, Karla. For God's sake the man just got here, and he's here to work, not socialize."

"I can see you haven't changed a bit, have you my friend?" Bill jested.

Karla rolled her eyes and smiled awkwardly at Bill. "I *am* trying to work. Here, I wanted to show you these." She reached down to pick up a photograph "Who's this? There's a whole box of stuff here that's from a different case. Do you know who she is?"

Ramone took the photo from her hand, "I think this must be the Denison girl, Suzanne Denison, I think I remember reading about that one on Trey's site. I need to look more into that, though, haven't had a chance to see why it's even in all this stuff."

"You mean there was another murder?" Karla's eyes suddenly shifted to Ramone's for clarity.

Bill chuckled a sarcastic but disgusted grunt. "More than just a couple. There were many in those years. It was a really dark time for this town. I know I missed all of the shit that went down that particular year in '75, but its effects lingered. And I heard about it for years to come. A few things anyway. Just scattered pieces of it all."

Ramone studied Bill's face, as if he was second guessing whether or not he had made the right choice asking him to help them. "That's right, you came on just a couple years later, around '78, was it? We probably

81

should've sat down and talked before digging right in. I'm sorry I didn't give you a chance to debrief with us before calling you up here. You didn't have trouble finding us, I take it."

Bill never lacked in confidence. He certainly wouldn't admit if he had gotten lost. "Are you kidding? U-Rent-It is one of the largest storage places in town. I've never used 'em before, but knew right where it was. I bought a car down the road at 28 ½ Road just last year."

For Ramone, the area was a puzzle. "You live nearby? I'm not sure I've figured out the grid around here. Karla told me we should've stopped by to see you first thing, you know, to be polite and all. But at least I checked the address, just haven't got my bearings yet. This is North Avenue, right? I recognized the name from some of the preliminary research. It seemed that this strip of town was hoppin' back then, huh?" Ramone took a breath to shake his head in a sarcastic jest, then continued his rant. "Not so much hoppin' now, though, looks like. But, back then, musta been. A lot of what I've read about showed some people of interest living out this way, with the exception of some who lived in the Whitewater region."

"Yep, you're actually right about that. It was just kickin' up at the time." Bill looked past Ramone, as if deep in thought to trace a memory or two. He elaborated with a sturdy nod. "Ya, the city folks were building businesses right and left up in this area when I got here. But no, I'm not living out this way. This area has clearly taken a turn for the worst. I live farther west, north of 1st Street, also known as 26 Road. Don't blame you for having trouble figuring out the layout. That's what we have MapQuest and navigations systems for, am I right? So, I was thinking that we can do dinner at my place, if you just want to follow me home when we're done here. I don't know why you bothered with a hotel. I told you we had room for you."

82

Karla was listening in on Bill and Ramone's chatter but had partially tuned them out by wandering out into the fresh air with an old magazine in her hand. She was scanning an article that seemed to have quite of bit of useful information. But mostly, it tugged at her heartstrings. "Hey, Bill, did you ever read this? Familiar to you at all?"

Bill made his way to her side and leaned over to catch a glimpse. "Oh, yeah, I know of it. Forgot all about it, but it caused quite a stir. People were spooked for years."

"Rightly so, it seems." Karla raised an eyebrow, still in a trance by the article's content.

Ramone followed suit and glanced at the article about the area's widespread murder rate in the 1970's. Bill did in fact have insight to offer, "Looking back, well, in those years, holy shit. I came here right after the worst of it all. Glad I did, but was here for the clean-up. Something wasn't right. Not here, not anywhere. Maybe it was the whole hippy, free lovin', drug totin' experiment with anything and everything era. I found out little bits as the years went on. Most thought it was Bundy, wreaking his havoc, you know. He came through here around the same time frame. Took a couple of victims on his way through. But your case seemed like an open and shut deal. Not Bundy at all. Not everyone was convinced Bakerson was guilty, though. But those folks were few and far between."

"So, moving out to this place wasn't what you thought it would be, huh?" Ramone referred to the time when Bill had left Phoenix to move to a more quiet rural setting to raise his family.

Bill made minimal attempts to hide his regret. "This place may have looked like Mayberry, but like any place with people, it's had its demons. And it was the '70's after all. And you and I both lived to tell about the 70's, didn't we?"

"True, we did. But the 70's turned into the 80's, and then so on. The drugs didn't die like their victims." Ramone's face went soft. Eerily soft.

Bill looked to him with compassion but continued on without dredging up unwanted conversation. "I know. All the shit that carried over from the older generation of secret crime wreaked havoc in their children, didn't it? It all changed for the 70's bunch. That new generation brought on a different kind of white-collar money that was as dirty as it gets. At least the old farts kept innocent people out of it."

Karla strolled back to her pile of debris that she had left on the floor. She plopped back down to fan several photos onto the concrete and make the connections between the photographs and the magazine article. She picked out a newspaper story that had been attached to the pile of photos with a paperclip. Karla's deep sigh spoke more than her words, "Shit, this one was brutal." She gulped back tears as she studied the smile of a child in one of the photos. Bill's face became more somber as he glanced down to her. "All of 'em are, sweetie. All of 'em are." Karla folded the pile back into place into an envelope and dug her hand into the box to retrieve a manila envelope torn at the top. She watched from her peripheral vision as Ramone and Bill pulled down a box of their own to go through.

They each worked in the drone of silence for a time, in their own way, getting caught up in the stories held hostage in cardboard containers. The sound of automobile traffic hummed and hissed in the distance, reminding them periodically of the present time and space. It was Ramone who broke the weight of thought that engulfed them.

"Check this out. Karla, hop up and bring me that box you got there." He met her halfway with a sheet of lined writing paper with handwritten notes scribbled on it. "That Denison case, it keeps coming up in a few interviews, and look here."

84

Bill turned to interrupt, "You know the Denison case was just solved a few years ago. The local cold case team was able to pull blood DNA from the archived evidence. Matched it to a serial rapist who had lived not far from here. It was pretty clear cut. Just like your Bakerson case had appeared to be."

Ramone laughed sarcastically, "We wouldn't be here if the Bakerson case was clear cut. So, why was Suzanne Denison's brother-in-law filing a lawsuit against Pitkin County?"

Bill was curious. "That never came out in the media, or in the trial that I know of. Let me see that." He scanned the words then thought out loud. "Jennifer, huh? She was Denison's sister? Says here that Jennifer was married to Pete Drake. Hmmm. I know that name, the name Drake anyway. What does a drug overdose have to do with the Sheriff Department in Pitkin County? And there was never anything in the media about the Bakerson thing having anything to do with drugs. It was painted as just a neighborly domestic thing gone horribly wrong."

Karla leaned over Ramone's shoulder to read for herself. "Looks like she and the husband, Pete, lived in Aspen. Jesus, she died too? What a tragedy for that family. Two women in two years. I can't even imagine."

Ramone kept the energy focused on the work at hand. "Karla, take that with you when you go do your public records search. I wanna know who this Pete guy was and what he was up to, and why he thought he had a case against Pitkin County for his wife's accidental drug overdose."

Bill followed Ramone's lead, knowing there was so much to be done. "Let's get some more information, there's a lot here. These two Bakerson boys sure have been busy collecting all of this. I'm glad they pulled all of this together, sure does make our job easier."

Karla, Ramone, and Bill spent over an hour sifting and sorting piles of archived files that were spread over a long folding table. Bill finally spoke up again, "Are we sure this Bakerson guy wasn't into drugs or something? Here's an email from one of the journalists who worked for the local paper back then. The Daily Sentinel has been the primary source for local news since the town was settled. This journalist says he doesn't buy the conviction and how it all went down. Says it was related to drugs somehow."

That caught Ramone's attention. "Well, I don't know. It all seems confusing. I've come across a number of interviews from records of the early investigation by the Police Department and it's weird. Doesn't add up. They never legitimately addressed the missing person's report. Didn't appear like they took it seriously. But, at the same time, literally, right off the bat, they had a tail on Bakerson from the get go. But, if they suspected Bakerson from the start, why aren't there any relevant connections of Bakerson's involvement showing up in interviews in the early stages of the investigation? And why weren't they looking into the missing person's report if they already suspected him of foul play?"

"Yeah, that seems odd. A bit contradicting." Bill admitted.

"There's a whole lot of scrutiny going on in these reports involving the neighbor, the Kendall woman, Betsy Kendall, with questioning about her involvement in drugs. But nothing about Bakerson's involvement in drugs. So, there's something there, at least as far as Kendall is concerned. They seemed to focus on her life right away." Ramone rubbed his face in exhaustion, twisting his neck side to side as he spoke.

Bill squinted in Ramone's direction, trying to stay focused. "So, I'm curious as to why they were following Bakerson around then, if there didn't seem to be any reliable ties to him and Kendall, or any drug ties that were being reported about him."

"Yeah, that's what I'm thinkin' too." Ramone continued his thoughts. "So much of what I'm reading seems to be about the neighbor, Kendall, so why look at Bakerson so early on? I've come across more than just a couple of things that ties her to the drug scene. And shit, she got around. I wonder how many boyfriends she actually had. You'd think that with so many people she was connected to, they'd have taken longer to investigate all of those possible suspects before honing in on Bakerson so early in the investigation. I mean the investigation was less than two months before they had Bakerson in handcuffs. How could they have possibly investigated all those people she was sleeping with, in that short amount of time? Yeah, it's definitely weird that they were following him around so soon, without initial reports of him doing anything suspicious, except that he was having an affair, which doesn't automatically make him a murderer. The actual line of questioning during the early stages of the investigation doesn't seem to shift to Bakerson until after the Sheriff's department took over. But I'm not seeing anything even in those reports that ties Bakerson to drugs, or solid ties to Betsy Kendall for that matter, aside from being neighbors. I mean, there are a couple of random statements from one or two people who clearly didn't like Bakerson, who said he hit on her a time or two- but it appears like a lot of men did. So, why focus on him?"

"I know, why follow him around right from the start? What was this guy like?" Bill was good at asking questions. Questions that mattered.

Ramone was quick with the answers. "He was the Vice President of an engineering firm. He must have been a real go getter, 'cause he made VP after only being there for a year or so. Also, a pilot, one of their primary pilots, and a clear workaholic. Loved to build electronics of all sorts of things. A Brainiac, nerdy type, but arrogant. Not well-liked at all. Kind of an odd duck, so it seems that's what people thought. Thought he was weird, but an asshole at the same time. He was the music director at his church. Sang in a quartet. Nothing in these initial reports would lead anyone to look at him as a suspect, other than people didn't seem to like him much. But yet they were following him around, before they even indicated or admitted, that a crime had been committed. The only thing that connects so far was that they were neighbors. That's all. There's something missin' here."

Bill walked closer to Ramone's pile of papers and read quietly over the mess, while Ramone compared, and cross referenced in a whisper of thought. Bill interrupted with his own thinking, "Well, it's standard to check out the life of a victim and all, but you're right, this stuff certainly doesn't match what ended up in the trial, as far as what they came up with in the end, as for a motive."

Karla finally spoke up, after only catching pieces of their conversation. "What about this? This goes back to the Denison thing." She handed over a copy of interview notes she dug out of her box.

Ramone scanned it and rubbed his chin with the tip of his fingers. "So, the families all knew each other. Bill, it says here that Denison's husband visited the Kendall residence after the missing person's report, looking for something that Betsy wrote. It says that he was looking for a handwriting sample, and some clothes, to take to Montrose. Says that Denison's husband took a letter that Betsy had written to someone in Texas. In the letter, she wrote that someone had tried to strangle her in her home, and that she was scared. She apparently had written in this letter that not only did she almost die in the strangulation attack, but also that others had been killed in a separate incident. But it doesn't say why Denison's husband was taking a writing sample and cloths of Betsy's to Montrose. That's odd to say the least. Wouldn't someone ask why?"

"That doesn't make sense. The media reports I've come across, and well the trial outcomes themselves, report these two cases as two separate incidents and completely unrelated. But clearly, they all knew each other. Bill, you said they nailed a rapist for the Denison case? Cut and dry? I'm confused." Karla shook her head in frustration.

Ramone was frustrated as well. "I've got a hunch there's something here that has to do with the drug epidemic. We just aren't on it yet. This place was swimming in the drug scene. Denison's sister was in Aspen, and drugs were especially problematic up in that area, as the feds were all over that pricey tinsel town trying to crack down on drug smuggling into the area. You know how rich folks liked their drugs in the '70's and 80's. I think that journalist who thought this was drug related was on to something."

Karla had a hard time letting go of things that didn't make sense. "Except there's nothing in any of this investigation shit that we have here that connects Bakerson to the drug scene. Clearly, he had a few strikes against him, being a crappy husband, liked women, a history of stealing, and well, hell, having a narcissist personality, which made him anything but popular. But nothing about drugs. Trey says he's been squeaky clean in prison. That's revealing in and of itself, isn't it?"

"Well, when it came to making money in those days, anybody could've been playing the game, and I wouldn't exclude Bakerson from breaking the law to make a buck." Bill added.

"Given that this city is the gateway between all major cities in this state, with the interstate running right through here and all, probably all sorts of illegal money-making deals went on. I'm sure it was economically profitable for everyone to get in on the game. Even the DEA recognizes the relevance of the interstate to drug trafficking. The DEA has special divisions specifically for Interstate cities. I did my research on this place, after all." Ramone grinned proudly to Bill.

Bill nodded lightly. "Yeah, the interstate was quite a big deal back then. It had just recently come through here at the time."

Karla shifted her gait, as she thought of everything they had so far. "Back to the lawsuit in Pitkin County. Could Bakerson have been a part of that somehow? There's no evidence that Bakerson was using drugs, but could he have been dealing? I mean, this statement says that this Pete guy was a known drug dealer. Probably why they were living in Aspen in the first place."

"Well, nowhere on record is there any indication Bakerson went near the drug scene. Aspen, maybe. He flew all over the place for his boss, who was no doubt running with the elite money whores of the area. Besides, putting Bakerson near drugs just doesn't fit with his self-righteous personality. All reports indicate that he thought he was above the drug scene. He saw himself as an up-and-coming high roller in the economic world. Thought he was too smart for everyone else." Ramone reiterated what had already been said as if Karla wasn't able to keep up. He paused and looked to Bill. "So, you think it's possible? That folks like him, you know, high-minded shits, had their hands in dirt like drugs?"

Bill was quick to respond, "It was a damn epidemic, it was. And there were certainly rumors. Not about Bakerson, though. Certainly, about others who fit that description."

"We both know how it happened back home, happened for years, still does, right?" Ramone hesitated, looking to Karla cautiously. "Anyone in particular in this place? That carried a fancy reputation or title, but didn't use it respectively?"

Bill stood still to think, and within just a few seconds remembered something. "Well, there was one case, but it was really nothin'. A black man with a badge didn't last long around here back then. Not a home grown local, obviously. He was from Chicago. He got tagged sellin' pot, fired and ran outta town. Rumor had it that it was all a set up. I'm not sure he had the reputation of being a big shot at all though. But it's interesting that it was at the same time that all of this happened. I think it was actually that same fall. We should find the report."

90

"So, anyone else? You said rumors with a plural. That was just one." Ramone wanted more.

"Well, the only other things that come to mind were from bar talk. I mean there was the occasional whisper in the department, but nobody would ever say anything directly or implicate anyone. Just when a job was assigned or a name I didn't know would drop, someone might laugh or clam up. Stuff like that." Bill was trying to dig deep, but he knew that rumors were hard to pin down.

That didn't stop Ramone from using these rumors as leads. "Go on."

"The bar talk, that was worth noting, I guess. Drunken bar talk of course." Bill let out a laugh as he recalled a particular incident, "There were a couple of out of control cops I had heard about once when I was out after work. They ended up in the newspaper for partying out-of-control, you know, drunk driving and the like. Got pulled over by one of their own, in a high-speed chase out in the boonies. Got a slap on the wrist. It was all downplayed. And really, why wouldn't it be. They were out in the country where no one was around."

Ramone still wasn't satisfied. "Bar talk is helpful if you can remember names. You got names?"

Bill shook his head in amusement. "You are persistent, aren't you? Well, yeah, like I said, it was in the paper, so of course I could get their names. I can't pull 'em up in my head this many years later, after all. But I have one even better. This one night, I remember overhearing something that was at the least curious. But unfortunately, no names, sorry. Had my mind wondering though. People I didn't know. Just loud and belligerent lightweights. The wife and I were out for dinner, and a man was at the bar, just a few feet away from our table. He was rambling on and on about the SOB feds butting in where they didn't belong. The bartender told him to quiet down several times, then he was escorted out. I was interested of course, so I excused myself and went outside. When I asked what was up, he carried on about how he had just gotten back from a trip over the mountains and how he had gotten pulled over."

Ramone laughed, nodding with familiarity.

Bill chuckled, "I guess they hauled him in and tried to tie a drug rap of some sort on him. He said he walked. In fact, he gloated that he always walked. He didn't know I was a cop, which I thought was funny. But he mumbled something about the feds not being able to touch this place. Then, he started throwing up, and I never got his name. When I mentioned it to my partner one night on patrol, he shrugged it off and said not to make an issue of it."

Ramone seemed intrigued by the story. "So, you never asked around for more? Why couldn't the feds touch this place?"

"Never dug into it. No, no. Not a chance. I figured out real quickly where my place was in this department. I came on after a big turnover and change up in leadership. People were uneasy, nobody trusted anyone, and I wasn't about to make waves. I was green in this department and just wanted to have a job. It was chaos in those days, for God's sakes. People were higher than a kite, free falling into the abyss of insanity. There was talk of some cult just outside of town, out in the Whitewater area. It wasn't a time to be a hero, Ramone. You know that as well as anybody." Bill talked fast to mask his own regrets. Like an out-of-control freight train, he just kept talking. "And then, there was all the other stuff, the prostitution, gambling and shit like that. We knew some of the working girls, but the Johns were hard to make. And besides, everyone knew that it was mostly women who ran it all. Well, except for a few motel and bar owners who wanted a little action. So much fell through the cracks, we just couldn't keep up with it all. We tried. We did our thing, we kept some control, but in the end, it was what it was. You of all people know how it was." With that, he stopped, and realized he had gone too far. He looked at Ramone apologetically and sighed. "I'm sorry, I just…"

"Don't. Not here." Ramone glanced over to Karla nervously.

The awkward pause was difficult to miss. Karla looked at Ramone and couldn't help but sense his own deep and uncomfortable regret.

I wish you'd talk to me more, Pop. What the hell was that, Pop?

"Just keep talking about this place." Ramone was visibly annoyed.

Bill paused to take a long breath. "Alright then. The gambling, well, that was on the radar some. Not that I cared much, since that shit had been around before any of us transplants ever set foot here, so I wasn't gonna question how the old timers got their money fix. The feds seemed interested. But I wasn't."

"Who decided what mattered? And how in the world could Bakerson have been connected to any of it? They had to have something on him. Being a shitty husband and having questionable character doesn't make you a damn murderer." Ramone's agitation seemed to be rising in his heavy chest.

"I don't know, Ramone. Bakerson was already in prison when I got here. And I don't know who called the shots before my time. The old Chief had just left shortly before I got here, taking a job with Pitkin County. But when he left, things were a bit of a mess. There were even rumors that the Chief had been under scrutiny for looking the other way on some prostitution things. Rumors of all sorts flew, like the one about lawmen taking time off the clock for hanky panky in that realm. I never knew if any of it was true. But I was told once that that the feds were looking into it. Who knows? I mean, a lot of really good men and women tried to do their jobs. But, those few who didn't, well, they made it hard for anyone to earn any respect."

Ramone took a deep breath, slow and methodical, downsizing the negative energy he was creating. "That does sound messy, if it were all true. Anything else you remember?"

"There was some tension between divisions. Sheriff and city patrol suits ruffling their feathers. Neither side appeared too fond of the other. I mean, both departments were housed in the same building, but from what I heard and experienced, it was hard to work together like a well-oiled machine. When it was necessary, it happened. Working together, I mean. There was in-house dating and personal disputes, stuff like that. And then, like I said, the feds out of Denver and even out of Salt Lake, kept trying to get their hands into local issues, which was fine, since that came with funding and even training. The undercover crap was hard to follow. Compromised undercover operations happened whether anyone wants to admit it or not. The programs changed names a couple of times, you know, with changes in funding as the DEA tried to re-organize and get a handle on the chaos all over the country. I heard that some of it around here was done off the clock. How would anyone track off the clock work? One particular undercover operation was completely dismantled, but I never knew why. Something about funding; but then one guy told me one program was dismantled because of something else but wouldn't say what. I don't know really what was going on, but I know in our day, we had to report to someone, and records were kept. And we couldn't work off the clock. We were watched like a hawk." Bill thoughtfully watched for Ramone's response.

Ramone simply looked past Bill and spoke with reservation. "Everybody reports to someone. Sometimes that creates its own chaos."

A brief pause created an awkward space. Glancing to Karla to check to see if she had noticed, Bill quickly subdued it, "So much shit, just so much. Most of it was long in play and had unraveled before I got settled in here. A lot of guys left the department right before I came on. Turnover was high then."

"Does sound like a bit of a mess," Karla chimed in. She had sensed the awkwardness, but subconsciously ignored it.

"Well, I just want to know how the hell Bakerson was nabbed for this particular mess. With all of that going on, how could he possibly have been the primary, or only suspect and how in the world would he have gotten a fair trial? I mean, maybe the process itself was on the up-and-up, as courtroom drama goes, legal at best. But if the investigation was sour from the onset, then what legitimate information can a jury make an honest decision with? I've compared the trial transcripts to what we are reading here, and most of this shit never ended up being presented to either jury."

Karla was tired, and simply had no way to respond to such a question. "I hope things have changed."

Bill seemed just as tired. "We certainly don't have eleven murders all in the same period of time anymore, like in those years, if that's what you mean. And that doesn't count deaths that were rumored to be suspicious, but never made public headlines as murders. Like I said, it was a dark time."

"That's how many there were? Official murders? You mean there were other deaths that people questioned?" Karla gasped.

Bill simply shrugged and sighed, avoiding the answers to her questions, because he simply didn't have adequate explanations.

Ramone rolled his neck in an attempt to stretch away the tension he felt. "We have a lot still to go through, so we can regroup in a while. I need to take some time to sort this shit in my head." Both Ramone and

Bill went back to their piles of papers, letting a span of silence settle the air.

Karla stood entranced, not knowing how to resume. "Holy shit," she whispered, as she picked up another box of history, moved to a corner of her own and slowly sat down. Placing the box in her lap, she crossed her legs around it. Her thoughts subdued her, as she looked around at the other stacks of boxes. *This is what we have. Boxes filled with remnants of people's lives. Just scattered pieces. They were once more than that. They were once whole.*

Chapter 10

Across the street from the upscale hotel that Ramone and Karla had been calling home for several weeks, a young woman and a child (a girl of about five years of age) stood at the corner waiting for cars to pass. The floor-to-ceiling picture window made it easy for Karla to get caught up in the outside activity of people passing by. The woman, whom Karla assumed to be the mother, held the girl's hand loosely. As the pair made their way across the street and toward them, they passed by the window Karla daydreamed through. Karla took notice of the way the young girl looked up to her mother as she talked. *Nice. She's listening, engaging. You don't see that every day.* When they passed, the woman ruffled the child's hair, and then rested her arm onto her child's fragile shoulder.

As she watched, Karla's mind drifted to thoughts of her own mother. *No memories. Not a single one. Certainly, there should be at least one.* She tried to picture herself as a five-year-old girl looking up into her mother's face; but nothing. All she had was the picture she carried in her wallet, and the identical copy she kept by her bedside.

Karla sat at a rectangular table intended for a group, in the open lounge area of their hotel. She was surrounded by several stacks of file folders and two cardboard file boxes at her feet. Karla could see the lobby from her seat, which was empty save for the desk clerk who looked up periodically when the sliding glass doors rolled open. Patrons came and went, in their own world, heading to and from the elevator. *Maybe I'd be less distracted in my room.*

The glare of the laptop prompted Karla to work. She glared back, not knowing where else to go. *I should know what to do here.* Taking a sip of her iced mocha, she sat still and conflicted. *There are snacks at the bar.* She was reluctant to order anything stronger to drink, given that her Pop could stop by at any time. Although she wanted to.

With another drink of iced chocolate mocha, Karla reluctantly began to tap her way back into cyberspace, using a different search site this time. Having access to searches that aren't typically accessible to the public, Karla felt confident in making some progress this go around. Glancing down at her notebook, which she camouflaged within a file folder, she typed in the name of an obscure city in California in one text box, followed by the name that Pop had said was her mother's first name, in another text box. She had assumed that they all shared the same last name, given that Pop had told her that he and her mother had been married.

Today, Karla was searching for the marriage license. Ramone had never told her they had been married in California, but she found a lead that had taken her there. *Ok, Pop, where did you two get hitched?* She scanned the hits glaring at her on the screen and clicked one. Reading intensely, she was drawn into yet another useless page. As time ticked away, she viewed a slew of useless pages, all catching her eye, but none retrieving what she wanted. *Damn it, just go to Facebook. Everyone's there. She could be there.* Although she herself wasn't there. Facebook was far too cliché.

After an undetermined amount of time had passed, she concluded that she needed something stronger to drink after all. She packed up all of her work and hoisted the boxes onto a luggage cart and loaded the elevator, with exhaustion taking over. As she exited the elevator, drudging the cart uncomfortably out into the hallway, she nearly ran into Ramone, who was rounding the corner and talking on his cell phone. "So, tell me again, how'd you get his name? I think I must have missed something. Hey Bill, let me call you back. I found Karla. We'll meet up with you later after lunch. Ok, thanks."

Ramone's breathing was quick and deep. He paused to take in a long heavy breath while still processing his conversation with Bill. "Where have you been? I thought you were stopping by my room an hour ago? Damn, Karla. This isn't a vacation."

This time it was Karla who took in a deep breath, for entirely different reasons.

Ramone lead the way to his hotel room, with Karla close behind, as he talked quickly, causing Karla to lean into him. "So, Bill has something for us. He struck up a conversation with a man down in the lounge last night."

"I thought you two were together last night?"

"Oh, we were. But, I had too much work to do, and he didn't want to go home yet. I don't think things are going well with the wife. Anyway, he said after I left, some drunk guy started making small talk. Turns out this drunk guy used to live here. What're the odds, huh? I guess the guy used to work for the railroad, but now he's got his own construction business up in Carbondale. Wants to retire closer to city amenities and is looking for real estate in town. So, while on the topic of real estate, as it related to the '70's and '80's, the guy says to look into investments going on north and west of town, and also into folks out in the Whitewater area with money to burn. He made some comment about 'Follow the money'. Interesting, huh?"

"Whitewater? Why out there? Isn't that just desert and ranch lands and all? I mean, what would any land investor want with that area? Doesn't look like prime land to me. I did do a little research, you know, since it's not too far from the Gunnison River. I figured we should look at possible locations for the shootings, since it didn't appear they had ever found the crime scene for that. If we could come up with the actual location of the shootings that could be something, right?"

"Yes, good thinking with that. You should let me know what you're up to. Don't be going off on your own, we need to work as a team, here. So, did you come up with anything?"

"No. Like I said, just old ranching families who have been there forever. And some family who bought up a shit ton of property in the '80's and '90's. Nothing alarming. I guess the land is good for developing, as it turns out."

"This is why we talk, Karla. So, it's true, there was a lot of investment building going on in the '80's and '90's. But, this guy from the bar seemed to think some of it was the result of dirty money. Especially out that way, where nobody paid too much attention. He says that in the '70's, those ranchlands were sometimes used as covers for growing and distribution sites of all sorts of drugs. Would make sense. Right? It's isolated and nothing but dirt and brush rolling on the hillsides as far as the eye could see. Who would notice?"

"So, did he give some names? Since he apparently noticed."

"Only folks he thought we could trust to talk to. Just people to hit up for information. Bill said the guy shut down a bit when he asked for more details."

"Well, that in and of itself is something. That whole six degrees of Kevin Bacon shit is true what they say, isn't it?"

"What's up with that? Bill said the same thing. I don't get it."

"It just means that mankind can be connected by six people, no matter where you are or where you go. They've done research on it and everything."

"So, what does Kevin Bacon have to do with it?"

"He was part of some of the research," Karla laughed out loud.

"Well, that doesn't matter; but in this town, it sure seems to be true. Maybe less than six people, it sounds like."

"I don't know, Pop. I think we need more than just some drunk guy spewing off about real estate out in the country. We're gonna go talk to someone, right?"

"Yes, oh, of course. And, I know. But what was especially interesting was that this guy said that there was a half-a-dozen cops living out in the area, there in the '70's. If what he was saying is true, then what were cops doing living out there? It's always bugged me that so much shit was hitting the fan all over the state with regards to the feds trying to bust up places. Except here. Major drug busts popping up all over the state, but nothing shows up here. I mean it's the damn gatekeeper to the state, and yet nothing goes down here that ends up in the papers? Feds can't make a single sting come up with dirt? Clean as a whistle?"

"Aside from an unusually high death rate in a few years' time span? Not so clean, Pop. Don't you think? Hey, were there any big busts in the Aspen area? Maybe something there will connect to here. With Denison's sister living there, and both of them had family here. Maybe there's something to that."

"I still have to do some cross referencing. But I do remember that we found that huge bust that the feds had made in '74 involving Aspen folks. It was on the national scale and it claimed eight different drug outfits were involved, some of which originated in the Boulder area. Maybe, there's some Boulder connections to this place that overlap."

"How could a place like this be connected to money like that? People around here are just, well, normal country folks."

"That's the whole point Karla, white collar crime isn't obvious. They stay in the 'normal zone' for a reason. This guy from the bar was really caught up in the fact that cops lived out there. He said that at least three of them had addresses in the city around the same time, while also showing up in Whitewater."

"Ok. People move."

"That wasn't just it. He said a few of 'em living out there also had city addresses not too far from the Denison girl, and a couple of these cops had gotten themselves stranded in a snow blizzard up above the valley on top of a mountain ridge. He called it something Mesa."

"Grand Mesa?"

"No. That wasn't it. Bill said he wrote it down and would bring me his notes later. I think it started with a P."

"When did that happen?"

"That's what Bill said was interesting. They were up in the hills not long after bodies turned up in the river, and right before Bakerson was arrested. They claimed to be coyote hunting but failed to tell anyone where they were. The place they were rescued was near an old timer's ranch. Except this old timer was doing more than ranching in those apple orchards of his."

"Still a lot of speculation, Pop. It wouldn't be unheard of for a couple of guys to get stranded in a snowstorm, huntin' coyotes."

"With one gun between them? And no family knowing where you are? These guys were law enforcement and lived out in the boonies. You'd think they would be more prepared than that. This guy from the bar, says he's an avid hunter, and he doesn't seem to think their story holds up."

"Maybe it was 'a going fishing on a broke back mountain kind of thing'." She let out a sly grin, hoping he caught the humor.

Ramone was talking fast, as his momentum was impossible to mask, so the joke went right by him. He had fumbled with his room key and was unloading Karla's boxes as he spoke, "And, while we're on the subject of cops, I also found verification of that other cop who was arrested for selling drugs. Interestingly enough, he also lived near the Denison girl. Here, take a look at this." He sat a box onto the bed, quickly shuffled through a pile of work laying on a pillow and handed her a newspaper clipping from a notebook he had been working out of the night before. "Compare the dates that he was busted. All of this happened, look, all in the same month."

"Interesting co-incidence. Seems like a lot was going on all around the same time."

As much as Karla wanted to speculate and dig deeper, her original plan to take a break was calling her. "I gotta get food, Pop."

"I got food in here."

"Not your kind of food. Real food. I'll be back soon."

"Just one more second. Before you go, will you finish unloading the stuff you were working on, and organize it all with my stuff on the bed, there? It won't take long. I just gotta use the john and want to have it all easy to get to when we meet with Bill later."

"My head hurts, Pop! Can it wait 'til I get back?"

"No. It'll only take a few minutes." He disappeared into the bathroom, as she reluctantly began to organize piles on the bed. She scooted his briefcase off to the side, and something out of place slid into view. Nervously looking to the bathroom, she pulled the small wooden picture frame engraved with a poem, hand painted in bright colors, into the light. She immediately recognized it, but was confused as to why he had brought it with him, and why carry it around in his briefcase? *Pop, you're so weird.* Hearing the water running, she instantly slid the frame back into its hiding place and resumed her sorting.

Ramone emerged from the bathroom scratching his head. "I don't know why, but this guy's name, a real-estate investor I came across, keeps tugging at me that we've read about him somewhere else. I can't place it. Bill's talk with this guy reminded me of it. It was a name I saw on that list of people found in Kendall's stash of writing. Craig was the name. Do you remember a Craig somebody coming up somewhere other than on that list of hers? But I've seen the name somewhere else. Damn it, why can't I remember?"

"Who's…what? What guy?"

"I don't' know why it sticks with me. The name was Hollister. Craig Hollister. Yeah, that was it."

"I know that name. He had his hands in a couple of small businesses. They went under, tax evasion or something like that, or maybe just got bought out, it was hard to tell. Came across the information when I was looking into records about that bar you told me to look into. It was quite the rabbit trail. I was just trying to look at who actually owned the bar, the paper trail was really sketchy, and his name came up as someone who had power of attorney over some other property. Now that I think about it, one of the owners was from Boulder. But he didn't have the bar long. Anyway, when I looked to see who he was, the other businesses pulled up somewhere in the mix. I'd have to go back and look at my notes."

"Well, I'd have to go back through some things, too. I can't place why he rings a bell somewhere else."

"Look, there was someone with that last name who went to high school with Denison. And he may have been related to Denison's brother in-law. Look at this statement. Hollister. Same last name. Could be related."

He took the file from her and scanned what she was looking at. After flipping a few more pages, he paused and looked up to her. "But, according to this, he went to college here in the early '70's. We should find out for sure if he was related to Denison's brother in-law."

"Yeah. But I'm still not making sense of the correlation and why it even matters. We can't even find a solid connection between these cases, anyway." *He looks tired.* "Pop, do you think that maybe you should break for lunch too?"

"Naw. You got this all sorted? Thanks. It helps me keep going if it's organized. Just go eat. See you in a bit." He glanced at her with concern in his eyes. "You've been having headaches lately, a lot. Are you getting enough sleep?"

"Yes, I'm sleeping fine," which was actually a lie. *I've been having headaches for a long time now, Pop.*

Out into the heat of the sidewalk, Karla's tension relaxed. The familiarity of city sidewalks, lined with mature trees overhanging the newly renovated hotel landscaping, calmed her. There were rows of flowerbeds, shrubs, and decorative art sculptures, which made her homesick. She missed the sun beating down onto the concrete, the large sculptures on every corner, and the street music at every turn. *I guess this will do.* She smiled as she strolled passed old brick buildings of times past. She could tell that these buildings were the earliest of the city's history. The beginnings of everything this place called its own. Demons and all.

Karla noticed a sign up in the near distance that spoke of a time from the 50's or 60's. This sign was a picture of woman, with the top of her head dawned in a mountain full of hair and large, fake eyelashes. The sultry seductress in neon sign form beckoned patrons into her establishment. Bubbles from a martini glass dangled from her long fingertips. The name on the sign completed its calling of "Quincy's Place".

Karla time-warped through the single frame door, the only window of natural light in the whole place. Brick and stone engulfed a dark room, with a single horizontally shaped light hanging above a well-worn bar. The solid oak that horseshoed itself around an island of liquor bottles, sinks and coolers, had lost its shine and smelled of wet and stagnant wood. The stools, intended to provide a resting place for patrons, were in desperate need of mending and looked anything but comfortable. Karla glanced around for signs of life, and the female bartender was all she could find.

Not that there weren't patrons. There were. A few anyway. Five to be exact. They could be counted at a glance. Each customer scattered themselves around the bar, mostly sitting alone, with the exception of a couple across the room engaged in a close and personal conversation. Karla took a seat on a stool nearest the door. It wiggled as she sat down. Balancing herself with her left hand, Karla made sure it would hold her before settling her weight into the stool. The lady behind the bar immediately laid a napkin in front of her, "So, what's your fancy, my dear?"

"I don't suppose you carry local wines, do you?" Karla smiled cautiously, looking around.

The bartender laughed. "Not this place, Sugar. Try the place down the street."

"No. That's ok, Jack and Coke is fine." *Maybe I need something stronger anyway.*

"Got an ID?"

Karla smiled wider, with a hint of laughter, "Of course." She dug into the outside pocket of her purse, letting her check it, and then watched as the bartender quickly went to the other side coming back within seconds with her drink.

"Not from around here, I see. What brings you in here? I don't get a lot of tourists in here." The woman glanced around and laughed. That put Karla at ease. *I can see why. But I think I might kinda like this place, anyway.*

"I'm not in this town for fun. Just here working. So, I guess that explains it, huh?"

The bartender glanced from side to side looking toward the others on each side of the bar. "You're in good company." She was as tattered looking as her clientele. Not as old as two of the gentlemen separated on each side of the bar. She certainly looked well lived. Seemed to be in her fifties or so. Her hair was slightly graying, and she could easily loose a few pounds, but who couldn't? Her smile was very much a contradiction to her somewhat rough demeanor. It was gentle. Genuine.

"What kind of work do you do?"

"I work in my father's private investigation firm. Well, I work for my father. I'm really a student. But, that's how I get paid."

"Yeah? Where you from?"

"Phoenix."

"So, you planning to go to the college here?"

"Oh, no, no. We're just up here for a case. I'm on break. I mean from school."

"What kind of case would bring you this far? Not much happening around here big enough to bring in out-of-state'ers." In her line of work, she usually knew all the happenings around town. "By the way, I'm Shannon." She wiped her hands before reaching out to Karla's.

"Hi. Nice to meet you. My name's Karla." She paused to take drink. "It's an old case. Not current. A private case from a client who used to live here. Long before I was ever born."

Karla took another sip from her drink and opened her purse to dig out cash to pay for it. As she opened up her wallet, she exposed several black and white photos lying loose in an open inseam pocket. One of the photos was of her mother and was secured within a clear sleeve. The others were simple loose paper copies, nestled close against her mothers'. Most of the women in the other photos were about the same age, with the exception of the photo that was most visible, near the opening. It lay in clear view as Karla placed her wallet open faced onto the bar to count out the bills. This photo depicted a girl who was clearly much younger than the others. All of these pictures looked as if they had been taken in a moment of times past. Simple reminders of life lost from the pages of old newspapers.

Shannon stopped short in a jolt, after she casually glanced down to the wallet. More accurately, she caught a surprise glimpse at the photo looking up to her. Shannon's eyes turned distant from an uncomfortable rush of emotion she hadn't felt in years. Karla handed her a ten-dollar bill, which she took in seemingly slow motion from Karla's fingers.

"Do you want change?" Shannon's voice was unusually quiet and her presence was eerily still.

"No. The rest is yours." Karla glanced up, feeling the awkwardness and attempted to smile it away. Shannon took the money and slowly made her way to the cash register, keeping her peripheral vision on Karla. She tried to slow down her out of control breathing, placing her hands onto the cash register to keep them from shaking.

Shannon stood for a few seconds, and Karla watched her body language with some confusion. *Did I say something wrong?* They both were distracted by the bell that jingled when the door opened. An older man entered, with a wobbly gait, and chewing tobacco behind his bottom lip. He nodded to Shannon with a cantankerous grunt, gesturing his hand to the bar. His thin bent- over stature indicated that he might not have needed another drink.

Shannon immediately went to a row of bottles and poured a glass full of straight whiskey. The man staggered his way past Karla and sat at a stool just one over from hers. Karla found herself feeling both uncomfortable yet intrigued at the same time. *As drunk as he is, I could knock 'im down with my pinky.* With this thought, Karla relaxed.

"So, who's this pretty li'le thing? She don't look like she belong...s here."

He thinks I'm pretty. Must be the booze talking.

"Hi." She reached out her hand for an introduction. "I'm Karla."

"Wha' a sweet name. You're too sweet to be in a...pl...ace like this. And what's this?" He pointed to her drink. "How can a young girl like you... take this shit so early in th' day? Don' you know it'll... ki' you? Hard on the liver...they say. They...do." He winked to Shannon, and she snickered, looking to Karla suspiciously.

He's endearing. Karla took a sip, feeling the coolness from the ice on her lips. It wasn't her usual glass of wine, but it was comforting. Shannon wiped the bar with a damp cloth. "She's just taking a break from some work. I'm guessin' she needs a break from the ol' man, am I right?"

"Why? He ridin' yer ass? My ol' man was'… hard ass if there ever was one. But I miss him. Son' a…bitch miss 'im. " He drank down his freshly filled glass, wiping his upper lip. "Get me what she's havin'. She's… showin' me up."

Shannon laughed and shook her head, making her way to the bottles to do as she was told. "By the way, Karla, this old fart is Randall. He'll grow on you. And as for you, my drunk old friend, this is all you're getting. Looks like you've got a head start." She stopped in front of Karla and slid the glass over to him. "She works for her father." Shannon hesitated again, looking to Karla. "Do you mind talking about it?"

Randall may have been drunk, but he still paid attention. "Talkin' about what? I think I miss' somethin'."

Karla shrugged. "It's cool. I work for my Pop. He's a PI. We took on an old case that just needs a second look."

Shannon shot Karla another cautious glance, "Why a second look? What was the case?" Shannon's chest continued to rise and fall in deep breathing. Something Karla couldn't help but notice but wasn't sure what was going on. *Why so suddenly guarded? What did I say?*

"Ya, like what kind…a case? I been around the block a time… or two." Randall leaned onto his elbow and looked at Karla, as if he were steady enough to stay that way for more than a few seconds.

Shannon grinned at him and winked, appearing to relax for a split second. "Just a time or two."

Karla smiled sweetly at the relationship between them. "Well, it's supposedly solved. But, our client questions the outcome. So, we're looking into it. It's how we get paid, you know."

110

"Ya? Anything that made headline...s? Prob'ly jus' a husband and wife thing. PI's usually take on those kinds... a... stupid things, don't they? Someone'...s... father... cheatin' on his mother, didn't he? Right? That's always...s...how... it goes."

Karla eyed Shannon as she cleaned up knowing that bartenders make a life of being in the know. Most patrons forget this. She could tell that Shannon knew this man well. No doubt he'd been coming in the place for years. No doubt he had a lot of great stories. And maybe some of them were true.

"Yes, you could say there was a lot of cheating going on," Karla smiled.

"I told ya! Nothin' more th'n cheatin' shit! I was hopin' it was somethin' more inter...est...in'." He slurred a bit as he steadied himself with the palm of his hand.

"I'm guessing it is a bit more than that. Or they wouldn't have come this far." Shannon looked to Karla with a serious gaze.

"Ya. Well, we don't need anything more inter...estin' around here anyway. We like it quiet." Randall's demeanor suddenly changed. He took a big and final gulp from among the ice and breathed hard. Shannon looked him in the eyes. His hard, tired eyes. They almost appeared to tear up. But, they hadn't a chance. Karla noticed. Shannon shot her a look that made her wish she hadn't.

Randall carried on without acknowledging that either of them had noticed.

"Well, don't get too caught up in what...ever it is you're doin'. Don't let it own ya. It's just... a case. Not like you can do anything about any of it anyway." Pushing the empty glass toward the opposite edge of the bar, he stood up, barely able to stand.

111

Shannon leaned over the bar and went to his aide by helping him steady his elbow to the solid surface. "You, my friend, are going home. I'm calling you a cab. Just sit tight, Randall, I'll get you some food."

"I'm sorry, did I hit a sore spot?" Karla whispered.

"No, he's just tired. That's all."

"Don't talk about me… like I'm not here."

"Don't get your panties in a wad. Here, drink some water."

Karla leaned over her drink and rubbed her forehead, realizing that she should get that food she knew she needed as well and then get back to her father.

"Headache?" Shannon asked.

Karla nodded. "You got anything to take?"

Shannon pulled a couple little pills from a drawer under the cash register. "Here. This should do the trick."

"Is it strong? Everything hurts these days."

"Like I said, it should do the trick." She smiled, setting Karla's insecurities at ease. "Do you want another drink?"

Karla indicated that she was done. "No, this is it. I gotta get back to work without Pop knowing where I've been."

"Listen, you seem like a smart and sweet girl, but ol' Randall here is right. He's a wise ol' son-of-bitch. Been around the block a time or two."

"Yes, he said that."

"So, really, about this case of yours. I've been around here a long time, as well. Maybe I could help." She looked to Randall. "Not now, though. Not when he's like this."

Randall sat up from what seemed like a sleepy stupor. "There.... you go, talkin' about me again. I'm fine. Reall...y."

"Yes, I could come back. And maybe I could help you improve your odds of enticing some new business. Tourists, maybe?"

"How exactly do you think you can do that?" Shannon chuckled.

"Well, for starters, you could add wine to your inventory. Local wines, maybe?"

"Not a bad idea, I suppose. Though most of our clientele aren't into the wines, as you can see."

"Indeed I do."

"You know, I don't mind it. These guys. I need them as much as they need me."

Karla smiled and nodded. "But they also need food. And that's where I can really give you a hand."

"Oh yeah?"

"I'm in culinary school. Pop hates it. Says I need to be doing something worthwhile. As if people don't eat."

Shannon laughed.

"I know, I look like I don't need to eat any more. Maybe that's why he doesn't support it. I've always had a weight problem. Not like my mother. She was so pretty."

"That's not what I was thinking at all. I think you're beautiful."

That's nice.

"I'm sure your mother is very proud of you." Shannon was sincere enough to almost make her believe it.

"I wish I knew if that were true," she looked to Shannon with reluctant hesitation to say more. Though she wanted to.

"Your mother not around anymore?"

"She never was. At least I don't remember. Pop says she just left one day. Just like that. Says he doesn't know why."

"They always know why, sweetie. That's just their own deception haunting them." Shannon quickly retracted, realizing that may have been too harsh. "I'm sorry. I over-stepped. I don't even know your father."

"No. You get it. There's more there, I know. Some of the things he says just don't make sense. I mean just today I found a silly picture that he usually has at home. It's stupid. It's not like him at all. I mean, it's a poem, for God's sake. My Pop doesn't even read poetry. *I* read poetry."

Shannon tilted her head and smiled. "Maybe there's more to him than you realize."

"No. It's just this one thing he's had forever. He usually keeps it on his dresser at home. It's been around since I can remember. I asked him about it once, and he just got all annoyed and told me it was something an old friend gave him. Clearly, he doesn't want to talk about it. So, I quit thinking about it. Until today. I mean, why bring it with him now? Here? On this trip? It's just weird, that's all."

"Well, you're not the first person to think their father is weird. I miss my father."

"Do you have a big family?"

"No. All that's left is me and my mom." Shannon took in another deep and slow breath and looked to Karla. Uncomfortable, she looked out towards the door, and then to Randall. "Wake up! Taxi's here!" She smiled to Karla as she moved around the bar to Randall's side, helping him walk outside. "It was nice chatting with you, sweetie. You'll be back, I hope?"

"Yes, I'm right behind you. See you again soon."

Karla walked out into the bright sunlight with squinted eyes and turned to watch as Shannon helped Randall into the taxi. *It would've been nice to have a sister.* She glanced around at her surroundings looking for a place to get some good wholesome food.

Up ahead in the distance, a young man with dreadlocks played a calming rhythm on his conga snug between his legs. She thought more about the poem within her father's keepsake picture frame. For all she knew, she could have written it as a child, and he was too embarrassed to admit that he liked it. After all, she liked it. It could have easily come from her. Even the frame itself could have come from her. The frame had been hand painted, with bright hues of blues and greens, and random shades of yellow scattered like hazy sun blotches. In a bold black, handwritten font it displayed the caption:

"Love is the music, flowing so free

Giving peace to the soul

Giving peace to me".

Chapter 11

Ivory keys danced precisely at the light touch of Ruth's fingertips. Each tap set free harmonious notes from out of the hymnal set upright in front of her. Her hands were enthusiastic across the piano keys, but her demeanor and the tension in her face spoke of anything but enthusiasm. *Why does he think he can do this? We have a life together. A life with music and church, and photography, so many things we share. What does he want from me?* Ruth's eyes were red and teary, as she tried to concentrate on the pages in front of her. That usually shifted her mood. A different distraction shifted her thinking instead.

"Tap, tap, tap!" The front screen door shook slightly with the quick knocking on its metal frame. Curtis emerged quickly from the master bedroom and opened the door. "Oh, it's you. You're not Greg."

Ruth stood up and headed toward the door when she heard Betsy's voice, "Well, not last time I checked." She was looking to him defiantly as she swept passed him into the house, carrying Blair on her hip. He stepped out of her way in agitation, "Oh, please do come in." His sarcasm amused Betsy, but she ignored him in spite of this. "Hey, you got some dish soap?"

Ruth was genuinely happy to see her. "Sure. Hey little man? What are you up to this evening? Where's Andrew?"

"He's watching T.V. I had to sneak out. If he knew I was comin' here, he'd just want to stay and play. I'm kinda in a hurry. My house is such a fucking mess, and their dad's stopping by. Thought I would at least do some dishes."

Curtis shot Betsy a glare and then a stern reprimand over his shoulder, as he headed back into the hallway, "I don't appreciate hearing that kind of foul language in my home."

Betsy ignored Curtis' glare, and continued the mission at hand, as she followed Ruth to get what she came for. Once in the kitchen, they heard a honk coming from a car out in the street. Curtis peeked his head around the corner, "I'm headed out. I think the boys should be getting ready for a bath soon, don't you think?"

"Of course. I was letting them play a little longer. You plan on being home late?"

"Not too late. Greg wants to take me out early in the morning to the new spot that he says is a great place for still shots. He's got some things to run past me for work before then."

"I thought he was showing you something he was working on tonight? Isn't that where you're going? To his place?" She was squeezing dish soap into a plastic container and didn't bother looking up to see if he had walked away. He yelled out to her just before she heard the click of the front door. "Tonight is something different. Tomorrow is the trip out by the river. I told you that!" And then he was gone.

Betsy was admiring Ruth's clean kitchen when she noticed Ruth blinking away tears.

She looked at Ruth intently. "What's wrong?"

"It's no big deal. I'll tell you about it later, when we don't have little ears." Ruth looked to Blair and leaned down to kiss his forehead. As they

117

made their way back into the living room, Betsy was comfortable prying for more information. "Who's Greg?"

"Curtis' colleague. He's a photographer too. But he's got a lot more clout than we've ever had. And he seems to know a lot of connections around town. Curtis is hoping he could help him do some networking. They're actually going into business together. A different photography business, I guess. One that doesn't include me."

"I didn't know there was that much networking needed to sell pictures."

"If you're serious about it, there is. Curtis is working on several pretty big jobs right now. Greg knows some people out in Whitewater, near the river. It's supposed to be nice and quiet for good photo shoots," she gulped down the need to cry, pretending to cough, then continued rambling, "they've been spending a lot of time together. I mean, I don't see why not. They have so much in common. I guess he's quite the gun collector, and you know how Curtis likes his guns. Not to mention they both love to experiment with building model airplanes. They're engineers after all, and that seems to be a real big deal to them. Just seems like toys to me, but they are pretty uptight about what they build."

Laying a tin of children's books onto the coffee table, Ruth sat down on the sofa, "So, are you headed out tonight? And by the way, how are you doing? You feeling ok these days?" Ruth made small talk, avoiding the subject of her recent argument with Curtis.

Betsy didn't play along that easily, "So, you're really not gonna tell me what's wrong? Nice job turning things back to me. I'm fine. I told you that yesterday. Quit asking about it." Then she switched Blair's weight from one hip to the other and sat down on the edge of the sofa to face Ruth, releasing Blair to the floor for him to toddle to the books with his cloth diaper loosely dangling to his ankle. "C'mon? You're not foolin' me. What did he do this time?"

"It's not that big of a deal. At least I hope not."

Betsy looked to Ruth with sincere concern.

"Ok. It is. But I've been trying not to think about it."

"I'm not tellin' you to think, I'm tellin' you to talk," Betsy snickered as she raised her eyebrows.

"Maybe you should be the one talking. You were the one who nearly died from that attack. C'mon, Betsy, I was there, I saw you. It was serious. And you won't even talk to me about it. You act like it never happened. Which is ridiculous. For heaven's sakes they had to hospitalize you. It was serious, Betsy. You need to talk about it so they can find out who did it."

Betsy stopped to think. Her face went somber. "No. That's not true. They won't. It's because I don't remember anything. That's pretty damn embarrassing. To not even remember what happened." She stopped again and looked sincerely into Ruth's eyes. "I'm glad you guys were there, though. If Curtis hadn't been up working....." She bit the inside of her cheek. "Never mind. The cops aren't gonna do anything, so there's no use fretting over it."

"I fret over it."

"Then stop. It's not gonna change anything." Betsy's demeanor took on a sudden change. A deliberate and distracting change with a forced smile. "You should go out with me tonight."

Ruth winced, watching her carefully. *Why won't she tell me what's going on with her? How can she ignore such a traumatic event? She would've died if Curtis hadn't gotten to her in time.*

Betsy continued to prod, bringing Ruth back to her endearing nagging, "I've even got a dress you could wear."

"What? You don't think any of my dresses are hip enough?"

"Just not short enough," Betsy teased.

"Well, I need to get the boys ready for their bath."

"You're always on a schedule, aren't you?"

"Of course. Routine is what makes a happy home."

"Really? 'Cause when I got here, you weren't lookin' all that happy."

"Ok, so you found me out. We'll make it all about me, since you refuse to talk about you." She paused. "Not really, I don't want to talk about me. Someone tried to strangle you, Betsy. I'm worried about you. I can't even imagine how shook up you must still be."

"I don't. It's over. I'm better. Just let it go. I'm ok. I promise."

Ruth smiled reluctantly. *Let's just be open to each other.* She scooted closer to Betsy, put her foot under her other knee and resolved to change the subject. "Ok. I give. So, am I making a big deal over nothing, if he's doing photo shoots with nude models?"

"So, that's what he's up to!"

"He says that kind of work sells. But I sell work, and I don't do nudes."

"You do great work. Of course it sells."

The room was silent for a bit. Betsy watched as Ruth gathered her thoughts. "What if he's still having the affair? I think he is, he says he ended it, but I don't know"

"Fuck him! He doesn't deserve you! Do you really think he is?"

120

"Shhshh. Not so loud. I don't know if it's really that important. I can't just walk away, Betsy. He's my husband. The father of our children."

"And you really think that's what matters?"

"I'm not so sure I know what matters. Not if he's cheating on me."

"You are gorgeous! And if he's stupid enough to ignore you for some slut? You deserve better. Besides, you're so smart. And your pictures? They mean something. I mean, check that out. That's so sweet." She pointed to a photo of Tristan that was in a frame sitting on the piano. He was standing on an old bridge overlooking the river, with a stick in his hand running it along the planks of the wooden crisscross side rails. The canyon walls in the background gave a scenic finish that only added to the photo's appealing charm. "I love that you caught him playing. You can almost hear the stick in his hand going clicking away. It takes a special eye to catch that. Any asshole can take pictures of naked women." She nudged Ruth lightly with the palm of her hand. "You really should go out with us sometime. It'd do you a bunch of good. And maybe you could get even. It's always good to have a backup plan, since men can't be trusted past their own dicks."

Ruth giggled. Betsy had such a way with words. *I'm lucky to have you. I hope you know that.* "You know I can't tonight. It's too late to get a sitter."

"You mean, you would think about it, though? Cause there's this fashion show thing coming up, out at the Caravan. Suzanne told me about it. It'd be so much fun! We could dress up and act like we don't live in this shit hole of a town."

Ruth smiled and bit her lip, "Curtis would hate it if I went out with you."

Betsy chuckled and widened her eyes, "Yes, he would."

"I'll think about it."

121

"Don't you dare change your mind. Promise?"

"I said I'd think about it."

"Alright then. It's a date." Betsy grinned, picking Blair back up onto her hip. "Off to do a bit of laundry."

"Laundry? I thought you were doing dishes?"

"Well, I'll do a few, at least. After all, I'm gonna have to feed them before the asshole takes them to his mother's."

"So, I'm confused. Where are you doing laundry? Why not just do that here?"

"At home in the sink, silly. I don't have time to do a whole load."

Ruth nodded slowly, secretly amused. *Of course. That should make perfect sense.*

As Ruth busied herself with the nightly bedtime routine, she was distracted away from the tug of her broken heart. She made mental preparations to pamper herself in the bathtub with a book, once the boys were asleep. She too, had something to look forward to this evening.

When night fell, Ruth was leaning up onto her pillow which was propped against the headboard of the bed. Garbed comfortably in her robe, Ruth quietly hummed the tune of *Amazing Grace* with her reading glasses in place. The light from Betsy's car shone through the bedroom window as it drove past. *Looks like Betsy is off for the night.* She glanced down to her watch. *She's running a little late tonight.* Ruth then flipped a few pages of her Bible that was lying in her lap. She plucked out a small piece of paper and jotted Betsy's name on it. As Ruth closed her eyes in silence, she rubbed the paper gently between her fingers. The conversation went unheard within the empty room, but Ruth knew that it had been heard. She opened her eyes, folded the paper and placed it back into its resting place, which was in the middle of the book of St. Mark.

The next morning Ruth heard Betsy's car pull into the driveway across the street. As Ruth wiped dishwater from her hands, she sauntered to open the front door, breathing in the early morning light. She paused, standing in the bright rays of a new day to watch Betsy unload two sleepy boys from the backseat of her car. Ruth grinned when Betsy gently placed Andrew to the ground to toddle unsteadily behind her, as Betsy lugged Blair in her arms, wrapped in a blanket. Betsy struggled to nudge the car door closed with her knee and was somewhat startled by Ruth's voice bellowing from across the street in the distance. "Good Morning!" Ruth called out.

Betsy squinted in the sunrays to see Ruth smiling.

"Can I come over and make a pot of coffee?" Ruth felt quite comfortable inviting herself over.

Tristan and Trey clung to Ruth's legs, peeking around them to look across the street, wondering if their playmates were with their mother. Betsy nodded in agreement and tried to wave with the hand less impacted by Blair's weight. Ruth whispered, knowing full well that Betsy couldn't hear her, "Thank you."

Chapter 12

The rhythm of musical energy bounced off the walls as Betsy jiggled her hind end across the floor, flicking the end of her cigarette into the kitchen sink. The radio perched on the refrigerator squawked a familiar tune. Mumbling the song lyrics, she twirled around several times, nearly tripping over Blair who approached her from behind. He had tears in his eyes and whimpered softly. She picked him up with a heavy lift. "Damn, you're almost too big for me to hold. Who's been feeding you anyway?" She giggled at her own joke and then continued humming.

Scuffling her bare feet across the dull hard wood floors, she sat him on the sofa to kiss the wounds the cat had made on his arm. "Stupi' cat!" Blair sniffled.

"Oh, you know she only scratches when you tease 'er. What were you doing with 'er?"

He hesitated but came clean. "'Drew made it. She won't come wit me." He pointed across the room. A proud grin surfaced at the mess of blankets folded onto a chair, held up by a cardboard box. She hugged him. "Well, she listens to me!" Betsy picked up the cat and tossed her inside the fort. She looked around the room and broke the unusual silence. "So, where's your brother now?"

Before she could find out the answer, she heard the ring of the telephone coming from within the kitchen. She plopped Blair to the floor and snatched the handset with the dangling cord twirling in her fingers as she spoke, "Oh, Hi! Yep, I think so, but I wasn't on the .... Ok, sure I will try...." Her demeanor changed as she processed the conversation. "Yeah, ok. I get it, you need me. But I don't have plans for the kids." There was a pause. "Yes, I wanna work. I need the damn money. I'll be there. Just give me time to get a sitter." She hung up without saying goodbye. "God, he's an ass," she whispered to herself.

Andrew strolled in and sat down against the wall watching. "We gonna go to Gamma's?" Sighing, Betsy immediately began dialing one circular number after the other.

"Hopefully," she sighed again. Within thirty minutes, Betsy had piled the boys in and out of the car and left them in Grandma's yard with Grandma standing in the porch watching her. As she drove away, she drove slowly, watching Andrew pick up a ball from the front lawn and tossing it to his brother, who wasn't paying any attention at all. The ball bounced from atop of Blair's shoulder and then back in his direction. She let out a giggle through the back-car window, blowing a kiss behind her.

As Betsy turned slightly toward the back seat, she caught a glimpse of a small plastic make-up bag lying on the floor, partially covered with the blanket she kept in the back for the boys. *Shit! How'd that end up in the back? Damn, I've gotta be more careful, the boys could've dug into it.* "Shit! Shit! Shit! I was supposed to take it down today." This time she breathed her frustration out loud. She made a swift decision to turn onto the highway, passing the bowling alley by. *This'll be fast. It has to be!* She watched the front of the building to make sure that her manager wasn't outside taking a break. Breathing nervously, she increased her speed.

Betsy parked right out in front of the bar downtown, despite the clearly marked no parking sign. With a quick slam of the car door, she hurried inside and looked around. Straightening up, and putting on her best fake smile, she waved The General down. The General slowly stepped over to her, with his cane supporting one side of his weight. He sported a pair of large dark glasses that complimented his mass of curly black hair, "Well, hello my darling child of beauty. I thought maybe you forgot about me."

"You know I'd never do that! Just off to a late start today, that's all." She gave him a slight hug, then sat at the bar, placing the make-up bag on the wooden surface beside her.

"So, how are those sweet little munchkins of yours doing?"

"They're wonderful, of course," she tilted her gaze as she smiled.

Making his way behind the bar he poured her a drink, sliding the bag under the counter so quickly that she almost didn't even see it. "Well, do give them my love for me."

Betsy leaned in and whispered, "I'm afraid I don't have time for a drink."

"Oh, but you do my love." He winked, which made her smile nervously.

Betsy sat quietly for a several minutes, taking sips every few seconds, as he excused himself into the back of the establishment. By the time she had nearly finished the drink, he re-appeared, leaning in close to plant a kiss on her cheek. "Well, I'm so happy you stopped in to see me. Please give my love to Suzanne." She clutched the make-up bag that he had laid in her lap. "Oh, and there's an interesting sale going on in the Penny Pincher today. You might want to check it out."

"I'll be sure and grab one and have a look. Have a good night." Betsy smiled at him and tried to mask her rush by breezing casually out onto the sidewalk. With a heavy sigh, she put the car in gear and focused on getting to work.

The parking lot had yet to fill up when Betsy pulled into her regular parking space. The big rush wouldn't file in until after dark, but she was anxious still. She opened her glove compartment and tossed the make-up bag inside, slamming it to make sure it was tightly shut. After locking both doors, she hurried inside.

By 10:00pm, splattered remnants of mustard, stale beer, and the sticky sweet of Coca Cola mixed into a tapestry that smelled of nothing less than nasty work covering her apron. Betsy set a series of glasses onto a round table and watched a group of bowlers not too far away. She could hear the laughter, and even some of the conversation. There was a teenage girl who looked out of place amongst a group of drunken adults acting younger than she, pretty, with long strands of dark hair flowing over her shoulders as she held a child on her hip. The girl sipped her soda from a straw, watching the drama unfold.

Betsy tended to a few other tables then headed back to the wait station to grab a cloth to clean up a spill. When she spun around, the girl was behind her, this time holding the hand of another, but somewhat older child. "Can our table get three more Pabsts?"

Betsy laughed, "Do you really think they need more?" She walked back behind the counter to reach into the cooler. The girl snickered, "Who says it's for them, what if it's for me?" Betsy was delighted with her wit.

"In that case I'll bring them right over," Betsy charmed back with a grin.

Approaching the group, Betsy winked at the girl and held up a virgin spritzer, with an umbrella in it. The girl came over and took the drink in hesitation, then sipped it, "What? You think I'm a prude?"

Betsy shook her head, "Not on my watch. What's yer name?" She bent down to say hello to the child at the girl's side.

"It's Cheri and I'm with them." She casually pointed back at the carnival in the distance.

"So, you must be the responsible one tonight, I take it?"

Cheri winced, "I'm cool, as long as I get paid."

A young woman approached who seemed to be approximately eighteen or nineteen years of age.

"Hey sis', d 'you get those beers for us?" She reached out her hand to Betsy. "Hi. I'm Shannon. I see you've met Cher'."

"Yes, she's doing quite a job with these kids. Any of them belong to you?"

"Oh, hell no! I'm here with my boyfriend's family. They all claim the bunch." Shannon grabbed a beer from the table. "Thanks sis'." She smiled to Betsy, "You got kids? Cher's a great sitter. I taught everything I know."

"As a matter of fact, I do. Stop by before you leave and get me your number, ok?"

Cheri grinned with a nod, first to Betsy, then to Shannon.

Betsy tried to stop and chat as much as she could to make small talk and watch Cheri clean noses and trek the youngsters to and from the bathroom. At one point she noticed one of the children crying and Cheri sitting him onto her knee in the chair, wiping his hair from his face. *Yes, I will definitely be getting your phone number.*

The sound of clattered bowling pins echoed inside Betsy's skull; as she rubbed her forehead. She looked to the group of revelers nearest her station and wished they would take it down a notch. An attractive woman sipped tauntingly from her bottle of beer, as her painted lips puckered around the bottle top. The woman noticed Betsy watching and

128

instantly looked away, leaning in to give her lanky man a kiss on his cheek. Betsy walked to the cash register to ring up her last order. *Insecure Bitch.*

"Can I get a burger? No mustard, just Ketchup." This same lanky man approached just minutes later. Betsy raised her eyes to make a tired and disconnected attempt at friendly customer service. She haphazardly responded, trying to finish her calculations on paper, "Ya, I got it."

The man didn't move, forcing her to make a more genuine connection. "Anything else?" Betsy asked, this time looking up long enough to see him, "Oh. It's you. Sorry. It's been a hell of a night. What'd you want?"

"Is that how you address all your customers? Don't know why you gotta be such a bitch to me." Grant had been drinking, and his demeanor was more confident than normal.

Betsy stopped short, a bit surprised that he brought the conversation in that direction. "You're the one who's shitty to me. Don't put it all on me."

"Alright, girl. Just trying to make small talk. You know, we could get along pretty well if you wanted to. I could help you get even," He teased with a grin.

"Not even in your dreams, or if you were the last man on earth, in your dreams." She grinned back.

"Ok, so does that mean it's a truce?"

"Sure. But your wife may not like us getting along so much." Betsy pointed behind him to warn him of his wife's arrival. Grant turned to recover a persona of integrity. "You want anything, hon'?" he asked over his shoulder to his jealous counterpart.

The woman leaned up to the counter announcing her position by placing her left hand into plain view. "Ya, I'll just get a basket of fries. And another beer." The whole thing amused Betsy, as she found nothing all that interesting in this gangly womanizer. *Stupid skirt chaser. I'd be a bitch too if I was married to him.* Colin approached, slapping Grant on the back. "Hey there! You're up, man. What's the hold up?" He asked Grant, although he was looking to Betsy with an inviting smile. "Evening," Colin nodded in Betsy's direction. She smiled flirtatiously back, recognizing him immediately. *He's just as good looking and polite as he had been the first time, I met him at lunch that day with Suzanne.* "Hello again. I don't know if I formally introduced myself. I'm Colin." He held out his hand to her.

You did, and yes, I remembered it. "Hello again. I'm Betsy, in case I forgot to tell you my name last time." Her smile was sweet and charming.

"I'll take a beer. Budweiser. I'll be over there, if you get a minute." Colin pointed in the direction where Grant and his wife had meandered.

"It's busy tonight. But I'm sure I'll get a minute."

Just then, someone came up to the side of the counter and slung a folded-up newspaper riddled with wet beer splashes into the trash can behind her, near the cooler. "Sorry, I gotta get back to work." Betsy went to get his beer, watching him walk away and making sure he was far enough away for her to move in the direction of the trash can. Betsy looked around cautiously as she pulled the newspaper from the trash and snuck it under the counter.

After several more trips around the room, picking up debris and unloading trays of sloppy, sour drinks, Betsy returned to her post to announce to the other waitress that she was taking a break. "I'll be back in a few." When the coast was clear, she pulled the newspaper out of hiding, tucked it under her arm, and stepped outside into the dark quiet of the parking lot. She scanned the rows of automobiles in the shadows as she made her way to her car. With a quick click of the door, Betsy leaned over the seat and stretched to the glove compartment, tossing the newspaper in with a thud. It rolled open, next to the make-up bag, revealing a large wad of cash loosely tied in a rubber band and taped to the inside of the newspaper with masking tape.

In a flash, Betsy was back to the building, taking a moment to rest against the brick wall, wishing she had a cigarette. Headlights pulled into a parking space near the side of the building, and she watched two men exit a truck, then stop to lean against it and light up, with smoke swirling into the darkness. Trying to ignore them, she looked up into the sky and closed her eyes. *I just wanna go home.* A voice broke her trance, "Hey sweet cheeks. You off for the night?"

"No. Not hardly."

"Too bad." The one with shoulder length blond hair grinned spit through his teeth.

"Hey. You should join us later. Don't you think she should join up with us later, Tony?"

"No thanks, I'm pretty tired when I get off work." Betsy looked in the other direction.

"You know, I could get you a job down at the shop. It'd be daylight hours. Then you'd be free at night to hang out with us. Plus, you could get that piece of shit wagon of yours painted for free."

"My car doesn't need to be painted."

"Did you hear that, Craig? She doesn't need a paint job. How 'bout I fuck it up for you? You know, a little dent here, a scratch there." His laugh made Betsy's stomach churn.

131

"Shut up, Tony. Let's get your fuckin' drunk ass inside." Craig didn't seem humored either.

The two obnoxious men walked past Betsy as she intentionally looked the other way. To her relief they quickly disappeared into the building. Unfortunately, Betsy knew them both, and figured she had better head back inside as well. Returning to the food station, she was startled by the noise coming from the direction of Grant and Colin's group of bowlers. *Shit folks, mello out, for God's sake. You're causing a scene.* She looked around for Tony and Craig, relieved at their absence. *Maybe they left as soon as they came in.* Betsy knew they didn't come here to bowl.

The night grew weary as Betsy carried a tray of cellophane potato chip bags and free sodas to Cheri's table. The grill was closed down by this time of the night, and it was all she could muster up this near to closing time. Two children lie with their heads on the table, eyes lagging, but still awake. "Long night, eh?"

Cheri looked up and smiled, anxiously grabbing a soda.

The four couples at the neighboring lane were whooping up out of control, and Betsy glanced in their direction instinctively. A woman coming to the frenzy from the bathroom nearly tripped down the steps, needing her friend to help her to a seat. Betsy kept a watchful eye and ear in their direction, glancing to the office across the room where the manager sat unnoticed to the patrons. She couldn't help but overhear words not intended for her ears. "C'mon, damit! You guys need to keep it down. There's eyes in this place tonight, you know. You're gonna draw attention, God damit." It was an attempted whisper, but the emotions were clear, and not all that quiet.

Betsy sized up the crowd next to her. She decided to make her presence known in a way that wouldn't appear confrontational. "Hey, there are children close by. Not that you guys can't have a good time or anything. Just keep it clean, that's all." Betsy smiled her sweetest attempt at kindness, and several of them nodded, getting the message.

Cheri shook her head in sarcasm, "Really? Does it look like anybody cares that these kids are here?" She ruffled the mop on the toddler's head and leaned back, "It's not a big deal, anyway. They're just having fun."

As Betsy cleaned up, her thoughts drifted. Something tugged at her to just go pick up her children and go home. Ruth came to her mind, as Betsy organized and tidied the workstation. She remembered watching Ruth wipe her kitchen counter down three times before placing the loaf of bread on top of the freshly dried surface. Betsy felt a sense of pride as she wiped the workspace clean before putting the Ketchup bottles in a parallel line along the counter. She had never cared before if the counter beneath them was clean.

Groups of exhilarated patrons stumbled out into the darkness, rambling about the next adventurous location where they would end up before the sun would light up the morning. Betsy waved at several friendly faces, as they seeped out through the exit doors. Cheri waved with the only hand she had free, as the other was holding a sleeping child. *I really like her.* Betsy fiddled with the piece of paper in her apron with Cheri's telephone number written on it. Only a few scattered packs of die-hards stayed behind until closing, making sure they were able to get in one last game before last call. As the night slowed down, she dropped off a tray of bottled sodas to the trash can and ran for a break to the bathroom.

Rolling her neck in an attempt to stretch away the soreness of the night, Betsy stood at the sink washing her hands and tried to peer into the dirty mirror at her exhausted reflection. She heard a noise from behind her, as someone entered the bathroom. The flash of movement caught her attention, and she turned to make out the image. It was out of the ordinary. Out of context. That's because it was a man.

133

Not just any man. Betsy knew him. Of course, everyone had to know him. He was nick-named 'Head Honcho' for a reason. And clearly, she had no respect for him, no matter how much he demanded it. Tony accompanied him, but stood in the periphery, leaning against the doorway, blocking any curious intruders. It was typical for Mr. Head Honcho to have a side kick or two close by for added intimidation, who typically did his dirty work for him. Fear gripped her as she backed into the sink slowly, eyeing her antagonizer intensely. *This can't be happening again.* "Just, get the hell outta here. You know I don't want any trouble. You know I'll just scream and draw attention. You'll never be allowed back. And what would that do to your glowing reputation?"

"Really? You're delusional, right? You think anyone gives a fuck about you? You didn't learn the first time? You really wanna end up in the morgue? You got lucky last time. You're just lucky the fuckin' neighbors were up. Don't think for a minute you're ever gonna be that lucky again. I can see to that. I will see to that."

He shoved her, pushing her so far backwards over the sink that it caused her back muscles to bow in anguish. Betsy's head slammed against the mirror. He reached to her chin and wrapped his fingers around her face, squeezing hard," You better watch your back, little girl. You and your precious little friend are walking on thin ice, and you've already been warned."

Betsy shoved his hand away. A daring move. "You don't know shit! You think you control things with your fake title and all of your pathetic little groupie boys following you around, but you're a pawn, just like everyone else." Her abrasive response only fueled him. This time he grabbed a handful of hair from behind her head, and with one sweeping force, threw her across the tile and through a metal stall doorway. Betsy fell to the floor and put her elbow up onto the base of the toilet to steady

134

herself. This time she didn't speak. She simply glared into his eyes, breathing heavily.

He composed himself, leaned against the stall door, and lit up a cigarette, his comb over hair style rustled a bit, revealing a small flaw in his well-tailored look. "Hey, Tony, do you know what happens to those who mess with a well working system?"

Tony folded his arms across his stalky chest and smirked, walking toward the sink in order to get a better look. A few seconds ticked away before Mr. Head Honcho straightened himself to a solid stance, his short stature elongated only slightly. His eyes burned into hers from the short distance between them.

Despite the attempted intimidation, Betsy didn't back down, "Not everyone plays by your rules."

"And that's a problem. 'Cause you know they're not just my rules."

Betsy looked up to Tony, as he meandered closer. She taunted him, "Where's Craig? You ditch, 'im? I bet he had better things to do. He's smarter than you, that's for sure."

Tony stepped forward, almost stumbling, with a sort of grit, clenching his teeth together. Mr. Head Honcho put his hand out to gesture Tony to stop. Standing as tall as his stature could muster up, he pulled out a pack of cigarettes and slid one into his fingers, tucking the pack back into the pocket of his over-priced corduroy jacket. After he lit up and took in a long puff, he tossed it to the floor and stepped on it, then gave the orders. He was good at giving orders. "Just ruffle her up a bit. I want her to remember it."

Tony picked Betsy up by her shirt and pushed her in place with force onto the rim of the toilet seat. Within an instant, he flung the back of his

135

hand across the side of Betsy's cheekbone, causing her head to turn sharply and fall against the wall.

Frozen in fear Betsy didn't move, leaning her head against the cold surface, looking up to him, not wavering her cold eyes away from his. The only thing that moved was her chest, in rhythm with visibly intense breathing. At this point, Betsy opted to stay silent, hoping he was done.

Tony leaned in close to her face and whispered, "You think ya know what you're doin'. Ya think you're protected. But I'm here personally to remind you that you're not. An' I don't have to remind you that this never happen', right? Are you clear on that?"

Betsy refused to answer, watching his dishwater blond hair fall carelessly across his face, flopping to and fro over his shoulders, as he tried to steady his gaze. "Right?" He pressed closer.

Betsy nodded slightly. *Just go away. Please just go away.*

Tony stepped awkwardly backward, eyeing her. "You should prob'ly clean up. Your hair's a mess." He slurred his words as he spoke, almost falling as he turned to walk away.

With that, both men disappeared from sight. Betsy heard the bathroom door open and then close. She sat up, slowly brushing her fingers through her hair, trying to tie the loose strands back up into the roll she had put them in before leaving the house. She brushed the fear away from her face with her hands, refusing to cry.

After padding her face with a wet paper towel and making sure her hair was smoothed back into proper form, Betsy exited the bathroom. She looked around and made sure no one noticed her. Taking in a deep breath, she straightened her shoulders, brushed her apron, and returned to work.

Chapter 13

Background chatter filled the space of the banquet room, as the noise moved its way through the crowds of people milling among the folding chairs. Most people were sliding their way into rows of seats that horseshoed around the 'T' shaped stage that would soon serve as a platform for local models to flaunt the latest fashion trends. Ruth glanced around at all of the activity. *I guess it's nice enough. I think I'm underdressed.* She scanned glimpses of sparkling halter tops baring slender shoulders and larger than life sleeves dangling from the wrists exposing hands decorated in gold. Ruth leaned into Betsy, adorned in a slender mini dress and with shiny white boots. "Do I look alright? I should have borrowed something of yours," she whispered.

"You look gorgeous. Stop being so hard on yourself," Betsy hushed back.

Suzanne caught an opportunity to give Betsy a hard time, "Yeah. At least you're not wearing gigantic sunglasses inside. Jesus, Bets', you trying to start a new fashion statement?"

"You're just jealous that you don't have a pair." Betsy grinned as she pinched the corner rim of her large framed sunglasses with the tips of her fingers in a sassy pose.

The three women found seats near the front of the stage. It was Betsy's idea to arrive at the local fashion show early enough to get seats as near to the front row as possible. She pointed out to Ruth that it was fun to be able to get an up-close look, so they could make fun of the flaws that were less apparent from farther away. Betsy whispered a play-by-play as they sat down, knowing this was Ruth's first experience at such a gathering. "It's not all the glamor and shit that a show in the big city would be, so the models aren't so perfect."

"I hear some of them are nothing more than local working girls," Suzanne chimed.

"We have working girls in this town?" Ruth often didn't know how to hide her sheltered upbringing.

"They're called escorts, sweetie." Betsy was typically in the know with such things.

"What's the difference?" Suzanne sat down and placed her purse in her lap.

"Escorts get paid more. Look around. Do these guys look like cheap-skates?"

Until Betsy had pointed it out, Ruth hadn't noticed the unusually large crowd of men that had showed up to this event. "So, this isn't really about the clothes?"

"For us it is." Betsy wiggled herself into a comfortable position and grinned to Ruth in anticipation. She looked up to the front of the stage to give Ruth the signal that the show would begin soon.

Ruth leaned her lower back in her chair and relaxed. It was just she and a couple of friends pining over clothes that none of them could afford. Only a woman would understand this sort of calling. *This is fun. Maybe I will get some ideas.* Ruth looked down at her simple blouse. She realized that her top was buttoned nearly to the top, where her collar bones met. She casually brought her fingers to the top row of buttons and fiddled with them nervously. One by one Ruth loosened three buttons, touching her skin lightly, and feeling herself breath.

The first half of the show wrapped Ruth in a cocoon of both admiration and confusion. She grinned ear to ear at the crazy ideas that only a world of modern fashion could dream up. "Alright, the last dress I liked, but this is simply outrageous. Who would wear plastic see-through pants? At least not in public." She whispered as quietly as she could as not to draw attention to her slightly humorous disapproval. Betsy laughed out loud. "C'mon, I could see you wearing them."

When the lights came on for a quick intermission, Betsy stood up and looked around. "I'm headed to the bathroom. Then does anyone want to grab a glass of wine?"

Ruth eyed Suzanne, afraid to speak up. Suzanne was quick to respond, "Come on Ruth, we'll grab one for you. Bets', meet us at the bar." Before Ruth could sputter out a rebuttal, Suzanne had grabbed her hand and was dragging her through the maze of people in the dining area of the restaurant. *I guess I'm having a drink. But I don't drink.* She bit her bottom lip and looked around for any familiar faces that may be lurking nearby.

While standing near the bar as Suzanne paid too much for cheap wine, Ruth noticed Greg in a crowd of people near the door. "Suzanne. Suzanne," she tapped at her arm gently and quietly got Suzanne's attention. "We should get back to our seats." Without waiting for a response, Ruth grabbed her glass of wine and weaved quickly back through the crowd, with Suzanne at her heals. They met Betsy in the doorway. "Oh, thanks ladies. Here. Cheers to us! The most beautiful women here!" Betsy didn't waste time with celebrating their time together, but sensed Ruth's reserved demeanor. "C'mon, take a sip. It won't kill you."

Embarrassed, Ruth defended herself, "It's Curtis' friend, Greg. If he sees me, he'll tell Curtis and he'll make big deal of it."

"Who? Where?" Betsy looked around.

"Back there. It's alright. I'm sorry to be this way. He looked busy anyway. I'm sure he didn't see me."

"Who cares if he did?" Betsy sipped her wine. "We only have a minute or two. Drink up, girls."

The coolness of the sweet tasting beverage soothed Ruth's edgy nerves. By the time she sipped her final drop, the lights were dimming for them to return to their seats. Ruth liked sitting in the middle, as it allowed her to hear every word of Suzanne and Betsy's hissing gossip throughout the show. "I think the place is being watched," Betsy whispered before another model took the stage, leaning into Ruth, as Suzanne leaned in close to listen. "What the hell are you talking about?" Suzanne spoke as she kept her eyes on the model sweeping down the runway.

Betsy squeezed in closer and whispered even softer, "They're all over the place. I saw undercovers. As if they're fooling anybody. My God, if I can make them, anybody can."

Suzanne laughed out loud, then put her hand to her mouth to stop herself. "You watch too much TV, Bets'."

Betsy rolled her eyes and grumbled in a whispered hush, as she sat back in her chair. "They're watching the place. I know they are. We can't go to the after party now." She slumped into her chair in disappointment.

140

Suzanne leaned in again, "You're serious, aren't you?" She looked around.

Ruth listened intently almost forgetting about the show.

"Yes. Of course I am. You know as well as anybody that this place is hot. Look. To your right. What'd I tell ya?"

Suzanne made a shifty glance over her shoulder. "He's not that inconspicuous. He might get what he's looking for in a different get up. You nervous?"

Betsy didn't answer. Ruth watched her carefully but wasn't sure if she should pry. At least not now. *Why would you be nervous?*

"Well, are you, Bets'? Don't ignore the question," Suzanne shot her a stern look.

"I don't want to talk about it here. We're here to have fun. Later." She shot a similar look back to Suzanne. "Later. Alright?"

Suzanne switched her gaze to the runway.

Another model took the stage. Ruth watched Betsy carefully examine the tangerine colored poncho with glittery fringe. She couldn't tell if Betsy was really that interested in the clothes, or just eluding the topic of conversation. Ruth followed their lead to let the conversation dissipate. One pretty girl after another strutted past them. She felt a tinge of envy, with all of the swooping hair and high cheekbones. Not to mention the ample supply of cleavage. She glanced down into her shirt once again. *No wonder he strays.*

Then Ruth saw her. The woman's presence on stage startled her with a wave of lightheadedness. She suddenly began to feel sick to her stomach. *Of course. She's a model. How on earth did she get that part?* She leaned over to Betsy, "How do these women get to do something like this? Do you know for sure some are working girls?"

Betsy gave a quick halfhearted answer, still watching the stage, leaning in close so as not to be heard "Usually they're friends of someone. They might go through the agency that's sponsoring the thing, but you actually pay them to do that. I don't think they get paid for this stuff. But, yeah, some get paid in other ways."

Ruth's mood darkened. She was distracted from the rest of show, pushing back her insecurities that the mere sight of Curtis' other woman had triggered. *He said it was over. Looking at her, I don't believe it, no matter what he says. She is pretty, I suppose.* When Ruth had confronted Curtis about her, he denied it at first. But then Ruth showed him the photo slides that she had found in the case tucked away in the closet. He tried to convince her that it was all professional. Nude photos can be professional after all. Then Ruth had shown him the pictures of the two secret love birds together, arm in arm near a tree. Curtis never did admit who had taken those pictures. Regardless, they told the whole story. As soon as the fashion show ended, Ruth got up quickly to excuse herself with her dignity soon to unravel.

Betsy noticed her panicked exit. "Wait! I'm right behind you." She followed.

"Don't forget about me!" Suzanne announced after them. Ruth barely looked back as she rushed into the bathroom. She escaped into a stall, with her friends at her heels, nearly falling into the wall. "Can't I go to the bathroom?" Ruth turned and asked politely trying to maintain composure.

"What's wrong?" Betsy looked at her like a big sister. Ruth sat onto the rim of the toilet seat and sighed, staring past them, holding back streams of tears with rapid blinks.

142

"She's here. Curtis' mistress." Ruth sighed again, with her lip quivering just slightly. "She's one of the models. The one in the flowery tube top and skimpy skirt. Toward the end. It's her." She melted into the back of the wall and breathed in deep, this time making eye contact. Betsy kneeled and cupped Ruth's face in her hands.

"She's a tramp and you're not. And he promised it was over, right? He chose you, right?" Ruth reached over to pull tissue from the roll, as she heard the door open and footsteps approaching. She sniffed back the tears that were able to escape and regained her typically gracious posture. "I'm fine. You're right." Sitting up Ruth pulled her shoulders up and back.

"It's ok. I can handle this. Let's go."

Ruth was so matter of fact that Betsy hesitated. "We can go home if you like."

"No. I'm fine. Are you sure we can't go to that after party? I can figure out something for the boys for the rest of the night." Ruth had a sudden inclination to do something highly out of character.

"Now you're just being irrational. No, I sense trouble at the after party. But, we can go somewhere else."

Suzanne smiled in agreement and helped Ruth to her feet. Ruth took a big breath and walked to the mirror to primp. She looked deep into her eyes and tried to convince herself that she was attractive. Betsy said the words for her, "You're absolutely beautiful, sweetie, all of you. Smile. It's your very best feature. And it makes your eyes light up. You have beautiful eyes." Ruth looked again. This time she smiled. She gave Betsy a glance of appreciation, as she fluffed her hair, blinking light back into her own reflection.

As they exited the bathroom, Ruth caught a glimpse of a group of men standing near the back entrance of the room. "Stand in front of me," she whispered to Betsy leaning in close to her.

Betsy was puzzled. "Why?" She looked around her shoulder.

"Because it's Greg again. He's sure to see me this time."

"Oh for heaven's sake, you're not doing anything wrong. Stop it, and don't let anyone intimidate you. "

"Just block the view, that's all. Please?"

"Of course." Betsy stepped in front of Ruth and tried not to make it obvious that she was eyeing the group across the room. "So, who's the big shot he's with? What's he here for anyway? If anything, you should be questioning him, as to why he's here."

"Looks like his brother. I've only met him once. I don't know who the other man is." Ruth spoke in almost a whisper.

"I know who the tall one is." Suzanne spoke up, reluctantly.

Betsy was more than curious. "Oh? The one with the fancy shmancy suit jacket? He's no local that I know of. Looks too high and mighty for my blood."

"He's not a local. Not anymore, anyway." Suzanne was watching carefully but staying behind Betsy. "We should go," Suzanne concluded.

"How so?"

"'Cause he's a Hollister. They got family all over the state. Don't know which one he is. I've just seen 'im with Craig around town and heard stuff about the whole family. They all have connections. And not the kind we're privy enough to be a part of." She stopped to look to Ruth.

"What's Curtis' work buddy doing with the likes of him?"

144

Ruth looked at Betsy and Suzanne with confusion, "I wouldn't know."

A man familiar to both Betsy and Suzanne, dressed to impress, strolled casually over to join Greg's group of elitists. The group of men stood with confidence, drink glasses in hand. Betsy's body stiffened, "Yeah. We should go. Wish I could tousle that ridiculous comb-over to the floor first, though. Someday, he's gonna topple from that high horse of his, and his title won't be able to protect him. Someday."

"Wishful thinking Bets'. Nobody crosses the Chief."

Betsy's face was pale. "Yeah. Like I said, let's get the hell outta here."

The silent trek through the parking lot shifted the mood, and Ruth began to second guess her decision to go out with them. She was startled by a car that zoomed past them and then cranked to a stop in a parking spot near the entrance of the restaurant. A series of whistles coming from inside the open window of the car prompted all three women to pick up their pace.

"Oh for God's sake!" Betsy guttered her disgust. "C' mon, hurry. I don't wanna hang around here anymore. Stupid assholes!"

Bradley and Travis emerged from the car and whistled over at them. "Hey, why you walkin' away? What's the matter? You not stickin' around? I know you want to!"

Betsy turned and tried to respond lightheartedly. "Just got better places to be. But you tramps have a good time!" She waved her fingers back at them recklessly, as she loaded into her car. "I'm so glad we decided not to go to the after party." She breathed heavy, putting the gear shift into place.

Suzanne leaned her head into the front of the car over the seat that separated them, as Ruth settled herself up against the passenger door to get a clear view of both men, feeling increasingly unsettled.

145

Suzanne folded her arms over the seat in encouragement to ignore them. "So, let's forget we saw any of them and just get back to what we came out for."

"So, who was that? You both seem to know everybody." Ruth couldn't help but feel out of the loop at times.

"You don't want to know." Betsy paused, as the car rolled from the parking lot and into the street. "You know, maybe I should fill you in about all the crap in this town. That way, with you being across the street and all, I could just flick the front porch lights on and off if I get into any trouble. That would keep me safe, right?" Betsy laughed as if she were joking. It was a forced laugh.

How could she be joking? Even after what happened to her? Ruth was confused.

"And then what do I do? Betsy, are you serious? Certainly you're not joking. Are you?"

Ruth looked to her sincerely, "Betsy, you nearly died. That's nothing to joke about. If you really are in danger, you need to let me know. You're not dealing with the attack. It hasn't even been a month ago, and you're acting like it was no big deal. Are you still in danger?"

Suzanne's tone became serious, "Bets' she's right. Stop making light of it. Stop ignoring the obvious. You're just trying to pretend it never happened. You can't pretend it never happened."

"She's right, Betsy, you never talk about it. You should talk about it. You said you didn't know who attacked you that night. How could you not.....?"

Betsy didn't want to ruin the night, "I don't know. Ok? I don't know who tried to strangle me. I don't. I wish I did. I just don't like talking about it, that's all. But...but, I do know who did this." Betsy finally took

146

off the big sunglasses she had been wearing all night, to reveal light bruising just under her left eye.

Ruth responded by putting her hand up to her mouth, "Betsy! Not again? What is going on? Who did that to you? You called the police didn't you?"

"It was bullshit! That's all. And no, not a chance. There's no one to call. Doesn't matter at this point. Don't think I'm gettin' any help from the cops. Trevor and Derek know about it, and they'll handle it. They're already looking into the attack from before. I don't need to involve you in my shit. We're just pissin' some people off, I guess. I can handle this, all of it."

"But, Betsy, someone attacked you. And that attack landed you in the hospital! You almost died! This is serious! And now this? You're scaring me, Betsy. This is not alright. None of this is alright. You need to get someone to do something! What is going on?" Ruth couldn't contain her emotions any longer. She held back tears by wiping her eyes with the back of her wrists.

"Alright. I am doing something. Keep an eye on my porch lights, that's doing something, right? You know how to use a gun. You can come over if I need help, right? Just like the last time. You were there for me before. So, if I let you know, with flicking the lights, then you can come help, and there won't be a next time. That'll work. I'm sure of it."

Suzanne sat back in her seat and sighed, "I don't know, Bets'. That's not enough. Maybe we should pull back. I'm feeling really scared for you. Maybe the attack wasn't just some random creep like we all thought it was."

"I don't know. And don't you think I've thought of that? But it doesn't matter, I'm not runnin' scared. So not a chance, girl. I'm not runnin' 'till I've done what needs to be done. And then, believe me, I'm gonna get a way to get the hell out of this town."

Ruth was more confused than ever. *I don't' understand. You're leaving town now?*

Betsy, you need to talk to me and tell me what's going on.

Chapter 14

The cord to the telephone coiled into a tangled mess as Suzanne moved from one end of the living room to the next. She was talking with one hand, rattling away her frustrations, unknowingly pacing her anxiety away as well. Betsy watched her intently from her perch on the sofa.

Suzanne stopped to stare out the sliding glass door through the view across her back porch, twirling the cord with her fingers, trying to untangle it. "No. Can't tonight. No. I'm not going to bother him with this thing. He's got shit to worry about with all the attention down at the Rider's Club, and he had to get on the road to work, so he rushed out. They had a suspicious man in there the other day, and he's been uptight about it ever since. Not to mention 'bout that raid down at the bar he was at the other night. He's just all shook him up, and he wanted to stick around for the weekend, but he just couldn't. I've got it under control, really, I do." Betsy wandered over to take a look through the sliding door to see why Suzanne was distracted. Betsy rolled her eyes at the two men she saw standing in the yard across the street smoking cigarettes. Suzanne looked over to Betsy, realizing she should wrap up her phone conversation, "Hey, Dwaine, I gotta go, man. Ya, of course. Ok, I'll touch base with you tomorrow. I will. Bye!"

Betsy glanced back across the street, "So, is Dwaine heading out of town at all this weekend?"

"Who? What do you mean?"

"Um, Dwaine. That's who you were talking to, right?"

"Oh, Ya. Sorry. I just wish they'd go away. I hate having that sleazy dealer right across the street. Do you think that cane is for show? I wouldn't put it passed him. He'd be just the type to use a cane to get him attention. I think he's counting on his color to win the City Council race."

"He's never done me wrong. It's the other one who's trouble."

"You definitely have a problem with your filter. Dwaine says they're both trouble."

"Since when do you take Dwaine's word over mine?"

"Sorry. I didn't mean it like that. I'm just edgy tonight."

"Well girl, get off the edge. It's a bad place to be. I should know. So when you're done with your yoga thing come out with me tonight."

"Ya. Maybe. I'd have to find a sitter, though."

"When I stop by the bowling alley, I'll see if Cheri's there." Betsy paused. "I can stop by after dinner and get you, if you want."

"I don't know, maybe. I may just stay in tonight and watch TV, though. Would you be cool with that?"

"Of course! Alright, girl. You do your thing. I'm gonna head on out. I'll call you tomorrow." Betsy pecked a kiss on Suzanne's cheek just before she headed out through the front door.

When Betsy pulled into her driveway, her mind was a flurry of anticipation. She hummed her way into the house and plopped onto her bed to daydream of the night ahead. *What will I wear? Trevor said to dress nice. Is he taking me out to dinner finally? Maybe we can go somewhere romantic since Suz' is bailing on us.* She giggled out loud, as if Trevor were right beside her. She leaned around to the side of the bed and grabbed her diary, flipping to a blank page. Stretching out on her back, she pulled the pen from the front sleeve and began to write. Betsy's thoughts began as doodling at first. Drawing always triggered the flow of creativity and eventually the pen poured out her deepest thoughts of the day in meaningful words:

In the light, the dawn filled light
I see the face of one true knight.
He rides on a horse of white and gold.
A sight of beauty, a sight to behold.
He saves the fair maiden, who fell to the ground.
He swoops her in sweetness, and sequence of sound.
He softens her heart as he speaks to her eyes.
He promises true love, with no more goodbyes.

As Betsy relaxed on the bed in a trance of imagination, she drifted off to sleep without intention, dropping her pen and diary to the pillow at her side. She quickly fell into a dream. A sweet dream. A well statured white horse galloped across the sun-drenched earth, with a man atop its back. He wasn't what she expected. No armor. No shield. No protective helmet. As he glided up to her, he reached a strong but gentle hand out to her. She reached for him, and he swooped her up to him. His face was familiar, but he was no one she could recollect from within her memory. Somehow, though, Betsy knew who he was. The dream faded, and slowly her eyes opened to hazy consciousness. *Nooo. Just keep going. I don't want to wake up.*

151

A bit disoriented, Betsy sat up startled, "Shit! Holy shit, what time is it?" She gasped with an anxious whisper and jumped up, rubbing her face. She could barely make out the sound of several swift knocks at the front door. "Shit!" Exhaling and stumbling to her feet, she responded, "Be right there!" Rushing toward the door, she pulled strands of hair behind her ears, and slid her hand down the back of her head to straighten locks of hair down over her shoulders. She flung the door open in a swoop and grinned with a giggle of embarrassment. "Sorry, I'm not ready yet. I actually fell asleep. I'm really sorry!"

Trevor made his way into the living room, putting his hand around her waist, planting a long passionate kiss to her lips, "Don't you worry about a thing."

He looked around the room, "Who says we have to go out anyway. Why don't we just hang here instead?" He wrapped both hands around her back and pulled her close into him.

Betsy breathed in the attention as he swept her away for the rest of the night. There was no need to go out after all.

He softens her heart as he speaks to her eyes.
He promises true love, with no more goodbyes.

The shrill of the telephone broke the early morning silence. Trevor sat up first, thinking he may be dreaming, and blinking his mind into the present space of Betsy's bedroom. The sun was beaming an early morning light outside the gaps in the window dressings. "Betsy, Betsy, wake up. Your phone's ringing. Hey, Girl…"

"Is that the telephone? What time is it?" She sat up and glanced to her nightstand to look for the time. "Who the hell is that? It's not even 8:00 o'clock yet!"

Betsy rolled out of bed just in time for the calling to halt abruptly. "Of course. Now that I'm up." Giving a frustrated glance through the door, she laid a knee onto the bed, initiating a crawl back into Trevor's arms, when the phone began to clang its call again. "Oh, dear Jesus, who the hell?" Marching out into the hallway, Betsy disappeared. She returned in the doorway, visibly concerned. "It's for you. Who knows you're here? It's a woman."

He jumped up and scrambled to put on his pants that had been left on the floor.

"It's not your wife. It can't be. How would she know you were here? Have you said something?" Fear was written all over Betsy's face.

"No!" He disappeared around the corner, and Betsy followed close behind.

Rushing through the house and to the phone, he grabbed it, expecting the worst, making him hypersensitive to the voice on the other end. The relief on his face eased Betsy's fear, but didn't wipe away the confusion. Betsy listened intently to the one-sided conversation. "What? What do you mean? How'd you know I was here? Wait, stop. Say that again?…Oh, God. Oh, dear God. How…? Who's there?…Ok. Ok. I see. What?!…Did you call Derek?…No. Oh, son of a bitch!…Yes, I'm fine. This is my fucking job! Don't undermine me…Yes. I'm fine. You just caught me by surprise. I was sleeping and…listen, I'll get in touch with Derek and head right over. No, not there. I know I can't go there. Those assholes will probably screw it all up, but I know I can't get in the way. I'll get over to Derek's. You at home?…Yes, I know. It'll be ok. Just stay there, and I'll call you. I'll stop by the station and find out the details. Someone there will know. It's ok. I'll find out. It's ok. I'll handle it." He was shaking his head as if he was trying to convince himself that it really was ok, all the while avoiding eye contact with Betsy.

153

Betsy watched every move of his face as he talked. She watched the very light of his eyes. She stood frozen in time, confused in a panic without a point of origin. *Must be a work thing. He's just being called into some job, maybe? Trev' talk to me.*

Betsy waited. She stood there, waiting.

Trevor hung up the phone slowly, without speaking. She stared into him, taking his chin into her hand. He looked right through her.

"Trev? What's happened? Who was tha...?"

Trevor pulled her close and breathed into her ruffled hair, twisting the strands in his fingertips.

"Trev', talk to me." Betsy began to shiver, only because he was quivering all over.

"Shshsh... give me a minute." His voice was calm, contrary to the rise and fall of his chest.

In that next minute, everything changed.

Sobbing, Betsy sat at the kitchen table, with her face burrowed into the hard surface, her head wrapped in her arms. Trevor attempted to console her, "Do you want to come with me? I need to get down to the station and find out what happened and figure this thing out. If you come with, you just have to stay in the car. Will you be alright in the car?"

Betsy tried lifting herself and failed; dazed, she stared into his eyes, "I can't move. I can't leave. This isn't happening, Trev'. It's a bad dream, right? Just another one of my nightmares, right?" She pressed into his chest as tears smeared onto his shirt.

"C'mon, girl. It's going to be ok. Let me go figure out what happened. You coming with?" Betsy shook her head no, light and shallow, blinking away the shock deep within her. She couldn't respond with words.

Trevor tried again to get her to come along, knowing that he had to get some information. "I don't want to leave you. I just can't leave you here, but I gotta…"

"I know. You gotta go find out. I get it. I'm fine. You need to go find out where Derek is. Is he on shift today?"

"No, he's off today. So, I don't know why he's not answering his phone. He should be home. I'll be back over soon. I promise. As soon as I…"

"Go. Get going. I'm fine. Just go. Just find out what the hell happened and who the hell did this…." Betsy folded her hands back over her face, and the tears couldn't be held back. She didn't even try.

"We'll do what we can, but you know it's not our jurisdi…"

"Fuck jurisdiction!"

"Ok, ok. I'll be back. Soon. I promise."

As Trevor reluctantly stepped out into the yard and looked back over his shoulder, Betsy watched out of the window in the other direction towards Ruth's house. She took a deep, slow breath and wiped the wetness away from her face. Swallowing hard, she managed to walk to her room to get dressed.

Once out into the fresh morning air, Betsy felt a tinge of recovery to her senses. As she approached Ruth's front door, she searched for words. She didn't knock. Opening the door slowly, she peeked in, "Ruth? Ruth? You're up, right? Ruth?" She knew they were. They always were.

Betsy didn't know what else to say. Her voice escalated with each call, "Ruth!"

Ruth came into the living room having just been out back feeding Bear.

"Oh! Hey you! How are you this morning?" The pleasant demeanor on Ruth's face immediately switched to grave concern. Her eyes softened, "You alright?" She sat down and patted the couch for Betsy to follow.

The air around them tightened.

"Sweetie, what's wrong. Are the boys ok? Where are the boys?" Ruth looked past Betsy, out through the open drapes and across the street, holding her breath.

Betsy gulped. "They're at Grandma's. No. They're fine. The boys are fine."

Betsy paused for a moment. She pulled the words out one at a time.

"Someone...*breathe*...got to her. I don't know..." She breathed in short shallow gulps of air. "I don't know what...how.... I don't....but, but they got to her...."

"Who?" Ruth's chest rose and fell in anticipation.

"Not just her..." It was a whisper. Quiet and hollow. Betsy's lip began to quiver, and tears streamed down her face, leaving droplets to fall recklessly from her nose. Her chest quivered, and her hands were unsteady. She gazed at Ruth, shaking her head slightly to and fro, with eyes dizzy from exhaustion.

Ruth sat silent, waiting.

Betsy breathed back more sobbing.

"Sweetie? Who? Please, honey, what happened?" Ruth was nearly in tears just watching her. Compassion spoke softly from her voice.

"Suzanne." Betsy paused and stopped crying long enough to say it. "Suzanne. She was found this morning. Her husband, he came home... he, and he found them."

Betsy buried her face into the palms of her hands and the sobbing resumed, this time escalating. Ruth shook her head in short sputters trying to clear the confusion.

"What?...what do you mean? Stop. Just stop and breathe." Ruth cradled Betsy's face in her hands and then reached around to lightly caress the back of her hair.

Betsy lifted her head. "They both...both..." She was breathing, one quiet and shaky word at a time. "...were...they were... stabbed." With the very words, Betsy leaned over and began to cry again. Tears escaped down Ruth's cheeks, no matter how much she appeared to maintain her typically calm composure. "You said 'them'. You mean...both, as in...?" Her voice was monotone.

"Yes. Tif' was found on the floor in the hall." Betsy whispered, as if by whispering, it wouldn't really be true. Ruth went numbly silent as she scooted near Betsy and wrapped her arms around her, pulling her close to her.

The words couldn't come. There were no words to say.

Chapter 15

Fragments of hissing whispers swirling around her head couldn't drown out the wicked laughter echoing in the distance. The noises drummed into her skull causing Betsy to curl into the corner where it was dark and dusty. The ringing in her ears caused a torment of confusion. A somewhat short, but stalky man, with messy dirty blond hair, and eyes glazed over, sat in a crouched position next to her. He smiled at her. She smiled back. *Do I know you? Yes, I do know you.* He smiled again, and something in his eyes pierced fear into her chest. He was still smiling, and the confusion heightened. *But, I know you. I like you. Your....* His face became clearer. Although she still wasn't quite certain who he was. Nonetheless, she spoke to him. "Oh, Hello. How are you? Aren't you....?" Betsy relaxed as she trusted him. He reached his arm around her waist, and she suddenly screamed, seeing his hand mutilated and twisted at the wrist. It was wrinkled and distorted. Blood dripped from his fingertips. Fingers from his other hand stretched out to her, and he was calling her name. "Betsy. Betsy, what's wrong? Betsy....?" His voice trailed away as her own scream woke her.

Betsy's eyes darted around the room in a panic until she realized that she was at home, lying on her sofa, blanketed in perspiration, and with the laundry scattered all around her. Rubbing her face to clarity and looking up to the clock on the wall, a different sort of panic set in. *God, how long have I been asleep?* Not the 'just waking from a nightmare' kind of panic, but the real kind. The 'Where are my boys, and why are they so quiet?' kind.

"Andrew?!" Betsy jumped to her feet and ran to their room. Rushing in through the doorway, she stopped short with relief. Andrew looked up from his perch on top of the toy box. He looked to her with wide eyes, as he jumped down and ran to her. "I was just looking for the bug, Mommy. It was gonna go out the window." He looked to her with such innocence. She simply smiled. "Where's your..." Betsy scanned the room to find Blair asleep on the floor at the base of the bunk bed. *At least he's getting a peaceful nap in before we leave.*

Relaxed, but still disoriented, Betsy sauntered into her room, rubbing the sleep from her mind. *I wish those damn dreams would stop.* Standing at her dresser, piled high with clothes, she lifted a shirt up to her breasts. Dropping it, she picked up another. The chiffon top was light orange, with small brown pin stripes. *Maybe too much color.* She paused and stared at it blankly. *But Suz' liked color.* Betsy tightened her grip around the shirt and made her way toward the bathroom.

Startled by a knock at the door, Betsy moved in that direction. Andrew had already opened the door and stood in the doorway dressed in nothing but dingy white under briefs and grinning up to Ruth. His hair fluffed around his face, and he held a toy train in his hand. Seeing Tristan, his smile broadened. "I got a new bag of trains from my grandpa. He found 'em in a house they were fixin'. Come on!" Andrew was running into the other room before Ruth could put Trey to the floor.

Blair waddled slowly into the room, clutching a baby blanket under his arm. Upon seeing Ruth, he ran to her with an unsteady waddle. "Hi ya, big boy!" She reached down to hug him. He wore nothing but a wet cloth diaper, and Ruth took it upon herself to unpin it and pinch it dangling from her fingers, allowing him to air dry. "I thought you were training him?"

159

"Ya. I am. Just haven't got him dressed yet."

Ruth looked around and saw a slew of clothes scattered amidst a pile of blankets on the floor. Dirty dishes from the previous night's dinner were on the coffee table with hard remnants of food scraps stuck to their surface. "You know we have to leave soon, right?" Ruth's voice was quiet, almost at a whisper. She leaned over and started picking up the plates.

"Yeah. I'll be ready soon. I was just getting' to it before you got here." Betsy stretched her arms to the ceiling as she yawned and sat back down on the sofa. "We've got time. You don't gotta do that."

"I know."

Betsy sat dazed, watching Ruth, still haunted by fears that had crept into her sleeping thoughts.

"You'll feel better when you clean up." Ruth sat down next to her and looked her over compassionately.

"Oh, I know. I'm just tired." Ruth noticed her notebook lying on the floor, as if it had fallen from the sofa.

"Looks like you've been writing though. Anything you'll let me read?" Her smile was warm and sincere.

Betsy reached down to the floor and picked it up, putting it on the end table beside the sofa. "I don't care. Why would you want to?" She became unusually tense at the idea.

"Did you go right to bed after you came by last night?"

"Couldn't sleep. That whole thing down the street at that business really freaked me out." Betsy leaned back against the pillow, lying flat to look up to the ceiling. "God. It was so weird. I swear to you, there were voices. But nobody was around."

160

"You said a light was on? It was late. I certainly wouldn't expect someone to be there that late. Were there cars in the parking lot?"

"I didn't see any cars, but ya, a light was on upstairs on the second floor of the building. Anyway. Doesn't matter. It's just stupid. I just don't like walking home from work that late. People shouldn't be in an office building that late. I could've just been letting my fears get the best of me. Who knows, I'm just freaking out over nothing." *I can tell by looking at her that she thinks I'm just crazy. I'm not crazy, Ruth. I'm scared.* So much so that she couldn't say it out loud.

"So, how was work? Busy?"

"Yeah. It always is during the summer, especially at night and on the weekends."

Betsy sat up straight and then stood, rubbing the darkness away from her face with the palms of her hands. "Will you keep an eye on 'em while I change?" It wasn't really a question of need, more a matter of making noise. Ruth looked to her with a smile. No words were needed. Betsy stopped short in the doorway of her bedroom and turned to shoot a glance back to Ruth, who was already thumbing through her diary.

Betsy put her fingers up to her lips to gently nibble on her fingernails as she watched Ruth entranced in the pages of her personal thoughts. *Maybe she can help. But, maybe she shouldn't. Maybe she should just stay out of it.* Ruth must have sensed Betsy watching her because she lifted her eyes and smiled at her again. "This is good. You should make your own book of poetry or something. Have you thought of doing something with this talent of yours?"

Betsy shrugged. *Maybe.* "If I get out of this hell hole, maybe I can go back to school and study writing or something."

"That would be good for you. So, you're really gonna go? Do you have a plan?"

161

"Sort of, just thinking of a way, though. Nothing solid. I'm not even sure yet what I really want to do. I really love Trevor. I don't know what to do with that. He's good to me, and I'm not sure I can leave him."

"You can do whatever is right for you."

"Maybe you should take your own advice."

"We're not talking about me, though." With a sly grin, Ruth put down the diary and stood to continue cleaning up. Betsy breathed in a smile of hope, desperately warranted, to tend to the needs of their morning timeline. The funeral was to begin in an hour and a half, and she wasn't moving as quickly as she needed to be.

Betsy emerged from the steam of the bathroom to see Ruth back on the sofa. This time, however, Ruth's face wasn't scanning the words of poetry, she was sifting through a stack of papers, papers that Betsy was more than familiar with, since she was the one who had written on them. "What are you doing? That's not my poetry." Betsy walked closer, her uncomfortable demeanor closing into Ruth, hovering over her within seconds.

Ruth twitched a quick response, looking up to her with confusion. "I'm sorry. They fell out from the back of the book. I just...."

"You just what? Thought it was ok to be nosey?"

"You said I could read...."

"My poems, not this stuff."

"Well, like I said, it all fell and scattered. I was just...."

"Never mind, just put it back." Betsy clenched her jaw, shot a look of disapproval over to Ruth, and then turned to go get dressed.

Ruth couldn't let it go. "So, who's the guy in the letter? And who are all these people here?" She held up a piece of notebook paper with a list of names on it. All men's names.

Betsy stomped over to her, leaned in, snatched the paper from out of Ruth's hands and scooped up the others. "None of your damn business."

With a quick turn Betsy started to walk away but retracted when she caught Ruth looking at her in complete confusion. She stood looking back at her, breathing while searching for words and fumbling with the papers in her hands. "Listen, you don't always have to know everything, ok? You sit in your perfect little bubble and pretend to care about my mess of a life, but sometimes, you just need to stay out of it."

Ruth's shoulder's stiffened as she stood up. "Well, first of all, I don't pretend to care. I do. So, that was uncalled for."

I know you do. I'm sorry. Betsy suppressed the tears that began to form with several blinks and swallowed the words that tried to form.

Ruth, on the other hand, had more to say. "And, what do you mean 'perfect little bubble'? You know of all people, that that's not true at all. Not to mention, you are the one who is always asking for my help, so, do you expect me not help then? How can I be the one to notify someone if you're in trouble, if you won't even be straight with me about the trouble that you're really in? That's not fair, Betsy, and you know it."

They stood silent for a moment eyeing one another- not so much a stare down, but more like a stare in. They looked into each other, saying more than words could ever say. Ruth broke first, "What is this all about? What's the MEG team? And why all the names? Why not send the letter? It's month's old. Why keep it, if you're not going to send it? I'm just confused, that's all. And worried. Worried sick. For heaven's sake, Betsy, someone tried to kill you! And you never even talk about it! Then, someone beats you up at work, and now Suzanne's gone? I'm

163

scared for you! Don't you get it? You're not dealing with whatever is going on. All you want to do is run away, but I don't even know why. C'mon. Let me be a friend and help you. It's not gonna go away by just running away."

"I don't know what to do. I'm thinking of....well, Pete says he can help. But he wants me to help him. I just want to do the right thing. That's all."

"Then do the right thing. And I will help you with that."

"I don't know what that is yet, Ruth. I don't know who I can trust."

Ruth bit her lip and softened her face. *She gets it. She doesn't know either.*

The air was still, and friends and family stood around Suzanne and Tiffany's burial site with deep aching pain evident throughout the crowd, as the sun drenched them all in comfort. The funeral had gone as well as any funeral could. Blinking in the sunlight, Ruth wrapped her two boys in one arm cuddled up against her shins. Betsy felt the soft squeeze of Ruth's hand on hers and looked down, and then up to Ruth. Betsy took in a deep breath and turned her head slowly to scan the crowd. "Where's Dwaine? I didn't see him at the church." She whispered. "I see Pete made it over. I should talk to him."

"Have you talked to him at all this week? You said he called a few days ago."

"Yeah. He wants to talk to me again about that stupid lawsuit."

"Are you going help him?"

"I don't know."

Words from the service splintered Betsy's soul in both conviction and confusion. *If God is good, why did this happen? I want to believe there's a God who cares. I want to. But this is so wrong.* Ruth's eyes seemed to pierce

Betsy's mind with understanding. "I know it's hard for you to understand. This wasn't God's fault. He doesn't make these things happen." Ruth whispered so quietly that Betsy had to lean in close to hear her. *But why didn't he stop it?* Betsy's silence cued Ruth to let it go.

Sadness pierced the air as each person walked slowly past the two caskets to say their final goodbyes. Betsy gulped her tears away watching Andrew and Blair put flowers on top of each casket. *This is wrong. This is just so wrong. Who could do this? Why would anyone do this?*

Ruth put Trey on her hip and led Tristan by the hand in order to place a bouquet of sunflowers tied with a bow on top of Suzanne's final resting place. Betsy stood at a distance, as she watched Ruth slide her hand across both caskets, then lay a single sunflower on little Tiffany's enclosed bed. *Tiff's casket is so small. Oh, sweet, sweet little girl.* Betsy held back sobs, wiping her eyes to maintain control. *She's handling this with such grace. How can she be so together at a time like this?*

Ruth led both families across the grass in silence. It was Betsy who broke it. "They're in heaven, right? They're both in heaven, they have to be. You believe in heaven, right?"

"Of course. I believe that they are. She believed in God, so yes. I do."

"So, it's true?"

"What?"

"Whosoever believes in God, in Jesus, has everlasting life? Isn't that how that Bible verse goes? Your church Pastor quoted it earlier. I think I got it right."

"Yes. That's pretty much it."

"Say it. The whole thing. I want to hear it again."

165

"For God so loved the world that he gave his only begotten son, that whoever believes in Him, shall not perish, but have everlasting life."

"Thank you. I just needed to hear it again. That they're really not gone. They're just somewhere else."

"You're welcome." Ruth shot her a sweet smile. "Do you believe in God? This hope of everlasting life, through the Son?"

"I do now."

"Would you like to talk more about it?"

"Not now. But, yes."

More silence.

This time it was Dwaine who ran up behind them and interrupted their contemplation. "Betsy, Betsy. I almost thought I was going to miss you."

Betsy turned around. "There you are. You doin' alright?"

"Such as anyone can. This fuckin' sucks. I'm sorry I haven't called. I meant to. Just that...."

"Don't worry about it. I understand."

"Did you see that Pete made it?"

"Yeah. I'm going to talk with him later, at the potluck. He's going, right?"

"Actually, he's not. Said he needed to get back on the road. But you do need to talk to him. He's pissed. He's going after somebody. I don't know what he's up to."

"Well, I kinda do. He wants my help."

166

"Be careful Betsy. Did you see who had the balls to show up?" Dwaine pointed in the direction of the parking lot, where she could see Tony leaning against his car.

"Why is he here?"

"I don't know, but my money puts him here to see who showed up or just to harass you."

"He can harass all he wants. I'm not afraid of him."

Ruth caught Betsy's eye and let her know without saying a word that she knew that wasn't true. *Ok already. I am. I am afraid of him. Just leave it be for now, will you?* Betsy tightened her grip on Andrew's hand while they crossed the lawn. She could see Colin in the distance, walking toward them. *I didn't know he was here. How did I miss him?* Betsy waved to him as he approached. When he finally met her gaze, she gave him a welcoming smile as he reached over to give her a hug. Colin pecked a kiss to Betsy's cheek, holding to her shoulders with care. "I'm so sorry for all of this shit. This is just crazy and so very sad. Makes you wonder what the hell is wrong with people these days. God, we gotta find the sick asshole who did this."

Betsy thanked him with another smile. "So, I didn't see you back there."

"Oh, I was just hiding in the back. Figured you needed your space."

"Well, I want to chat sometime about what you said a few weeks ago. You said you may be able to help me with a cash flow problem."

"Oh, hell ya. I'd do whatever. You know, I can hook you up with whatever, or whoever you need. I got your back, sweetie."

"Ok. So, I'll call later this week then?"

167

"Absolutely, girl." He gave her another kiss on the cheek. "I'm sorry again. This must be so hard. Just know, it's gonna get taken care of. We'll find the S.O.B. We're on it." Betsy kissed his cheek back, with a tear wiping from her cheekbone to his. She stood still, watching him walk away. "See, they're not all bad. He'll make sure they find out who did this."

Ruth was skeptical. "I thought you said he was a bit of an outsider down at the department. That he made some people uncomfortable, and that many folks down at the department really didn't like him much."

"Well, that was coming from someone I'm not sure is all that trustworthy. I mean, you can't put a whole bunch of men into a single building and expect them all to get along. Besides, there's enough jerks down there that I don't like too much, so if he's the outsider, then he's the one to trust."

They resumed their slow pace, as Betsy took notice of the warm earth under the soles of her chunky high heels. Silence engulfed them as they walked to where Betsy's car was parked. They drove through the iron gate of the cemetery, and a quiet peace engulfed them. Betsy's eyes stared straight ahead as Ruth's thoughts slid from her tongue, "Are you going to help him? Pete, I mean?"

"Yes. I'm thinking so. Maybe. Then I'm getting the hell outta this town."

"It'd be the right thing to do, I think. How's Colin going to help with getting you money?"

"Let me worry about that. Will you help me too, though? You said you would help, if you could."

"Of course. Anything you need. I'll go anywhere with you if you need me to."

Betsy rehearsed the words of a poem she had recently written. It was engrained in her memory like a fresh dream. A good dream. She was trying to focus on the good ones.

Echoes of darkness trickle, drifting to dust.

Confusion settles, defusing my trust.

Once it made sense, or so it did seem.

It was so long ago, it seems like a dream.

Laughter gurgles muck up from the past.

Taunting my giggles, releasing my grasp.

At one time, so genuine, honest, and true.

At one time so often, but now only few.

My hopes, my dreams, my song, my dance.

Filtering aimless in a sea of chance.

Sometimes I see, sometimes I know.

That hope is returning and destined to grow.

It pitters on tiptoes, not tainted by time.

It patters my heart like a drum in sweet rhyme.

I know when I see them, their laughter still pure.

That I've not been forgotten. I'm not that obscure.

I reach to a place where certainty stands.

Where love's not forgotten, secure in his hands.

The echoes now trickle, drifting dusk into dawn.

Confusion is filtered in the light until gone.

Clarity splinters the pain from the past.

My soul sees its hope. Hope at last

Chapter 16

The Sunday church service let out at noon as usual. The Bakerson's rushed home so that Ruth could unload a cooler full of ice and set up a long folding table in the carport. It was Ruth's idea to host a summer picnic for the folks at their pint-sized church congregation. Curtis would not have typically agreed to such a plan had Ruth not mentioned it in front of their pastor, who was emphatically in favor of the idea. Ruth had compelled Curtis to invite a few work friends as well. Then she could invite a few friends of her own to attend, hoping Betsy would come. It could be a pleasant distraction.

Ruth anticipated the afternoon and took a great deal of care as she smoothed out the plastic cover along the metal surface of the table. She carefully taped the corners in place, then brushed the dust from her hands. "Have you lit up the charcoal?" Ruth peeked her head through the screen door. Curtis was leaning up against the kitchen counter casually sifting through the Sunday paper. He glanced back at her above the rim of the newspaper. "Of course. It's all ready. I'll be out shortly."

Within minutes, a station wagon, a four-door sedan and two pickup trucks had parked along the curbside in front of the Bakerson house. People of all ages streamed into the backyard bearing homemade dishes, platters of raw vegetables, and paper bags filled with an assortment of condiments and utensils.

A wooden picnic table had been set up in the center of the yard, the centerpiece for all of the iron framed lawn chairs that had been sprinkled amidst the chatter. Umbrellas were set up along blankets to allow for shade where the single tree in the yard could not reach. Ruth emerged from the kitchen with a large plastic bowl in her hand, delicately balanced as she scanned the yard, quite pleased with what she saw. It didn't take long for the guests to begin mingling as they tasted goodies from the ample supply of food spread across the table. Two teenage boys had agreed to man the barbecue, which left Curtis free to roam at will. He had dug out one of his remote-control airplanes from the shed and was proudly entertaining a group of men in the front yard.

As Ruth busied herself dishing up plates for the boys, she watched Trey toddle his way into the front yard to catch a glimpse of what the men were up to. Trey stood directly behind Curtis in awe of what he saw. Ruth, standing just around the corner, could check on him if she looked over every few seconds. She was amused by the way the men entertained themselves so easily. Trey took tiny steps to get closer, so close that Curtis nearly toppled over him in a backwards tilt, barely catching his balance in midair.

"What are you doing out here? Where's your mother?" Placing the controls to the ground, he stiffened his tall stature and led Trey by the arm into the carport. "Ruth! Ruth, keep an eye on him, will you? He's wandering. What are you doing that you can't keep him in the yard?"

"I'm making them a plate. I had my eye on him, I saw the whole thing."

"Then why didn't you come get him?"

Ruth ignored the latter statement and didn't bother to look up. "Here, sweetie, stay with me. Let's go eat back here." Her friend Dorothy met them at the backyard gate. "Oh, Ruth, dear, let me help you. You look like you got your hands full."

"Thanks. Really. Have you seen Tristan?"

Dorothy pointed into the backyard where Tristan had found a quiet spot in the dirt, near the row of tall sunflowers. He seemed quite content with the plastic bowl in his lap, a spoon in his hand, and a pile of small rocks at his side.

"Here, will you help them both to that blanket over there, so they can sit down to eat? I'm going to grab them some lemonade."

"Always obliged to help, dear."

Ruth slid through the screen door into the kitchen and felt the presence of someone behind her. As she reached to open the refrigerator door, she was a bit startled to have a hand grab the door for her. "Can I help you with some things?"

"Oh, hello, Grant. I'm just getting some lemonade. Can I get you some as well?"

"No, I've got a soda outside."

"I'm glad you could make it. Your brother's around here somewhere, I assume? He had said he thought you might join us today. Were you in church this morning? I didn't see you."

"Oh, no, I didn't make it. You know I'm not all that into that stuff like my brother. Besides, I had a late-night shift last night."

"I hope it was a light night for you."

"It wasn't too bad. Given that things have been a bit sketchy around here these days."

Grant watched her carefully and shifted his gait to lean into her as she poured lemonade into two paper cups. "I wasn't intending to eavesdrop,

172

but I couldn't help but overhear. Curtis seems a bit edgy. Does he ever let up?"

"Oh, you mean with Trey? Oh, it's alright. He's just looking out for him."

"Well, it seems a shame for him to be out there with a bunch of sweaty men, when he could be at the side of such a pretty lady instead."

Ruth smiled uncomfortably. "Well, thank you. That's kind." She politely nodded as she led the way out into the carport.

"Have you been able to make yourself a plate?"

Glancing up at him nervously, Ruth hesitated to respond as he offered to help again.

"Oh, thank you, but I will eat with Curtis when he's done out front." *He certainly is persistent. And handsome.* She could feel her face blush and quickly slid through the gate into the backyard.

Ruth was relieved to sit down onto the blanket to help Trey with his lunch. Dorothy sat with her feet tucked under her and scanned the crowd. "No Betsy today?"

"No. She wasn't sure if she wanted to stop over. She said she wasn't feeling up to it. I was hoping she would at least stop by. I really wanted her to get out and meet some different people. She's still a little reluctant to get to know everyone from church. And she had to drive to Montrose this weekend, anyway. But I'm still trying to get her to come to church. I'm really worried about her, Dorothy."

"Of course you are. She's a damn mess! For God's sake, how did you get involved with the likes of someone like her?"

"What do you mean? She's a gem. So, she's got herself mixed up into some things. But, she's really quite sweet. And she means well. Her heart is in the right place."

"Well, just be careful when you're with her. I say she's trouble with a capital T."

"You don't have to worry about anything. Not with me, anyway. I don't go out with her, or anything like that. We just go shopping sometimes and hang out at home, mostly. But I'm really concerned about her. She's getting worse, that's true. She called the other night, convinced that someone was in her yard. Curtis and I went over there, and there didn't seem to be anyone around but the cat, anyway. It was after midnight, though, and she was really spooked. She says she wants me to watch her front lights, and if she flickers them, then that means she needs help. I know that's pretty ridiculous, even though I can easily see her house from my bedroom window. But, how in the world would I even be able to help? I really think she's into something serious."

"I think she's just crazy. If she were really in trouble, how's she even gonna get to a light switch. It's crazy. She's crazy. That's all." Dorothy flippantly shrugged.

Ruth chewed her food slowly, looking around the yard. *She's not crazy at all. If only you knew.* She was distracted by Grant entering through the gate and watched him walk across the yard to join his brother with a group of men sitting in lawn chairs. *I wonder if he could help. Certainly, he's got connections. He could watch the house or something.* As she brushed away crumbs from her denim shorts, she stood. "Hey, do you mind sitting here with them for a bit longer?" Dorothy nodded in agreement with a smile.

Ruth walked over to the group of men and inched her presence into the conversation.

"Do any of you need anything? Can I get you more sodas?"

"Just sit and relax, for God's sake." Grant suggested.

Just about that time Curtis stepped up behind her and placed his arm around her waist.

"There you are. Have the boys finished their lunch?"

"They're working on it. Over there." Ruth pointed in the direction of the blanket, with Dorothy. Greg wandered over and sat in a chair next to Grant, who took a swig of soda before making small talk. "So, Greg, how's things up there at Tri Star now that this guy's got the VP position?" Greg shifted in his seat, looking to Curtis carefully before answering. "He's not so bad." He teased, with a casual nod and a forced smile. "It's pretty much a team thing we've got going on. We just let him think he's got some power." Greg laughed, tilting his soda can to Curtis in jest.

"You guys ever get away for some fun?" Grant glanced over to Ruth. She noticed and glanced away.

"What constitutes fun in your mind? I hear you like to race cars?" Greg's interest was purely polite.

"You bet I do. You should come by the shop and take a look sometime."

"Curtis and I like to play while we work, don't we Curtis?" Greg nodded again.

Ruth watched intently the dynamics of male social hierarchy, trying to determine who fit where with this particular group. *Greg certainly wants to be the alpha male. Hmmm, I'm not sure where he fits.* She looked up to Curtis as he answered back.

"I hear you to like to fly." Curtis looked to Grant with a look of indignation.

"Yep, I do. I love the Gunnison River area. Nothin' like takin' a spin through the canyon above the river." He snickered with pride. "You know, get as low as you can go. Hell of a rush."

"That doesn't sound too smart. That's a tight canyon. A more experienced pilot would know better. You get a more intimate view from the river itself, anyway. You ever took a kayak down it? You see more when you're not in a hurry."

Greg sat forward to inch his way into the topic. "It's quite amazing, actually. With a kayak or any kind of boat for that matter, you can get some beautiful sights from inside the canyon."

"Do you ever take Ruth down the river with you?" Grant looked in her direction.

Ruth smiled at the thought of being invited to be a part of this conversation, though she sensed that Curtis became annoyed at the question. "We travel to all sorts of places together. I'm helping her get into the photography market and such. So of course we go together some. Maybe not so much with the kayak, but we go to the river together all the time. We take the children and make a family affair of it." He tightened his grip around Ruth's waist, just slightly.

This time Grant looked to Greg. "So, do you kayak too?"

Greg reluctantly answered. "Sure, some. I'm not much of a swimmer, but if you're good with the boat, you don't need to be, am I right?"

"The Gunnison's a nice river. Nice and isolated, if you like it quiet. I'm more into exciting ventures." Grant's eyes caught Ruth's and she looked away just as quick.

"Well, of course. That's the point of kayaking. To enjoy the quiet space." Greg eyed Grant suspiciously. Ruth noticed.

"So, if you spend time out that way, do you know anyone in the Whitewater area? I've got a neighbor who has family out there. I go out that way to his family's place sometimes to target shoot. It's plenty isolated. But once the guns get popping, not so quiet." Grant laughed a cynical sneer.

"Oh, sure. I know folks that are as good as family who live out that way. Curtis and I use the landscape a lot for photo shoots. The isolation makes for contemplative work."

Grant nodded. "Yeah, this guy I know, you know, my neighbor friend, he has some old homesteaded acreage that he allows folks to use for hunting and shooting and shit. He's a little rough around the edges, but I like to be able to have access to his family's place, so I tolerate 'im. It's even got an old farmhouse that he lets people use for all kinds of stuff. Sometimes, when I go grouse hunting up there, I just take a sleeping bag and crash out on the floor of the ol' place. Keeps the rain out, even if I gotta fight the critters off, you know, 'cause it doesn't have windows or nothin' like that. But that way, I can get an early start in the morning and get all the kill I want. You guys do any of that? Hunting and sorts?"

Greg sat up and leaned in. "I hunt a little. Collect, mostly. Most of my guns are just for show. Know of a couple of really good places to get some great buys, if you're ever in the market."

"The Rider's Club on Main Street is probably the best place I've found for a good selection." Grant gloated, shifting his ankle onto the knee of his other leg.

There was a gap in the conversation. Ruth heard Trey whining from behind her, and politely excused herself as she glanced hesitantly over to Grant. She could sense his eyes on her, and the attention made her

177

curiously uncomfortable. She walked away with the sound of Greg's voice bragging about his gun collection that he had built up from his connections to a local Pawn Shop on Colorado Avenue. Normally she wouldn't have paid all that much attention to the male rantings of such things, but she had some sort of stored up knowledge regarding a Pawn Shop in town that Betsy had shared with her a few months back. Not that it mattered much. Betsy was full of useless gossip, and it was hard to keep track of everything she rambled on about.

When Ruth entered the kitchen, she noticed Dorothy at the kitchen sink placing a plastic bowl on a towel to dry. "What on earth are you doing? You're not allowed to clean up." Ruth jested.

"I do what I want, dear. Oh, and I took the boys to their room to play. I hope that was alright." Dorothy winked. Almost in the same breath, she continued, "So, are you still planning to give my granddaughter piano lessons? I'm supposed to find out if you're going to be available in the next few weeks."

"Well, I was certainly planning to get started soon. I don't know when, exactly. I'm planning a trip in the next few weeks, so I should make sure when we are heading out of town before I make definite plans."

"You going with Curtis on a trip? It's about time he takes you along."

"No, that's work for him. It wouldn't be appropriate for me to travel with him." Ruth hesitated, biting her bottom lip and looking around, slightly glancing behind her before continuing. "I'm taking Betsy to testify for some case that has to do with Aspen."

"Oh? Whatever for?"

"Just something that has to be done." She shrugged her shoulders. "People around this town sure will be really shocked when it all gets out, though."

Dorothy tilted her head and began to ask for more details, but then the screen on the back door clattered, causing Ruth to turn around. It was Grant. "Bathrooms in there, right?" He pointed into the direction of the living room.

"Right hand side, once you're in the hallway." Ruth smiled awkwardly.

Dorothy wiped her hands dry, then announced her departure. "Well, dear, I need to head home. Let me know what to tell my daughter about her piano lessons, when you get back from that trip with Betsy. I'll talk with you again Wednesday night for prayer service."

"Speaking of prayer service, will you keep Betsy in your prayers? All the mess she's gotten herself into really does have me worried about her."

Dorothy gave her a quick kiss on the cheek as she hugged her shoulders. "Of course. That girl sure does know how to get herself into the wrong places at the wrong time, doesn't she? God help 'er."

"She doesn't mean to. She really is a good girl. I just want to help her, that's all."

"Well, don't go getting in too tight with her. You have your own dealings to tend to and all." Dorothy smiled a soft warning of concern of her own. Ruth escorted Dorothy out the front door, waving her away with a smile of her own. As she closed the door, she noticed Grant just coming out of the bathroom. He shot her a flirtatious grin. "Thank you kindly." Her heart almost stopped at the way he looked at her. She instinctively shot passed him and headed to the boy's bedroom to check on them, finding an excuse to hide. *I'm so thankful that Dorothy brought the boys inside. They needed a break as well.*

Ruth sat cross legged on the floor in the isolation of the boy's room, as Tristan colored from his train coloring book. Trey had clearly had enough fun for the afternoon and lied on the bed with his fingers in his mouth, kicking the wall. *He needs a nap.* Before climbing onto the bed to lie with him, Ruth heard Curtis and Greg in the hallway, sounding as if they were standing in the doorway of the master bedroom. Curtis' tone of voice caused her to stay put, out of eyeshot of either of them. "What do you mean, I wouldn't want to know? What makes you so sure I wouldn't want in on it? You're making money, aren't you? What makes you think I wouldn't want in?" Curtis seemed agitated but kept his voice low.

"Just trust me. This is a project I'm doing on my own. Not like the other things we got going on. I mean I'm ok building shit with you that we can market as legit. Or even the jobs that aren't. But that's all business you got buy in for. This is a different deal. You wouldn't want in."

"So, you don't have to share. That's what this is really about, isn't it? Keeping the opportunity to yourself, are you?"

"No, Curtis. Let it go. God, we're better friends than that. You just need to trust me when I say this isn't something you want to get involved with. It's complicated."

"Making money always is. You know I can handle it."

"You've got enough going on with all the other business and all. I told you we were good working together on all that. Let's just you and I focus on what we've already got going on together. Besides this job's with law enforcement and you can't stand anyone from down at the department. This is the last thing you want to get your hands into. Let me do this one. Let me do something on my own. Stop asking so many damn questions."

By this time the sound of their voices had faded away into the bedroom, and then out again, as if Curtis had just gone in there to get

180

something as they talked. Ruth almost felt guilty for eavesdropping. She stood to her feet and set her mind on more present matters. *Let's get you down for a nap, sweet boy. Your routine has been meddled with enough for today.*

Chapter 17

The image of Karla's reflection in the mirror stared back at her through the glare from the bad hotel lighting. She was on a time crunch. She sighed, stretching her neck from one side and then to the other. *Really, why does Pop always insist on getting such an early start?* Karla pulled back the shower curtain and stripped down to enter the shower, deliberately ignoring the larger image on the reflective wall. The warmth of the water penetrated Karla's skin, relieving tension from a poor night's sleep. She began to hum her thoughts into order. *I wonder where we're headed this morning. Breakfast first, I hope.* After ruffling away the wetness from her hair and brushing it into a ponytail, Karla was dressed with no time to waste.

Thud, thud, thud! "Housekeeping!" The voice on the other side of the door clamored with enthusiasm. A male voice. Her father's voice.

"You're hilarious." Karla grabbed her bag from the floor as she opened the door. Ramone was endearing, standing there grinning. She couldn't help but smile.

"Good morning, Sunshine." He handed her a cup of coffee as they walked to the elevator.

"Please tell me this isn't breakfast."

"We don't have time to eat, Karla."

"But the buffet is still open, I'll just grab something to take on our way out."

"Karla, you're not supposed to take it with you."

"Oh, for heaven's sake, Pop, lighten up. People take food up to their rooms, why can't I just grab some for the road?"

"Suit yourself. But if they say something, I'm not sticking around to help."

Why ya gotta be so difficult all the time? Shit, Pop. Karla held tight to her cup of coffee, and let the issue go. "Can we at least take an early break for lunch then?"

He looked in her direction but didn't respond.

They boarded the rental car, which still smelled of newly polished vinyl. "Are you going to give me an agenda? You usually give me an agenda." Karla settled herself into her seatbelt.

"We must be excited to get to work, are we?"

Karla purposefully ignored him by reaching around into the back seat to grab a notebook that she had left there the day before. Ramone sent a nod in her direction. "Open my briefcase, there. There's a summary for you and a list of questions. On the backside of that is what we're working on first."

Karla was gazing through several pieces of paper, as he tried to maintain focus on the road. He rambled on in the background, as she sifted through some of the newspaper copies in a different folder. One particular write-up caught her attention. "Wait. I know this girl. I've come across her before. There was another picture of her in that box with all the Suzanne Denison trial stuff. I didn't get a chance to really read up on it. Was her death a murder, too?" Karla felt embarrassed to share with him that she had cut clippings of all the women she had come across and kept them in her wallet. She had carried this girl's photo with her for weeks but still didn't know what happened to her. She wasn't sure if she really wanted to know.

He stopped to glance over. "No. Hers was reported to be an accidental drowning."

"So, why is there stuff on her in all this research? What's the relevancy?"

Karla couldn't help but to allow her eyes to stare at the young girl in the photograph. She was so young. The girl's eyes grabbed hers and wouldn't let go.

"Yeah, I read up on it a bit. If I remember right, it was drugs, though, that caused her to drown. That's the printed version, anyway. Some weird off the wall drug of some sort. I can't remember exactly what it was."

"Drugs? She doesn't look like a druggie. She looks so, well, so innocent and young."

"She's a girl posing in a photograph. What did you expect?"

Karla's stereotypical image of a 1970's drug addict was distorted. This child was no long-haired hippy with bad teeth and shallow cheekbones with flowers in her hair holding up the peace sign. Not at all. Karla's gaze couldn't stray from this sweet face. *So soft, and her structure so perfect. So pretty. And so young. She's younger than me. So young.*

Shaking away the emerging tug to drift into a trance with this girl, Karla tried to gain clear perspective. *Keep unattached*, her father would always say. *Keep it about the facts, and what we know. She's just one in a*

184

million of a mirage of faces who's lived on this planet. But her eyes. Her innocent eyes.

Looking ahead Karla scanned the road. "So where are we going?" The silver four-door sedan mingled with an eclectic plethora of SUV's, high riding trucks and compact tin cans. They turned onto the two-way street of North Avenue, with a concrete median between the opposing two-way traffic. It seemed like one of the city's main business districts, although hopefully not the sustaining one. It was lined with fast food chain restaurants (some in desperate need of upgrading), several cheaply lighted used automobile dealerships made over as if they had held a past life as something else, and other scattered remnants of a once thriving economy. The old single-level motels made of brick and stucco now housed insurance agents, chiropractic massage therapists, and single-family entrepreneurs cutting hair or reading palms. There were only signs of human life (aside from the traffic) when they passed the tire store. A patron sat on the curb talking on his cell phone.

It wasn't until they made a left hand turn that Karla met a welcoming sight. The local, well-groomed college loomed above the aged landscapes around it. Although much smaller than the university back home, it still emitted the modern stature of intelligent building design and a tailored look. Stopping at the command of flashing lights, Karla watched students cross the newly installed crosswalk. A brand new parking garage was their destination. She felt more at home seeing the starkly built structure power up from the underground.

"You thought you were done walkin' a school campus for the summer, didn't you?" Ramone grinned. She grinned back at him. *This is my world. And he noticed.* They squeezed into a parking space with a careful halt.

Exiting the car, Karla grabbed her bag, fully equipped with all the technology they needed. The walk across the campus caused her shoulders to relax. Despite the insecurities she felt being in a new place, it was the familiarity of being around her own kind that settled her nerves a bit. No one seemed to notice her within the crowd of students. And she had learned to take comfort in that.

Karla followed Ramone into one of the privacy rooms of the library, where he quickly and silently set up his own mini workstation, equipped with a white board, a pile of sticky notes, his laptop, several files, and a city map. He handed her a pad, with several lists on it. "Ok, here's what we got. Each is a separate list that doesn't seem to be connected. Let's go through all of this and see if we can find something that connects any of them." He picked up one of the files and tossed it in her direction.

Karla didn't have to ask too many questions, as he was a master at making lists and giving her a starting point. She knew how to take it from there. Karla sifted through interview reports, lists of names equipped with addresses, possible relatives, employment histories, and letters. Within a half hour, she was in full swing. Silence was all that absorbed the room for what seemed like hours.

Karla glanced over at her father and laid a palm over her squeamish stomach. She scanned the white board and realized that between the two of them, it was nearly covered with scratches of notes and yellow paper squares. She checked her cell phone for the time. *Lunch time.* "Hey," Karla whispered, as if she was avoiding any interruptions to Ramone's thinking, "I'm really hungry. Can we break?" She shuffled her papers back into a folder. Ramone didn't respond. "Or maybe we should review all of this before it gets out of hand? Do you think?" She leaned back in her chair to stretch.

"Ya. I'm up for food. Bill is expecting to hear from us soon anyway. Says we can regroup at his place this afternoon. Maybe we can do lunch at his place." He pulled his phone out and began to tap in Bill's number.

"So, we just pack this out like it is?"

186

"Why not? Just be careful sliding it in there." He pointed to the large carrying case, usually used by artists to transport their form of work. Ramone was already talking to Bill, as she carefully packed everything up. "Oh, if it's ok, will you ask him if I can make lunch? We can stop by a grocery store on the way there, right?"

Ramone nodded in agreement.

Good enough.

Once outside in the warm dry air Karla was tense as her brain was spinning with thoughts. She passed a group of young students who seemed aloof and off in another world. She needed to relax, and she just couldn't shake it on her own. "Hey Pop, do the grocery stores here sell wine? I'd like to pick up a bottle to go with lunch."

"Why? Really Karla, why do you have to make things so difficult?"

"Because, Pop. I just want a nice lunch. C'mon. Just don't give me grief. Let me have a glass of wine for God's sakes!" Her agitation was on the rise, and Ramone didn't have the energy to fight it.

"Alright, Jesus, Karla. We'll have to stop at a liquor store. I don't think they can sell wine in stores here."

"Bill said it was cool that I make lunch?"

"Of course."

"I knew he would." *At least Bill doesn't give me shit.*

As they pulled the car into Bill's driveway, Karla breathed in a sense of relief. Hotel life was getting old, and she anticipated the chance to sit on the patio of an actual home to enjoy a real meal, surrounded by a lush green yard and a nice breeze.

Karla rushed into the kitchen with bags of goodies in hand. "Hi Bill!" She nearly ran into him, sweeping by him.

"Hey, kiddo! Let me give you a hand."

"Mind if I just help myself to the wares?"

"Nope. Mi casa su casa." Bill winked in her direction. "Hey Ramone, I got something to show you. If you need anything sweetie, we'll be out on the porch."

Although they left Karla's field of vision, with the sliding glass doors wide open, Ramone and Bill were close enough that she still could hear everything that was said. She fumbled through a drawer to retrieve a paring knife and sliced a colorful blend of yellow, green, and red sweet peppers while listening to words that were brought to her on the trestles of air blowing into the kitchen.

"So, I was able to track down someone who attended the Suzanne Denison trial. There appeared to be some questions in the way that they nailed that guy for both murders." Bill wasted little time to get down to business.

"Why? The guy left blood DNA all over the apartment. And he was a convicted rapist. That's pretty much a slam dunk. Why the questions?"

"Well, yes, true. But there was talk of a possible second person in the apartment that night."

"Oh, yeah? How so?"

"There was another blood sample that was found in the kitchen sink that didn't match his. And, when I asked where his blood was found, he said there weren't any reports of his blood being anywhere near the little girl. The state's theory claimed that he cut himself while killing Suzanne.

188

So, if the DA's motive of attempted rape were to hold up, he would've killed the little girl after her mother, right?"

"Well, ya. That would seem most likely." Ramone squinted his eyes in thought. "So, none of his blood was found anywhere near the child at all?"

"He said he was confused by that. I can see why."

"So, let's think this through. If he had tried to rape her, she fought back and heathen killed her, he'd see the girl after the fact. The girl's death would've been a spontaneous after thought. Out of panic."

"Yeah. So, it would be an instant reaction. He wouldn't've bothered cleaning up first. That was what I thought. Maybe he washed up before going after the girl? But, why do that?

"Clearly, if he saw the girl in the hall, which is where she was found, he wouldn't clean up first. So then he would've left blood somewhere on or at least near her. At the least it would've dripped some on the carpet or on her clothes. If they were able to find and identify his blood everywhere else, they should've found some, even a little, in or around the child."

"No shit. That's what I mean. And to add to that, the wounds from the girl and her mother were not from the same knife."

"Ok. He carried two knives around with him, then? Or found one in the kitchen?"

"Well, the knife he was known to carry was never recovered. But there were two knives in the sink, neither of which were his. Some of the wounds were made by a knife that wasn't in the sink at all, though. They couldn't match some wounds with any knife that they had in evidence. As far as what he said, anyway. Remember, this is just a man

189

at the trial proceedings. He's not privy to details that weren't brought out or discussed."

"It is interesting that the wounds weren't all the same. Not sure what to make of all that. I'd like to see the actual transcript, not just secondhand reports. Sometimes testimonies can be difficult to decipher. It's never an exact science. Can we get the transcripts?"

"We could certainly look into it. But it'd take some doing. And we'd need help. The guy also said that the DA mentioned in his closing arguments that there could have been someone else there. They just couldn't prove it."

Karla leaned around the corner, peeking her head around to share her thoughts. "Hey, I read an email that may have gotten overlooked. I thought I showed it to you, Pop. But, didn't get why it was even in the file. The case seemed open and shut to me too. But, now that you got me thinking, this email was weird."

Ramone scratched his mop of hair. "Hurry and finish up in there so you can join us."

"So, what was it? I haven't heard about this." Bill leaned over to hear her better.

Karla stayed inside, yelling loud enough for them to hear. "Some guy said he was a friend of the Denison family. Was concerned about his uncle, who also knew the family. He had told him that his uncle was threatened at a gas station when he was looking into their murders, just out of his own curiosity. I thought I mentioned it once, didn't I, Pop?"

"I don't think you did. So, when was this email sent? And to whom?" Karla took a quick break and stood in the open doorway. "I'd have to find it, but I think it was right around the time of the Denison trial. That was just a few years ago, right? I think it was written to someone in the family, but don't remember the name. I'm sure I could find it again. It's in that box of Denison documents."

There was a brief moment of silence, and she peeked around to catch Ramone rubbing his forehead. "I wish she'd hurry. I'm hungry."

"I'm done, Pop. Just relax."

Bill laughed.

Karla sauntered in with a plate of sandwiches arranged so meticulously that it could pass for a piece of art. "Holy shit, girl! We have to eat those? Where'd you learn to do that?" Karla smiled with pride at the attention that Bill gave to her work. Tomato wedges wrapped in curls of cucumber skin rings lined the plate to add aesthetic flavor. Ramone grabbed one as she laid the plate in the center of the table. "Do we eat these?"

Karla rolled her eyes. "Do whatever you want, Pop."

Bill chuckled and grabbed a sandwich.

"I'll get the wine." Karla disappeared into the kitchen and back through the doorway in a flash.

"If it's all the same, Karla, I'll just drink my beer." Bill winked in her direction and tipped his beer bottle to her in appreciation.

"Suit yourself. I got a bottle of local stuff, and it goes well with the meal."

Ramone appeared skeptical but allowed Karla to poor him a glass. He took a bite of sandwich, as she stood at his side and waited. "Well…"

Ramone looked up to her as he chewed. His words were slurred and mumbled, but clear enough to Karla "Ok. Sit down. It's good. Sit down damn it. It's just a sandwich."

Bill nudged her as Karla took a place at the glass table next to him. He had already gulped down a bite as well. "I like the sauce, kiddo. Can't say I recognize what it is."

"That's because I made it. And you can only get the recipe from me. It exists only in my head." She smiled, tapping the top of her head.

"Well, you should bottle it. I'd buy it." Bill glanced up to Ramone and back to Karla.

Ramone chewed as he talked. "So, what about that email? Some guy said he was threatened. How, exactly?"

"Well, the email was third party, so it probably couldn't be used in any court proceedings, but it reported that this guy was in line at a gas station when someone approached him from behind, whispering in his ear a reminder of what happened to people who 'know too much'."

"What the hell? Karla, that's big. I would've remembered you telling me that. You have to show me these things."

"Well, the guy was clear that his uncle couldn't collaborate 'cause he died a few years before. So, it's not like it'd be really useful. Besides, he said his uncle was really scared and got rid of whatever information he had gathered up. I guess he must have suspected something unusual, otherwise why would he be digging into it? And if someone said that to him, he must've known something noteworthy. I mean, that'd scare the shit out of me, too. Oh, and another thing that I thought was weird, but, of course may not be anything of worth, is that this guy, the one who was threatened? He worked with the Chief of Police's wife. Wouldn't you think that he would mention it to her, if he was worried about his safety? She was a co-worker of his after all. If it were me, and I was concerned, I'd at least mention it to see if anything could be done about the threats? Right?"

192

Ramone shook his head in frustration. "Hmmm. Well, if that's all true, I wouldn't know right off what to make of it. Something out of the ordinary was up, though. Would it do any good to try and follow up on that, if the guy is deceased?"

Bill leaned back and took a swig from his beer bottle. "I doubt it. If we've got the email, it's a piece of the puzzle, but that's all. It's just something to know, I guess. There's a slew of things about that whole ordeal that don't add up. Just brings up more questions than answers." He took in a deep breath. "I don't care if they nailed someone for it. I'm still not convinced it was truthfully solved." Bill paused. Then leaned forward, carefully choosing his words. "When I went through Denison's autopsy, Suzanne's, I got a creepy feeling as to how they found the body."

"Yeah, she was naked. But, reports from friends said she always slept that way. And that only fuels the theory that it was an attempted rape."

"No, that wasn't really it. It was the cuts in her chest."

That statement made Karla shiver. *That's why I avoid reading the autopsies.*

Ramone was curious. "What'd you mean? It was clearly a passionate crime. Stabbings always are."

"No. These wounds were deliberate. There was some sort of cross or X carved into her chest. They weren't just random stab wounds."

Karla felt nauseous. "I don't like the sound of that. Why would a rapist carve a something into victim's chest? That's beyond creepy."

Bill sat back again with a thoughtful stare. Almost saddened that he didn't have adequate answers. He gulped down more of his beer. "I don't know. Just don't like it. Don't like any of it. I can't help but think that if someone else was in that apartment, and he wasn't alone, then

193

that means someone is out there. Someone who never got served for his part. I hate the thought of injustice, especially where women and children are concerned. When anyone is murdered for that matter."

"Do you really think every case that goes to trial ends in justice?"

Karla looked to Ramone with compassion. *Wish this job didn't make you so hard, Pop.*

She added her own version of discontent to the conversation. "Well, I don't know about either of you, but I sure as hell don't buy that friends getting murdered just months apart from each other are completely separate circumstances with different motives and completely different perpetrators. Just sounds too coincidental. That's all."

"I certainly don't believe in coincidence." Ramone placed his glass of wine to the side, near Karla. "Would you just grab me beer? I'm not sure I like this."

Bill kept up the momentum. "Did the husbands know each other? The women were no doubt friends, but were the husbands?"

"No indication that I know of that the husbands were friends. I read that Suzanne's husband was out of town when she was killed. At work."

"Yeah. He had a solid alibi. I don't think they considered him much of a suspect anyway."

"Well, if he had an alibi, I guess that counts him out. But with what we found out about all the gun buying, gambling, and drugs that was going on, I just wonder if any of that was ever sufficiently explored. I mean, I know that the obvious theories are caught up in the whole drug crap. But, drug dealers need guns. Guns that can't be traced. And, money. Easy money. And at least this husband was clearly into guns with a passion. Remember, he was a member of that gun club? It was called

194

the Rider's Club or something like that, right? And we both know that there's always a market for guns where there's a market for drugs."

Ramone nodded. "True. But, didn't you say this city is a valley full of country folks? Country folks like their guns. Bill, you gave me the impression that people around here, particularly in those days, all had guns, right? And besides, Curtis was a gun collector, too. So, does that mean he's automatically suspect? He didn't even deny that he had possession of stolen guns. After all, that stolen gun he hid in his crawl space was a huge reason he was convicted in the first place, even I think that made him look guilty as hell."

Karla settled into the table, leaning on her elbows. "We can't be making assumptions based on a person's hobby of gun collecting. Curtis' gun was never determined by any means at all to have even been the murder weapon. It was a theory, based on behavior alone. There was never any evidence that actually put his gun at a murder scene. And stealing guns is not murder. So, neither husband should be considered a suspect based on just that. To get a conviction, you're supposed to show that a gun was in fact the murder weapon, and then be able to show who had possession at the time of the murders, at the crime scene. None of that happened in this case at all."

"You're such a sensible girl." Ramone teased.

"So, was Curtis really that hung up on all of his possessions that he'd hide a gun just because he liked it and he didn't want to get busted for it being stolen?" Bill shook his head in disbelief.

"With his narcissistic personality, all caught up in possessions? Sure. That's not a stretch at all. Plus, we know that he was warned by a friend that some of the cops were looking at him from the get-go, and the investigators made it a point to get the word out that they were looking for a .22. No doubt he was feeling a bit defensive to get them off his back. That'd make anyone hyper-sensitive, even paranoid, if you were under stress or trauma."

"What about that whole thing with that cop, wasn't his name Grant? He confiscated Curtis' guns earlier that summer. That just seems odd. I mean the way it all went down. The DA tried using that against him. But it doesn't make sense to me. It actually makes the department look bad. The way it was done and all."

"No. I'm not sure I can put my finger on what that was all about. I mean that cop, Grant, testified that he took Curtis' guns because the wife was afraid of him. But then he gave them back, without ever checking them into the department through proper channels. If he was really protecting her, he wouldn't have given them back so soon. And he would've checked them in, so it would've been documented. But it wasn't and he didn't. Seems fishy to me."

"Yeah, and, do you think there had really been an affair between this Grant guy and Curtis' wife? That's what I read in an interview that folks suspected. I don't see a strait-laced woman like her falling for a womanizing cop like him."

Ramone took in a deep breath. "It's possible. He was supposedly charming, according to the report. She could've been lonely, married to Curtis and all. Doesn't seem that farfetched."

"Yeh. Curtis himself said in our interview with him that there was no possibility. It bothered him that people would say that Ruth was unfaithful but remember there were several men sweet on her during that time, who knows. Ramone reached into his bag to retrieve a notebook. "Let's take a look at what we came up with today. Karla, go get that board."

Karla dismissed herself momentarily, while Ramone cleared the table of all of the lunch wares by pushing everything down to the end of the

196

table. At the same time, he gathered his thoughts. Bill seemed to read his mind. "So, you really think these cases are connected? I'm thinking something was amiss. Just can't put it all together."

"I know, that's where I'm at with it. There's this name I keep coming across, but just can't figure out why. This Hollister guy, Craig Hollister. We can't find any direct connection to any of the victims, but he seems to have been in the middle of something back then. Here, look at this. That interview I did yesterday, the guy said that this Hollister character was in cahoots with some big time drug dealer, and Karla told me that she read scribbled in a notebook that was used to take notes at the Denison trial, that this Hollister was in the parking lot of Denison's apartment building the night Denison was killed. He was an actual witness, apparently."

"Is he important?"

"I don't know."

"Could be someone to talk to. Especially if he was a witness in Suzanne Denison's deal."

"Yeah, I think I'll have Karla try and find him. He could be useful."

Karla returned with the white-board case in hand. "Who could be useful?"

"Oh, this Hollister guy. He seemed to be in the know. You should try and find him."

"Oh, yeah. I know that guy who was in the parking lot the night Suzanne was killed. He said he had seen someone leaving the apartment, holding his shoulder."

"Why was he there again? In the parking lot? It was the middle of the night. Was he just sitting in his car?" Bill shook his head in confusion.

"Nobody seemed to ask, or at least documented that they had asked." Karla looked to Ramone, who had become suddenly quiet. *I wish I could read your thoughts, Pop.*

Bill piped up again, breaking the silence, "I wish I could've been there to see that scumbag rapist give his testimony. I mean, I think they had plenty on him to put 'im back in jail. Hell, he said himself that he saw the bodies and then just left. Who does that? Let's say, even if he hadn't killed her. Who steps over the body of a five-year-old little girl and then just leaves?"

Ramone looked through the notebook as he spoke. "I might buy it. Maybe. He had just come from the bar. It was in the middle of the night. So, he was most certainly drunk. A self-professed druggie, so he was probably high, too. I don't know about the part that he said he was attacked going into the house. It would be more reasonable that he gave this other guy a ride so he could get drugs. He wouldn't give just anybody a ride home, without knowing he was getting something in return."

Karla snatched up the notebook from Ramone and examined it for herself. Ramone took the opportunity to stand up and reach down the table to grab another sandwich and quickly began to gobble it down. Karla glanced up and noticed. *So, he likes them after all.* She resisted the urge to say something smart-alecky. Bill also took advantage of the break to reach down into the cooler for another beer. Karla finally spoke of her own thoughts. "So, you think he really went to get drugs? I think I might be with you on that one. But, if that were true, then that could make Suzanne a drug dealer. She wasn't. Was she?"

"No. Nothing in any testimonies or reports indicate that she was, other than being married to a man who had known associates that had been in prison because of drugs. So, who knows, could just be a glitch in yet another theory. Unless, the drugs were coming from somewhere else

198

near her apartment, and his story about the door being open was true. After all, he admitted that there were drugs in it for him. He didn't deny that at all."

Bill chimed in. "Or maybe there was a price other than cash to be paid for those drugs. Drugs breed other evils, as we well know. What if the guy that he gave a ride to needed his help? And that's how he got his drugs, or even paid an overdue debt. Who really knows? Bottom line, he was there. He left traces of himself all over the place. That's really all we know. And that's why he got convicted."

Karla wasn't satisfied with that conclusion. "Ya, but who was with him? Who else was there? There was someone. There had to be. The evidence says so. Why wasn't that more of an issue to anyone?"

Bill was realistic and practical. "They got somebody. Why would they try too hard to look for a second man?"

Ramone was simply frustrated that they didn't have all the answers. "I just need to get up and move for a bit. We're still missing too much. That's how it is Karla. As long as they got somebody. The aim in so many cases isn't to get to the truth. It's to convict somebody and appease the fear of the people. Clearly, it was a scary time. If that weren't the case, more people would be talking about the truth, and not just the convictions. Let's face it, we still can't piece together how these cases even fit together. So, the victims were friends, and they were killed in the same summer. That's all we got. How does it help that there was someone else in Denison's apartment, if we can't find the pieces that our case was connected to hers?" Ramone slipped out from his chair and shuffled out onto the grass, with is hands on his hips.

Karla fumbled with the stem of her wine glass, then took a sip. *Because there was someone else there. And that means it wasn't attempted rape. Because you of all people know that the truth matters, Pop. The truth matters.*

Chapter 18

Karla sat up in bed in a cold sweat, her chest rising and falling in panic. A slivered stream of light peered through the heavy polyester curtains and faded into a dirty haze. The pounding at the door brought her into a dizzy state of reality as she squinted into the beam of light to gain clarity. Her cell phone was buzzing beside her and she realized that she hadn't turned the volume up the night before so that her alarm would wake her. Fumbling with the phone in her hands to try and view the time, Karla breathed away the annoying knock at the door. The buzzing continued and she saw that her father was calling. Still not knowing the time, she reluctantly answered. "Is that you making all that noise? Holy shit, Pop, I'm coming. Give me a minute!" The exasperated whisper gave herself away.

"You're not up yet, are you? C'mon, Karla, we're burning daylight here."

"I'm coming. Just give me a sec."

"I'll be in the lobby grabbing some coffee. You've got fifteen minutes."

Karla hung up without saying goodbye and her placed behind her back to lean up against the headboard. She tried to rub away the recent images piercing her thoughts. Breathing in deep, they were still there. Eyes.

Not her eyes. Multiple pairs of eyes, staring at her, calling to her. Eyes that waded in a shallow sea of dark, milky water. Water that swirled with hues of purple, gray, and reds. *Who says people don't dream in color? Or maybe that was with dogs, or cats, or something.*

Karla blinked several times to try and make sense of the images. Then she remembered the screams. *God, screaming eyes? So weird.* She slid the palm of her hands over her face to try and make sense of it. *It doesn't matter. It was just a dream. I'd best be up and get going.*

Scattered amidst the blanket and crumpled sheets were the remnants of last night's study session. Clippings and photocopies of pictures layered themselves in several disorganized heaps, as well as a file balancing near the edge of the bed as if trying to escape. Karla crawled on her knees, gathering up the mess, trying to put things in order as she scooped. *Damn, he'll be pissed if this stuff is out of order.* She sat back in a cross-legged pose and sifted through each piece, trying to remember how they had been sequenced.

Karla stopped short when she came upon a black and white photocopy depicting a young woman. It was a posed photo. One that looked to be like a school senior portrait or something. Her hair was well-groomed, and her shoulders were primed at just the right angle. She had a subtle lean with her chest pushed up ever so lightly. She was half smiling, not over the top, but it was there nonetheless. *Is it real? The smile doesn't look real. And those eyes.* The eyes were looking right at Karla. Looking into her. Calling her.

Shivering slightly, Karla continued her sorting, realizing that there were at least a dozen photocopies she had browsed through the night before. Many had nothing to do with the case they were working on, just the dark happenings of the time. Some were victims of Ted Bundy, the infamous serial killer of the 1970's. *I don't know why I bother with all of these.* Her father would say it was a waste of time. "Stick to what's relevant," Ramone's police wisdom would say.

Not all of the photos were of women, but women with their children as well, depictions of smiling, giddy children who didn't necessarily know how to pose in dignified statures. Karla came across an image of two little boys playing in the grass, with giggles written all over their faces. *Refreshing.* As long as she focused on the smiles and not the eyes.

Karla realized that she was in fact wasting time and quickly gathered the piles into some form of order. Stuffing the contents into the folder, she pushed her way into the bathroom to collect herself. A shower was out of the question, but the dark layers under her eyes suggested that she at least wash her face. With water trickling from her nose Karla leaned into the mirror and didn't like what she saw. Her forehead ached from the alcohol she had consumed before going to sleep. It was just a few nightcaps that had settled her nerves. That's all it was. Karla stood back away from the mirror. She stared deep into her own eyes. *I look like shit. I'm in the prime of my life, and I look like shit.*

Karla wiped away her insecurities with a towel then proceeded to brush her teeth and wrap her hair in a ponytail. As she adorned herself in a cartoon character tee-shirt, her phone began to buzz its annoying reminder that she was not on her own time. "Oh for God's sake, I'm coming." She reached for it and turned off the buzzing in a pinch, ignoring her father's call. Swiping up the backpack with the day's work tightly squeezed inside with the laptop, she rushed out of the room. Passing doors in the long hall gave Karla time to compose herself.

In the lobby, Ramone was leaning against the counter with a cup of coffee and a smile as he chatted with the hotel clerk. Karla approached and immediately leaned into him to give him a kiss on the cheek. "Morning Pop." She sighed when he didn't return the greeting

"What's with you?" Ramone tried to cover up his impatience with idle jesting by including a smile as he spoke.

"I was up late and didn't sleep well. I had this really weird dr..."

"I came by your room to get some of those documents and you didn't answer. It wasn't that late. Why didn't you answer?"

"What time was that, Pop?"

"Around 9:00 or 9:30."

"Hmm. Must have been in the bath. I took an early bath before going over all those letters you gave me." Which was a lie. Karla wasn't in the room at all at 9:30pm.

Ramone reluctantly accepted the explanation and handed Karla his briefcase as they walked to the car. "Do we have any interviews today?" Settling into the seat, Karla laid his briefcase on the floorboard of the car and messed with her backpack in her lap. He watched her from the corner of his eye. "I need you to get out my laptop. Google a map site. We're going for a drive today."

"Ok Pop, but I wanted to show you some inconsistencies I came across last night. Let me get this stuff out first."

The car pulled out onto a two-lane highway in an outskirt community. "So, where we going again? Can I get some breakfast, or at least stop and grab some coffee from a gas station?"

"If you'd been up, Karla, you could have eaten at the hotel, you know." He grinned over at her, letting her know he was teasing.

"Please," she grinned a quick, fake smile in his direction.

Ramone caught a glimpse of a gas station up ahead and pulled in for a quick stop. While he waited, he grabbed his briefcase and proceeded to do what she hadn't. She was climbing back into the car within minutes.

"So, where we going again?" Ramone didn't respond. He appeared caught up in his own thoughts as he pulled out onto the road. Taking a deep breath, she looked out of the window and didn't bother repeating herself.

As they crossed the bridge that hovered over the Colorado River to the outskirts of town, Karla scanned the map that Ramone had pulled up on the screen while sipping from a cheap Styrofoam cup with a plastic lid. "Oh, I see where we're going. We'll drive right through the Whitewater area, right? Are we going there? Please say we are. It'd be nice to be able to picture the area, since we keep hearing so much about it."

"We are. Just relax."

"Should be a nice drive. Are we meeting anyone there?"

"Not there. In Montrose. I called a couple of the locals and got some pretty positive responses. No one wants to talk about what I want to, though. Just old timers wanting to tell me stories of their own lives, minus the small details of what was going on around them, of course."

"They're just old people who raised families trying to earn a living. They don't want to remember any of the bad shit. For them, none of this affected them. Life went on. Why would they talk to you about any of it?"

"Well, there was some real shit going on in their peaceful little community. There's no doubt. And when shit ends up with someone dying, multiple people dying in fact, you'd think somebody would care enough to want to know why."

"As far as everyone in this town is concerned, it was already settled, Pop."

"Except that there are people who know that it really wasn't."

Karla felt the images of her nightmare return to her in a flash, then they were gone just as fast. She closed her eyes to try and blink the images away for good.

"We did get one hit, though. The wife of an old retired rancher who used to go to church with the Bakersons. They moved out of the Grand Junction area in the '80's and settled in Montrose to retire closer to the mountains. The old man is deceased, but his wife, she said that her husband had a friend who worked in law enforcement in Pitkin County. Seemed a bit reluctant, but willing to at least talk to us."

"So are we going to the bridge sometime, on the way there or on the way back, maybe?"

"Yeah, soon, on the way. Bill's meeting us there in an about an hour. But let's drive around some, just to get a feel for how far away folks lived from the river."

Karla took in the sights of the surrounding landscape. They passed fields and fences and newly remodeled farmhouses. A quick turn brought them facing the base of the area's most notable mountaintop, towering slightly ahead and above them. The infamous flat top mountain of the Grand Mesa. *It's beautiful. I can see now why people like to live out here.* Karla took in the fields of grass, trees and shrubs, and a few homes scattered across the hillsides, many acres apart from each other. *Peaceful indeed.* She wondered out loud, "How could anyone possibly determine where the shootings took place? If it didn't happen at their homes, or at the bridge, finding the location of the shootings around here is like finding a needle in a haystack."

"That's why we have to talk to people. People are where the leads are gonna come from. What people remember are pieces to the puzzle."

They drove upward, on a winding road where newer houses had replaced older farm homes. Ramone waved out of the window an arch into the air to point out a large acreage of land. "All of this used to belong to a railroad worker who was said to have quite a flourishing crop of marijuana going in all directions. He lived simple. But he was making his share."

"Where's he at now?"

"Died awhile back. He was a local hero of sorts. Everybody liked him. At least it appeared that way. It seems like folks out here are nothing more than homesteaders who have generations still living here. I read a book about the area. Pretty cool history. You should check it out."

Karla sat back and tried not to think too hard. That was her father's job. She was still feeling uneasy. She decided to sit back and enjoy the scenery. They drove in what seemed like almost a full circle, as Ramone talked continuously about the various families of the area. *That must have been some book.* Karla completely tuned him out. *I thought we were supposed to stick to what was relevant?* Ramone turned to her and questioned her attentiveness. "Karla, Karla, did you hear me? Are you even listening?"

"Wha…what? I heard you. Of course." She glanced back out of the window, somewhat annoyed. "You were talking about some ranching families, that this place has had families that have been out here forever. Or something like that."

"Well, yes, I find it interesting. The history, and such. That's all. I mean, wouldn't it have been something to be able to pass land down through the family? To have a home passed down through generations. There was a family I read about whose son still lives here, not at the old house his father was raised in, but still, to be able to have access to a place that has so much history to it. I guess no one lives there now, it's just an old abandoned house. But I just think that would be something to be proud of."

"But somehow not connected to anything we're doing, though, right? That's unlike you, Pop."

"Ok, fine. You got me there. Maybe this town is growing on me some."

Hearing him say that actually made Karla smile.

They pulled to the side of the road a few times to take pictures. At one stop, Karla took an intriguing picture of an old makeshift storage cellar. It was made of large river rock and well-weathered wooden posts. The cobblestone formation had clearly been hand built, with remnants of muddy mortar securing the stones in place against the rustic wooden frame, which had tilted slightly at varying angles through the years. It had been dug into the side of a hill, which made it barely visible, almost camouflaged. It caught her eye, nonetheless. The most visible form of the cellar, from the distance of the road, was the door.

Splintered and faded from years of exposure to the elements, it made her curious as to what would be stored inside. *So cool. There could be some hidden treasures in there. It's like going back in time.* Karla zoomed her camera in as close as the lens could get. Detail. Something this rustic and authentic deserved adequate detail. "We don't see things like this in the city, do we Pop?" She took advantage of the ability to get out of the car and feed her imagination, feeling grateful for her Pop's changed demeanor. "This is kinda cool, Pop. I didn't know people still used cellars." Karla glanced into the open window of the car where Ramone was writing down some notes. *Ok, so it was short lived. Never mind.*

When they returned to the stretch of highway, miles from the next turn off, Karla found herself drifting into memories of her own time's past. It wasn't a cellar, but it was a door. A uniquely distinct door. *Was it to a bedroom, maybe?* She remembered the door because of its one-of-a kind charm. It had a large painting of the sun on it. Yellow and orange, with the sun rays winding from its center in a snake-like fashion. Karla thought she remembered words spiraling in circular lines, winding their way into the center. The image was cloudy, and she wasn't sure if it had actually been real or dreamt up.

"Pop, did you ever know anyone who was a painter, like an artist or something?"

"What? What are you talking about?"

"I don't know. The door on that cellar made me think of an interesting door I remember from somewhere when I was little, really little, I guess. I think I may have actually dreamed about it before, so maybe it was just a dream. But I swear it was real. It had this beautiful sun painted on it, with words on it, like a poem maybe? I was probably a dream, though, unless you remember it. Did I just dream it?"

Ramone stared out to the road ahead of them. "Yeah. You must 'ave just had a dream sometime" They both suspended their conversation and passed the time in silence. Karla took advantage of the quiet to think, to contemplate. *If only I could remember.*

Suddenly the tone of Ramone's cell phone broke the trance that had settled amidst them. Ramone's disappointed voice gave away the content of the conversation. "Hey there…Oh, that's too bad…No, No. We can head out there tomorrow, if that works better…No problem…Ok. Give me a call first thing…Oh, of course. I bet it gets hot really fast. You said it was a bit of a walk, right?…Oh, yes, I know. Nothin' like back home. But still, wouldn't want to be out there in the heat of the day…Alright. Will hear from you in the morning, then." Ramone clicked the call to an end and shrugged to Karla.

"So, Bill's not meeting us out there?"

"No. We'll go tomorrow. Just make sure you're up early."

Approaching the quaint and well landscaped double-wide manufactured home neatly lined with rows of red and yellow flowerpots with river rock leading the way, Karla felt a sense of comfort. She was getting accustomed to the welcoming feel of the country. An older woman answered the door, cordial, but a bit abrasive in her demeanor. Dorothy's face roughly bore the scars of life. She broke out in a smirk, with firecrackers for eyes, which indicated to Karla that she had handled the scars of life just fine.

"Well, hell, I wondered if you folks would make it. The day's half over you know." Dorothy sent a wink to Karla. "You folks come on in." She invited both of them to the sofa with a gesture of her hand. A plate of cookies beckoned them as well. A small tin of cream with a cup of sugar added to the charm of the coffee table in front of them.

I wonder how often she gets visitors.

"I hope you like coffee. I can make tea if you'd like that better. They say I'm not supposed to drink coffee. And I really don't like it. I just drink it to spite what the so-called experts say. Experts, my ass."

Ramone nodded with a slight chuckle, not sure how to respond. "Coffee's good. And thank you." He sat down and pulled up his laptop, then handed it to Karla who sat still beside him, waiting to follow his lead. Dorothy went to the kitchen and returned with two cups of coffee.

"C'mon, child, eat a cookie. I don't bake that often."

Karla grinned. "Well, you ought to. They look perfect. I bet they're good."

"I guess you're about to find out." Her mischievous grin relaxed the tension in the back of Karla's neck.

"We sure appreciate you talking to us. Can I start with asking how you knew Betsy Kendall?"

209

"Oh, I really didn't know Betsy, not personally so much. Poor girl, though. Knew a lot about her, on account that Ruth told me everything."

"You said on the phone that you were concerned about the kind of lifestyle that Betsy was involved in. So, you knew this because Ruth told you?"

"Oh, yes. You know since Ruth and I, we went to church together, and she was always asking everybody to pray for Betsy. That Betsy was sleeping with everyone in town, it seemed like. Especially men in uniform. Cops, Sheriff deputies, firefighters, the whole lot of them. Oh, not just the uniformed ones, though. Lots of 'em. How does a girl who doesn't eat or sleep right have such energy? For God's sakes, I could only handle one man."

Karla grinned, almost a snicker.

Ramone wasn't amused. "Did Ruth ever talk about Betsy wanting to leave town? Were she and Betsy planning to leave together? We heard they were taking some sort of trip together."

"Oh, no they weren't leaving together. I mean, yes, they had a trip planned. But Ruth was planning to go back home to her family once they got back and all. She was leaving Curtis, that was for sure. I told her to. He wasn't good to her, after all. And yes, Betsy had some cockamamie idea to get money so she could get the hell away from all of the shit she had gotten herself into. She was gonna take her boys and get away. I think it may have been on account that she was scared. She was sure as hell scared of someone. Ruth said that she was always asking to have her yard or her carport checked for some intruder that she thought was poking around. She had gotten pretty paranoid. And, then, of course, she was attacked twice, after all. The one time, it nearly killed her. Some man tried to strangle her. Landed her in the hospital, it did. Ruth also said she had been beat up once. Both instances happened within three or four months of each other. And then, that friend of hers getting' killed and all. So of course, she was scared as hell, she surely was."

"Do you have any idea who of? Did Ruth ever indicate that Betsy had told her who she was scared of?" Ramone glanced over to Karla as if to check to make sure she was taking notes.

"Oh, no. That upset her, though. I mean Ruth did ask, but Betsy wasn't talkin'. Said she didn't know who it was. I know one thing for sure, all that should've been dealt with better. I'm not sure any of it was taken all that seriously. For God's sake, she nearly died the one time. Had it not had been for Ruth and Curtis the night she was strangled, she might've. You've looked into that, right?"

"Yes. We've looked into that extensively. Did Ruth ever indicate that she had any suspicions as to who might have attacked Betsy that night in her home?"

"No. Like I said, Betsy wouldn't talk about any of the details as to who was responsible. Ruth said something about some dirty blond-haired man that Betsy talked about a little. Never like she accused him or anything, but Ruth said he seemed suspicious. At least in Ruth's eyes."

"Anybody you know that Betsy was sleeping with that fit that description?"

"No. I stayed clear of all the party crowds. Betsy was quite a partier and knew everyone."

"Any chance you could narrow it down?" Ramone was getting impatient with the rumor mill. He wanted something he could narrow down to anything resembling a fact of some sort.

Dorothy released a rough and gutted grunt. "Holy shit! If only I could narrow it down."

211

"But you just said she was sleeping with law enforcement. Were any of them partiers?"

"Well, hell ya, there were so many damn rumors, even I couldn't keep up with them. I even heard that the Chief himself was gettin' outta control. Had people around him like damn groupies, always at the bars doin' God knows what. There was some elitist crowd that he ran with, always havin' parties out in rich man's country. Betsy didn't likely party with them. They were too high and mighty for her. You know, all the money folk with their drinks in one hand and girls on the other. I heard they always had girls around. You know what they were for. And these weren't the street kind. They wore nice clothes, probably given to them from the high-end dress shops in town. I know for a fact that shit was going on 'cause I had a niece who was part owner is some modeling agency. She ended up on the losing end, but she went to some of these parties. Never would give me the juicy details. She's gone, though. Sad story, her life was. Boy, I'd be rich as hell if I knew the likes of the men who were at these parties. Money mongers don't like to kiss and tell. You know, that's what bribery is for."

Karla laughed. "Did these rumors give any indication that drugs were in the midst of these parties?"

"Of course drugs were in the mix! Had to be! Hell, it was the '70's after all. Besides, my husband was friends with a law man, you knew that, right? He knew a lot about all the rumors. Even his friend couldn't do nothin' though. He wasn't high enough on the totem pole and certainly wasn't in that groupie crowd. Frankly, he didn't want nothin' to do with any of it."

Ramone made another attempt to narrow it all down. "Did you ever hear whether or not Curtis or anyone he knew was a part of this circle?"

212

"Oh, for heaven's sakes no, not Curtis, not a chance. Curtis thought he was better than anyone else. Including those who were in charge with money in the mix. And he couldn't stand law enforcement. Practically loathed them. Well, he did have a mistress who was all into that scene, though. So, maybe if he was with her, then maybe. But I doubt he'd be seen anywhere near runnin' with law enforcement. I mean, he wanted to run with the big shots in town, but they didn't seem to like 'im. But, now that you mention it, some of his coworkers, they were big shits around town. His boss was on the City Council, after all. Curtis was too self-righteous, though. The other woman, the mistress, though, I don't know. I have my doubts about her. Well, she was some model of some sort and had friends who weren't as upright as they wanted everyone to think they were. So, I suppose he may have secretly entertained the idea, if only to impress her, if only for her sake. But, Ruth figured that he thought he could save this troubled woman. Thought he held some special powers over the 'weaker sex' as he perceived them, I guess. My guess is that's why he was with her. To save her, and of course to use and control her. Well, that's the obvious reason, of course. The mistress was certainly beautiful. I don't know. Ruth never indicated that he had anything to do with the party scene, even with the likes of the mistress. But like I said, a few of those co-workers of his could've easily been wrapped up in that scene. They were known to run with the socially upscale derelicts. That Greg friend of his, for example. Ruth said he had some things going on that Curtis talked about but acted as if it was all secret and stuff. Actually, Ruth thought maybe Curtis was trying to get in on all the action that Greg was doin'. Had some things up his sleeve with Greg, and Ruth suspected it was illegal. She said they were both sometimes flying lawyers and shit to all over, places like Aspen. So, no doubt, I'd put that Greg fellow in that sketchy white-collar money scene."

Karla was enthralled with Dorothy's ability to ramble on without even taking a breath. *She's so endearing.*

"Yes, we know a few things about this Greg friend of Curtis'. And, well, the mistress seemed to be feeding the investigation, according to one of the retired officers we spoke to. It seems like from the way he talked, they were taking everything she said as gold. Like the whole investigation against Curtis hinged on her statements. Some people seemed to count her words as the sole reason they think he's guilty. Makes me wonder, if she was in the drug or prostitution scene at all, whether or not she was given some sort of deal to keep herself out of the limelight in order to get dirt on him. I was in law enforcement and that's how it worked sometimes."

"Well, Ruth knew this guy pretty well too. Counted him as a friend. She talked about him like he was some sort of genius or something. I guess you'd have to be, to be an engineer and all. That's what I was sayin', you know, about him workin' on the side doin' some sort of peculiar side job. Ruth said it really bothered Curtis, 'cause it involved law enforcement somehow. And like I said, Curtis didn't think too highly of law enforcement around here. I often worried about her, though. You know, she seemed to know about people that she really didn't have any business to. That was mostly because of Betsy, of course. Betsy knew everyone it town, so I guess she knew a lot. That's not always a good thing, you know. Yep. I sure worried about her a lot." Dorothy's voice trailed to a slow stop as she sipped from her coffee mug.

Karla couldn't help but notice Dorothy's hands jittering, as if her old age had taken over her central nervous system. *God, she must've seen so much life. Has to be in her mid-nineties at least. Her mind's so sharp for her age. Must be hard to have a sharp mind in a body that's not. I want to be like that at her age, with that sort of mental clarity, even if my hands shake. We need more time with her. I need more time with her.*

214

Karla was taking notes, even though they had the recorder on the computer going. That was a good thing, as Karla's note taking wasn't going all that well. She was simply enthralled with Dorothy's way of telling things. "So you and Ruth were close, I take it? Seems like she was more like a daughter than a friend."

Ramone glanced over to Karla with a look of disapproval and interrupted. "We found a piece of notebook paper with a list of men's names on it. It was in Betsy's handwriting. Do you know why she would have a list of names? If we showed it to you, do you think you could recognize any of the names? Most of them are first names only."

"Oh, hell, I don't know. There was some diary that was a big deal in the trial. I'm sure you read all about that, already. She was keepin' some sort of record of things. Don't know for sure why, though."

"Yes, yes we have read all about the diary. But we have reason to believe there was more than one. The one that seemed to matter was destroyed by one of her boyfriends. A Sheriff's deputy."

"Oh, ya! Shit, can you believe that? A lawman destroys evidence, admits that in court, and nothing's made of it? I never could figure that one out. If that isn't suspicious, I don't know what is. God, I bet you would love to have that diary, wouldn't you? Burned and thrown into the river like that. What a shame and a complete mockery of a woman's deepest thoughts. Do you keep a diary child? You should. Good for the soul, you know. Good for the soul." Dorothy nodded to Karla with pride in knowing that she could be helpful to a young girl's inner development. Karla seemed to read her mind. *I'd like to know what's in Dorothy's diaries.*

Ramone's impatience was beginning to show. He pulled out his cell phone and checked the time, glancing back over to Karla to end the chit chatting. Karla ignored him, instead leaning forward in her seat to be

215

closer to Dorothy. "Did you keep a diary? I bet you could have some wonderful stories to share."

"Well, hell yeah, when I was younger. I had many over the years. I have a hard time writing these days, though." Dorothy looked down to her unsteady hands.

Karla smiled sweetly to her. "So, did you keep any of 'em? Anything you'd be willing to let others read? I bet you have a secret or two." Karla tilted her head in jest, with a grin that raised her eyebrows. She vaguely could see Ramone from the corner of her eye shift his feet, then pull out a folder to retrieve a piece of paper. He leaned toward Dorothy and handed it to her. "So, here's that list. If you could just glance through it, and maybe see if any names jump out at you?"

Dorothy took it politely and scanned it thoughtfully. "Well, some sound familiar, but without last names, how would I know who they were? This one here, this Craig name, Ruth said once that Betsy dated someone by that name. Even said that Betsy's youngest child may have been his. But, how the hell would I know for sure if that were even true?" Glancing down again, Dorothy slid her finger across a few other names. "Well, and here are a few names that maybe could match a couple cops I knew of. She slept with a Bradley character according to my husband, and this guy here, this Tony name. My husband said that there was a drug dealer with that name around town. My husband's friend arrested him once bringing in a shipment of drugs in this ol' beat up car hooked up to a trailer. Said he got off scot free with nothin' at all. Happened all the time, he said. Makes me wonder why anyone would bother tryin' to nab these guys, if all they do is get set free again."

Ramone stood abruptly and put out his hand to take back the piece of paper. Dorothy handed it back to him, while taking in a breath to mask the slight annoyance written all over her face. Ramone's tone was as abrupt as his stance, "Well, I'm sure we could talk all day, but we have

216

another appointment, so as much as I'd love to stay and visit, we should be on our way. Thank you so much for..." Ramone reached out his hand for a polite exit handshake toward Dorothy's, who failed to notice. She was standing up to lead them to the door, as she watched Karla scramble to put Ramone's computer away. "Well, it was good for me, too," Dorothy smiled politely. Karla awkwardly stood to her feet to follow them, smiling to Dorothy apologetically.

Ramone nodded to rush them along. "We appreciate your time and are quite grateful for your information. We just a have a tight schedule. We don't mean to rush away. May we call you to follow up, if we have any more questions? Could we send you that list to see if any more people come to mind? I'd love for you to be able to review it without any pressure."

"Do whatever you like. You have my email address. Any way I can help, any time."

As they departed, Dorothy had one last word, facing Ramone.

"Schedules will be the death of you, you know. You'll never be at peace, until you let yourself relax. Life's about letting go of the pressure to have everything all in order, young man. When you're my age, and the only schedule there is, is breakfast, lunch, and dinner? Who gives a shit about schedules?" Karla grinned at Ramone, as she waved back to Dorothy. *I like her. I wanna visit again. But without Pop next time.*

Chapter 19

The door jingled as Karla entered the small tavern. She glanced across the empty bar stools. "Where's the old man?" No longer a stranger, Karla settled onto her own self-proclaimed barstool and nodded a grin to Shannon as she was wiping her hands with a dirty dishcloth.

"Well, good afternoon to ya, my love!" The florescent lights above Shannon melted into her hair, illuminating a few small strands that settled around her eyes. "He was here earlier, but I haven't seen him since then." She brushed the hair strands back away from her face with the back of her wrist. While grabbing a glass from the shelf to begin the routine pouring, Shannon coughed hard into her sleeve. Karla studied her as she worked. *She should stop smoking. That doesn't sound so good.* Karla let out a breath of life into the muggy dead air around them. *She's really quite beautiful, with her hair a bit of a mess like that. She could use a break. And maybe a doctor.* "You should quit smoking. That cough would go away, you know."

"You should quit drinking." Shannon grinned with a wink as she placed a glass in front of Karla.

"Then who would pay your medical bills?" Karla grinned back.

Shannon stopped short, pausing in the middle of a task to look at Karla with sincere contemplation. Immediately, Karla hesitated her own motion with anxious expectation, responding to Shannon's thoughtful gaze. "What?"

"Can I ask you something?"

"Of course."

"Do you really think your client is innocent?"

"Well, actually, our client is the son of the man convicted, and yes. Yes, he does."

Shannon smiled and relaxed. "Ok. Let me restate. Do you think your client's father is really innocent?"

"Of course. Pop would never take a case he didn't believe in." She studied her motives for asking. "Why?"

"Can you pull out your wallet?" Shannon was serious but not in a negative way.

"Oooh…k?" Karla reluctantly grabbed her wallet from her purse and laid it out in front of her. "Why? What's going on, Shannon?"

Shannon smiled away her apprehension. "The pictures. You have pictures in there, right? I've seen them."

"Oh, ya. Here." Karla pulled out the photos and fanned them across the bar.

Pointing to the photo of the youngest girl, Shannon looked up to Karla and paused. Karla noticed tears forming, but Shannon blinked them away. She slowly rubbed her finger back and forth across the photo her eyes had landed on. Shannon breathed in slow steady breaths, her voice almost at a whisper, keeping her gaze on the photo. "She was thirteen when it happened."

Wha…What? "You knew her?"

219

"I should say so. We shared a home, after all." Shannon finally looked up and smiled. "Oh, and DNA as well."

"Oh! Holy shit!" Karla stopped short and studied her face. *That's right. You had a sister.* Karla looked to her in confusion. "Why'd you not say anything before now? Shit, you let me go on and on, and never said anyth...?"

Shannon crinkled her mouth in apology. "Oh, I don't know. Just didn't seem like the right moment. Besides, didn't want to talk about it when Randall was around. And, well, he's always around." She chuckled. "He's touchy about it all."

"Why?"

Just then, the door jingled open again.

Karla watched cautiously as Randall stumbled to his regular stool beside her. He was no longer just a man at the bar. He was the man at the bar that she had become quite fond of. He was oblivious that he had walked in on a conversation of which he was unwittingly a part. "Alright, girl. I'm up for a rematch!" He shuffled a stack of cards he pulled from his back pocket and laid it down beside her drink. Karla glanced to Shannon to see her shaking her head with a silent warning. She looked back to Randall, heeding the warning with a shrug. "Well, hello to you too...." He teased her. "Don't think you're gonna get me this time."

Karla shot a sensitive smile to Shannon who simply smiled back.

So, 'till later then, I guess. We'll resume all of this later. "What d'ya mean this time? How about every time." Karla teased back.

"You know I let you win."

"If you say so." Karla's mood lightened with every word.

"So, how's your ol' man? Still givin' ya shit?"

"Pop is Pop. He's so tied up in knots right now, I'm guessing he doesn't even know I'm gone."

"You don't give 'im enough credit, girl."

Karla gave him a look of protest, frowning in his direction.

Randall wasn't steered from his point. "You said he's been alone all these years with you, right?"

"Well, yeah. So, what're you saying?" Karla was shuffling a new hand, as she didn't like the one she had.

"Hey! Just 'cause you're cute, doesn't mean you can cheat!" He growled through spattering teeth.

Karla giggled. "I love that you think I'm cute. What am I, ten?"

"You might as well be, always talkin' shit about your father like you do. Quit'ch yer bitchin' girl. He's a hell of a man to raise you on his own."

"Ok, ok. I get it. I'm a spoiled little brat. I bet you were quite the hellion yourself. Am I right?"

"Ha! There! Full house. I gotcha again!"

"Oh, wait, I've not folded. Hmmm. Ok. I fold." Karla spread her cards face down in front of her and smirked a response with a shrug of her shoulders.

"See? How about we do a game of 21. That's all luck and no skill. Maybe you can actually win a round."

"You didn't answer my question."

"Huh? What question?"

"You were a little shit, weren't you? You said once that your father had to be a bit hard on you. I'm sure you needed it."

"Ok. I fold an' own up. I was. But I turned out ok."

Shannon placed waters in front of them both. "Yes you did, my dear friend. Yes, you did." She winked and reached over the bar to pat his shoulder.

"And he was a good man, he was. I deserved every ass whoopin' I got." Randall tapped the wooden bar to emphasize his point. "So, whatever happened to yer ma' anyhow? You don't talk much about 'er. Why the hell not?"

Karla stopped short and looked directly at him, almost offended. But then, she relaxed. *He sure does have a way about him. Can't blame him.* "Well. I guess 'cause there's not much to say. I never knew her. I was too little when she left to even have any memories. Wish I did, though."

"No pictures or nothin'? Your Pop doesn't talk about 'er? That musta been some breakup."

"I don't know what happened. He doesn't say. I ask. But he always changes the subject."

"Has he always been a PI? I'm sure he worked long hours. Maybe she just got sick of it."

"No, not a PI. A cop. But I suppose being a cop took its toll on her maybe. Pop was in law enforcement all his life. Didn't open up the agency until after he retired."

"Huh. I'll be damned. That'll do it alright. It's a tough job. Most marriages don't make it through the bullshit of the job."

Karla looked up just in time to see Shannon's face take on a contemplative demeanor as she gazed at Randall. She tried to ignore the

222

awkward silence that had suddenly settled around them as Randall sipped another drink. Karla broke the silence with her own thoughts, "Well, I'm not even convinced they were actually married. I've been trying to find out. Searched everything I can and still have yet to produce a marriage license. Not to mention, I can't find her to save my life."

"So, you're lookin' then? Does the Pop know?"

"Yeah. But he doesn't approve. He thinks I should just let it go."

"If he really believed that, girl, he wouldn't be in the business of snoopin' out other people's dirt. Nah, he don't wanna talk, 'cause he don't want you to know about her."

"Why not?" Karla was taken back by the thought.

"How the hell would I know? You're the PI."
"PI assistant." She nudged him with her elbow.

Another awkward pause.

"So, do you guys think I should be looking?"

Shannon stood in front of her, then leaned closer into her with her elbows on the bar. "I think you do whatever you have to, to be at peace with where you came from." Shannon blinked encouragement into Karla's soul.

"You would've been a good mom. Why didn't you ever have children?"

Shannon simply smiled and turned to put a few pitchers onto a shelf.

Maybe some questions are just meant to go unanswered. Maybe I should just.....

Randall brought her thoughts back to the present. "Listen. If your mother is supposed to be found, she will be. In my book, keep looking. It's in your blood after all. You know, to look for shit."

"What if I don't want that? I mean, yes, I want to find my mom. But that's because it's personal. I'm not my Pop. Searching for justice, whatever that is, and nitpicking someone's life apart to get to the bad guy? That's him, not me. Always about the details, the facts. I just like to see people happy. These cases he chases, I don't even think he knows why he does it. Aren't they more than cases? Aren't they about people? Sometimes, I'm just not sure."

Shannon came back to join in, "So, you don't want to work for him? Then don't. Why work on this case with him, then? Just tell 'im no. What about it makes you do it?"

Karla sifted her fingertips through the scattered photos that she had piled next to her, a few only somewhat visible to Randall. She looked up to Shannon with a serious gaze. *We should talk.* Randall sat up slightly on his stool, just realizing the photos were even there. He shifted again, then leaned in to take a closer look. "Well, I'll be damned." It was all he could muster up. He looked up to Shannon, expecting a response. "So, you knew what she was up to, and didn't tell me?"

Shannon watched intently as Randall studied the faces in the photographs visible in the pile. She shook her head back and forth, shrugging her shoulders. "Why? No reason to. You made it clear a long time ago that it was off-limits. Besides, she knows I'm Cheri's sister." She winked at Karla, then looked to him. "You're up to bat, my friend." Shannon folded her arms, crossing them under her breasts and stood back.

"I ain't got nothin' to give 'er," he said quietly with reservation.

Karla blinked the confusion into focus as she watched the two of them with intense intrigue. *Oh, hell no. You both are gonna fess up. C'mon guys, don't do this to me.* Questions emitted from her face, floating into the quiet tension of the atmosphere. "Is someone gonna tell me what the hell is going on?" She looked to Shannon and then back to Randall. "Randall?"

Shannon looked to Randall and shrugged her shoulders again, blinking away the awkwardness. Karla persisted. "Randall? You know something, don't you?"

"Listen, I ain't got nothin' you don't already have. I wish I could help."

"Bullshit. I call bullshit, my friend. I win this round."

Randall rubbed his face with the palm of his hand and took in a deep breath. "Alright. Here's the deal. I ain't got nothing to say. Ok? I don't wanna talk about it. That good enough for ya? Nobody does. It was bullshit. You're absolutely right. I saw too much. It was a bullshit time. And I just don't wanna talk about it. So maybe your ol' mans' onto something when he ignores you and wants you to let it go. I mean, with your mother an' all. Some things just don't need to be brought up again. You ok with that, girl?"

Karla stared into him, and he stared back. He blinked several times. She didn't. Randall stood to his wobbly feet and looked to the floor. "I'm sorry. You're such a sweet girl. I'm sorry. Really."

Randall shot a somber gaze to Shannon and addressed her disappointment with his own silence of regret. He spoke up after several long seconds passed. "Just add it to my tab. You know I'll be back in later. I just need a walk." He tossed one hand into the air and brushed by Karla without looking up, still clutching the drink glass in his hand.

Karla and Shannon watched him stagger out to the sidewalk. Karla scooped up the photos and placed them gently back into her wallet. She looked to Shannon for some sort of explanation, as she took out a twenty-dollar bill and a ten to pay for her drinks, as well as his. "He's got a drink in his hand. Aren't you gonna stop him? Chase him down or something? Couldn't you get into trouble for that?"

"Give 'im time, Karla. He's just broken… And, he'll be right back in with it. Just watch. I'm sorry I didn't say anything before."

"What d' you mean? Sorry about what? He hasn't said anything of value."

"He wants to. Really, he does. He was a cop in '75. This was his world back then. The big shots wouldn't let 'im work any of these cases, and he left the department the year your man was convicted. He knows all about it, Karla. And there are reasons he won't talk about it. You just gotta give him time."

"This man, the one in prison? This man and his family? They don't have much time left, Shannon. He's been in there for forty years. And what about Cheri? What if her death wasn't an accident? Don't you want to know that? Don't you want to know why she was wandering the backwoods of the neighborhood that night? Why her shoes were found on the back deck of the neighbors' house? Why her body wasn't found for two weeks, and why they didn't search the pond in the first place? Don't you want to know?"

"Karla, maybe you're more like your father than you want to admit. 'Cause actually, no, no I don't want to know any more. I used to. But, not anymore. I don't mind that you do, though. That's why PI's exist. Because someone has to seek out the truth. Justice doesn't happen any other way but through people who do jobs like yours. It's ok to be like your Pop, even if just a little."

Karla's eyes began to water. She blinked the flood of emotion back inside. *Ok. So just a little.*

226

Chapter 20

Betsy's former sister-in-law, Renee, sat cross-legged on Betsy's sofa as the two carelessly chatted away the afternoon. No ill feelings were felt between them, even after Betsy's most recent break up with Jeremiah. Blair's cries from in the other room put Renee onto her feet in a flash. Betsy casually shook her head in a humored response to the familiar sound. "They're just fighting. They'll work it out." She reached into a bag sitting on the coffee table for a handful of greasy barbecue potato chips. Renee ignored her and had already disappeared around the corner before Betsy could start chewing. When Renee returned, Betsy was licking salty orange remnants from her fingertips. "So, what were they fighting over?" She grinned.

"Andrew was trying to color and Blair had the box of crayons, taunting him. I guess. At least that was Andrew's version."

Betsy chuckled and reached for more chips, chewing nervously. She was startled and jumped when the telephone's ring blared from within the kitchen. Licking the mess from her fingers once again, Betsy darted from her perch to answer it.

Leaning against the wall of the entrance way between the kitchen and the living room, Betsy anxiously twirled the phone cord in her fingers. "Hey there!" She turned to face the kitchen window, to avoid direct earshot of Renee. "I told you, I'll be there.... No, he's not staying the night tonight. I already told him that....Yes. By 11:00. I know. You've told me already, and I know. He'll be gone by 11:00. All right? Yes. Ok....I'll see you later then. See you then." Betsy turned back to face into the living room and hung up with a sigh.

Renee raised her eyebrows. "Is everything ok?"

Betsy was careful with her choice of words, fiddling her fingers to her mouth, looking past her. "Oh, of course. Nothin' big. Just have some things I gotta do later."

"How much later? Is Grandma taking the boys then? I thought she couldn't take them this weekend?"

"No. She can't. They're comin' with me. It's nothin'. They'll be able to just hang in the car. It's just a quick thing I gotta do. I'll have someone with me, so they can just chill in the car."

"Oh. Alright. If you need me to watch them, I can. You said you were having company tonight, right? Is he gonna just hang with them then? Will it be late?"

"The boys will be fine, Renee. That's what I keep the blanket in the car for. They'll be asleep the whole time. Let it go, will you?"

It won't be long. I'll be away from everyone. Just me and my boys. I can take care of them myself. I can, and I will.

"Just letting you know, I can help if you need me to." Her reluctance to let it go was written all over her face, so Betsy smiled and changed the subject. "Hey, did Jeremiah happen to mention to you when he'd be back in town? He didn't tell me before he left on that run."

"Tomorrow, I think. Why?"

228

"Oh, no reason, really. I guess I just like to know if I should expect him to stop over. Sometimes he does that without telling me."

"He just likes to check in on the boys. You should be grateful for that. Not all Dads do that, you know."

"I know. And, of course, I am. He should just let me know that he's comin' by, that's all. No big deal. Just want a heads up."

Betsy anxiously pulled back the curtains to glance through the living room window to Ruth's house across the street

"What's   wrong?"
"Just lookin' to see if Curtis is home. I wanna see if he can get the car running. I can't get the damn thing started again."

"You really gotta have it tonight? Can't it just wait?"

"Yes. I do." Betsy stood to her feet and breathed hard once again. "I guess he wouldn't be home yet anyway. It's still early." Renee stood up as well and headed toward the door. "Well, I should get home. I need to get home and start getting dinner ready. You probably do too, I imagine."

"Yeah. I thawed out some hamburger for spaghetti. It doesn't take long, though. The boys love spaghetti."

"Is that guy you got comin' over gonna join you all for dinner too?"

"Should be. If he gets here in time. He said he'd be over by 7:00 or so."

"Well, have a good night, then," Renee turned to the hallway and yelled toward the giggles coming from the bedroom. "Bye, boys! Love you munchkins!"

After Betsy escorted Renee through the door and waved her on her way, she went into her room and stood above her bed, glancing around. Her heart sank a bit, as she fought back a rush of conflicting emotions. *I should start thinking about how to pack up. I don't need to take all this shit. Keeping it light shouldn't be a problem, I don't want any of it, anyway.* Opening the closet door, Betsy pulled out the overnight travel bag she used for her quick overnight trips and headed into the bathroom with it. *Maybe I won't need this. I don't know. It might not be big enough. Still, I don't want to take much. Oh, hell, never mind. I don't want to do this now. It can wait. I still got plenty of time. God, could be weeks. I hope not.*

Just as Betsy came through the doorway, Blair let out a lightning bolt squeal. Dropping the bag beside her in the hallway, she rushed into their room in a panic. "Oh, God, what have I told you both...?" She sighed in both relief and frustration when she saw Andrew jumping from the top of the toy box, with Blair holding his finger, which had been jammed underneath the lid. "I'm sorry Blair. I di'in't mean it!" Andrew was holding him from behind, looking to his mother.

"Let's get some cold water on it. C'mon you two. None of this. You know you're not supposed to be standing on that." She led Blair into the bathroom. "Grab me washcloth from up there. Ok Andrew?" Soaking the cloth with cold water Betsy made a crude compress to wrap around Blair's finger. "Alright you two, just play for a while. Mommy's got some things to do for a bit."

With the mini crisis under control, Betsy sat back down on the couch to smoke a cigarette. She glanced up at the clock, and then out of the window again. Lying down with her head facing the ceiling, she blew puffs of smoke up into the air to watch them swirl into a picture-perfect dance that put her mind at ease and into somewhat of a trance.

I guess the sorting can wait.

After she felt grounded, Betsy rolled over and with a stretch of her arm, put her cigarette out into the ashtray sitting on the coffee table. Lying flat again, she closed her eyes to imagine she and her two boys walking along a beach, then her daydream evolved into another scene where they were looking up to the sky at night under a well-lit moon with only a slight breeze to cool the warm temperatures. Betsy relaxed with the thought that someday they would be free from her troubles. *I won't always be afraid. Thank you, God for this peace. For making it ok, no matter what. Please take good care of Ruth. I know you will. Thank you for her. Our trip will be good. This is going to be good. Everything will be good.* Her mind settled, even if for a moment. And with that, she sat up and reached for the pen and her diary lying on the coffee table where she had left them the night before. She pulled her knees into a cross-legged position on the sofa and began to write.

A piece of paper slid from Betsy's diary, and she picked it up from the floor. Scanning the letter she had typed several months earlier, she paused in thought. *Even Ruth wondered why I never sent this. I don't know why I kept it. She was right. She's always right.* She laid it beside her, intending to toss it out. *Maybe. It's so silly, maybe. I should just chuck it. I do miss him though.* The nostalgia of the letter (written to a previous lover who had moved away), prompted her to sift through the scattered pages of her thoughts. Several loose pages had been inserted into the back, tucked away safely for her, and her alone. At least that's the way it was supposed to have been. *What if Ruth hadn't seen all this? She doesn't have to do this for me. I'm glad she's there for me. 'Do the right thing', she said. I'm glad to. It feels good to do the right thing. It's time to.* It was, after all, because of Ruth that she would be sharing all she knew. Soon. Very soon.

Chapter 21

"Betsy needs to use the jumpers tonight." Ruth was startled by the sudden sound of Curtis' sharp voice. He kept talking, not missing a beat. "Will you take them over to Mr. Franklyn's and ask him to get her car jumped for her? I'm sure that's all it is. But make sure you get my cables back. And don't forget to put them away in the shed." Ruth turned away from her stance at the stove. *Why's he home already? Dinner's not ready yet.* The steam rose up in curls from the pan as she stirred. She went toward his voice and forced a smile when she saw him. "You're off work early. I...."

"Well, of course. I need to be heading out soon. I have that appointment at six. I told you about that. Is dinner ready?"

Hello to you too.

"So, did you get that? About the jumpers? I'm so glad we have good neighbors like Franklyn. Always can be counted on. I know he'll get them back to you right away. You got that right? I don't know what she's up to now, but she just caught me in the driveway and says she needs her car running. Something about having to leave later. That woman is always up to something."

"Well, yes, of course. I'll run them over. I'm sure he will give her a hand." Ruth ignored his negativity toward Betsy. *You won't have to worry about helping her much longer anyway. I will certainly miss her.*

Ruth knew more about Betsy's plans than she would ever let on to him. She kept particularly evasive with regards to their upcoming girl's trip. Ruth would eventually have to tell him, as the trip was coming up soon. And naturally she would have to share with him her own plans to leave him and move away to her family back East. Of course she planned to take the boys.

"Ruth? You didn't answer me. Is dinner ready? I need to load up and get out of here soon."

Of course you do.

Blinking back tears Ruth chose not to respond. Once she was feeling secure, she turned to face him, hoping to make eye contact. *See, I'm fine. I really am fine. I don't need you anymore.* Curtis was already headed out of the back door to the shed. It didn't matter if she had answered or not. Tristan approached her with his usual sweet grin, all teeth and eyes in awe of her. It was a nice distraction. "You all cleaned up for dinner? It'll be ready in minutes."

Ruth kissed Tristan on the cheek and patted his backside as he shuffled away to the table. "Oh, but where's your brother?" She looked past him, into the living room. "Trey!" She followed the sound of playful squealing from in the bathroom. "What are?...Oh, boy. What is this? So, you've found my shampoo I see? C'mon 'ere, let's get cleaned up." Then she whispered, not to him, but above him. "Before your father sees you."

Getting most of the thick bubbly liquid from out of his hair, Ruth toweled Trey as clean as possible. "We'll have to give you a bath later. This will do for now." Carrying him into the kitchen, she could see Tristan waiting patiently on his usual chair, watching his father move in and out of the back door. Back and forth, back and forth. Then finally back again.

Placing Trey on a chair to keep him from beneath her feet, Ruth went to gather the dinner dishes. "Sit. Don't move." She warned with her forefinger. He wiggled in his chair, rocking lightly back and forth, giggling across the table at his brother. She quickly placed down the chicken, beans, and corn on the cobb. The kitchen smelled of its flavor, and the moist heat from the oven created fog on the back-kitchen window.

Ruth sat down beside Trey and dished him up a plate. "So, you'll be home sometime tomorrow, you said?" She avoided looking at Curtis directly.

"Yes. I have to stop by the church and take care of some things with Pastor for church on Sunday. I'll be here by dinnertime, though."

"Still no chance that I could tag along? I... have time get them to grandma and grandpas? They said if we needed them to...they could watch them for the night." She talked hesitantly, as they had already had this discussion.

"I said not this time. I've got other things to do besides the picture shoot. It'll be a bore for you. Why so persistent?" It was his persistence that she *not* go with him that made her so persistent. She fought the sense within her to question his real motive.

The rest of dinnertime was quiet. Clinking of forks against the cheap white dinnerware, and an occasional slurp and gulp when one of the boys took a drink of their milk, was all that penetrated the air. Curtis finished quickly and laid his silverware on his plate, then scooted away from the table. "It's time for me to head on the road. Don't forget the jumpers for Betsy's car." He darted out the back door with a quick peck on her cheek. He also managed to wave to the boys before he left. *At least he made an effort.* Strolling to the front door, Ruth could hear the loud rattle of his revved up 4x4 through the screen door.

The tears that Ruth had held back earlier began to surface, welling up like tiny balloons, as they escaped through the corners of each eye. Standing in the open doorway, with her arms folded and her heart broken once again, she watched him slowly drive past the house. With teardrops rolling down her cheeks Ruth looked deeply through the space of the yard to the glare of his windshield hoping to see his face. *Look at me, just look at me.* And this time, he did.

Ruth sat on the sofa in silence, studying the wall clock above the piano. *Barely after 6:00. Dishes are done. I mowed the lawn earlier. Boys are playing contentedly in their room. Now what?* She sighed and scanned the empty room with regretful eyes. *I could call Grant. Maybe he would stop by. I'd have to find a sitter for the boys. Cheri might do it. She's been so busy lately, though. But I wouldn't have to explain my plans to her.* Ruth sat still for a few seconds, then pulled back the curtains in the living room to see if Betsy still had company. When she saw that the car (that had been parked in front of Betsy's house most of the afternoon) had left, Ruth jumped to her feet. *The jumper cables. Oh, yes, gotta take the cables to Mr. Franklyn.* "Tristan! Trey! Boys, c'mon! Let's go see what Mrs. Betsy and your buddies are up to?"

Both boys rushed around the corner from the hallway in a dash toward her voice. Tristan grabbed her legs at the knees and looked up to her. "Where we go…in'?" His eyes twinkled. She picked up Trey who was bouncing awkwardly on his feet in excitement.

"We just need to help Mrs. Betsy with her car."

When she stopped into the carport to grab the jumper cables, Ruth spotted Tristan's new bicycle leaning up against the wall of the carport. "Hey boys, maybe we can go for a ride in a little while? Would that be fun?" Tristan grinned in agreement skipping at her side as she led them across the street.

Betsy greeted them with an open door. "Oh, thank God. Good to see you. I was hoping he'd follow through."

"Well, he said to have Mr. Franklyn come over and do it. Are you able to walk over with me? I was thinking about taking the boys on a bike ride after he gets it running. You wanna come with us?"

"Oh, I'll have to go over and ask him in a bit. I've got someone coming over soon. Maybe he can even help me instead. As long as I have cables, he should be able to help me. Maybe I don't even need to bother Mr. Franklyn."

"Ok. Sure, as long as I get these back. You know how he gets about his stuff." Ruth handed her the cables, glancing down to Tristan as she fiddled her fingers around his tiny little hands.

Betsy sensed her hesitation to leave. "You ok? You wanna come in?"

"Oh, I'm fine. I just.....it's just that..."

"C'mon, out with it. Obviously, he wouldn't let you go with him. What was his excuse this time?"

"Same as always. Nothings' changed, Betsy. It's time, isn't it?"

"Past time, girl. Past time."

"I'm not sure what to do now. I mean. I guess I should start planning instead of taking the boys for a bike ride. I just thought getting out for some fresh air would do me some good."

"Get out of the house, for God's sake Ruth, he's not gonna be home 'till tomorrow. Besides, it'll take you some time to come up with the money you'll need. And you can't leave until we get back from our trip,

236

anyway. You got plenty of time to plan, Ruth. Any ideas how you'll get enough money?"

"Not at the moment. I suppose I could borrow some."

"Why not get rid of some of those pictures? You said Greg's wife wanted a few, right?"

"That's a good idea. She did say that. Thanks."
"Probably better than my plan." Betsy shrugged her shoulders.

"You're not following through with that are you? Bets' I told you...."

"Don't preach, girl. I'm gonna do what I need to do."

"I thought you said that both Derek and Trevor talked you out of that. You said yourself that Trevor didn't like the idea."

"They tried. Trevor doesn't know that I'm doin' it anyway. Damn it Ruth, I don't have much else I can do. It needs to happen soon. I don't have anything else to fall back on. It'll work. Don't worry, it's a foolproof plan. I promise, it's gonna work. By tomorrow, I'll have most of what I need."

Ruth looked long into Betsy, realizing that nothing she said was going to change her mind. Betsy shook her head and took Ruth by the arm. "Worry about you. Do what you need to do. Let me do what I need to do."

Ruth bit the bottom of her lip and in an instant knew exactly what to do. "Ok. Ok. I think I'll go see Greg tonight. Maybe he'd be willing to loan me some money. All I have to do is tell him it's for the business."

Betsy grinned. "Are you gonna tell a fib? Ruth, you little devil, you."

"Oh stop it! I know how to do what needs to be done as well, you know." Ruth smiled. It was a hopeful smile. Then her face turned

237

serious. "Be careful, Bets'. I know how your foolproof plans go. The sooner you're out of this town, the better."

Betsy leaned into her and kissed her on the cheek, while squeezing her shoulder. "I'm gonna be fine. And the sooner we both get out of this town, the better." She looked to Ruth with a reluctance for words and admiration in her eyes. "You're gonna be fine, too."

Ruth blinked in agreement. "I know. You're a good girl, Bets'. Don't let anyone tell you differently."

Betsy lifted up the jumper cables into the air. "Thank you. And I'll be over tomorrow to bring these back."

"You sure you're going to be able to get someone to do it? You know Mr. Franklyn will be glad to help."

"Yes. If I need to, I can run over there myself. Go! Go give those boys that bike ride! Go talk to Greg. I know he'll help you out."

Ruth smiled sweetly. Endearingly. Almost with tears. "Alright. I did tell them we may go for a ride. So we better. Have a good night and see you tomorrow." Ruth hugged her again, then winked as she stepped down into the grass. She took Tristan and Trey's little hands in hers and strolled into the carport to attach the wagon to the back of her bicycle. Tristan eagerly climbed onto his bike and led the way with an unsteady roll. Ruth glided slowly at his side, careful to position herself nearest the street to keep him at a safe distance from traffic.   .

Chapter 22

It's after 8:00 o'clock already. My, what a hassle the evening has turned out to be! Ruth and her boys returned home tired and on foot, as the evening hadn't evolved completely as planned. She glanced down at her watch, anticipating an end to the mayhem soon. "Ok, boys we'll go back to Mr. Franklyn's to pick up my bike in a bit."

Ruth led the boys into the house, then headed straight for her bedroom to put away her pocket purse. At least one thing went as planned from their nearly five-mile round trip jaunt. *Now, where do I hide it?* She pulled out a wad of cash from her bag and counted it. *Still short. But they said they could see about a loan. I knew I could count on them. Just hope he doesn't ask Curtis about this. He said he wouldn't. At least for a few weeks.* She came into the hallway just in time to see Tristan scuttle into the bathroom clearly in a hurry. Trey whined at her feet, so she picked him up for a squeeze of security. "Alright, little guy. Let's get you in here with a book for a bit."

Ruth's plans to read to the boys were interrupted by a knock at the door. She welcomed their church pastor standing on the porch, holding a wooden box. "Hello, there dear! I thought I might miss you again! You just got home, I presume?"

Ruth paused. *How did you know that?* "Well, yes. We were out riding, just an errand. But Curtis said you were stopping by, so we tried to hurry. My bike got a flat, and that delayed us quite a bit."

"Well, I was here a few minutes ago, and you weren't here, so I figured you were on your way soon. I just circled the block a few times and came back. Hey there little guy? Did you enjoy your ride?" Tristan stood at his mother's side, wrapping his arm around her leg. Trey was trying to crawl between her legs, and she reached down to pick him up.

"Well, I don't want to keep you too long. Just needed to bring this back to Curtis before I forgot."

"You'll be seeing him tomorrow, right? He said he was stopping by the church before coming home." Ruth had grown accustomed to verifying nearly everything Curtis told her.

"Oh, yes, he said he would be. But I wanted to get this back as soon as possible, while I was out and about. I'm afraid I'll be wrapped up in work tomorrow and just didn't want to forget."

Ruth thanked him and without much thought took the box into the bedroom closet. It was a music recorder, and Curtis was particularly protective of anything electronic, so she didn't want the children playing with it.

Since the door was open from the Pastor stopping by, Ruth glanced out to the street to be reminded that her bike was still at Mr. Franklyn's house. "Alright, let's go see if my bike is fixed!" Ruth rounded the boys up for another trip outside, ushering them to the front yard. As they passed by Betsy's house, she couldn't help but notice that Betsy had company once again. A different car was parked in front of the house this time, although one that Ruth had seen before. *Well, as always, she's got no shortage of suitors. So much for being in love with Trevor.*

Tap, tap, tap! Mr. Franklyn answered the door with a frown. "Hello, Ruth. I'm sorry I wasn't able to get it fixed. I thought I had a tube. It turns out, I don't after all. Curtis by chance wouldn't have one in the shed somewhere, maybe?"

Ruth's shoulders drooped in disappointment, but she was gracious, nonetheless. "Well, that's alright. You know, I was wanting to run by the store anyway to get ingredients for cookies." She looked down to the boys who were standing close to her.

"Cookies would be a good way to wrap up this crazy night." Ruth looked back up to Mr. Franklyn. "I'll just pick up a tube while I'm there. We could be back within thirty minutes or so."

"You're not going to drive?"

"Oh, no, my car's not running these days. It's not a problem. We love to ride our bikes. I'll just take Curtis' bike. Thanks so much for your help. We'll be back in a bit."

Just as she had predicted, Ruth took off on Curtis' bike and returned within thirty minutes when she leaned it (with the wagon still attached) against the house under the protective covering of the carport. "Alright, Tristan, dear, put your bike away in the shed. I'll put Daddy's away later." Ruth pointed to the shed, then unloaded Trey and the paper bag of groceries that she bundled tight under her arm. As they headed up the steps and into the house, Tristan turned to glance down the street behind them. "Is....is... he gonna, gonna fix it, Mamma?"

"Of course. That's why we took him the tire tube. I'm sure it won't take long to fix. We can walk down there after we make cookies. I'm sure he'll have it done by then."

Ruth quickly dumped the bag to the counter. "Have a seat, boys. Let's get started!" She was already feeling better. The boys were perched in chairs at the kitchen table ready to help.

Ruth hummed a soft rendition of *In the Garden*, as she helped each child take turns plopping spoonfuls of sticky goo, embellished with chunks of chocolate, onto a flat greased pan. "Ok you two, let's clean this up." Trey had remnants of tacky batter smeared from his upper lip and across to his cheekbone, half dried with strings of his hair sticking to his face. *Thank you, God, for the simple things.*

After cleaning up, Ruth lifted the plate of cookies onto the palm of her hand and moved the party into the living room. The boys each carried a glass of milk, although with some leaning and tipping along the way. It wasn't often that the boys were allowed to bring drinks into the living room; but tonight, Ruth bent the rules.

Ruth set the tray to the floor and crouched down cross-legged with an assumed invitation for her children to join her. She scooted a basket of miniature cars, trucks, and motorcycles over for an easy reach. Tristan wasted no time settling in beside her and snatching a cookie from the tray. Ruth carefully tugged Trey in close onto her lap, allowing him to do the same. Tristan scooted in close as well. "Mamma....when we...when we gonna go...go to bed?"

"Oh, sweetie, it's still early. We have to go get Mommy's bike first. You must be so tired. We rode a lot tonight, didn't we?" Tristan leaned his head onto her. "I like...like my bike. We crossed a road...you know, the...the big...big road, way down that road." He took a toy motorcycle and rolled it back and forth, grinning up at her. Ruth chuckled and plucked another toy motorcycle from the pile of toys to demonstrate her own rendition of their ride. "Oh, it was surely a long ride, huh? Across the road, then back again..." She drove the toy up over his leg, and this time it was Trey who giggled.

"Then, oh, no! Mommy got a flat! Oops! We have to come all the way home to get Daddy's bike. Gotta get it fixed, too! Oh no! We have to go get a tire at the store! Darn it! Let's go over the road again!" Both boys burst out in laughter at the sight of their mother acting so silly.

Their fun was interrupted by another knock at the door, which surprised Ruth. She looked up toward the door, confused. She wasn't expecting anyone. *Who's visiting after 9:00pm? Betsy wouldn't be knocking. She never knocks.* She pulled the curtain back to see a small sports car parked in front of Betsy's house. *Can't be her.* When Ruth opened the door, she was surprised to see Curtis' friend Edward, from church, standing in the moonlight. His car was still running, and his wife sat in the passenger seat of the car, waiting. He had a black leather bag in his hand, in the shape of a small handgun, resting at his side. She recognized it immediately but didn't want to seem impolite by questioning what he was doing with it.

"Well, Hello! What brings you two out this way tonight?"

His demeanor was nervous, although he tried to hide this with a crooked smile. "Just dropping this off for Curtis. I borrowed it a few weeks ago."

"Oh. Well, he's in Ouray tonight. Remember? He's working on some scenery shots for the calendar early in the morning. Won't be home until late tomorrow. He told you, didn't he? I thought you guys talked about it last Sunday at church?"

"Oh. Oh, ya. I just forgot. Well, just put it away for him. So, so, how's it going tonight? You having a good night?" He glanced behind her, into the house, then over his shoulder, quickly and sporadically.

"Well, we just made cookies. That makes for a good night, right? You two want to come in for a bit? We have plenty."

243

"No. No. But thanks. You know, the wife's in the car…" He pointed behind him. "…. wants to get home and get to bed. Not feeling well." He shifted his stance, almost at an angle, as if he had one eye looking backward. *If I didn't know any better, I'd say he was looking toward Betsy's house. Weird.*

"Is she alright? I mean, is she sick?" Ruth nodded toward his wife in the car.

"Oh, no. Just tired. You know how it is."

"Of course. I'll add her to my prayers tonight, that she gets a good night's rest."

"Thanks. She just needs to get to bed, that's all. I suppose you need to too, huh?"

"Well, sometime, I suppose…"

"Well, ok. Just put that away, you know, away in the drawer, and let Curtis know I got it back to him. And have a good night, now."

"Alright. We certainly will. Thanks for bringing it back." She waved him back to his car, blinking away the awkward spirit of his anxious behavior. She took the leather case, with the handgun nestled carefully inside, and laid it on top of the dresser in her bedroom, out of reach of the boys, noting to herself to be sure and lock it up in the drawer before calling it a night. Curtis liked to keep this particular gun in the drawer near the bed for the safest of keeping. After all, it was his favorite. *I'm surprised he let him use this.*

Before returning to her children and the tray of cookies that was quickly disappearing, she glanced to her watch. *Time flies. Already almost 9:20. Better get to Mr. Franklyn's before it gets too late.* "Alright, boys, let's go. I know you're both really tired, and we need to get ready for bed still. So, hopefully this will be quick."

244

The short walk to Mr. Franklyn's and back went faster than expected, even though Ruth walked her bike with the boys taking mini steps trying to keep up with her. They came through the doorway with Trey close against Ruth's breasts. Trey insisted that he needed to be held once she parked her bike. Ruth sighed in relief to be calling the evening to a close. She whispered to Tristan, as Trey's eyelids were weighing shut. "Alright, head on in there. I'll get him changed and in bed while you get your jammies on and find a book to read." Once she dressed Trey and tapped a kiss to his sleepy eyes, she sauntered into the living room to turn on the TV. *The news should be starting any minute.* Tristan didn't want to wait. He was rubbing his eyes as he stumbled in her direction. "Mamma, I want....want....to go...go to bed. Now, Mamma." She smiled and hugged him. "Yes, of course. C'mon." She turned the TV off again and led him by the hand to his bedtime routine. *I suppose I can forgo the news tonight.* "Alright. Let's get you both down to sleep," she whispered.

"Pray, now, pray mamma. Don't....don't forget to....to pray." *Yes, of course.* Ruth stood at the foot of the bunk bed, folded her hands down in front of her, and bowed her head to the floor. "Now I lay us down to sleep. I pray the Lord our souls to keep....."

"The....the other one. Do....do the other one.... Mamma."

"Of course. Can't forget that one." Ruth's smile warmed the room. She took a long breath. "Our Father, who art in heaven, hallowed be thy name. Thy kingdom come, thy will be done, on earth as it is in heaven. Give us this day our daily bread and forgive us our debts as we forgive our debtors..." Ruth whispered as she talked, looking up periodically, watching them. When the prayers were done, she flipped the light switch to leave shadows of peace throughout the room, then stepped away slowly, leaving the door open only an inch or so.

Ruth's own bedtime routine was more of a chore. It was personal. She was alone with her thoughts. Peeling her shirt over her head, she couldn't help but stare into the mirror. She straightened her shoulders and tilted her head. *What doesn't he see? Grant must see something that he doesn't.* She smiled at herself in the reflection. *His loss.* Opening the top drawer, she started to grab a plain white tee- shirt. But then she saw it. Nestled amidst the pale colors of night shirts. The red nightgown her mother had bought her recently. It had yet to be worn. Still on the small plastic hanger. It was simple, but red, which made it almost too much for her. The skimpy shorts attached with metal clips would certainly reveal her thin legs. *My legs may be thin, but they're strong. I'm strong.* Ruth smiled at her reflection in the mirror. *Just put it on.*

The silky fabric felt clean and fresh against her skin. Ruth imagined herself standing in front of Curtis. *No, not Curtis, maybe Grant. No, not even him. Maybe him.* But then there was the doctor she had been growing fond of. He had even given her keys to his office so she could find a little escape now and then. *Yes, he would appreciate this.* But he was a secret. So was Grant. She too had secrets these days. Ruth resolved that no one but her would be seeing her in the likes of this attire any time soon. Not anymore. She sighed. A good kind of sigh. *No one will know but you. And after all, that's all that matters.* This thought lightened her eyes as they ricocheted from the reflection of the mirror. A fire she hadn't seen in a while.

In spite of feeling empowered, Ruth reached into the closet and pulled down her mauve colored night coat. Wrapping herself tightly, covering more than just the daring nightgown, she buttoned the large plastic buttons and then tied the wrap tightly around her waist so as to make sure it didn't come lose, just in case her boys may need her attention any time soon.

246

Walking into the living room, Bear followed her. "You need outside, girl? C'mon, let's go outside for a minute. Just until I'm done reading." She led the dog to the door and opened it, breathing in the warm night air and letting her run free in the back yard. The fresh air smelled of life, adding to her current mood. *I'm so grateful, God.*

Anticipating her nightly reading, which always prompted a peaceful night's sleep, Ruth made ready her sleeping space before closing her eyes for the night. The ritual of folding her blankets back into an angle, taking her glasses from the bedside nightstand, and carefully placing her pillow up ever so slightly prepared her mind and soul for rest. Ruth lied back on top of her bed against the headboard with her book in hand and began to read.

"Oh, Bear, what's wrong?" she whispered, breaking the moment. Ruth could hear the faint bark of a dog coming from the backyard. *Shoot. I guess she wants in now.* "Alright, I'm coming." Still speaking in a whisper, so as not to disturb the tranquility of the house. She laid the book face down, but open so she could save her place. Her tennis shoes were left not too far from the bed, so she slipped them on without tying them into place.

Shuffling to the back door with a yawn, Ruth opened the screen door, and stepped down the step to call for Bear. Distracted by her thoughts, she failed to notice Bear growling with her wide eyes looking past her and no longer barking. "C'mon girl!...hey...uh..wha...uh...uh..."

Confusion engulfed her in a startled and instant panic, as Ruth reached behind her and into the dark to grab at the hands that held her from behind. They were big hands. Strong hands. She kicked the back of her shoe at the legs that stood attached to those frightening hands. Trying desperately to scream, Ruth only managed to quietly squeak out shallow spurts of air, whispers that escaped into the still night air. "Oh... dear God!" *Get to the telephone....No! The gun! Get to the gun!* In a lucky

247

split second, when he became off guard as he kicked the dog away (sending Bear running to the fence whimpering), Ruth managed to break free from his unsteady grip. She fell into the house clinging to the hard surface of the floor on her knees, with hopes on getting to the bedroom. This shadow of darkness pressed her to the floor, inhibiting her clarity to make sense of what was happening.

Squirming to her knees, Ruth escaped again, this time enough so that she was able to stumble in a staggering walk, almost a run. She wanted to see his face, but the fear was too gripping to look behind her. Instinctively she wobbled toward the hallway but losing her stance in the living room instead. *The boys! Need to keep him away from the boys! It's there. If I can just get it!* She imagined the gun in her hands. She knew how to use it. Curtis had taught her how. Something he had done right.

Fear commanded her. She was unable to scream. If only she could scream. Behind her, her attacker's hands were grapping at her hair, pulling at her. She felt his breathing spatter onto the base of her neck. She could feel his presence pressing against her. Heavy, hard breathing. It smelled of wet and poisonous alcohol with the stench of cigarette spice. The weight of his body pushed into hers, knocking her face down with his force pressing her ear into the carpet with a sting. *Please, God, don't let the boys wake up.* Ruth thought about the porch light. Then the gun. And the porch light again. *Just push up and run! The gun! The light! Get to the porch light! Oh. God. Please. Don't let them wake up.* She and Betsy's plan to flicker the lights in times of trouble had never been intended for her.

Pain gripped her shoulders as her attacker reached under her squirrely frame to grab her arms, cross them around her chest and sharply up against her sides. The pressure of her small breasts being squeezed by the force of her arms not within her own control made it difficult for her to reach through the carpet fibers for air. He was sitting

248

on her, his knee plunging through her back and into her lungs. Lungs that tried to grapple for life. The pressure kept the sound of her desperate pleas from making their way to her lips. *Please, don't hurt them, please, please....* The lack of air made her head spin. She couldn't move. Her eyes were losing clarity.

The room was dimming, but even so, she clawed sporadically at anything within her reach, frantically clawing, if only from her fingertips. *Oh, God... can't ...breath, can't breathe, can't.... God...protect....them....*

Bear was still barking. In the distance outside, Ruth could faintly hear her. That's all she could hear. *Bear. Bear... Be....uh...uh...uh."*

Then it was silent. Dark, sick, disturbing silence. Within mere moments, the life within her was gone.

Chapter 23

The man reached under Ruth's limp body and carelessly pulling her over his shoulder, clenching the heavy weight with both hands. One of her shoes fell lightly to the floor unnoticed as he turned to leave the house through the back door. He carefully stepped through the house with his hands shaking and his blood pounding through his veins. *This was fucking unexpected.* It wasn't supposed to happen this way. This wasn't supposed to happen at all. *Why the hell wasn't the dog inside already? Son of a bitch!* He hated unexpected problems. He quickly slid out through the back of the house in such a panic that he slammed the screen door far too wide, catching a piece of bent aluminum on the sloping step. It never even occurred to him that the door hadn't shut behind him. The gate was a bit more difficult to maneuver, as he awkwardly balanced Ruth's weighted figure, while slipping the latch up, and then back in place behind him. Still lacking focus, he hadn't felt the sting to the back of his hand that had been scratched from the side of the wired post attached to the house. Small trickles of blood escaped, which flowed to his fingertips unnoticed. As he closed the gate, he brushed his hand across the top of a roll of wire draped over the gate's metal décor. His mind raced in all directions, landing on one thing and one thing only. *Get her to a hiding place.*

Latching the gate closed, he jumped just as Bear ran at him with an angry bark, standing with her front paws on the gate. "Shut up! Stupid dog!" He whispered with an aggressive hiss as he stumbled backward, almost losing his stance. The weight of Ruth's body was beginning to be too much for him even with the broadness of the shoulder that she engulfed. His head was spinning, and he pressed his thoughts to determine what to do next. *Gotta get her out of here. Fucking Dog! Shut up! God Damn it! Shut up! Just get her out of here! Quietly. Quickly.* He could hear his own heavy breathing, thinking maybe the whole street could as well. Sweat saturated his back and under his armpits. *This wasn't supposed to happen! Dammit! She was supposed to be asleep already. Fucking dog!*

He leaned against the compact car in the Bakerson driveway, holding her with both arms at this point, kneeling tightly up against the front bumper, hidden in the shadows. Releasing the weight, with a roll to the ground, he rested his jittering body against the car. The street was dark. There didn't appear to be much life around. No one except Betsy had any lights on that he could see, as he twisted himself to peek up over the car's edge. But Betsy was surely occupied. *Get a grip.* His breathing was getting under control with each deep heave that he forced through his lungs.

Kneeling to a crouched position he blinked several times to gain clarity. He stepped low, as close to the car as he could get. He was relieved that Ruth's car was there, parked useless in the gravel, as it hadn't run in months. He leaned around it to sneak a peek across the street, then glanced back behind him. The dog had stopped barking. He noticed that he had left the door to the shed open when Ruth's presence startled him. *That was a waste of time. Nothin' in there I need.* He was looking for anything that could be useful in order to get Betsy out to the river in the boat. Ruth's unexpected entry into the backyard changed everything. *Shit. Now we need to make two trips. Fuck! Two bodies will complicate things.* He glanced again through the carport and across the

251

street. *I wish that guy would leave. Just wanna get this shit done. If I hurry, surely no one will see. Take 'er out the back. Come get 'er later. No, can't, that fucking dog's there! I need to think. Jesus, this is all fucked up! Just make a fucking decision. No one will know she's back here, and this'll be nothing more than just a distraction. Keep with the plan, dammit. I can't leave 'er here all night. Someone will find her in the morning. It'll fuck up the whole thing. Can we come back later? Fuck! I need some help.* The situation had changed. The plan certainly would have to change.

Nauseous and feeling the need to cough, he looked again in both directions at his surroundings. He took note of Curtis' bike leaning up against the side of the house. He quickly unhitched the wagon, knowing he had to hurry. Breathing a sigh of relief, he loaded himself onto the bicycle, unstable at first, but then after a few strides, he leaned in with a quick jolt and bolted ahead down the street. He was exceptionally careful to look in every direction for any signs of life, which to his relief, there wasn't any. Except for Betsy's porch light. Shining still and steady.

The air was fresh on his face, which relieved his uncontrollable sweating and calmed his nerves. The lights from the upcoming parking lot brought him back to the reality of the situation. He knew he had fucked up and would definitely hear about it. But it was too late. They needed to come up with a plan B.

Colin then methodically sped into the bowling alley parking lot, sliding to a halt, and tossing the bicycle up against the side of the building. Before he emerged into the light of the neon sign, he straightened his shirt, fluffed his fingers through his hair, and wiped sweat from off his face. He briskly shook his hands at his side before pulling the heavy glass door open. Reaching into the back pocket of his jeans and out again, he clapped a pack of cigarettes between his hands with more force than is usually needed to bring the sticks to the surface. As he approached a group of bowlers one particular man turned, gave

252

him a nod, and walked in his direction. Tony held a beer in his hand and took a drink as he walked. He sensed something was wrong. "What are you doin' here, man? You look like shit."

"Fuck you. Shit's changed. We gotta change plans." Colin lit up his cigarette and inhaled a deep breath of much needed relief.

"What the fuck are you talking about?" Tony was whispering and stood close, trying to be inconspicuous.

"Just take my word for it. I'm not goin' into it here. I gotta make a phone call and you need to follow me over there."

"What? Is he still there? What the fuck's going on, man? How'd you get here?"

"Shut up, and just do what I say. I'm on a fucking bike. It was a bitch not being seen."

Tony shook his head in confusion, knowing the longer they stood there and talked, the more attention they could draw. He casually strolled back to the group that he was with, made a respectable exit, and proceeded to lead the way outside. Once outside, Colin stopped at the pay phone and turned away from the front entrance to talk. "Hey, man, we had a glitch, but we'll be back on track in no time. Meet us out there as planned.....Yeah, I know. Don't worry....Ok. But hey man, listen, don't freak, but expect a little more work....no, I mean another one....Jesus, man, I told you not to freak. I got it under control. Fuck you man! Just meet us up there and don't fuckin' get all self-righteous on me. Shit happens, man. It's just a glitch.....No. Just see you there. I got it." He hung up the receiver with a sharp click, almost losing his cool. "Fuckin' doesn't want any problems, but I don't see him doin' this shit himself!"

They walked to where the bike leaned up against the cinder brick wall, out of sight from the dim streetlights. Tony stopped to light up a cigarette for his own calming and nodded. "Whose bike is this?"

Colin shot him a look to stop asking questions.

"Alright, asshole. What the fuck do you want me to do?"

"Just go down the street to the parking lot, at the end, and wait for me. Make sure your lights are off. We'll still take her car. We just may need you, though."

The two men exchanged nervous looks, and each went to their own modes of transportation, as if robots on a routine mission.

Arriving onto the grass of Betsy's front yard, Colin lighted off of the bicycle with a trot, careful to move with as much silence as possible. He let the bike lean against the brick wall, not paying any attention to the damaged gears he had caused, riding it so aggressively. With the sports car still parked in front of Betsy's house, Colin didn't want to take any chances being seen as he crouched down in the carport, hiding behind her wide-square backed station wagon. *Once he leaves, this'll be easy.* He had no doubts Betsy would be drunk by now.

Colin held his breath, when the side door opened. It was a shadow of a man. Colin could hear Betsy in the kitchen. "I'm tellin' ya, I heard something. You sure there's no one out there?" The man blew a few puffs of cigarette smoke into the carport, then shook his head and closed the door. There was the sound of mumbling voices that quickly disappeared. Colin's heart began to pump in rhythm once again.

The wait was only a few minutes but seemed like an hour. Betsy's visitor eventually left her alone for the night. The loud rumble of the sports car soon dissipated down the street. *It's time to get her the hell out of here.* Colin glanced down the dark street to see the shadow of Tony's truck parked inconspicuously in the graveled lot at the end of the block.

With Betsy's company finally out of the way, Colin composed himself with a breath of fresh August air and straightened his shoulders up and steady before knocking on the back screen door.

After several attempts, Betsy opened the door. "Hey…! I didn'… know *you* were comin'? Where's…" Her words were slightly drawled but clear enough to be audible.

"He told me to come get you. There's been a little change in plans. You ready?"

"Well…actually, no. I haven' had a chance to…"

"Doesn't matter. We gotta go. Why the fuck aren't you even dressed? Fuck, get your clothes on and let's go."

"But…, I gotta get the boys. They're…they're asleep."

"What? I thought they were at their grandma's?"

"No…. not this time. I'm not goin' to leave the house without 'em, what the hell…?"

This was not what Colin wanted to hear. *Jesus, no more glitches.* "Alright. Fuck, alright. Why do they gotta be dressed? Jesus, we're comin' back."

"Le' me be a mom, for heaven' sake. What if they wake up an'… I have to take 'em in? They can' go anywh' in their undie…s…"

"Ok. Just…just hurry. That's all."

Betsy shuffled into her room and threw on a pair of shorts and a pair of canvas tennis shoes. She was feeling unstable from the fair amount of wine she recently consumed. Failing to sense the urgency in his voice, she meandered her way into the boys' room and dressed them carefully, taking time not to wake them. Colin was standing in the doorway, smoking a cigarette, and trying to hide his anxiety.

"Hey, so... when we ge' back, I got more to tell ya." Betsy whispered. Colin ignored her, let out a sigh, and rolled his eyes. He was trying to come up with a plan as to what they were going to do with the unexpected passengers. All of them.

Betsy reached across the bed and snatched a baseball cap to toss it in Colin's direction. "You left tha' here the other night. Andrew got ahold of it and has been playin' with it." Pinching his cigarette between his lips, Colin picked up the cap from the floor and ran his fingers through his hair to place it onto his head. Betsy looked up and laughed. "If I were a bitch, I'd le' you walk around with tha' on your head. It's... filthy. Andrew go' jelly all over it." She laughed again. "Now you're gonna have sticky hair." Colin frowned as he ripped the hat from his head and tossed it back onto the bed. "Just hurry the hell up, will you?"

Once she was satisfied with preparing the children for the ride, Betsy gently pulled Blair up onto her shoulder and rubbed his back to keep him asleep. "Shshsh... we're just goin' for a li'le ride." She whispered into Blair's ear and smiled to Colin with a sense of misplaced trust that she didn't understand.

"You know, you were supposed to be ready to go." Colin ignored her smile.

Betsy shot an angry look back in his direction. "Well, grab 'im then, if you're in such a big hurry an' all. Don' gotta be an asshole. Why you all actin' 'is way? You don' usually act like such an ass. Jus' be nice." She smiled and giggled, hoping he'd tease back. He didn't.

Clinching his cigarette between his lips, Colin lifted Andrew up onto his hip, holding him in place with one arm. As they passed through the kitchen, he couldn't help but take notice of the remnants of a spaghetti dinner still visible on the kitchen table. "Do you ever clean up? Jesus, Betsy."

"I was... gonna ge' to it."

In the shadows of the carport, Colin opened the back door to Betsy's car and laid Andrew onto the seat, watching him curl up against the blanket already there. Andrew, with his eyes still closed and in a groggy stupor, pinched the end of the blanket between his fingers and into his palm, falling back into a deep slumber. Colin reached out to take Blair from Betsy, but she protested. "I can do it'!" She began to show signs of agitation. Betsy gently placed Blair at Andrew's feet with his back against the seat. "Shshshs...I don' wan' 'em wakin' up." Then she carefully latched the door closed and made her way to the passenger side of the car.

"Just get in. We're gonna be late." After Colin made sure Betsy had loaded the car without incident, he glanced across the street to remind himself of some unfinished business.

"Oh, shi'!" Betsy's voice from inside the car startled him as he climbed into the driver's side.

"What's wrong?"

"I... I hope the car starts."

"Why wouldn't it?"

"I...I was suppos' to have 'Ole Franklyn jump it. That was hours ago. It's...been being a shit again. You could try. I was gonna go down and le' 'im know. I mean, I, I di' trie' to get someone. If it doesn' work, you're good with cars, right? I think Curtis' jumpers are out by the side...O'r there." She pointed out of the windshield toward the house.

"Let's just try. Where are the keys?"

"Ummm, well, like I was sayin', I had 'em ready for Franklyn to come by, an' had 'em on the table by the couch." Betsy reached her arm across the seat and laid her head into her elbow. "It's hot in here." She then sat up and began twisting the knob to roll down the window at her side and then lean out into the breeze. Betsy was oblivious as to how her demeanor was impacting Colin's patience.

"I'll go get the goddamn keys and make a phone call to get some help in case it won't start. Don't fuckin' move."

"For heaven' sake what the hell is wrong wi' you?" Betsy sat up to speak, then rested onto her arm that was draped out of the window. She closed her eyes to wait.

Colin snuck around to the back side of the car, careful to watch for signs of movement inside, and waved his arms toward the truck at the end of the street. *Thank God I had him stick around close by.*

The lights from Tony's truck slowly crawled passed them, then stopped in front of the house across the street. Colin ran to him, looking back to make sure Betsy didn't emerge from the car. "Turn off yer lights and go grab something real fast. Well, more like someone." He whispered and pointed toward Ruth's carport. "She's behind the car. And hurry the fuck up. Just get 'er in the back of your truck for now."

"What the hell? What do you mean? Get who?"

"The neighbor. Who else lives over there?"

"Are you shitten me? That wasn't in the plan!" Tony had no idea why they were whispering, but figured it was necessary.

"No. Shit! Just do it, we don't have time for this! Where the hell else are we gonna put 'er?"

258

With that, Tony quickly backed his truck into Ruth's carport up next to her car. Within minutes he was parked back in front of Betsy's house. Tony was clearly distraught, and his agitation showed in the rise and fall of his chest. Colin met him at his open window, with Betsy's keys in hand. "What the hell happened?" Tony barked in a low voice.

"Like I got time to explain now. Just help me make sure this car starts." As Colin jolted in the direction of Betsy's carport, he saw something lying at the edge of Ruth's driveway. He ran over to it and found her shoe in the gravel. *Fucking pay attention, moron.*

Grabbing it, Colin ran back to Tony's truck, lifted it slightly in the air, and then opened the back door of Betsy's car to toss it in the back. Betsy sat up to the noise. "What 're you doin'?"

"Nothin', just checking in on the boys. We're gonna get this car started, ok? Just relax."

After Colin attempted to turn the ignition with only the repeated rumble of the starter failing to make the engine start, Tony bailed from his truck to open the hood to Betsy's car. With all of the activity, Betsy opened her eyes to see Tony standing beside her car. "What... the hell is he doin' here?" She blinked a few times and opened her door to stand up. "What the hell is goin' on, Colin? Why's he here?"

Colin moved in close proximity, causing Betsy to sit back into the seat. He leaned in and whispered a surprisingly gentle warning. "Don't blow my cover. I called him to get us there. He's part of the plan, Betsy, just roll with it." She looked into his eyes to study him. Reluctantly, she sat back and watched out of her window as Tony pulled his truck next to hers, and the two men hooked the jumper cables between the two cars.

With a turn of the ignition, the car rumbled to a start. *Jesus, it's about time.* Colin climbed back out of the car to let Tony know to follow them.

When Tony tried to question him as to where they were going, he barked at him. "Just follow! Fuckin idiot." Colin nearly ran into Tony as Tony had just flung a gas can into the grass of Betsy's front yard. "What was that for?" Colin inquired.

"I grabbed it from across the street. Thought maybe it just might be outta gas and grabbed it in case we needed it. Found this too." Tony lifted up a roll of wire to show Colin what he had found. "It was on the gate. Since you went and added more to the mix, we're definitely gonna need this shit."

All Colin could do was nod a show of approval, recognizing the wire from a coiled roll he had noticed laying over the gate at the Bakerson house. *Should 'ave known that'd come in handy. Glad he grabbed it.* Betsy could hear that they were squabbling but couldn't make out the words. "So, we're headed to the bowling alley, firs', right? Did he tell you I had t' pick up the stash that I hid…there?" Betsy mumbled as she opened her eyes and sat up to clear her head and prepare herself for the next few hours." Colin thought quickly on his feet. "Oh, well, ya. Sure. I just got in a hurry and forgot." His heart pounded, and he began to sweat again. *So, now we stop by the bowling alley. Fine. Damn if this night isn't over soon.* As Betsy's head began to clear she became mindful of his unusual behavior. "Why did you come instea', again? I thought I was meeting up wi' you tomorrow so we could set up the final drop?"

Colin shook his head, trying to hide that her questions annoyed him. "I can't explain right now. Just roll with me, remember? This is how it's done, Betsy. You gotta roll on your feet and not ask questions."

The men separated into each vehicle and drove down the street without much notice from the neighborhood. Neither man realized that the Bakerson shed was left open, as well as leaving behind the bicycle and the gas can in Betsy's yard. As they drove down the street, the neighborhood was quiet.

260

The only neighbor who gave any attention to the activity was an old woman who had been woken up in a delirious sleep induced stupor of her own. With her significant vision loss, and lack of clear state of mind (due to her current regime of medication and confusion from the lateness of the hour), Colin and Tony had no reason to worry. She could never possibly recount what she had seen with any degree of accuracy.

They were soon pulling into the parking lot of the bowling alley. Colin checked his rear-view mirror to be assured that Tony had followed him. *Don't blow this, man, just stay in the damn truck.* He looked over to Betsy with impatient eyes and heavy breathing. "So, you gonna go get it?"

"Well, ya. Give me a sec' to freshu' up. Haven' you heard that patience is a virtue? Hell, you're 'bout ta piss me off, you know." Betsy fluffed her hair with her fingertips and went to grab her purse from her side. "Shit! Where's...where's my purse? What the hell?"

"What d' you need yer purse for?"

"Oh, dammit! I didn' grab anything, did I? Why'd you have to rush me so fast? Dammit, Colin, now....now we gotta go back!"

"Not a chance, Betsy. There's no time."

"Are... you kiddin'?"

"No. You'll be fine. Just get in there and do what you need to do. But, don't draw any attention."

"You're joking...you have to be. I can't...can't jus' go in there without a reas'n. That'll draw...attention."

Andrew was crawling to a sitting position in the back seat from all of the noise Colin and Betsy were making. He rubbed his eyes and blinked. "Mommy? Mommy, what we doin'?"

Betsy leaned around to greet him, sitting on her knees to reach out to him. "Just goin' for a ride, sweet pea. Go on...go back to sleep. I'm righ' here."

He laid back down and stretched. "I'm hungry, Mommy. Is there more subsketty?"

Betsy chuckled. "The spe...ge...tti's at home, silly boy. I'm sorry, we can ge' some when we ge' home."

"But, Mommy, I..."

"Oh for Christ's sake, Betsy, get 'im somethin' from inside."

"But, I don' have my money, Colin. Re...member?"

"Oh, hell, here. Just get in and get out." Colin reached under his seat to grab and open his wallet and hand her a five-dollar bill. Betsy grabbed it with a jerk and opened her car door.

"I'll be righ' back with some fries, love bug. Jus'...sit tight." She blew a kiss to Andrew and disappeared in the darkness.

Before Colin could open his car door, Tony approached flicking a cigarette between his fingers. Colin quickly got out and shut his door with a quiet click to keep from waking up Blair as well. He stepped in between Tony and the car, to keep Andrew from seeing him.

"What the hell are you doin'? Stay in the truck."

"What's yer plan, man? Havin' her back there is makin' me nervous. You at least got something to cover 'er up with?"

Colin shifted his stance, then turned to get into the car, reaching over the top of the seat to grab the blanket in the back. "Sorry, buddy. Just gonna borrow this for a minute. I'll get it back in a jiffy." He smiled

262

awkwardly to Andrew who was staring at him with childlike confusion, as if he may be dreaming.

Colin followed Tony to the truck and tossed the blanket over the dark shadow of the form barely visible against the front corner of the truck bed. "So, just follow me. But stay back some. I got help comin' and meeting us there." Colin began to give orders when Betsy rounded the corner with a paper bag clutched to her side and a paper basket filled with french fries in her grip. "So, are we leavin' or wha'?" Colin and Tony turned and shot each other a glance of near panic. Colin made it appear that they were leaving Tony behind at the bowling alley. "Yeah. We're done here. Later, man."

Climbing into the car somewhat unnerved that Colin was talking to Tony, Betsy did not hide her frustration. "So, I got it, but wha's the plan? Wha's the deal with him?"

Colin blinked a story into play. "He's the go between. Set it up for us. We're ditchin' 'im here."

"So, where's the real meeting, then? I wasn' expect...in' you."

"I know that! Quit harpin' on that. We're meeting them at a more isolated location."

"Why?"

Colin shot Betsy a look that made her retreat.

God, girl. Stop your fuckin' questions. She did, with the help of the lingering intoxication, even though it was beginning to wear off.

"Here, Pum'kin." Betsy leaned over the seat and gave Andrew the french fries. She then reached down to place the few dollar bills and change that she got back into one the boys' shoes that she had laid on the floorboard in her rush. She glanced outside her window to see Tony still sitting in his truck. "Why's he still here?"

So much for shutting your mouth.

"He's goin' into the bowling alley in a minute. Just getting' high first." He put the gear shift into reverse and backed out of the parking lot and onto the empty street, glancing cautiously behind him for his headlights. Betsy leaned her head back against the seat and watched out of the window as they drove. "So, we're goin' to meet them now, right?"

Colin breathed in deep before answering. "Yes. That's what I said."

Andrew spoke up with a groggy whisper only Betsy could hear. "Mommy, the blanky. I want the blanky."

Betsy leaned over close to him. "Wha's wrong sweetie? You wan' the blanket?"

Colin's face froze as he barely turned to watch, afraid of the direction this conversation may go. Betsy had already crawled over the seat, sifting her hands across the floor of the back seat. "It's gotta be here, baby. I know it was here."

Colin spoke up. "No. I didn't see it when we loaded them. You're lookin' for the blanket, right? I don't think I remember it being there."

"I'm sure it was ou' here." Betsy looked at Andrew, who was looking at Betsy with confusion in his eyes. Colin sensed Betsy's unsettled spirit, breathing deeply to monitor his own anxiety. Betsy finally gave up. "It's ok, pum'kin. We'll…we'll find it when we ge' home." Betsy puckered her lips and sent a kiss of love toward Andrew, then situated herself back into her seat while looking to Colin suspiciously.

Fuck, let's get this night over with. She's not buyin' this shit.

264

Chapter 24

"So, why are we heading this way first?" Betsy's eyes scanned the Orchard Mesa community landscape through her window as they traveled through the darkness along the highway. She was sobering up a bit, and the clarity only increased her anxiety. "I was s'pposed to meet them at the Caravan before heading up to Montrose for the exchange. Why are we going there now? I still have to....."

Colin sighed a heavy gesture of frustration. "I already told you, the location has been changed. It's on the way there."

"Well that doesn' make sense. There's nothing between here and Montrose, unless they're meeting us in Delta. But, I've never done tha' before. Why has it all changed, Colin? Why didn' they let me know?"

"I told you I'd explain later."

"It IS later. It's jus' us, so why all the secrets?"

"Just because." He looked out of his window, gritting his teeth.

Leaning back against the seat and gazing out into the shadows of street signs and billboards, Betsy put her confusion to rest. In the side mirror she noticed headlights behind them. She glanced behind her shoulder to check in on the boys, while getting a better look through the back

265

window, then concentrated her eyes back to the side mirror again. The headlights moved close enough for her to see the shadow of the truck in the near distance. *What the hell? Why's he following us?* Betsy looked over to Colin, who seemed increasingly anxious. *This isn't right. Something's not right.* The confusion resurfaced.

With a sudden inclination to be with her children, Betsy climbed into the back seat. Colin eyed her suspiciously, as she clumsily curled herself next to her boys. She leaned sideways in the seat and tried to casually glance behind through the rear window to get a better look at the truck following behind, just to be sure. That was when she saw a shoe. A tennis shoe, very much out of place. Ruth's shoe. *What's that doing there?*

Betsy's heart sank into her stomach, although she didn't know why. She suddenly felt like throwing up. *I need to call Ruth. Something has gone wrong.* She scanned her surroundings, recognizing that they would be out of city limits within minutes. A small town tavern blinked signs of life in the distance. Betsy leaned forward awkwardly. *Play cool, girl. Maybe I'm wrong.* "Can we at least stop up here and let me get some cigarettes?"

"I got one for you." Colin plucked his pack from the console and tossed it back to her.

"I don't smoke that kind. Those are disgusting."

"Fine. We'll stop." His jaw line was tense, and his words, sharp.

"I don't got any money, remember? You're gonna have to front me again."

Without looking back, Colin held a bill behind him for her to take. "Here. Make it fast."

The car came to an abrupt stop in a graveled parking lot in front of the downstairs basement entrance of the tavern. Betsy looked into the back seat to check in on the boys another time, and then reluctantly to

Colin. *I'll be right back. God's looking after you.* She looked over to Colin again and closed her eyes to say a silent prayer over her children. *They'll be ok.* A car pulled up beside them, and a couple exited, meandering to the door to make small talk with a man leaning against the entrance wall. *There's people right there. It's well lit. It's ok. It's gonna be ok.*

Betsy stepped from the car, leaving her side door hanging wide open. Her fears hardened when she saw Tony's truck parked along the side street, with its lights off, but still running. *Holy shit, Colin? Dammit, what's going on? Why won't you tell me what the hell's going on?* Fear crept into her soul and began to take hold.

Hurrying down the steps into the bar with her gut in full churn, Betsy knew she had to stay calm. She abruptly asked the bartender if she could use the phone and dialed Ruth's phone number, trying to control her jittery hands. When the ringing on the other end of the phone continued without a response, her fear turned to panic. *Ruth would never ignore a phone call this time of night.* She clicked the base of the phone to hang up and nervously tried again. *C'mon Ruth! Still no answer? C'mon!* Betsy's hands were shaking out of control, and her heart rate was so fast that she thought the bartender must be able to hear it. *Something is so wrong! So very wrong!* Looking to the bartender in an attempt to maintain composure, she asked for a pack of cigarettes. "Ya, those are the ones. Thanks." She paid so quickly that Betsy didn't even know whether or not she received her change.

Scurrying back into the car, she was relieved to see her boys nestled safely in the back and still sound asleep. *I'll get us out of this, boys. We'll be fine. I promise.* She looked to Colin suspiciously, fearing that he was not who she thought he was. Nonetheless, Betsy tried to maintain a persona that she trusted that everything was going as it was supposed to.

"You happy now?" Colin chided.

Betsy lit up a desperate attempt to relieve her fears and took a long drag, blowing rolls of smoke into his personal space. She breathed in deep to keep her hands from shaking. "Of course." Betsy forced another smile, holding back tears.

"No change?"

"What?"

"Change. I gave you a five."

"Oh, well, I tipped 'im."

"What the fuck? For cigarettes? Why the fuck would you do that?"

Her smile was clearly sarcastic. "Because it wasn't my money." Betsy watched his response to her teasing, but when she didn't get any, her doubts about him were solidified. *Stupid Son 'a bitch, I'll keep your damn money.*

The deep darkness of the night took on an eerie form as they left modern civilization and rounded a hill into the ranchlands of Whitewater's oldest settlements. Vacant and desolate boxed houses scattered the hills, while a small community of residents continued to make a life here. She watched for lights on the front porches of houses, wondering if there would be a way to find help out here. *The nunnery's not far from here. I wonder if they'd remember me.*

Colin turned the car off the main highway and onto a winding road that Betsy knew well. She was glad the area was familiar. In spite of that, she held back the urge to throw up. Unfortunately, the only lights that indicated civilization were their own headlights, and the distant stream of lights wavering in the rear, barely visible. Betsy began to chew on the inside of her lip. She knew what went on up in these hills. She knew who lived up in these hills.

268

As they turned a sharp corner, Betsy shifted toward the front seat. She could no longer contain her tears. Nor her fears. She muttered softly, with several rolls of teardrops escaping down her cheek. Despite that, her tone was stark. "Where are we going, Colin?" He looked into the rear-view mirror and stared into her. Betsy sensed a darkness in his eyes that she had never seen before. His own emotional energy began to surface. But it wasn't fear. Anger showed itself, despite that his body was still and controlled. His words and eyes were not. "Stop asking so many fucking questions. I didn't ask for this. You put yourself here, God dammit! So just shut the fuck up! If you'd 've just kept your fucking mouth to yourself, you wouldn't be here, and neither would I!"

Betsy took in a deep breath and held back the tears trying to escape. She sat back into the seat and turned to her boys, hoping they hadn't woken up. Sliding her fingers behind each of them, she caressed them softly. *Thank God. They're still asleep.* Betsy gulped her own explosive words back into her soul, sensing it was best at this time to keep quiet and think of a way to get to some place safe.

Silence consumed the car for more than twenty minutes. The only thing Betsy could hear was the sound of her own heartbeat, which she desperately tried to control. The car finally came to a quiet stop, after drifting away from the paved road about a quarter mile into the thicket of cottonwood trees, pine nut shrubs, and rolls of sagebrush. They settled atop the faint remnant of a dirt driveway, which over the years had grown over with desert foliage. The old, once upon a time driveway twisted its way around the hillside, making the old abandoned farmhouse barely visible from the road. Betsy's chest rose and fell as she sat otherwise frozen, trying to come up with a new plan of her own. Her thoughts were broken by Colin's cold and sharp voice. "Get out."

Colin climbed out, facing toward the back end the car, as Betsy turned to see Tony's headlights pulling in close behind them.

269

"Not without them." Betsy was cautious but stern, as she kept her hands on each of her children.

"Then lay them down inside. There's a bed. They can sleep. They'll be fine."

Betsy moved as if she were sleepwalking, slow and steady, trying to control the urge to shiver. She carefully reached around Andrew to hold him tight to her. He was heavy, but somehow she didn't feel the weight. Inside the old house, she saw an aged and filthy mattress on a flimsy metal frame up against the wall. She laid him down, bending at the knees. Her knees were shaking, and she hoped it didn't wake him.

Andrew stirred a bit, rubbing his eyes and trying to open them. "Shshsh…go back to sleep. It's ok. Mommy loves you. I'm right here. Shshsh…there now. That's it." Betsy spoke softly, as if she were almost singing a lullaby. Andrew responded as she had hoped and dozed back into oblivion.

Back into the mountain air, Betsy reached into the back seat once again, and this time tears were streaming down her cheeks. She imagined herself finding a weapon of any kind and putting an end to all of this, for good. *I could do it. I know I could.* Betsy was diligent to look for something she could use, as she carried Blair inside.

This was a well-worn and run-down house, with scraps of junk scattered here and there. *All I need is a piece of sharp metal. That would do the trick.* She had read once that you could kill a man with any sharp object if aimed in the right spot. *The throat. That was the place.* Once it was over she could scoop her babies up and drive home. Not to her old home, a new home. Some place where things like this never happened. Betsy cradled Blair in her arms. He never even flinched. Even in his dreams, her arms were his refuge.

After gently placing him beside his brother, Betsy whispered over them. "I'll be right back. I love you. I love you both so much." She gulped back her fears. "Mommy will be right back." They were sound asleep and peaceful. She sat on her knees and blew them kisses as she suddenly gained a sense of power. Betsy wiped her tears with her fingertips. There would be no more tears. Now she was angry.

Standing to her feet Betsy could hear men's voices out in the dark. The sounds were gruff and holding back, so she couldn't make out their words. As she stepped into the moonlit night, Betsy emerged with an old piece of splintered wood, sharp and deadly at the tip. She had also picked up a large river rock about the size of her foot and held it behind her clutched tightly in the other hand, just in case.

Emerging out from the doorway with a vengeance, Betsy was ready. Not running, not jogging, but walking at a swift pace, preparing herself for a full throttle attack. The two men were standing at the back of the truck, which was parked behind her car, with the tailgate down and the rear of the truck toward her car. Toward her. They seemed agitated and talked under their breath, heavily breathing with frequent puffs of their cigarettes. As she neared them, Betsy caught a glimpse of the blanket she had looked for earlier. It was draped off the end of the tailgate, as if it had been dragged to the edge. With the tailgate down, Betsy could clearly see what was inside the truck. Who was inside the truck?.

Betsy halted with a sudden jolt. All of time stopped. It happened so very fast. She saw her. Ruth's frail body lying there, motionless. *What? What's...oh my God! God no!* Nearly falling to her knees, something within Betsy kept her in a stalled stance. Ruth looked like a China doll, with her red silky nightgown lying softly on her smooth skin. Ruth's silhouette of a body was visible as it emerged from underneath the heavy, dull night coat. Reality hit Betsy like a grenade. Explosive and painful. Ruth's eyes were closed, and she was pale. Betsy opened her mouth with

271

a violent scream and lunged at both men, weapons in full throttle. She attacked with a fiery passion, flailing her arms at the enemies before her. Her mind was in too much of a blur to remember where to aim.

Betsy's fist held tightly to the rock in her hand, as she attempted to pound at Tony's face. He wasn't much phased, taking it from her in a quick twist of his wrist and tossing it to the ground. With her brutal attempt at survival, Tony was angered into action. The stick in her hand poked splinters into her skin as Betsy tried to break free from his grip, taking aim at whatever, she could feel. "You fucking bastards! I'll kill you! I'll kill you both! You son-a-b....." Spit flung from her lips in sync with her flailing hands. The hand that clutched the stick pierced feeble stabs at whatever flesh she could see or feel.

It was Colin who grabbed her and pulled her away from Tony's angry grip. Taking her from behind he attempted to gain control. His immediate plan, although not at all thought out, was to get her in his grip and carry her into the house. Not for the purpose of rescuing her, however.

Tony, bleeding from the scratches left behind from the rough splinters of wood, was cursing under his breath as he smacked Betsy across the face with the back of his hand, knocking her away from Colin and onto the ground. A mere haphazard attempt to knock her out. It didn't. Betsy fixed her eyes with his and scrambled to her feet, pulling her arm free from Colin's grip with sloppy attempts to claw at his face. As Colin took hold of both of her arms, he glared at Tony and tried to maintain some control through spurts of forced air through his teeth. "Goddammit, asshole, there's an easier way to do this. The last thing we need is her blood all over this place. Get a grip, man!"

Colin reached around Betsy's waist to gain momentum and to subdue her once and for all. With a grunt, he flipped her to the ground, face first. Sitting on Betsy's back to keep her from being able to move, he dug his knee into her and pulled on both of her arms, which were crossed around her chest underneath her. Colin maintained physical control of Betsy's wiggling frame in robotic fashion, responding quickly and methodically to her every attempt to break free. Betsy made one last attempt at a kick. Colin's grip tightened as he breathed heavily over her. Within mere minutes her fight for life was resolved, as she melted into the ground.

Chapter 25

Colin stood to his feet, clumsy and almost dizzy. He stepped back, nearly tripping over himself and shook his hands vigorously, as if they would lock up if he didn't break the spell. "Son of a bitch!" He leaned over to cough forcefully.

Tony stood staring at him, numb, blinking away the horror that he had just witnessed. Colin seemed annoyed by this. "Quit acting like you've never seen a dead body before. Fuckin' get a grip."

"I'm the clean-up man, asshole. Just haven't been in it like this. You can be a real fuckin' asshole sometimes, man. A real fuckin' asshole!"

"I just do what I'm told to do. Otherwise, I end up like this. It's the game, man. Never said I liked it." Colin stood over her for a few seconds, almost regaining a sense of dignity. Almost. "I liked her. Such a fuckin' shame. God dammit, why'd she have to go and do this? She should've done what she was told. Kept 'er nose where it belonged."

In all reality, Colin felt like throwing up. He just couldn't let anything get to him. It was a matter of survival. He took in a deep breath and nodded to Tony. "I'm gonna go smoke a bit. Make yourself fuckin' useful." His voice was monotone and empty of humanity. It was just a job at this point. "Load 'em up and let's get done with this shit." Tony's jittery hands followed orders, as he struggled to breathe.

As Colin walked away into the darkness, Tony lifted Betsy's body into the truck with a roll. A third set of headlights moved its way toward them. "We got help!" He called out, not surprised by the oncoming visitor.

The car rolled lightly to a stop. Once the headlights returned the dark air back into its hiding place, a shadowed figure emerged from within the square form of the vehicle. "We done here?" He was smoking, and you could see the orange dot radiating from off of his fingers.

"Just about. What the hell took you so long? You missed the chaos. We could've used you."

"What chaos? This wasn't complicated, unless you're an idiot."

"Shut the fuck up! We had a few mishaps. It happens."

"Mishaps? Oh, hell. So, you fucked things up, then?" The large frame of the man kicked a branch out of his way with the steeled toe of his heavy boot. "Never mind, I don't wanna know." He tossed his cigarette into the dirt as he approached Tony. "Did they clean up shit inside from the last shipment? We can't be leaving shit around, you know." He was acknowledged with a negative nod. As he passed by the truck, he looked inside. "Why the hell are there two? You dumb shits fuckin' get greedy?"

"That would be one of the mishaps."

"No need. I don't give a shit. Let's just get done. I got shit to do still tonight." He disappeared into the house but came back out almost as fast. This time, he was pissed off. Highly pissed off, as evidenced by the way he carried himself and by the long quick strides across the thirsty field grass. "What the fuck did you guys do? Why are they here? A few mishaps? What the hell happened tonight?"

275

"Hey, man, we didn't know they were home this weekend. They weren't supposed to be there. They're usually gone on the weekends. Don't get all bent outta shape on us! And quit your damn yellin'. You don't wanna wake 'em up." Tony was trying not to yell himself.

"You gotta plan?" His body was tense, and his eyes were ready to blow.

"Ya. We'll take 'em back. Someone will find them tomorrow."

He pressed forward, right up to Tony's face and tried to whisper through his angry teeth. "That's your plan? You fuckin' idiot!" He was nearly spitting, trying to keep from raising his voice. "They've no doubt seen you two. Are you really that much of a fucking moron?"

"They've been sleeping the whole time, man. Fuck. Calm down."

Colin strolled in from the darkness, around from behind the house. "What the hell, you two. Get a grip. They didn't see us. And if they did, they wouldn't remember. They'll think it was all a dream. Man, let's just load 'em up and get outta here. I need a fucking drink, man."

"Oh, no. You two morons aren't giving me a fuckin' death sentence. Get in there and load all the fuckin' boxes full of that paper and shit that those assholes left in there and get it all into the cellar and outta sight. And get in the fuckin' truck. Fuckin bullshit, nobody can do anything right! And make sure that cellar's shut tight. I'll get someone over here another time to finish cleaning all this shit outta here. I'll be right behind you. Don't leave yet. Son of a bitch! I got this." He darted into the house before either of them could take another breath, not to mention to follow his orders.

One pop! fired, and they could see the flash of light come and go in a split second through the empty frame of the broken window. The air was still. Another pop! and another flash. Neither man moved a single muscle until he came out through the doorway, putting his gun away

276

inside his waistline. "Now clean the fuckin' mess up! Get shit put down in that cellar and get all this mess cleaned up. Get to work! Wrap 'em up in that." He pointed into the back of the truck at the blanket.

"Wasn't that for her?"

"Do you think it really matters, now? Use your fuckin' head. You want blood all over in your truck?" He walked with a brisk gate back to his car and leaned against it to light up another cigarette while they worked. The rest of the night, there was very little talking. Even necessary whispers seemed unnecessary.

Tony drove the truck as quickly as possible, bouncing lightly with each divot in the rocky dirt road. He tried to control the washboard effect that carried his tires down the desolate path to the river. It was quiet, except for the sound of their own breathing, with an occasional inhale and exhale from their cigarettes. The man in the car had followed them but just to the turn-off of the highway. He chose to wait along the roadside, to keep intruders away. There was only one way into this secluded entrance down to the river, and his job was to make sure no one else turned into it. Sometimes reckless teenagers liked to hike these woods and walk the river late at night, and he would certainly be a diversion.

As they approached the railroad tracks to turn toward the bridge, the truck came to a stop. They each bailed into the darkness, and without thought or confirmation of words, they picked up four railroad angle bar irons. They were heavy, but not too heavy that they couldn't lift their share. They dropped them hard onto the sturdy surface of the truck bed. The thuds broke the silence, but not the tension. They were back on the road within seconds.

The robust and rustic wooden bridge towered over the moving water with the respect that only a bridge this aged could demand. Its crisscross architecture of strategically tapered boards running along both sides were visually inviting, but the well-worn planks that supported the massive structure was not so convincing, if you hadn't crossed it before. The ranchers on the other side used this bridge regularly, as did the hired hands of the local railroad. So, it was safe enough. Despite the darkness of its shadows.

Anyone who knew the area knew the bridge. It was a celebrity of sorts, as far as bridges go. Although it was in reality a thoroughfare to the working ranch on the other side, it was commonly used by the locals. The family who owned the ranch preferred to keep the gate closed to protect their dogs from chasing nearby trains. But, for those who knew that a closed gate doesn't necessarily mean a locked gate, it was fully accessible.

On this particular night, the bridge appeared to sway. It weighed a heavy sigh as the truck parked near the entrance of its threshold and unloaded its passengers. The glowing moonlight shown its spotlight into the water's steady forces, creating hasty shadows as if to warn the river. The walls of solid rock and earth layered high on each side of the river leaned inward to watch, with its crevices opened up wide to swallow up the darkness. Everything within this silent country canyon seemed to moan a sad but watchful eye.

A bird watched from its nearby perch nestled among the tall protective cover near the water's edge, keeping silent in fear that he too would become prey. Shadows of wildlife scuffled into holes to hide. The men worked frantically, sensing the skittish eyes around them. Wrapping and tying knots of awkward metal wire, attaching each body firmly with fiercely quick hands, they secured their victims to the weighty irons. The wire needed minimal snipping, as some of it was already cut in sufficient lengths. Coils cut into Betsy's flesh, but neither of them cared. Finally, Tony spoke up, almost under his breath. "I thought we were supposed to use the boat." He motioned to a small fishing boat, nestled below them in the brush at the base of the river.

"Really? How the hell do we get four bodies into that thing? Things have changed, in case you didn't notice. They go down from here."

They didn't seem to have enough room to roll the bodies through the wooden slats, so they each took an end and hoisted the first one up and over the top of the railing. It didn't seem all that far to the center of the river. With a heavy and awkward roll, a quiet splash interrupted the stillness in the air. Another heavy hoist, this time accompanied by a struggling grunt. Then another splash. The two smaller bundles were not as difficult to maneuver, and with another roll, they were plunged into the blanket of water as one. Together. As it had always been. With the final splash came a final groan from down below. The river murmured its sorrow, as it engulfed them in its compassionate embrace.

In the river waves, wetness wrapped them as if to console them, to caress them, to hold them. Betsy's hair swirled across her face, as she floated with one thud after another over the smooth stones and flittering life at the river's bottom. As she lightly tumbled with the current, Ruth's arm broke loose from the wire's grip and dangled in the wash of the floodwaters around her. Her hand unwittingly reached for Betsy's face, dancing amidst the rhythm of the water's rush and rippling song. Her fingertips reached out to accidentally brush lightly across Betsy's cheek. Lightly, softly, and maybe not so accidentally. It settled there, for a brief moment, caressing Betsy's cheekbone. The river sang what Ruth surely must have been singing to her from somewhere:

When peace like a river attendeth my way.

When sorrows like sea billows roll.

Whatever my lot, thou hast taught me to say,

It is well, it is well, with my soul.

It is well, it is well,

oh my soul.

Chapter 26

Karla rubbed her face with the palms of her hands and then ran her fingers through her hair at the top of her head. *Damn, my head hurts.* She and Ramone were sitting on iron lawn chairs in the enclosed patio that extended the length of the hotel lobby. Karla picked up a photograph, pinching it between her fingertips, trying to focus. Her eyebrows squinted in concentration as she examined all of the details. "So who took this?" Ramone glanced in her direction. He had earplugs in both ears and wasn't sure what she was saying. But he could tell she was asking him something. He paused his computer and pulled one earpiece free. "What's that?"

"Do we know who took this?" Karla turned the photo around for him to have a better look. He snatched it from her, nodding that he recognized it. "This is somethin' isn't it? Yeah, I asked Trey, and he said his father didn't take it, so must have been Ruth."

"How does he know that his father didn't?"

"Curtis was particular about what he used. Trey asked those who knew him best, and everyone said that he thought he was too good for a basic 35mm. That was taken with a 35. Ruth was taking a lot of photos during that time, even had a studio at a friend's house. A friend of hers, apparently, not theirs".

"So Ruth used a 35? I don't know the difference. Didn't know there was anything else back in those days. Do you think it means anything?"

"Only that the family liked to visit the river, like a lot of people, sounds like. What I'm learning is that the area was remote as far as tourism goes, but a hot spot for locals. Every time the county would put the sign up, someone would steal it. Then there's some tree on the side of the highway, gets decorated every Christmas. A real local thing."

"So, it's nothing more than a weird coincidence."

"No. You know there's no such thing. But, to answer your question, the family did like the area. So it's not a coincidence that there would be photos taken there."

"Ok, smart ass, but this is the exact place that the, that they, that she…."

"I know. That doesn't make it a coincidence, it makes it, well sad. Heartbreaking, in fact. He was just a child. He didn't know the significance of that bridge. He was just playing."

So you have emotions after all.

Tristan Bakerson was a mere five years of age when the photo was taken. It was a moment snapped in time. Young Tristan stood upon the planks of a wooden bridge facing the camera but not looking at it. He was playing. He had a small stick in his hand and was running the stick along the sides of the rustic railing. Even as a still photo, it was easy to imagine what he was up to. Clickety clack, clickety clack. Click, click, click. Clickety clack. It was clear that he was fully engaged in what he was doing.

The family dog stood in the foreground. She was looking back to him, as if telling him to follow her. His face was a bit blurred, as he faced toward the rail and tilted down a bit. He may have been looking into the water down below, curiously watching the current as he played. But it was hard to tell. In the background, the scenic canyon walls, trees and tall grass lined the river's edge like a painting.

It was a serene shot. Pleasant. A family treasure to mark the joys of childhood.

"Does Trey know when it was taken?" It brought tears to her eyes. Tears she quickly suppressed as soon as Ramone answered. "I don't see why it matters. Since Ruth clearly took it, it had to have been taken before she died." He had put the earpiece back in its place and seemed annoyed that she was still asking about it.

Afraid she'd say something she'd regret later, Karla slid out from behind her chair and opted to take a break. She walked into the hotel lounge and folded her arms as she glanced around at the artwork on the walls. A particular painting caught her attention. It too was a depiction of a river. Done in pastel watercolor, the green hues brought a sensation to her memory that she strained to clarify. Grass. Grass dominated the painting, with all shades of green. Tall, spiky grass blades. Karla brushed the thought away, having nothing in particular to attach it to. Ramone's voice startled her. "What're you doing in here? You didn't even let me know you were leaving."

"Sorry. You just seemed preoccupied and I just needed a walk." She paused, then turned to him suddenly. "Hey, Curtis was a kayaker, right? He rode that river all the time, didn't he?"

"Yes. And…"

"Ok. So, here's what I'm thinking. So he's this genius, everyone knows that. He's meticulous and has a photographic memory. And he knows the river, really well. Bragged to everyone about how much he knew. That was the whole thing about that damaging testimony, you know, what he said about the river currents?"

"Karla, get to the point. You're losing me."

"He *knew* the river. As well as anyone could."

"Yes, part of the reason he got convicted."

"Well, I overheard a group of people at breakfast this morning, talking about tubing down the river. Sounds like fun, if you ask me. But the one thing that stuck with me, I didn't know why then, but now I do, is that the river is always low in August, and so that's the safest time of year to tube down the river. They talked like it was common knowledge. At least for anyone who lives around here."

"Wait, you're on to something. Curtis would know not to dump bodies in the river at the end of August. He would know the water would be low, and the bodies would soon surface. That bullshit story that the river was lower than normal that year because of that draining they said was done, and that he wouldn't know it would be low, that's a crock 'a shit. Yeah, it would make sense for it to always be low in August. Check the history, it'd have to be. Curtis rode that river enough to know exactly what it was like that time of year. His perfectionistic nature wouldn't allow him to make a mistake like that." Ramone looked to her with a grin and nodded. "Damn, if I didn't know any better, I'd say you're pretty good at this. Thinkin' just like a cop."

"I'm not a cop. You are."

"I was."
"Okay, whatever. I don't wanna be a cop."

"I'm not having this conversation with you, Karla, no one said you had to be a cop."

"But, you want me to be."
"You're good at this."

284

"No. You are."

Silence. Tense silence.

"Alright. I'm sorry. Let's just stay on track. It was a good point, that's all I was saying."

Ramone turned to walk away, avoiding any more conflict. Karla followed him back to the table out to the patio, still thinking about the area that the bodies were found. She continued to speak her thoughts as she sat down. "Ok, Pop, so it's a fairly remote area. Kinda out of the way, right? It's not like it's right off the highway or anything. I mean, unless you already knew how to get there, well, you wouldn't know how to get there."

Ramone nodded. "The locals would know. And not to mention, there wouldn't be too many people who would pay much attention to the tie irons, unless you were there enough to already know they were there."

"Were they easy to spot?"

"Not according to the preacher. He said they were off to the side, piled near the railroad tracks. The way the road turned up and over the tracks, you'd have to have already known they were there. Wouldn't be able to see them at night. Headlights would miss them with the angle of the turn."

"Ok, so we're talking someone who also knew the area. Someone who was familiar with the bridge and that there were tie irons near the railroad tracks."

"Clearly." Ramone started sifting through a stack of papers he pulled from a box at his feet.

"What?"

285

"I think I remember reading that there was a boat at the river too, when the bodies were found."

"A kayak?"

"No. I if I remember right, it was some kind of fishing boat, maybe. No, not really a fishing boat. Something small, like something a child would use. It was out of the way. Hidden a bit, almost under the bridge."

"Was it searched? Or used as evidence?"

"I'd like to know. But, wouldn't be surprised if it wasn't." Ramone shook his head in frustration. "Damn, pages of shit went to the CBI for testing. Next to nothing from that list was used in the trial. Ridiculous if you ask me. I mean, what did they use? Wire from Bakerson's house? Hell, there are reports that say the shed door was wide open. Bakerson was as compulsive and materialistic as they come. He doesn't leave his shed open, ever. And that whole deal with the wire? Of course the wire on the bodies was cut with his wire cutters. It was his wire, for God's sakes. He said so. Ruth cut it down from her garden, using his snips, of course. There were reports, in writing, that she told people this. And besides, they had no way of showing that the cuts were new or old. Hell, it all was in the river for over a month, they didn't have decent technology back then. And they couldn't even match all the snips with his cutters as it was. Some cuts flat out didn't match up at all, meaning some of the cuts weren't with his snippers at all."

He's rambling. It's not like him to ramble.

Karla sighed the tension away and hesitated before speaking. She spoke, nonetheless. "Do you want to go see a show or something, Pop? I saw a flyer advertising some live music up the street later tonight."

Ramone stared at her with confusion all over his face.

286

Ok. Never mind. "Forget it. I just thought maybe it was time to call it a night."

"Why would we do that? We're on a roll." Ramone reached over to his briefcase and pulled out a folder. "Take a look at that. The prosecutor never even let the jury see the wire. He just drew a picture of it on a big board, even though the wire was sitting right on the table, all rolled up, right in front of him. Why not just show them the actual wire? Why draw what it looked like, and how he presumed it was cut, when it's sitting right there?"

"I wouldn't know, Pop." She gave him a passive half smile, looking out of the window for a distraction.

"You know, I tried to call you last night, and you didn't answer."

"I probably just had my phone in my bag. I went to sleep to the TV."

"Well, that's not too good for you." He paused. "So I called since I wanted to show you something. I found some evidence that matched up to a description of the guy that Betsy had reported to one of her friends that she was scared of. A blondish fellow, dirty blond, with shoulder-length hair."

Karla leaned in thoughtfully. *Ok, Pop. I'm still here.* "Could that be the guy that tried to strangle her a couple months before? I thought she never said who that was?"

"She didn't. Claimed she didn't get a good look at him. They tried pinning that on Curtis, too. Couldn't stick, though. No evidence at all that it was him."

"Except the neighbor, who said he was lying over her in the front yard."

"Because he heard her scream. Ruth heard it too and was out there almost as fast as he was. She reported that to several women at her church. By the time Betsy was in the yard, the damage was done. Evidence clearly indicated she was attacked in the house. She went out front for help. Use common logic. Why would the attacker follow her out into plain view, after attacking her and her getting away? What a ridiculous concept. Plus, she cut her hand on the attacker's big belt buckle. Curtis wore slacks and was too conservative in how he dressed for big belt buckles. It was a simple explanation: Curtis was hovering over her in the yard because he was helping her."

"Yeah, and not to mention the nurse at the hospital reported that Betsy told her the Bakersons saved her life. Why wasn't her testimony used?"

"Because they conveniently couldn't track her down."

"Seemed to be a lot of that happening."

"The question is, why?"

The tapping of her pen on the table drummed the rhythm of Karla's thoughtful trance. "So, we're looking for someone who may have had shoulder-length dirty blond hair, someone who knew the area around Bridgeport Bridge, and someone who knew Betsy? How do we narrow that down, when she was so very popular among the gentlemen?"

"Ok, let's go this route. Who do we have from that list of names that she had made?" He dug around his work box and retrieved a copy of a document that they had nearly memorized.

Karla rubbed her forehead. "But most of these don't have last names to them. How can we be sure who they are?"

"Go back to what we already know."

"Alright. This guy. Grant something. Someone with that first name bowled at her work, flew planes for fun, and bragged to his bowling buddies that he loved to fly through the canyon above the Gunnison River. What'd he look like, do we know?"

"No, but we could find out. Don't forget, this same guy was rumored to be pretty friendly with Ruth. Some thought they were sleeping together."

"Ya, but we can't prove that. People closest to Ruth say no. It seems like a rabbit trail and nothing more."

"True. And we can't link him to a motive, either."

"So then, this Craig Hollister guy. Had Whitewater connections, some reports that Betsy's youngest son was his. We found out that he's in jail, right? Has been for years."

"His ties to people in Whitewater were later on, not that year. And yes, he has a criminal record. Again, what's the motive?"

"Shit, Pop. Don't ruin it for me. Felt good finding possibilities."

"We need a motive. That's what's going to ring it in. A motive. This Craig guy is certainly someone of interest but can't be a suspect without a motive to kill both women. And there isn't anything that even puts him near the neighborhood that night."

Karla sat back into her chair and stretched her neck. "Remember that transcript you showed me? Have you been able to track that guy down?"

"No, that's been a wash."

"Too bad. That guy seemed to have something. Can the transcript be used without his testimony?"

"Not if we don't know where it came from. Trey has no idea where it came from. His brother had it in some of his stuff. I wish we could follow up on that." Ramone laughed out loud. "His statement is pretty powerful, though. Just kept saying that he 'saw too much'. Over and over again. 'I just saw too much.' He kept on saying it. God, what the hell does that mean?"

"I don't know, but it's something in and of itself, isn't it? I mean, he obviously was holding something back. One only holds back if they have something to hold back."

Ramone's frustration appeared to grow even stronger. "And then, he said that Betsy 'wasn't where she was supposed to be'. What the hell is that all about? Doesn't make any sense at all. I wish we could find this guy."

Karla eyed Ramone carefully. *You look tired. C'mon, let's call it.* "Pop, do you think he'd talk if we did find him? I'm thinking not too many people want to talk. Around here, it's a done deal. Are we wasting our time?"

"The truth is never a waste of time, Karla."

"Not everyone sees it that way, Pop. I mean, let's face it, that prosecutor was a smart one, he was. He got the job done, and people bought it."

"He was more than smart. He was as slick as they come."

Slick indeed.

Chapter 27

The buzz of the florescent lighting penetrated Karla's ears, which made her numb. She could see people in front of her talking, but their words flittered passed her unaware of her presence. Karla waited idly in line at the grocery store, neither patient nor impatient. Just there. Her phone in her purse began vibrating, and after glancing at it, Karla knew she would have to lose her place in line. She needed to take this call.

Darting past moving obstacles dressed in sweatshirts and baseball caps, Karla made her way around the bend of the building and leaned against the brick wall's shaded seclusion. *Please don't hang up. I got it.* Karla's breathing was heavy as she answered. "Hi. I thought you'd never get back to me. Any news?"

"Well, hello. I wasn't sure if I'd be able to reach you. I'm guessing you've been busy. Having any luck with the case?"

"I suppose. Maybe. It's a tough one. So what's up, anything new? Anything good?"

"Well, actually, yes, I found a couple of things. I don't know if it's good or not. I don't know how you'll view it anyway."

"I guess any news is good news, right? Just give me what you've got."

"Well, no luck with the marriage license, but I got in contact with the hospital that you were born at. I'm glad I had you do a release, they almost wouldn't give me anything. Tried to say I didn't have your authorization. I had to produce a contract of services to get it done. Anyway, all they would give me was her name, and from that I was able to locate a valid birth certificate. But her name's not what you said. It's Bethany Lincoln. That's the good news."

"Which means there must be bad news."

"Well, I don't know what to make of it. It's about your father. He's not on the birth record. There isn't a father named at all. And there is no marriage license."

Karla stood still. *That's not possible. The hospital version he gave me had his name on it.* She was confused. *You have to be wrong.*

"Karla, your father is not on your birth certificate. The certificate you gave me doesn't match any of the records at all. And there's more."

"Ok."

"Take a breath. Don't panic, just listen."

"I am. What's wrong?"

"When I searched her name deeper, I found an adoption record. And a death certificate."

The blood left Karla's body from head to toe. She went empty. Her heart stopped. She couldn't have heard correctly. *That can't be...he's said.. but he...*

"But, my birth certificate...it said..."

"Karla? Karla, you ok? Listen, this will be ok. You need to ask him. This information should come from him. Ok? Clearly, you don't see this as good news. But there's gotta be a reason. Karla, your birth certificate that he gave you, it's not real. But, still, give him a chance to explain. Don't jump to conclusions…"

"Jump to conclusions? Who's jumping to conclusions? He's lied to me! How is that jumping to conclusions?"

"Alright, alright. But he's your father, and he loves you…"

"My father? Apparently not. That's what you're saying, right? He's not my father….you just said…"

"Karla, c'mon. We don't know the details. There has to be more. He's raised you. Get a grip. He's your father. Take a minute and just breathe. Let him talk to you about it."

Karla took in a deep breath to hold back the tears. She blinked away her surroundings and tried to process the words. "But I have a picture…" She paused to gulp down the panic. "Do you suppose the picture is even real?"

"Honey, of course it's real. Just, please, go talk to him."

"Sure. If he will talk. He's gonna be pissed that I hired you."

"He'll understand. He's more reasonable than you think."

"Then you don't know him."

"I know you. And, I know that you are the woman that you are partly because you had him as your father. So don't make any assumptions and go talk to him."

"Sure. I'll give it a try. Any chance you can send me those documents? I think I'll want them to show him. He always wants the evidence, you know. So I'll give him evidence. Then he can't argue with me. He can't lie to me."

"Yes, I'll email them right away. You're gonna be fine. This will be fine. Call me, soon. Ok?"

"Sure. Thanks, really. I mean that. Thank you for all you've done."

Her surroundings were silent. Everything moved in slow motion. Karla wasn't even aware that she was standing in the parking lot, until a honk blared its obnoxious intrusion. She glanced around for clarity, finding a sense of reality to the present. Moving slowly to the sidewalk Karla looked up the street to her hotel in the distance. *Fine. There's a good reason he's lied. There is. There really is. There has to be.* She straightened her stance and determined that she would put aside her doubts and her questions and get back to work. After all they were in this city to do a job. And she would do it, so she could get home to where things were normal. Whatever that is.

I have to be his child. I'm even acting like him.

Chapter 28

Tap, tap, tap! "Hey, Pop! You ready?" Ramone opened his door with briefcase in hand, knowing it was Karla at the door. Karla studied his face. It was strained. She was distracted by his face. *He's gotta be my father. We look alike.* She jumped right into work to push the thoughts out of her mind. *This'll perk him up.* "I've got the notes on that audio that we did with the preacher's interview. I'm not sure there's anything there that we didn't already have, other than solid confirmation that Curtis can't be a valid suspect on the strangulation attack of Betsy earlier that summer. The pastor clearly states that Betsy said Curtis and Ruth saved her that night. So what do you got for me now?"

"Well, let's walk and talk. Follow me downstairs. I need a big table to line some things in chronological order. Everything Ok? You're early." Dropping a folder that was loose, Ramone seemed disheveled. "Shit! Would you grab that, Karla? I want you to read through something on the way." He stopped (dropping his briefcase) to bend over and retrieve the mess, sorting as he collected, then handing her a few documents, poorly copied, but clear enough to read.

"What are these?"

"Interview reports. And a couple newspaper stories."

"Who did this one?"

"I don't know which one you have. Check the bottom. Could be Sheriff, but most are from PD interviews." He glanced over her shoulder. "Oh, that's PD. You'll love that one."

Karla was scanning the interview and raised an eyebrow, careful to multitask her steps into the elevator as she read. "This is weird, Pop. Check it out. This guy's clearly covering his ass. Why would he feel the need to do that?"

"Not the brightest this city has employed, apparently. Look there, at the date."

"Oh, shit. Whoa, wait a minute. They supposedly didn't take the missing person's report seriously, so why is this cop claiming he had nothing to do with where they were?"

Ramone laughed sarcastically. "No shit, Karla. You can't tell me something isn't up, when you got a city cop making a written statement that he had nothing to do with the disappearances of women who supposedly left on their own accord. God, he wrote that report the same weekend! Shit, the more I dig, the more bullshit I find."

"Wow. Is this name on her list?"

"Could be, there were three on it with that same name. Wish we had the last names to go with the names on that list."

"Where's this guy now?"

"That's what we're going to find out."

By this time, they were headed into one of the hotel's smaller conference rooms. Ramone dumped his briefcase onto a long folding table. Karla watched him struggle to get organized. His hair was in disarray, and he was sweating. "Pop, you ok?" *Are we ok?*

"Of course, why?"

"No reason." Karla struggled to take her eyes off of his face but quickly looked to her work when he looked up. She spread the documents in her hands across the table. "So what else we got here?" She picked up a piece of paper and scanned it. "What 'ya know. There were sunflowers in the backyard after all. I don't know why the prosecution made such a big deal to discredit that."

"Because it gives credence to the wire being left on the gate."

"I never doubted that. More than one person said so."

"Yes, but this is from a journalist. It makes the statement more credible."

Karla's eyes shifted to another story, a clipping from the Grand Junction Daily Sentinel. This one was especially interesting. She gazed at it in disbelief. Ramone elbowed her and startled her. "Sorry, I'll move."

"No, you're fine. Just thought I'd lost you for a minute."

"Oh, sorry. Do you know what this was about? Who's this cop? I haven't come across him before." She was curious for more personal reasons.

Ramone peeked over her shoulder. "Oh, yeah. A young rookie cop. Made the papers a time or two. Turns out, he lived in Whitewater that year. Well, actually for several years. Once I found this, I looked more into him. He seemed to be getting into all kinds of predicaments in those years."

Karla's heart began to beat so hard that she was concerned Ramone could hear it. She took in slow breaths to mask the sudden realization she was faced with. "What's the back story with this guy?"

297

"Well, he got fired from the department in '76. His name was Randy…something."

I know. It says so, right here.

"Seemed to be in the wrong place at the wrong time, all the time. I'm not lookin' to him as a suspect or anything. I mean, every time he showed up in the newspapers it was because he was on the law end of trouble, not causing it."

"This clearly appears to be a threat toward him. Why would a relative of Betsy's threaten a cop right out in the open like that?"

"It was a relative of her ex-husband. Not hers."

"Still. This happened just after the bodies were found."

"My question is, why didn't anything come of it? Holy shit! A guy points a gun out his car window at a cop. Better yet, a family member of the ex-husband of a recent murder victim, points a gun in broad daylight at a cop. And nothing? A slap on the wrist? What the hell was wrong with people around here back then? Am I the only one who finds that disturbing?"

I find this very disturbing. "Why was he fired?"

"The documented version, or my version?"

"Both."

"He was in some kind of high-speed chase in Debeque Canyon. At least that's what he claimed. His windshield got shot out, and he was nicked by a bullet. The official report says he made it all up and was careless with his own firearm, shooting his own windshield."

"And your version?"

"He was fired to keep him quiet."

It apparently worked.

"I'd like to find this guy. Maybe enough time has passed, and he'll have something for us."

Apparently not.

Ramone rubbed his temples. "This shit's starting to get to me. You got any aspirin or something? Have you ever come across anything that may make Betsy's ex-husband suspicious?"

"No. He had a solid alibi. I've not come up with anything suspicious on him."

"Just is so weird. This poor woman. God, she had so many men in her life. And it doesn't appear that any of them really cared about her. I can't help but feel for what she was going through. She had no idea who she was. So insecure. I guess men tend to be drawn to women like that." He looked the other way, as if deep in thought.

Karla was confused by his sudden change in demeanor. *He does care about more than just the case shit. What's up with you, Pop? This is all just too much for me right now. It's all getting to me too, Pop.*

"My head is spinning, Pop. I've got something I gotta do." Karla watched as he rubbed his forehead and nodded. "Alright. See you soon, then?"

No protest? No questions? Something really is wrong with him.

Chapter 29

The door of the tavern jingled more forcefully than usual. Karla flung herself up to the bar, approaching Shannon's back side. "Where is 'e?" Before Shannon could even turn around, Karla was pacing to the other side, looking into the back room. As Karla made her way back to where Shannon was posed (dumbfounded at Karla's behavior), she asked again. This time with better clarity. "Where's the old son of a bitch? He's got some serious explaining to do." Shannon gave half a grin, with eyes wide open. Not the happy kind of grin. The 'What the hell is wrong with you?' kind. "Karla, you alright? Have a seat. Take a breather."

Karla slumped into her barstool with a frustrated thump. "Shannon, he was fired. Did you know Randall was fired from PD? And he was threatened. Did you know this? You know all about it, don't you?" Shannon put down the glass she was wiping down and leaned onto the bar on her elbows. She looked closely at Karla and breathed in deep. "Listen, there's nothing here I can say that will make things right. Yes. He was. And yes, I know. But he's got to come to terms with talking to you on his own. I'm not stepping over that line. I care too much about him."

Karla's eyes began to tear up. Shannon took Karla's hand in hers. "I'm sorry. Get a grip, girl. This is just an old case that was already solved."

You too? You're just like everyone else in this town.

Shannon smiled sweetly. "Honey, I'm not sayin' you're not right, I'm just sayin' I got over it. I moved on. So did he."

"You really believe that? I don't. He's drinking his life away. Have you looked at him? He's not ok. He's not moved on. He's hiding in his booze."

Shannon stopped and thoughtfully nodded. "Ok. You got that much." She looked over to the door, then back to Karla. "Well, I haven't seen him in a couple days. Which is unlike him. I even went by his place, after calling a few times and getting no answer. His car was gone, so at least I know he's still alive, and somewhere. He'll show up."

The silence was comforting this time. Shannon walked over to the bottles to pour Karla her regular drink. "Here. I got you." She poured herself one as well. Putting her glass up into the air to clink Karla's, she nodded a sign of friendship, of understanding. "To Betsy, to Ruth, to Suzanne....and to Cheri."

"And don't forget about those beautiful, sweet little babies who were the most innocent of all."

"I wish I could."

"Me too."

They both gulped a simultaneous stress relief, and glasses clinked again.

Their moment was clipped short by another jingle of the door. Randall made an abrupt entrance, already unsteady and fired up for trouble. Shannon took a wise step toward him, and immediately defused what could possibly come next. "Hey there friend! I've missed you!" She looked to Karla with a clear warning to keep it low key. He took up his

301

spot next to Karla without responding, simply looking at Karla with endearing eyes. "So, you're still here, I see. I figured you'd given up and gone home already."

Karla shook her head with a clear answer of 'not a chance', searching for the words she needed. Shannon slid his usual drink into place, stood back, folded her arms across her chest, and leaned against the center island inside the bar. "She knows you were a cop. She knows you were fired. She knows you were scared. Just call a truce."

He looked at Karla and grinned wide, showing that he needed serious dental work.

"Well, hell! Then I got nothin' to say after all! Drink up, little girl!"

Pondering her next move, Karla pinched her bottom lip between her teeth. *Alright, you ole' fart. Another time.* Grinning back, she reluctantly retreated. *I'll get to him. He won't know what hit him.* "Ok. Fine. I'll let it ride, for now." She glanced up to Shannon, who nodded a silent note of approval. Karla settled into her seat more comfortably and took in several deep breaths to help her let it go. For now. "You got cards on you? I'm up for a rematch."

Shannon turned from her perch with a chuckle and resumed doing the dishes. The time went by quickly and Karla failed to notice when several hours had passed. Not to mention, she was slurping down her fourth drink. Her mood had lightened, and her head was anything but clear. Karla hadn't noticed that the last drink was significantly watered down. Shannon watched her cautiously, as she watched the clock. "So, I thought you said you were meeting your father for dinner? When did you say that was?" Karla shot her a glance that she didn't really care but giving a grateful smile.

With a slap of a card, hard onto the bar's slick surface, Randall slapped his knee and almost fell off of his stool. "Ahaha! I ain't gonna let you have this one!" Karla giggled. "I might."

"I think you're both pretty much done." Shannon announced graciously, taking the glasses from each of them. Karla reached for it, not realizing that she wasn't joking. When Shannon used a small amount of increased force to take the glass from her hand, Karla pulled back harder than planned and knocked her purse to the floor. "What's that all about?" Karla whined, bending over to pick up the mess at her feet.

"Oh, let me get it, girl! She thinks she's got me on a leash, and she's gonna put you on one too, it looks like!" Randall bent down and scooped up the scattered contents, shoving them back into her purse. *I can do that myself.*

"No, it's ok. I got it." Karla tried to intervene, then sat up and looked up to Shannon in disbelief. Shannon merely shrugged. "You got 'im drunk. Don't look at me."

"I ain't drunk, you ol' hag, you! I'm a real cowboy, and I can handle my shit!"

"You also ain't as young as you think you are, either. I'll get you a Coke. And here, eat this." Shannon had already prepared a sandwich on a paper plate and slid it in front of him.

Karla's journal peeked out from the inside of her purse, having not made it back all the way in from the mess. Randall took note of it and reached to take it out. "Hey, girl, what's this? Is this one of those diary things?"

Karla slapped his hand away. "Hey, keep your paws off! I got it." She tucked the journal deeper inside her purse.

"I was just bein' hel'ful" he slurred.

303

Karla raised her eyebrows and snickered. "If you say so. Besides, it's a journal, not a diary." She moved her purse to the other side.

"Aren't they the same thing? Wha's it doin' in there? Someone might get their hands on it, you know. Maybe, ol' Shannon here could get her hands on it and read it? You know, people are snoopy like that. You should keep yer secrets at home. Tha's all I'm say'in."

Karla shook her head and rolled her eyes. "Who says I got secrets? It's just a journal."

"Everybody's got secrets." He stood up. "Don't tell any, while I go to the jon." He slinked away into the darkness of the room.

Shannon watched Karla closely as Karla watched him leave. "I know what you're thinkin'. And you should really just let it go. He's never gonna give you what you want."

Karla took another drink, grinding ice between her teeth. Randall was winding his way back to the bar with only the sound of his own breathing to break the quiet. "Who? What? You guys talk 'in about me?" He plopped back to his perch. "Will you get me a cab?" He looked over to catch Karla's somber face, "Did I miss somethin'?"

Shannon shook her head and smiled. "Yes. I'll get you a cab. You should get home and get into bed. Don't do any work or anything. Got it? It'll be dark soon, so just go straight to bed." Shannon leaned in closer to make her point.

Randall leaned side-to-side to keep upright as he shook his head. The uncomfortable invasion of her personal space caused Karla to lean back a bit. He stayed his course. "Keep that diary thing to yourself. Nobody ever needs to read it. You hear? I mean it. Nobody needs to read it. Ain't that right Shannon?" He was wobbling to the door. With his back to them he was mumbling, shaking his head, "Saw too fuckin' much. I just saw too damn much...."

"Yes, my dear friend. I know. Go home and get some rest, Ok?" Shannon grabbed a wet cloth and wiped down the area near where he had been sitting.

"Is... he gonna... be ok tonight?" She talked slow as she pushed another ten-dollar bill toward Shannon.

"As ok as any of us are." Shannon winked and looked up to the clock. "You missed dinner. Has your father called?"

Karla reached into her pocket and retrieved her phone, glancing at the screen. With a few clicks and taps, she winced. "Looks like a bunch, to be exact."

"Better go make it right."

"Sometimes I think it's too late for that." She slurred.

"It's never too late for that." Shannon watched her leave, wishing she didn't get people drunk for a living.

Peeking out into the street, she caught a glimpse of the sun just beginning to drop behind the horizon. The walk back to the hotel was hazy, slow, and disconnected. Words from the last three hours swirled aimlessly in her mind. *Maybe we should just call it. Maybe we should just give up.* She wasn't simply referring to the case.

Karla shuffled her way back to the hotel without daring to make contact with Ramone. She knew he'd still be at the restaurant and wasn't in any condition for him to see her. Once in her room, Karla sat on the bed and fanned her fingers through her journal. She hadn't written in it for a few days, and maybe she could write something tonight. *I could work on that song some more.* Not mustering up enough energy, she laid her purse beside her. *It's probably all mixed up and in shambles.* Shifting her position Karla dumped the contents of her purse out in front of her, making a genuine attempt to sort and put it all into order. When she saw a plastic room key that her father had given her, she examined it. *This is his. Why'd he give this to me? I'd never give him mine. Maybe he's back to his room. I should go talk to him.* Without giving it any more thought, she left her room to go to his.

At first, Karla knocked. But then, recklessly, after realizing that he wasn't there, she clicked her way in. She was scanning the room, not even knowing why. Just being there, among his things, in the presence of his space, gave her comfort. *Why did you lie to me, Pop?* Tears escaped down from the corners of each eye and rolled down her cheekbones. She slowly sat down to rest briefly on the side of the bed. Her distorted mental clarity had no plan in place in case he was to walk through the door. Staring straight ahead, Karla was blank of conscious thought. Then, something she saw brought her back to clarity. A framed photo lied on the nightstand next to the bed. It was upright and facing the bed.

Holy shit! It's her. And....

She reached for it. She gazed at it. *....and me.* Karla was just a baby, not even a year old, it appeared. She was holding her. Her mother was holding her. They were in a room like a garage or shed of some sort. The walls behind them were raw and dirty. There didn't appear to be much in the way of furniture, but a waist high bench that she was standing in front of. It too was jagged and old, with a splintering surface. There were things hanging in the background and a guitar leaning from the bench, up against a wall. A poster of some strung out rock star and a painting were clearly visible. It was hard to tell what the painting depicted, but it had long strands of flowing fields of grass, green and yellow, as if blowing in the wind. The image and shades of green seemed to engulf her and her mother from behind. On the bench, she could also make out plants scattered all around. They didn't look like house plants. *Shit, where the hell are we? Doesn't look like anywhere Pop would hang out.*

Karla wished she could keep it. *He keeps her with him. After all these years. He loved her. He really did. So why not talk about her? She must 'ave really hurt him. But, why....why the adoption record? She's not alive anymore. I wonder when she died, and why Pop never told me. I wish she'd get me those documents. I need to call her. Why hasn't she sent them? Hell, I can't trust anyone.*

Something sensible jolted her mind into action, causing her to remove the photo from the frame. *Take a picture of it on your phone. He'll never know you have it.* When she held it in her hands, rubbing it with her fingers, she caught a glimpse of the backside.

There's writing on it.

Karla slowly read the words, hoping for something. Anything.

'Crossing paths may be all we are, but my love will forever shine like a star.'

Yours in spite of it all, Beth.

Karla's mind nearly went into a tailspin. *She was right. Her name was Beth! Why did he say it was Janet? What the hell?* Karla turned the picture back over again, laying it on the end table, pulling her phone up to its surface and carefully clicking a shot. She checked it to make sure it took. When the lighting wasn't right, she shifted the position of her phone, turned the photo away from the lampshade, and snapped again. This time she lit up with a smile. *This'll do. I should get out of here before he gets back.* She swiftly put the photo back into its frame and snuck back into the hallway. *I guess everyone has secrets after all.*

Chapter 30

The hotel lobby was buzzing with a group of elderly tourists who had sauntered into the cool shelter from down the street at the train station, only a few blocks away. They toted several bags each, and they were tagged with handwritten name tags upon their cotton shirts to identify them as visitors.

Ramone leaned against the counter and watched the mayhem, glad that in his mind, he hadn't quite arrived to that state of retirement. Though he feared he wasn't too far away. His cell phone buzzed, and he reached in his trousers and haphazardly peeked at the number. Karla eyed him carefully, watching his every move. "Is that Bill? Is he joining us for dinner later?" She followed him out into the courtyard. "No. I mean, yes, he's joining us later, but no. That was Trey."

"Oh. Good. When did he say he was headed up here? His email seemed like he was excited to dive right into things. He's flying right?"

"No. he's driving."

"Oh. Well, I guess that's alright. I guess I'm just anxious to sit down face-to-face and go over everything."

"It's not like we have a lot, Karla. We're far from wrapping it up."

"Well, I think it's coming along quite well."

"Karla, all we have is circumstantial. We need something solid that is admissible in a legal proceeding. We don't have the money to just pull out the archived evidence and start testing for DNA. We'll have to be able to convince a law firm or the state to do that. And after two trials, and no legal way to re-open this case, we need more than circumstantial evidence to prove actual innocence."

"So, what you want is a nice little predictable murder case that you can hand over, wrapped up and tied in a neat little bow, right? Pop, that's not like you. And it certainly isn't this case. You're a better investigator than that."

Ramone looked at her in pleasant surprise. "Ok. Ok, I get it. Call me out on my shit. I can handle it." He smiled, reassuring her that he hadn't sold out his true passions to mediocre expectations.

They chose to sit at opposite sides of the round table to sit at, and Ramone leaned back, breathing in the fresh air. He had his eyes closed, and Karla studied his unusual relaxed presence. *He's not digging right in. His briefcase isn't even opened yet.* "So, I did some checking on that friend and coworker of Curtis'. Greg something. He was the one Ruth went to see that night. You know, in his interview, it was never reported what the purpose of her visit was, except to just see their new kitchen cupboards. It seems strange to lug two small children, one riding his own bicycle, the other in a wagon pulled by nothing but bicycle muscle power, all that way to see cupboards. I question why more wasn't reported about that."

"That's probably because no one asked for anything more." He was still leaned back, with his eyes still closed. His hands were in his lap, as if to be resting.

"Well if they prodded for more, it didn't get written down. You'd think they would've asked for more. I mean, looking to the events prior to the murder seems basic. Who did she see, why did she see them? But the report says the bare minimum. Only that she went there to see cabinets. Really? Her husband just left on an overnight trip, she was upset, probably because she knew he was going to be with the mistress, and she rides her bike all that way to his coworker's house, with kids in tow, to look at their new kitchen cabinets? Pop, I don't know about you, but I don't know too many people who would be riding young children that far, with a five-year-old riding his own bike, just to take a look at someone's new kitchen."

Ramone just nodded. "Yep." He sat forward, eyes blinking, and pulled his notebook open onto the table. "Ok look, this guy was up to something. Don't know what, yet. I asked Trey to find out whatever he could. He went through some old letters and found a statement about Greg that is interesting. So, then I took it a bit further. Yeah, he was up to something. And as much as Curtis wanted in on the action, Greg kept him out of it."

"I thought they were friends."

"They were business partners. That we know. We just can't say for certain what that business actually was about. They were photographers and engineers, but there was more."

"Well, what was he was up to?" Karla was reading from the notebook that Ramone had pushed her way.

"Read it for yourself. Look at the transcript from that interview. The old retired cop verified it. Greg was building surveillance equipment on the side. And according to this statement, he was doing surveillance work for law enforcement."

"Which branch? It doesn't say."

"We don't know for sure. But it would make a difference, wouldn't it?"

"Hell ya. It would help us understand which circle Greg ran in." This time it was Karla who sat back in her seat and closed her eyes to soak up the sunlight. "He had money didn't he?"

"It appeared so."

"So, he wasn't runnin' with people like Betsy. She was as broke as they come. I mean, an engineer building surveillance off the clock, that's a big deal. Out of Betsy's league."

"No, he was higher on the money totem pole than the likes of Betsy. But don't forget, she was going somewhere to give up some sort of information that had ties to Aspen. That old lady insisted it was an issue. People with ties to Aspen would be more up his alley."

"But, then how would Betsy know anything that was that high up on the money ladder? What kind of information would involve anyone or anything from Aspen? We can't find a single thing that puts Betsy in that crowd. Or Ruth, for that matter. Maybe the ol' lady is just crazy and full of delusions."

"No, there's something there. The only thing that is close is that other case. You know, Suzanne Denison and the little girl? You seemed pretty intent at finding out how all of that mattered. You come up with anything? Anything that puts Greg in the mix?"

"Other than it seemed odd and suspicious, not so much. The whole thing. I mean yes, Suzanne's sister lived up there and all, and she died under suspicious circumstances. Her husband seemed like he could easily have been trouble. These women were all friends, and they all died in a short time period. And, well, you know I'm not convinced the convicted rapist committed his part all by his little lonesome. I've not

311

found anything that would bring this Greg into the picture or shine light into why Ruth went to his house, then wind up dead hours later."

"Well, clearly, she'd had enough. She was wanting to end her marriage. Greg had money. She didn't."

"And she just wanted to go home to her parents. That takes money. Why not just ask her parents for money?"

"I don't get the impression that they were supporting her divorcing Curtis."

"How, Pop?"

"Oh, hell. I don't know. Don't most church folks think divorce is wrong and all? I mean, I know we're working to get an exoneration for a man innocent of murder, but he was far from innocent. At least when it comes to being the good church going man he claimed to be at the time."

"Well, Pop, even I know that people are people, no matter what they believe about God or the afterlife."

"You believe there is such a thing? I never taught you that. What makes you think there even is such a thing?"

"I have a life, Pop. Not everything I believe comes from you." She stopped and watched him closely. "So, you don't believe that there's more?"

I wanna believe my mother is still alive. She's not just gone. Existence can't be that shallow.

"Oh, hell, I don't know. I never gave it much thought."

"You work murders, Pop. You have to have thought about what's out there after death."

"No, not so much. I don't give it much thought at all, Karla. We all die. Good or bad. And those who lived a good life, end their lives in peace. Those who didn't, well, I guess they'll never be at peace. That's all. Don't make more out of it than that."

But I'd like to think we have more purpose than that. That none of them died in vain.

They both sat in the silence of the street for a few minutes, disregarding the traffic and people laughing across the street. Karla spoke first, bringing Betsy's sweet smile and her careless eyes into the forefront of her thoughts. "So, I'm still not sure what to make of Betsy. So many people think this was all about drugs, and it sure does appear like she had some sort of connection to that scene. But all the interviews we read from those who knew her don't seem to implicate her with using or selling drugs, either one. Unless weed counts, but this wouldn't be all over marijuana, would it? I don't get the impression she was into anything more than that, do you, Pop?"

"Regardless what she was into, it was going on all around her, either way. And it all made money. People die for money, no matter the source. I mean she worked at one of the biggest hot spots in the whole drug scene."

Karla nodded in agreement, then paused. "Oh yeah, that reminds me, did you ever find out who that guy was who was trying to off-load that drug shipment? I heard you and Bill talking about that on the phone yesterday. That was that same week, right?"

"Yeah it was. Don't know for sure about it all. He was apparently trying to get rid of some sort of shit in a hurry. Didn't just go to the bowling alley. Went all over, to several different bars. Seemed like he was in a real hurry to off-load something. The drug business creates fear like that." He was scanning through his notebook, almost distracted, but looking like he was multitasking pretty well.

We could use some help here, God. Karla scanned her surroundings and then looked up to the sky. She hadn't given up on the idea that God existed. She had to be able to trust in something.

Chapter 31

"You're a sight for sore eyes!" Karla reached around Randall and squeezed his shoulder. Even his familiar smell of gross man sweat and booze didn't thwart her affections. Randall was grinning oddly and swayed lightly to the left, as usual. Shannon breezed by behind him, coming back to the bar from the stock cooler. "Don't knock 'im down, Karla. He's a bit fragile."

"Oh, can it! Ain't nothin' fragile about me!"

I believe that. I really do. Karla chuckled, as she sat down at the bar. "Alright. I went shopping today."

"Really? New clothes? I thought you had something new and spry on."

"Ok, yes, I got a few things for me, but I also found a couple of things for the two of you." Digging into her purse she plopped a brand new deck of cards down onto the clean surface of the bar. "I went into this little gift shop down the street. I know it's a bit too cliché for me but thought of you and had to get them anyway." It had the clear plastic wrap still intact, and even though the graphics spoke clearly of cheesy tourist, he was touched. He didn't dare show it. The cover of each card was a different horse, posing so perfectly one would think they knew they were on display. "Well, thanks kindly, little lady. We should break them open and break them in. But, first, I gotta pee." Karla tilted her head

315

and laughed. Even with the smell of sour whiskey on his breath, he was a breath of fresh air.

Karla looked up to Shannon, who was bent over a sink, rinsing a round of clear glasses. She wiped her hands on her apron and smiled up at Karla. "That was sweet."

"Your turn. This is for you. I thought of you, too." Karla swallowed hard, hoping she wasn't crossing a line of any kind. She pulled a small lightweight cardboard box from the gift bag in her lap and gently lifted the lid. Nestled inside the box was a cross pendant. It was the kind with a circle at the center of the cross. The circle had a latch on it, barely visible. It was so tiny, Shannon had to almost squint to see that there was already a small photo placed delicately inside. As she peered closer, putting the pendant up to the light, her whole body stood motionless, and tears filled her eyes. Karla held her breath.

Shannon held the pendant in her fingertips, laying the box and bag on the bar. She looked at Karla and blinked away the tears, several times. Then she leaned in and gave Karla a tight squeeze around the neck, leaning awkwardly over the bar.

With a soft whisper, Shannon took away Karla's anxiety. "Thank you." Smiling graciously at Karla, she took the gold chain and clasped it around her neck. Shannon tucked the pendant down into her shirt as she mouthed the words 'Thank you' again and then proceeded to wring out a wet washcloth from the sink.

Karla and Randall played hand after hand from the new deck of cards. Shannon stopped every so often to tease him about his hand of cards and to give Karla the advantage by secretly sharing with her what he had in his hand. He knew this but played along anyway. "You know, I wouldn't allow that shit if I were making money off you."

316

"You can't make money from someone who doesn't have any." She giggled back.

"C'mon, you should be raking it in. On TV the PI's have all sorts of cash flow."

Shannon chimed in. "Really? You know better than to believe everything you see on TV. Since when does anyone other than the lawyers make any money in this fucked up system we call justice? You know that as good as anyone."

"Yeah. But you know, back in the day, there was money to be made in this game. I never made any, though. 'Cause I wasn't ever invited to those games."

Shannon raised an eyebrow. "Watch out for this guy. He's full of shit most of the time."

I don't mind. Keep talking. Just keep talking.

That didn't slow him down. "Oh, hell yah! Lawyers, judges, bankers, shit, even doctors got in on it! They all made their fair share!" He began to cough amidst his laughter.

"I thought that only happened in the movies." Karla knew him well enough by now that she could keep him going as long as she kept it light-hearted.

"Don't be fooled by the Mayberry looks of this place, my dear. It has its fair share of secrets." Shannon looked up and stopped. Karla glanced over to her, then back to him.

Please don't clam up. Please, just out with it already.

Randall looked to both of them in drunken confusion. "Like I gotta tell either of you that! Oh, for God's sake, deal another round! Don't

317

get all sappy and wanna talk shop. I'm not goin' there, and you both know it. Give it a rest and give me that deck."

"Alright, old man! You get another shot at me! But, don't think I'll be easy on you. I know when you're bluffing." Although she was subconsciously referring to more than just cards, at the moment, she didn't care much about anything but filling time, so she ordered another drink. In here, time stood still. And it was easy for her to forget the time and everything else that was wrong in her world, in a place where time stands still.

Chapter 32

It was well past dark when Karla turned the corner to trigger the automatic doors into the painful florescent lighting of the hotel lobby. She was slightly wobbly and lightheaded, but not obviously intoxicated to the naked eye. Unless of course, you were her father. Ramone knew her state the minute she walked through the arched entrance into the hotel lounge, looking in his direction.

Ramone and Bill were in a booth nestled in the corner picking at the final remnants of dinner. They were engaged in intense conversation. Initially, Ramone ignored Karla as she approached their table. Ramone was focused, listening closely to Bill's words. "Ok, so they all did more than ignition work. They were smart businessmen. It wouldn't be all that surprising that Greg was doing some work on the side. They were all about the money. You know, anyone worth their weight in business was. Still is, that's how it works."

"Ok, yeah. Of course. But Curtis' boss was even sued over his little side jobs. White collar crime never gets into criminal court. Not to mention, Curtis' other co-worker, he had a couple of renegade sons who were said to be knee deep in all the drug shit going on. I just found out that one of 'em dated Betsy."

"So, Betsy did have connections to people Curtis worked with after all. Why would it surprise us that she dated someone related to someone Curtis worked with? It's two degrees of relationship connections in this town after all." Ramone paused to look in Karla's direction as she settled in. "Hey, nice of you to join us. Did you hear that? Turns out there is a loose connection after all between Betsy and the money shits around town."

Karla pulled up a chair and slowly sat down, careful not to give her unsteady stance any attention. "That's a really loose con...connection, Pop. And tha' could tie Curtis, too... then. Since he worked with th'm. I don' think... tha' can help us."

"There has been nothing at all that says Curtis was doing anything on the side, like those jokers were. In fact, it explains why none of them were there for him once he got arrested or during both trials. I always thought it was strange that they all knew he was in Ouray. Knew he had an alibi and yet, they pretty much abandoned him once he got arrested. It almost seems like they bailed any loyalty just to keep their own shit from getting into the limelight. Curtis was a talker. Wanted to play with the big boys. This guy, Greg. He really did, as well as Curtis' boss. They weren't playin' with petty cash at all. But Curtis hadn't had a chance to get in tight with the big boys in town, being the new kid on the block and all."

Bill shook his head in doubt. "We don't know enough about that ordeal that was hacked into. All we know is, that this operation, what was it called again?"

"MCNET. I think it was called MCNET."

"Yeah, according to the old cop, the program was compromised because the unit that stored and monitored all of the narcs, was tapped into or something like that, and that they had to shut the project down. At least that's what he said."

"But, other reports say that there was more than one undercover gig going on within those same years. MCNET could've been a county thing, maybe even a state thing, but not specifically by the city. And we can't ignore that official reports, well newspaper reports, say that the federally funded drug programs were shut down due to funding issues. The county's programs wouldn't have involved Greg, since the interview report said Greg worked with city cops, not county folks. But I guess just the one interview alone is enough for me to put Greg somewhere in that scene. Just not positive where. Let's face it, if you're building surveillance, you know how to tap into surveillance. Can't deny that. And it appears like that's what may have happened. We know they shut at least one of the projects down that year."

Karla moved her gaze from Bill to Ramone, Ramone to Bill, then back to Ramone again. *Slow down, holy shit.* "I must 'ave miss' somethin'...."

"You've missed a lot, Karla. Where the hell you been? And for God's sake, you smell like shit. You been hanging around a bunch of homeless drunks?"

Karla glared at him, then looked to Bill. "So... what's all this abou'? This...s is new. Wha's Mc...MCNET?"

Bill glanced over to Ramone who seemed agitated. "It was an undercover operation of some sort. Stood for Mesa County Narcotics Enforcement Team. I'm still unclear if it was separate from city PD or Sheriff, or both but overseen by the state. Maybe it was something all on its own, handed down from the DEA. Could've been a multidisciplinary thing from a state or federal grant or something like that. Anyway, that year, there was a problem with the program, all of the informants were compromised, and the program was shut down. One report said it was due to lack of funding, but others say it was a breech in security."

"So then, how does this Greg character play in?"

"He built surveillance on the side. We don't know who for. He could've been a part of this all somehow."

"How would we know for sure?"

"Talk to someone, I suppose, but who? Programs like that aren't easy to get information on. 'Undercover' means it's not common knowledge. It supposed to be secret."

Ramone slid over to the edge of the booth to stand up. "I'm gonna go for a walk. Fill her in about the alibi shit. I don't want to go back over it, just 'cause she couldn't get here on time." He glanced down to her. Karla looked at Bill and winced, instead of looking up. She leaned into him, scooting her chair up closer to the table. "So, what'd I miss?"

"Well, you already know Curtis was in Ouray with an alibi until 10:30 at the earliest. But the DA was able to show that he had time to get back into town from when he was last seen there before the estimated times of death, which the DA said was around 1:00am."

"Yeah...but Pop says they were wrong abou' the time Ruth.... was killed, isn' that wha' he said?"

"True. The prosecution's theory only works with a sketchy timeline using the autopsies from the boys. Because they ate later, if you stretch out the time to a full four hours, you might be able to get a 1:00am time of death for them, only if you use the full four hours. Still a stretch, since they still had food in their stomachs."

"So...you don't even buy the 1:00am time...s of death for the boys?"

"It's iffy for them. But there's no getting past Ruth's autopsy with regards to her time of death. It's clear cut. It proves that Curtis' alibi was legit, no doubt about it. Even if they convinced a jury that it wasn't."

Karla leaned almost too far into Bill's personal space, and sat up quickly, hoping he hadn't noticed. He had; but he smiled compassionately and kept talking to avoid the awkwardness. "The only reason the timeline worked in either trial was because Ruth's autopsy wasn't talked about much. I read those transcripts. It was mentioned only slightly, with no argument from the defense."

"Why? Why wouldn't they use it? Pop said somethin' was off …you know with Ruth's time of death, but…I haven' got a good ex…explan…ation from him. He's been actin' distracted the last few days. Have, have you… noticed?"

"Well, I suppose so. But you haven't exactly been cooperative, and around much. You think that could be why?"

"Well, that's convenient. Blamin' me an' all." Karla turned her face away to hide her own agitation, just in time to catch Ramone's presence from her peripheral vision.

Bill sighed as Ramone took his place back in the booth. "So, we all caught up?" Ramone smiled over to Karla, who didn't smile back. He and shook his head in exasperation in Bill's direction, who laughed trying to lighten the mood. Karla wasn't the least bit amused. Bill sighed again. "I don't know why the defense team didn't jump on that. Ruth's activities that night completely legitimized his alibi. An early autopsy said she died one to two hours after her last meal. Then the autopsy was modified, and testimony went to two to four hours after her last meal. There was ample evidence that she didn't eat past 6:30pm, with the exception of cookies. I mean, when you really look at the evidence used, the Prosecutors' case was weak. Convincing and circumstantial in the right hands maybe, but in reality, really weak. And let's face it, it continues to get weaker the more we know, and the more time goes on."

"It's what the Prosecutors didn't use that matters here. What was omitted in a crafty theatrical performance?" Ramone shook his head in frustration.

Bill leaned in, displaying his own emotion. "No shit. There were clear reports that Ruth was out and about from the time that Curtis left, and then there were those visitors at her house intermittently until little Tristan told the detective that she put him to bed, right when the news started. The trail of events reported that night make it crystal clear that she didn't have time to have eaten a full meal any time after cleaning up dinner. Which was around 6:00pm. In fact, all those reports simply support that she ate exactly when Curtis said she did, by 6:00pm. Ruth was a busy girl that night. Tracking her activities and the witnesses who saw her, the condition of her bed found the next day, little Tristan's story to the investigator, all of it screams of an earlier time of death. Plain and simple. There's no way she could've eaten during all of her comings and goings, with two little boys in tow the whole time."

"Yep, that's the one clear thing in all of this. Her autopsy. She still had recognizable food in her stomach after all. Recognizable, for God's sakes. After thirty days in the river, half decomposed and shit. There's no way in hell her time of death was one o'clock in the morning. Early notes say she even had food substance in her esophagus, I wonder why that didn't make the final report? Clearly food hadn't had that long to digest. Even using the modified testimony of the time of death, it puts it at a more accurate time of death to be around 10:30 pm."

"Oh, I meant to tell you earlier, that I read that the original autopsy reports had actually been destroyed in some fire. I gotta go back to that

324

and get more information to clarify the details. I find that difficult to wrap my brain around."

"No, I read that too. Sometimes its mind blowing how things can get lost in the mix."

"You said it. I can't get past the way her bed was left and all, not slept in, with her book and glasses on the bed. How'd the facts get left in the shadows of all the courtroom drama like that?"

Karla tried desperately to mind her tongue as they talked. She sensed that Ramone was really upset with her, so she listened intently, but still wasn't following everything that well. Leaning in closer Karla tried to slow the conversation down, or more accurately she just leaned. She caught herself and sat up abruptly.

Ramone sat back and glared at Karla. "You know what, if you can't even sit up straight, just go to your room and go to bed. You seem to be doing a lot of sleeping these days anyway. Why bother even showing up?"

Karla looked into her lap to contain the emerging need to explode. Instead, she stood up and walked over to the bar. Ramone watched her suspiciously, then sent his voice in her direction, trailing her with guilt. "You sure you need any more? We're kind of on the clock still." Karla simply ignored him, as she waited at the bar to order a drink.

Slinking back into her chair, with a drink in hand, Karla interrupted a conversation she immediately presumed she wasn't privy to. She only caught the tail end. Just one word. "....mother..." Karla stopped short and looked at Ramone, who was looking like he wasn't even breathing, but making a suspicious glance to Bill. "What about my mother?"

Ramone sat back in his seat and grimaced. "No one said anything about your mother."

"You did. I heard you." Her weakened senses suddenly woke up.

"You heard wrong."

Bill leaned in to talk quietly and still be heard. "Listen, you two. I've known you both far too long. I know you don't know me much, sweetie. But I knew you before you were even born. And I don't wanna be in the way. But, really Ramone. Talk to your daughter. Ok? From on old and trusted   friend.   Communicate.   Both   of   you."

Karla's eyes began to well up. She watched Ramone sitting there quiet, deep in thought. *Oh shit. Here it comes. Just breathe.* She waited for him to speak, but it didn't come.

When Ramone continued to sit silently, Karla finally burst out in anger. "I think he's right! You do nee' to talk to me. For starters you can explain why you've been lyin' to me my whole life. An' instead, you could actually tell me abou' her!" Ramone and Bill shared a look between them. Ramone's face was pale. Bill spoke up, wishing maybe that he'd kept his mouth shut. "Karla, you seem really upset about something. Maybe after a good night's sleep, maybe then it will be a good time. I didn't mean...now. Maybe this isn't the time."

"You wanna talk about a good nigh's sleep? I don't sleep. Does that surprise you? Ok? So let's talk now."

Karla glared at Ramone through wet and hurting eyes, who was looking helpless and dumbfounded. His lost gaze only fueled her frustration.

Karla sat back exasperated against the pleather cushion of her chair and stared desperately into Ramone's eyes. "Just tell me, Pop. Tell me abou' her. All I have is a lousy picture. And the fact that you gave me a fake hospital birth cer...certi...thing, and that her name was really Beth, and that you two weren't even married, and tha' there's some sort of adoption papers I know nothin' about and that, oh, wait, how about tha'

326

she's dead! Pop! What abou' that she's dead! Isn't she? She didn' leave me. She didn' leave you! Or did she? I don't know, 'cause you're a liar! Wha' the fuck, Pop!?" Karla put her face into her hands on the table and started to cry, then suddenly sat up again, turning to Bill, with tear streaks speaking more than words could say. "You know, he jus' gave it to me after I begged to see what she looked like. An' you know what he said? 'Here. Here she is. Now leave me alone about it'. I was eight! Bill! Eight! Who the hell says that to an eight-year-old?!"

Ramone's eyes began to leak, and he blinked several times to suppress them. "I'm sorry, Kar…"

"Sorry? You're sorry? Now? You're sorry? Really Pop? Oh an' by the way. I found the picture you keep of 'er. Why get annoyed with me, when you keep 'er around? You disappear behind your badge and your gun and your work and…."

Karla's tears had already let loose like a dam had just broke free.

"Karla, I couldn't…."

"Couldn' what? Deal with it? Couldn'' look in my eyes and say, I loved her but…. But, what? What couldn' you do Pop?" She hid her face into her hands again and leaned down into the table for support. Through the sobs, her words were faint. "Please, please just tell me. Tell me that you really are my father."

Ramone took in a deep breath and looked around the room, wiping his face casually, hoping to salvage his pride and dignity. To his relief, only the bartender looked on in curiosity. He was the only person in the room this time of night. "I am, Karla. You're my daughter. And I didn't run her off, Karla." He stopped, and then quickly and unexpectedly he snapped out the truth. "She did die. Ok? She died Karla." His voice was sharp, almost cold. He didn't mean to spit it out so abruptly.

327

Karla blinked away the confusion within her. Bill put his hand on her shoulder. "Karla, Listen, sweetie. There was a reason he couldn't talk about it. At least at first." Karla lifted her head to see Bill glance over to Ramone as if he was reprimanding him. "He would've lost his job. The very means that you were raised from. He was alone with you. You gotta cut him some slack."

Karla looked deeply to her father again. "Then, tell me. Jus' tell me." She whispered with quivering lips.

Ramone gulped and took a deep breath. "I'm sorry. I am really, really sorry. I never wanted to hurt you. I should've said something. I know, I should've said something a long time ago. But by the time I retired, it didn't seem to matter anymore."

"Didn' seem to matter?" Karla was crying and holding back the need to collapse under the table.

"I mean, what happened. What happened didn't seem to matter after all those years."

"But it matters to me, Pop!" She wailed, this time raising her voice even louder. Bill started to lean into her. Tapping her back and whispering for her to calm down, that the bartender was going to call security. It didn't work.

Ramone tried to make it right. "Ok, Ok. I'm sorry. I said I was sorry, Ok? I should've seen that. But Bill is right. I couldn't talk about it. I would've lost my badge. Kid's talk. You would've talked."

Silence. *Just tell me about her. Stop making fucking excuses and just tell me about HER. I just want to know who she was.*

Taking in another deep breath, Ramone seemed to read her mind. "She was a prostitute, Karla." He whispered. "One of my street

328

informants. It was a part of the job back then. Not that it was right. It was just the job."

"What?! Jus' the job?! Right. Right. Just the job. You used her for information. You slept with her for information? Oh, for Fucks sake, Pop! Wha' the…"

"No, it wasn't right. But it's what we did. It's what everyone did. And besides. I fell in love with her, Karla. In the end, I loved her. I did. But I couldn't do anything about that."

"Oh, I'm sure you couldn't. And I'm sure you did, Pop, such a sweet love story. Really? Everybody was doin' it? That's your explanation? I haven' used that one since I was twelve, Pop. I can't believe…."

"Karla, Please. Just let me finish…"

"No! I think I've heard enough! You son of a bitch!" Karla started to stand to leave, nearly falling down with her unsteady balance. She caught herself by putting her hand on the back of the chair and turned back around. "So, how'd she die, Pop? Did you take me from her? Did she kill 'erself? Is that why you never tol' me? Why didn't I just stay with her or her family? And how'd you get me without anyone findin' out I was yours, anyway?"

"She died from a drug overdose, Karla. I knew you were mine all along, and I'd look in on the two of you regularly to make sure you were cared for. I'd give her money and hired a babysitter for her and everything. I worked it out, so it was part of her payment for helping out. Kept it all legit.

Karla started to laugh a sarcastic, hateful laugh. "All legit…that's classic. You kept it all legit. Wow, Pop. Of course. That's what's was important. It was all legit."

"Oh, for God's sake, Karla, don't get all self-righteous. It was my job, I was in love with her, and I did what I thought was best at the time. And

329

then, she, well, then she.…..." He took in a deep breath. "I didn't know what to do. And I couldn't have you placed into foster care. No one else knew, well except Bill here. So, I lied and said that I had grown fond of you and arranged for a legal adoption. It was all legal, Karla. I swear, I just couldn't lose my job or you. I had already lost her. It was a different time…"

Karla was dumbfounded, numb. Her lips tingled and her hands shook. Tears streamed down her face, as she swayed gently, leaning up against the tall beam behind the booth. "All legal. That's all it ever is to you. Right or wrong, as long as it's legal. I'm sure sleepin' with your informant was never legal, Pop. Just because it was the way things were done? Oh…." She breathed through a cruel laugh. "…and you fell in love with her. So, that made it all ok? You're a fraud, Pop. A fucking, selfish, insensitive, lying fraud!" Karla grabbed her bag in a flash and ran from the lounge disappearing into the lobby and into an elevator, holding her face from the crowd of onlookers in the lobby.

Once the elevator doors closed, Karla pounded the button to her floor and leaned against the wall, sobbing. When the doors opened, she darted through them and rushed to her room, shaking while trying to get her key to light up the lock. "Fucking bullshit!" She whispered. The door clicked and she dropped to the floor, just inside the door, pounding it with her fist until it closed. *This is all just a bunch of fucking bullshit! All you assholes are just a bunch of fucking bullshit!* Karla buried her face into her hands, then wrapped her arms around her head, closing her elbows down around her face, tucking in as tight as she could into the corner of the wall. *She's dead and buried. There's no finding her. Just like this whole case thing. Buried. Why are we even here?*

330

Chapter 33

This isn't all there is. It can't be. Karla stood outside in the garden area of Pastor Hanson's home, surrounded by flowers and a stone waterfall. He had been Curtis and Ruth's Pastor in 1975. He was older now, a lot older, but his memory was pretty much intact. Karla was watching the sky, when he offered her a chance to sit down. This startled her from her thoughts. "There's a bench right there. Please, sit."

"You have a beautiful place." Karla smiled a gesture of thanks as his wife came through the back door and handed her a cup of tea. He didn't hesitate to start right in. "I've thought of Betsy often over the years. Hard to believe it's been about 40 years. I don't know how much I can really help. I was a friend of Curtis'. Ruth, too of course. It'd thrill my heart for someone to prove he didn't do it."

"Well, that's what we're working on."

"I talked to Trey just the other day. It was really good to speak with him. We actually have spoken some over the years, his brother too. Such good children. So very sad. How it all went down. Just so sad." He shook his head in somber thought.

"I know. I actually called him before calling you. I have some questions. He said you'd be the best person to ask."

"I don't know what more I can give you. I talked to your father already. He said you weren't feeling well the day he came over. You seem well today."

"Yes, I am. My reason for being here, well, it's a little different than my Pop's'."

"Oh, how so?"

"I know Ruth had a belief system, well, a faith, so to speak. Did Betsy? Is there a chance people have an afterlife, even without having any kind of faith to hang it on?"

"That's quite a question. I'll do my best to help you."

"It's just that Betsy didn't seem to have it much together. She wasn't exactly a saint, or religious, and I never heard anything about her going to church. But, I just, I find it hard to believe that God, well, if there is one, that this God would ignore the person that everyone said she was and focus just on what she did."

"Oh, well that's an easy one. God loves everyone, so much so that he gave his Son, Jesus, to make right everything that is wrong in us. She didn't have to be perfect, act a certain way or even go to church. She just had to have faith, that God is, and that God's life, his physical form, was given for her. It's just a matter of God's forgiveness and healing of her soul. It's not God's wrath or expectation that we are perfect on our own."

Karla smiled at the thought. Not just for Betsy, not just for her mother's sake, either.

She allowed the preacher to elaborate for some time. Simply nodding as he spoke on and on about what could have made all the difference for Betsy. *It was a bit too late for that. She's gone.* Karla questioned his reasoning. She questioned everything. *She still would have died.*

Her haphazard nods, and questioning looks in her eyes, didn't slow him down. "You know, when I was with her in the hospital, that time she was first attacked and lived through it, I just kept telling her that she needed to be thinking about her relationship with God, the afterlife, and who she was in Christ. It was all so scary for her. And you know, I think she took it all very seriously. She really seemed to. I hope so. I really do." He was sincere, and it was clear he was passionate in his beliefs.

Karla tuned in to his sincerity. It struck a chord with her, this sincerity. The preacher kept using the word 'relationship'. Relationship with God. *Such a strange concept.* The thought of a God who wants a relationship with his creation confused her but intrigued her all the same. *Interesting. Ruth, no doubt had this. Everyone spoke of it. So why, then, did she die like that? She still died anyway. In spite of believing. She still died.*

He seemed to read her mind. "It's a personal decision, very personal. You may never know if someone has faith or not. And it doesn't mean life here is perfect, or devoid of pain or even death. It just means life after death. Faith is hope that there is more than this."

Hope. What an idea.

"And it's the forgiveness, you know. It's what does it. What makes it possible. Forgiveness makes so much possible, you know."

Forgiveness. Karla thought about the song written by Don Henley from the popular band, the Eagles, who started their musical phenomena in the 1970's. Her father used to listen to that album a lot. She had a sudden image of being held by someone, a woman's hands, swaying to the song. She had an inclination that she may have danced with her to that song. The image was more than she could bare. It seemed to be a real memory. *It couldn't be. The times and my age wouldn't fit. But it feels good to pretend that it was.*

She was only half listening now. She heard the word 'heaven'. He was talking about heaven. *Heaven. Is that what has drawn me to the photo of little Tristan on the bridge? Was he in heaven? If so, he must have so much to talk about with Ruth. Tristan and his mother.* That thought struck a nerve. A soft, but damaged nerve. *With his mother.*

Karla was brought back to reality with the buzz of her cell phone. "Oh, do you need to take that, dear?" He was polite. Karla was polite back. "I should. I'll call right back, though. I'm sorry. Can I get in touch with you this week? I'd love to chat more, but this is a call I need to return, and it's getting later than I expected." She sincerely didn't want to leave. Once in the rental car, she sat in silence. The call was actually from Ramone. And she didn't call him back. She drove to the nearest park and wrestled in her own thoughts. She didn't want to go back to the hotel. She didn't want to see him. She wanted some peace of mind that this isn't all there is. *I want more than this. I don't want to just solve a case. I want the hope that they are still alive. Somewhere. To know that Tristan, as a grown-up man, is able to look to his mother as he used to do, while she sings the songs he remembers. I want the hope that two playful young boys are sitting beside Betsy unusually still and content by the sound of her voice, as she tells them a story. I want to see the image of a little girl named Tiffany holding her mother's hand and giggling, as they splash water at each other in fun. I want that hope. I want to be that little girl.*

Chapter 34

I can't take this anymore. Ramone tried to maintain his momentum, not giving up on his pursuit for justice, especially after his most recent telephone conversation. Too many thoughts whirled within him, all disconnected and scattered, which was highly unusual for him. Clarity was a trait he flaunted. A trait he carried plastered to his chest like the badge he used to hold so dear. *This has to stop. This lack of concentration is going to make me insane. It simply has to stop.*

Standing at the service counter and glancing behind him, he looked first to the front lobby doors, then to the elevator. Again, he looked back to the doors, scanning the sidewalk outside through the wide glass, and then again to the elevator. The clerk returned with a new set of room card keys. "Here you go. We do charge for lost keys. It will simply show up on the final bill. You said another week, right? Thank you for your extended stay. We love having you." Her smile seemed to be a part of her meticulously tailored uniform.

Slipping the cards into his pocket, Ramone loaded the elevator. He felt so many things: anxious, annoyed, frustrated, confused, and reluctantly guilt ridden and sad. He suppressed the latter emotions, which were emotions he wasn't accustomed to admitting having. Not to mention, he was worried. That one was at the forefront. That one

335

brought fear so deep into his soul that he suppressed it more than the others. He couldn't give in to fear. *Get it together. She's fine. She has to be.* But as his hands began to shake when he placed the key into the doorframe of Karla's room, he thought that fear just might take over. *What if she's there? Worse yet, what if she's not. She's surely to get angry. I have no right to lie to the front desk clerk and gain entrance to the only place where she could hide.* It wasn't right. But he entered anyway.

He slowly pushed the door open into the darkness of the room. *I hope she's not here. She'll attack, thinking I'm an intruder. I taught her well. I guess I am an intruder. She might just attack anyway, even if she knows it's me.* Coming in through the door, he peeked. He stood and was quiet. The room was silent. She wasn't here. *Where are you?*

Gazing around the room, he was sickened by what he saw. The room was in complete disarray. Laundry was all over the floor. On the bed were files shuffled across the bed in piles, and scattered papers milled amongst disheveled blankets and sheets. Photocopies of photographs were haphazardly stacked next to a pillow. Despite the mess, the piles of work were a welcomed sight. *She's been working.*

What bothered him was the number of mini-bar bottles, the plastic kind with the screw-on lids. They were scattered everywhere, all over the room, on the bed stand, on the floor near the pillows. And three empty bottles of Nyquil stood amidst the used tissues on the dresser, near the T.V. Two left over paper bags from Burger King and a plastic City Market bag with an empty box of trail mix peering out from within, all made the room look as if she was homeless. *At least she's been eating.*

Ramone stood at the end of the bed. *How did I miss this? How did I not know that she was this much of a mess? Worse yet, how do I not know where she is now?* It had been almost a week since their fight. Well, not his fight so much. He had struggled with the words to say. She had done nearly all of the yelling. And he couldn't forget the crying. He never dealt well

336

with the crying. That's because he never cried. A thought in the pit of his gut told him it was time to pay attention to the elephant in the room that was his soul.

A sigh gave him the energy to gather all of the remnants of her most recent study session. It seemed she had been searching for something specific. She had what appeared to be piles of sorting, and each group seemed to be categorized somehow. He scanned a few papers now in his hands. One was a copy of Ruth Bakerson's autopsy. Not easy reading and not for the light of heart. Then he found reports from the autopsy of the two young boys who had been shot in the head at a very close range. He hadn't remembered giving her these. *When did she make copies?* Then something he hadn't seen before caught his eye. *How did she get this?* He was told he couldn't get these reports without going through more complicated channels. And that's if they could be released to him at all.

Karla had scrawled a question across the top of the first page: *'They were dressed?'* He thought about this and remembered that this had been mentioned in a police report. *That's right. They were found dressed. One even had a shoe still on. A pair of the boy's shoes were found in her car, on the floor of the passenger's side, with money tucked inside one of them. Betsy's male suitor on that night had said that the boys were put to bed in their underwear earlier that night. So, why were they dressed when they were found?*

This was relevant since the prosecution claimed that Curtis killed Ruth because of marital problems, then Betsy and the boys were killed because they got in the way somehow and could identify him as Ruth's murderer. It was proposed that he then carelessly and haphazardly loaded them all up quickly for disposal. *Curtis wouldn't take the time to dress the children after killing them. That's absurd. They were put to bed in their underpants. But then, they went somewhere. Somewhere alive. Betsy took the time to dress them. Meaning she prepared them to leave after her male suitor left.*

337

As Ramone kneeled onto the bed, he glanced over each document that he placed neatly into a pile, trying to get an idea as to what angle she was following. The folder that contained all of the witness testimonies in the trial fell from his arms and to the floor. *Why did she need to go through these? I had scrutinized every one of these testimonies meticulously myself.*

He scanned a copy of the primary witness testimony for the prosecution. The testimony given by an old woman across the street was nothing short of a mockery to any respectable trial procedure. He hadn't given that one much consideration at all. He was disgusted that her testimony was even used, and more absurd was the fact that her testimony was taken seriously by any respectable lawman. He had no doubts that her words were the Prosecutor's words, not to mention that when the victims were first reported missing, all the neighbors had been initially interviewed, and this woman hadn't reported anything unusual happening that night, at least not at that time. Not until the Prosecutor had gotten a hold of her.

Ramone sat down to review the material. *It's possible I missed something. Slightly possible.* He read through her testimony and mulled briefly on a few of the others. *I already know what's in these. We've talked about all of these things.* In hindsight, he realized that he had done most of the talking.

Ramone came across another neighbor's testimony, this one much more credible. Karla had highlighted a section regarding something that was heard by a neighbor around 1:30 in the morning the night of the murders. 'Oh no!' was what the neighbor had said she had heard. *I remember this. It was odd.* The prosecution had claimed that Curtis Bakerson killed four people around 1:00 in the morning, then drug them into his vehicle between 1:00-1:30 am. But then, a neighbor hears this outburst of shock shortly after they had supposedly just been killed. Not

338

a scream, nor the sound of a struggle. No gunshots, nor fighting. But simply, *'Oh no!'*

This report seemed so out of context for the given scenario. The witness said she saw a vehicle stop, a man get out, walk to Betsy's house, back to the vehicle, then drove away with the lights off. The witness then went back to bed. It was after she had fallen back to sleep and had woken up later that she heard it. *"Oh no!"* That was all it was.

He read the report more thoroughly, making note of what he already knew about the other witnesses and what they reported. *Wait a minute. Her boy came home from being out with a friend. Said he was at the drive-in, then went and got food, and his buddy dropped him off in his truck. Another neighbor heard a car door slam, near the same time. A third neighbor hears a loud vehicle. Another hears loud noises, like yelling. But all of these neighbors were on the far west end of the street. Not near the Kendall home, but down the street. The only one who heard any kind of actual scream was the young man next to the Bakerson house. And he described it as a nightmare-like scream. It's so simple. The neighbors on the west end of the street heard this woman's boy coming home from being out. The "oh no!" came later. The neighbor near the Bakerson house hears one of the boys having a nightmare. The reports don't actually tell of any screams near the Kendall home at all. No one from across the street or down on the east end of the street testified, except the blind lady on medication. Jesus, this is so logical, it's ridiculous how I'm just figuring this out.*

Ramone continued to scan through Karla's mess to gather up and organize everything. He sifted through a pile of handwritten investigation notes that he hadn't seen before. *Where is she getting this new stuff from?* He was somewhat annoyed that she hadn't been keeping him in the loop. Even though he knew it was his fault. A report written by a sheriff's investigator caught his attention. It spoke of a relative of the Kendall family who had called in a tip about Suzanne and Betsy. It stated that the two women had crossed a drug dealer and that he was sure that this drug dealer would be out to get them as soon as he got out of prison. *What the hell....did anyone follow up on this? How many references is this now, from completely different people indicating this was about drugs somehow.*

Ramone paused to process and clear his head. He had to keep going. Karla had all this stuff out for a reason. He went back to the neighborhood witness reports and re-read the report from a neighbor near the Bakerson home who had heard whining, or whimpering sounds, sounds that were described by the witness as "nightmare" sounds. Again, not screaming, or sounds of a struggle, but whimpering. This verified his line of thinking. *Yep, this guy's bedroom window was on the same side as the Bakerson's two bedrooms. He could have easily heard them crying.*

In a flood of thought, Ramone began making connections he had missed. *'She wasn't where she was supposed to be.'* He remembered this comment from an interview and realized something important. He connected the dots to a report that stated a man had called Betsy that evening. A man who fit the same description had been seen at her home two additional times later that day, and that evening. A red truck had been seen parked in front of her house that day as well. *Betsy was supposed to have been meeting someone that night. Something important enough that someone was hounding her about it, making multiple trips to her house looking for her. When she didn't show, wherever she was supposed to be, he came by looking for her again. But she was already gone when he got there. They were all gone. What were you up to Betsy? What were you up to?*

Ramone stopped. His shoulders dropped, and he lowered his chin to his chest.

Karla is gone. Karla, where are you? What are you up to, Karla?

Ramone almost got lost in his despair. But only for a moment. He quickly realized that he was wasting time. *I've memorized most of this shit. Just figure out where she could be.* As he filtered the piles and piles of

340

carefully typed or handwritten information into smaller piles, daring a sense of organization, a yellow piece of lined notebook paper slid from the folder in his hand and landed in front of him on the bed.

The last name of the well-known district attorney who prosecuted the case was written at the top of the page. *What's this? I don't remember this, either.* It had gotten lost in the mayhem of the thousands and thousands of documents he had read. *How did I not remember this? The writing is my handwriting for heaven's sakes.*

As Ramone read over the scribbled page, it began to come back to him. *Oh, yes. The diaries. The ones that had been admittedly burned and thrown into the river by Betsy's Sherriff Deputy boyfriend. This evidence that had been destroyed by a sworn-in county official. Who could forget this? How did I let this one slip?* The words had been hand-copied from a memo hidden away in a remote and forgotten file at the courthouse. Karla had highlighted the date midway down the page, but he read the entire memo to take in the context of its purpose:

"*Page 195   Article 556   # 7*
Criminal action # X-10065
Letter   May 3, 1976
Gerry McAlister to Stephen Fielder:
No objection to your requests. I thought you already had inspected the diaries in our possession. If not, they are available to you. The information you requested has just recently been turned over to you."

Ramone was dumbfounded that he had missed this. *Son of a bitch! They had the diaries during the trial investigations? After the arrest? What the hell? If they had the diaries during the investigation, and there had been anything in there about Curtis, they would've used it in trial. But they didn't. Information*

341

in those diaries wasn't about Curtis. The sworn-in testimony that "the" diary was destroyed before it went into custody was false. Ramone needed to find Karla. *What the hell was she up to?*

Ramone scanned his cell phone for Bill's contact name. With a click, the phone was ringing on the other end. "Hey, are you busy?"

"No, just came in from watering my plants. What's up? Have you talked to her yet?"

No, I haven't found her. I'm in her room, and she's been here recently. Looks like she's been working."

"You broke into her room? jesus man have a little bit of dignity. What if she had been there? You could've ended up with another fight on your hands."

"She wasn't. And what difference would it make at this point? She's never going to speak to me again anyway."

"You know that's not true. Hey, listen, I wanted to talk to you anyway. Remember that guy you interviewed right at first? The one who left the department that same year? Ya, I found out that he was in the hospital, so I went to see him."

Ramone held the phone in place with the top of his shoulder snug tightly to his ear, while he finished gathering up papers and stuffing them into folders. He stuffed each folder neatly into his now open briefcase, listening half-heartedly.

"You still there?"

"Yeah. Go on."

"Well, he didn't remember me, but I told him I was helping you with all of this, and he seemed surprised that you were still on it. But, in his medicated stupor, he made a comment…"

"Get to the point. I'm headed out of here, and I wanna come see you. I've got some things to run by you."

"Ok, Ok. Did you ever hear from anywhere that the Chief had a fling with Betsy?"

"The Chief? No. Why?

"Well, he made an off-the-cuff comment about 'that son of a bitch was sleeping with her' and then he said 'he beat'er up, you know', but then when I tried to get him to say more, he went off onto something completely different and I couldn't bring him back. This guy didn't like the Chief much, and he made no apologies for saying so. But, then, he rambled on about other cops too. I wasn't sure exactly who he was even talking about at first. I just thought if you had come across him somewhere else, you know, someone else that said he knew Betsy."

"Well, I did talk to an old railroader awhile back who somehow seemed to think he knew the ins-and-outs of department gossip. He made an off-handed remark that everybody knew down at the department that the Chief was being investigated by the feds. He said they had some kind of file on him. But he too wouldn't go on about it. Changed the subject real fast and all. I asked him to clarify and tried to get more, and he said 'Clarify what? No, that isn't what I meant.' Like I heard him wrong or something, even though I know I didn't. And then he wouldn't say anymore. I couldn't substantiate it with anything or anyone else, so I chalked it up to useless gossip. You think there's something to it?"

"Well, maybe. Not admissible if we can't verify it."

"Yeah, well, I'm not comin' up with much that's admissible. I need some help you know. You got any contacts I can look into? I need to get someone else on this. There's shit out there that can clear this thing up, and we both know it. I just can't get my hands on it. And the reason I

343

called, something I forgot, so, I'm sure I never mentioned it, but did you know that the DA had possession of Betsy's diaries in May of '76?"

"What? I'm confused. I thought those were destroyed? What? How'd?...ok, just show me. I've got a mess here with my garden I gotta clean up. Water all over the place. Let's meet for lunch. I'll buy this time."

Already outside loading into the car, Ramone clicked the call to an end. He leaned back into the seat and breathed in deep, trying to calm his nerves. *Karla, where are you?* He drove the car east, heading down Main Street, the tourist trap of town. Ramone then passed a line of narrow two-story brick buildings, not having any reason to take notice of the peculiar sign portraying a woman with a tall fluffy hairdo dangling a martini glass that hung above the front door of a quaint little tavern. The door to the bar was inconspicuous, which is why Karla chose this place to hide out in the first place.

Chapter 35

Karla sat on her barstool, holding a tinkling glass in the palm of her hand. Shannon leaned over the bar on one elbow. "So, have you talked to your Pop, yet? You know, you need to settle this thing. It's not healthy. You gotta forgive 'im."

She took a sip. "Yes, I know. One thing at a time, though, right?" She opened her purse and rummaged through her wallet, pulling out the old photo of her mother.

"She's pretty, isn't she?"

"Like mother, like daughter." Shannon winked. Karla admired the photo with pride.

Shannon watched Karla study the photo as if she'd never done that before.

"He's human, you know." Her tone was low and sincere.

"Hmm. I know." Karla's eyes didn't flinch. "Her eyes were soft." Then she looked up.

"Get me one more for the road. I've got a few things yet to do before I call him."

"One more Coca-Cola for the road, it is!" She smiled at Karla genuinely. "No need to cut you off today, do I?" Shannon sprayed a hiss of soda into her glass. Randall was sitting beside her and leaned into to her with a nudge. "Who am I gonna drink with, with you all going clean and sober on me?"

"Well, you just gotta stop all your nonsense then, I guess!"

"Not 'till hell freezes over." Shannon teased.

"It could happen. Well, prob'ly not." He snickered, his rugged teeth showing without apology. "So, if you're headed back home, is your Pop gonna stay and wrap things up?"

"I don' know. There's a lot more to do. But, I don't know how we can....he can, do it alone. It's so complicated. No wonder they rushed into an easy conviction so quickly. I get it. People were scared. They needed someone fast, to appease the community. I don't have to tell you, but it still seems crazy that they arrested him so quickly. Managed to get all the evidence they needed in a matter of less than two months. How do you get enough evidence to convict someone of murder in that short of time? That poor thing. She was in the middle of so much. Like a damn spider web. A very big, tightly knit, spider web. They all got caught up in it. I guess that's what happens, huh? People just get caught up in shit."

"Some wiggle their way out of it, and some don't." The old man's eyes teared up slightly, and then he cleared his throat. "You're best to head home. In the big city, at least people can hide from the past." Today, Randall was unusually somber. If Karla didn't know any better, she thought he might be sad to see her leaving. He took a drink from his beer bottle and tipped it in her direction.

Shannon broke the mood of the room. "You've been keeping track of your thinking, right? You know they say that when you write things down, things seem to make more sense." As bartenders go, her advice was always practical.

346

"Well, yes, as a matter of fact I have been. My journal is full of my thoughts. Mostly useless crap. And still pretty muddy. I guess it helps. But this thing, this whole thing, it's just muddy. I don't think there's any way around that."

"You'd be surprised. Go back through it. Just keep going back through it. It'll come together. It'll make sense in time. And I'm not talking about this whole case you're working on."

Yes, I know. You mean me, pull me all together. I get it. She rubbed the new cross pendant that she had purchased for herself between her fingertips. And hers had a picture of her mother in it. *It is well, it is well....with my soul.*

"You're wearing jewelry now? That's new." Shannon wiped drops of condensation from around her glass with a dry towel.

"Yeah. A gift of sorts, you could say. I mean, I bought it. But there was definitely a gift involved." She slid the tip of her forefinger onto the smooth surface of the stone carving, as her thumb held it still against her skin. She gulped down the last of her soda and stood to her feet. "Well, I'm burning daylight. I got places to go. You guys take care." She winked and looked to Randall reaching out for a hug. "You'll have to find a new a poker buddy, but I'm sure you'll manage."

"Wait." His abrupt hesitation startled her. "I gotta take a pee. Be right back."

Karla looked at Shannon and giggled. "Oh, this is new." She sat back down, only partially, with one leg still in the upright position, but the other leaning against the frame of the bar. Shannon busied herself while Karla idly waited. Randall scuffled back within a few minutes and reached out to hug her again. "Sorry. You know, some things just can't wait."

"I know, Randall, you gotta go when you gotta go."

His big bulky jacket pressed into her with unusual tightness. *He's sad I'm leaving.*

How cute, but sad. She stepped back and glanced at his face. *Someday, my friend, you'll be calling me. I just know it.*

Karla stood on the sidewalk, almost wanting to go back inside. She looked into the sky for strength, while tucking her larger-than-life handbag up close against the right side of her rib cage, where it nestled in comfortably. She fixed the loose straps tighter on top of her shoulders and walked confidently back toward the hotel. *Time to make this right.*

Karla decided to call him instead of just barge in on him at the hotel. While digging into her bag for her phone, she felt something out of place. She pulled the large manila envelope into full view, unsettled. *Strange. What is this?* It was sealed shut.

Confusion gave way to intrigue. Not trying to make too much sense of it, but just trying to figure out what it was, Karla poked her forefinger into the loose grip of its seal and slid it across the top, revealing an old book of some sort on the inside of the envelope. She knew it was old, as it smelled of that attic smell, almost as if the moisture from a hundred years ago were finally escaping through the cracked pores of the cover. Pulling it from its protective hideaway, she ran her fingers up and down its wrinkled surface, front and back. Well worn, with holes and lines randomly breaking across the material, it wasn't soft, like a new leather-bound book should be, but hard and coarse. This made it clear that it wasn't real leather, but an imitation, now thin and brittle. The pages were well worn, with faded splotches of dirty yellow that had been tinged with the stains of time.

She quickly, too quickly, sifted through the pages. It wasn't a book after all. The handwritten images of words and sentences on the lined

348

paper began to clear her path to discovery. There were dates affixed at the top of each page, as each page was revealed. Some dates were on the top right side of the page, high in the corner, but some were written on the first line at the left of the page. The writing was neat on some pages, but messy on others. These were clearly paragraphs, and even with the inconsistent writing patterns, clearly written by the same person.

The dates sparked a sudden sense of gleeful panic, striking her central nervous system with glitches of activity that made her chest rise and fall at an increasing rate. Flipping through the pages, scanning each date, created anticipation that Karla could hardly contain: March 23....March 31, 1975.... April 2, 1975....April 10, 1975....April 28....June 15....July 18, 1975....She turned through the pages skimming faster and faster, then slower and slower. As Karla scanned through the contents on each page that she came to, she turned the pages back over to the front inside cover. Her hands were shaking. *Holy shit. This can't be...this is....is this...? Oh Lord, I gotta call Pop. Now. No. wait. Just take it to him. Show him. That'll be better.*

Karla's excitement gave way to reality as she bolted into the lobby of the hotel. She had nearly sprinted all the way there. Something tugged within her to slow down. To think this through. *Just read it. Read it first.* She impatiently waited for the elevator to climb to the floor of her room and fumbled with the key getting it to unlock. When she entered her room, she felt a sick sensation that something was wrong. Her room had been invaded. All of her things were gone from her bed. *Son of a bitch! Oh, shit, what the hell?!*

With her hands shaking, she reached into her pocket to call her father. *He's going to be pissed. But this is serious. My things are gone! I'm sorry I threw such a tantrum. Forget all that! He just has to hear me out.* She knew he must be worried, since he had left her a bunch of messages, every day, all week long, and especially since she refused to answer when he came to her room. She pushed those thoughts of guilt aside. *I'm the one who's mad at him, after all.*

Background music played on her end of the phone while waiting for Ramone to answer. Karla rummaged through her workbag, thinking maybe she was just losing her mind. *Had I just put all of the work away and had simply forgotten?* Her phone lid loosely in her hand up to her ear, waiting, but more focused on the knowledge that someone had been in her room. Things were missing. Then her father answered, which startled her. She paused, putting her phone on speaker "Hello? Pop?" *Just breathe.* "Ok Pop…Hi…I, Umm… I'm Sorry, I…I'm so sorry…"

"Oh good God, Karla. It's you. What the hell…?

"Pop, I know. I'm sorry. I should have let you know that I was ok. I'm ok. I am. Really. I am. I'm sorry. I know…Ok, just listen…please?…Just hear me out, ok?"

"Where are you? I went by your room. They let me have another set of keys. I know you like your space and all, but God, c'mon Karla, you wouldn't answer my calls or my messages, or even my texts. My God, Karla, I've been worried sick. Please, where…."

"I'm up at my room. You said you were here? Did you get my…"

"Damn, it was a mess, Karla. Yes. I gathered it all up. I have it. I'll be right there."

"You have it? All of it? For God's sakes Pop, I was freakin' out! No, no. Just wait. I have something to do first. I'm headed out again. I just lost my shit when all the stuff was gone. You should've let me know."

"I did. Check your damn messages. Where are you off to? Just meet me at the hotel. I'll be right there. I mean, what the hell are you after? I went through some of it and you…"

"The same thing you are, Pop. The truth. They were loved. They meant something. Just let me do what I need to do. I won't be long. I

350

won't be at the hotel. Please, just give me a few hours. I promise. I just need a few hours. And, well, Ok. Here's the deal. Can you meet me at the bridge? I know it's a bit of a drive, but I will explain there. Let's just say in a few hours? Just give me that much time. I won't ask for anything ever again."

He was tired of fighting. He needed her back. She needed her time. He gave in.

"Ok, Ok. You sure you don't need a ride? I could...
"Pop, I'm good. We really do need to talk, though. Ok?"

"But, you're ok, though? You don't hate me?"

"I never did, Pop. I'm sorry you thought that. I'm fine now, really. See you later, ok?"

And she was fine. *You just have to trust me, Pop. We have to trust each other.*

Chapter 36

Ramone hung up the phone and leaned over, putting his face into the palms of his hands. The weight of his mid-section made it hard for him to catch his breath. Bill scooted forward on the sofa, sitting across from him and leaned in. "I told you she would call when she was ready."

Ramone looked up with relief all over his worn and tired face. "I'm too old for this, Bill. What am I doing? Thinking I could make sense of her?"

"She's all grown up. You gotta let her be grown up."

"Ok. Ok. It's fine, right. She's fine. Ok." He wiped his face, embarrassed that he had begun to break down like that. Gaining his composure, he went back into the place he knew best. Work. It was a quick shift back to the task at hand, but Ramone didn't know any other way. He paused briefly before continuing. "Now that that's ok. She's ok, right? Where were we?"

"That's it?" Bill chuckled. "Where has she been?"

"Didn't ask. She's all grown up now, right?"

"Alright,   then."
They sat silent for a moment. The only sound was their breathing.

"Ok. So, we have this list of evidence, but only a small handful ended up being used in the trial." Ramone paused, looking down at the paperwork on the coffee table in front of him.

The coffee shop style deli was nearly empty at this time of day. They were both pleased with this. It gave them the chance to talk freely and openly. Ramone rubbed his forehead. "Why is that? I mean, really, they didn't have much, so why ignore all of this other stuff? They certainly couldn't put him at the scene. Not him, nor his wirecutters, nor his gun. They couldn't even identify the crime scene. Nonetheless, they tried to put him there."

"They speculated it was at the houses."

"Except the houses were cleaned, lived in. What are the chances that evidence collected after that much time could be of any use?"

"There had been activity at Betsy's house, per a witness."

"The witness. One who was old, blind, on medication, and who had been woken up, meaning she was in a sleepy stupor. Not to mention her story changed multiple times. She may have seen some activity. Activity. Lights, a man carrying something bulky, then a car, and a shadow of a man. Of course there was activity. There would've been activity at Betsy's. She had company, then he left, then she dressed the boys and left. Somehow, maybe with someone. That we don't know. We know she was planning on needing her car. And there's evidence the car was used that night. With her keys still in the ignition the next day, the boy's shoes there, and not to mention Ruth's shoe was found in her car. Jesus, how'd that get by everybody? Anyway, no doubt there was activity with her car that night. If the neighbor really did see a man loading something, then someone had helped her load her sleeping and dressed children into her car. But nobody saw Curtis. They saw someone. No one saw *him*. Ok, so the neighbors down at the west end of the street heard some

353

things, saw a car with its lights off, saw someone get out, walk near the Kendal house, get back in. But no one actually saw Curtis. They didn't hear a woman screaming, they heard yelling, a nightmare-like scream and whining, and someone yelling "Oh no!" If you look at the facts and only the facts, there's nothing pointing to Curtis. On the other hand, though, Curtis was seen by several people in the town of Ouray between 9:00 and 9:30 and then again, by another man and woman around 10:30pm. That place is over 2 hours away, if you drive over the speed limit, which his 4x4 could barely go 50 without the alignment shaking all over the place. Nearly two hours it would take in his 4x4. We have no problem showing Ruth's time of death around 10:30. It's all on record."

"You're right. Can't get past it. The times of death that the DA insisted on were wrong. Simply wrong."

"So, his alibi should've stuck."

"Ok, So what about the blood on the mat in his 4x4? That one is just as bizarre. Curtis was as meticulous and OCD as anyone can be. Isn't that what they call it now? Obsessive Compulsive Disorder? Anyway, he had been seen washing his car multiple times since they all disappeared. They even tried to use that against him, to say he washed it to cover up the smell of dead bodies away from the dog. I guess they didn't know him as well as they thought, did they?"

"Yes, I got this one. I double-checked the dates again that they had the vehicle in custody, just to make sure. It had been about a month and a half gone by when they found the spot of blood. And that was after they had the vehicle in custody for a complete search already more than once. In fact, they had the vehicle in custody a few times for complete searches before finding the blood."

"Ok, so it had been thoroughly cleaned, it had already been searched multiple times by law enforcement, and let's not forget that Curtis had his dog back there several times, had the boys back there, had loaded wood and equipment back there, all before a droplet of well intact blood was found, in plain sight. Beyond bizarre."

"It's almost comical when you put it like that."

"Not comical, really. A man's been in prison over it for nearly all of his adult life."

"How do people miss stuff like this? I mean, they didn't find a splatter or a smear, but claimed it was a perfect round little droplet that they had just accidentally missed. Then, when after the prosecution examined this droplet of blood, there was coincidently nothing left for the defense to examine, which isn't even supposed to be allowed."

"So, I guess around here, the courts don't have to follow the rules."

"Well, he did get a second trial because of all those bad calls by the judge. Nine counts of prejudice to be exact, is what the Colorado Supreme Court ruled."

"But we know the second trial was nothing more than a repeat of the first. There wasn't anything new in the second trial. They just rehashed the same shit, pretty much the same way."

"It must 'ave sounded good to the jury."
"It always sounds good to the jury when presented in the right way."

"So, what does that leave us? The gun? That was a big one, you know."
"And incredibly self-incriminating. He hung himself on that one."

"But, he was a gun thief. Of course he's gonna lie about it."
"But, why hide that one? He had stolen other guns."

"Besides that, he was a selfish son of a bitch, and he liked that damn gun? And it was in fact stolen. He's always said so. Besides, remember that he had heard from people at work that they were looking for a .22. The investigators asking around made no attempts to hide that fact. And he also knew they were tailing him and watching him like a hawk. Jesus, he was scared. Wasn't gonna admit that, as cocky as he was. He was scared they were going to pin this on him. So, he did what scared people do. Something stupid."

"Besides, they could never prove it was a .22, anyway. There were no slugs removed. Just fragments."

"So says the reports. Not the ex-cop who thinks Curtis is innocent. He says there were slugs."

"Well, the reports say there weren't. And that's what we have to use. Unless this guy wants to come forward. Which you and I both know, he won't."

"Ok. But even still, let's say it could be proven to be a .22. They still couldn't put him where the boys were shot. And they didn't have an actual murder weapon anyway. They couldn't put his gun at the crime scene or put his fingerprints on the murder weapon. They couldn't put any gun at all at the crime scene or in his hands. At all. They didn't even have a crime scene, for God's sakes. It is so preposterous that it makes my head spin. They convicted him solely on character. Now-a-days, it's called character bias."

"So, what do you make of that cop, Grant was his name, right? He testified to taking Curtis' guns because he said Ruth was afraid."

"Oh, yeah, Karla and I went over that pretty carefully. True, it didn't look good for him. But, still, isn't evidence that he killed anyone. Ruth only gave Grant some of Curtis' guns, not all of them, which kind of puts holes in the theory that she was afraid of Curtis having guns. The guns that were taken were never checked into evidence through the right procedures, and Grant gave them back pretty quickly, making me question if it was for Ruth's safety that he took them in the first place."

"Well, I guess he's just one of many in the never-ending list of people that we've got questions for. Nothing more than a simple person of interest, as far as I can see. We do solid work and just want some questions answered."

"We need more money. More pull." Ramone was visibly tired and frustrated.

"Then get it."

"You gonna help me with that, right?"

"I said I would."

"Well, I'm gonna call it an afternoon and try and go meet Karla. I've already got calls into that number you gave me. I'll try and see if I can just head over there. Maybe then, he'll respond."

Ramone gathered his things and parted ways with an ever-draining spirit that he just couldn't shake. At the same time, he felt so close to closing up this case. After all, the job was to find information that put Curtis' conviction into question. Not actually find out who really had committed these murders. His spirits lifted as he thought about seeing Karla. He loaded into the car, hopeful to see Karla soon. He had so much to say to her. He just didn't know where to begin.

Chapter 37

The drive was bumpy, but Karla didn't mind. She had been out to Bridgeport Bridge only once, just a few weeks back. It seemed much longer this time, though. The views of the landscape intrigued her, allowing her mind to wander. At first it was merely a deserted array of dry hills. But, as she got deeper in toward the river, the rocky terrain became alive with color, sharp edges, and vegetation. The gravel parking lot, at the entrance of this narrow canyon, was quiet. Only the sound of the river trickling past her broke the silence.

There were three vehicles parked along the cable divider, marking the parking lot, and intended to keep people away from the railroad tracks on the other side. The entrance to the boat ramp trail was clearly marked. Metal signs posted along the row of 4x4 studs planted deep in the earth warned of the legal ramifications for anyone treading anywhere but along the designated trails. Karla didn't have much experience walking near train tracks, so she gladly conceded to the warning signs.

Taking a swig from her water bottle, she knew the walk wasn't a mere hop skip and a jump away. Karla may have been raised a city girl, but she knew to drink sparingly on a walk of this length.

The trail was well marked, as it was literally a dirt road. The gated entrance that led to the water's edge, and subsequently to the bridge, had not always been blocked. Safety regulations now required a locked gate, only accessible by railroad personnel and the ranchers still living on the other side. However, foot traffic was still allowed, being public lands and all. It occurred to Karla that the road wasn't always such a highly restrictive path. In the 1970's, when the gate wasn't there, any vehicle could have used this road.

Life surrounded her in majestic scenery. *I can see why Ruth and her family loved it here.* Karla felt alive as she walked at the base of the canyon surrounded by rock walls. There was something magical about the red, yellow, and black stone surfaces dotted with green, yellow, and brown hues, providing homes to so many critters. She hoped to see some along the way. Life was everywhere, bringing life within her to the surface.

As she carefully crossed the railroad tracks, Karla could see the bridge up ahead and vaguely another one further up in the distance. There were two bridges now. Most people used the newer one to cross to the other side. The old bridge was now primarily used by the ranch. She wondered if the ranchers felt an invasion by people like her, being led here by such a dreadful cause.

Karla slowly approached the old bridge and shuttered unintentionally. It was an oddly intimidating structure, even though it wasn't a large bridge, as she was accustomed to in the city. Somehow this bridge held a respect all its own. It was old and wooden and held a history that stood the hands of time. That deserved a different sort of respect.

Walking onto the planks and facing downstream, Karla leaned over its barrier and peered into the running water below. She kneeled and then sat down on the edge with her legs dangling over the water. Her tennis shoes teased the water as she swayed them back and forth in the air. With anticipation, she pulled the diary from out of her bag. Karla lost herself in its contents, in its reality. She lost herself in them, in Ruth and Betsy, and in everyone they knew. She had already scanned it. She couldn't contain her curiosity. But here, at this place, at their initial resting place, she absorbed it, taking her time with it. It became too emotional for her to contain. The tears flowed freely, gently without restraint, but oddly with an undefined sense of tranquility.

Karla was hooked from the very first page. Well, actually on the page marked March 2, 1975. Her eyes scanned slowly at first, taking in every word. As she turned each page, she was more and more involved, and her reading rate increased. She lost track of time and had no idea what time it was at all when reached the page marked June 4, 1975.

By the time the page titled August 21, 1975 came and went, closing with the last words that Ruth Bakerson would be allowed to write, Karla couldn't bring herself to close it shut. She sat still, with tears streaming down her cheeks, holding it frozen in time in the palms of both hands. Almost in fear that if she closed it, the thought of who they were would disappear forever.

Blinking away the glare of the mid-day sun, Karla suddenly sensed that she wasn't alone. She hadn't heard anything, not consciously anyway. Karla turned slightly and saw him out of the corner of her eye. Ramone stood at the edge of the bridge, as if he was afraid to come near. He walked slowly toward her, his feet unsteady on the terrain, with his heavy frame difficult to maneuver. "Hey, princess." His voice was soft. Sincere.

She smiled, but didn't get up.

"Can I join you?"

"Of course." Karla finally and ever so gently closed the contents between her hands. *He doesn't need to know about this just yet.* She inconspicuously slipped it back into her bag, before he got too close.

Ramone walked to where she was sitting, and Karla stood to her feet to meet him. He reached out to her, hoping she would respond likewise. She did.

"Karla, I'm so sorry. I really am. I don't...."

"Stop. It's not necessary. I know."

"I'm not perfect." He whispered.

"Me neither. I guess I held you on some sort of pedestal or something."

"Well, not that you shouldn't." He laughed.

"Don't push your luck. Forgive me for being such a brat? You didn't deserve any of that. I didn't mean what I said. I really am sorry." She nudged him.

"Isn't forgiveness a byproduct of love? At least that's what I've heard. I'm no expert, and the jury is still out. I do love you, despite everything I kept from you."

Karla let out a deep laugh. "Smart ass." She put her face into the hollow of his broad shoulder and closed her eyes. "Did she love me?"

"More than you will ever know."

"Was she kind?"

"Yes. Very."

"Will you talk about her more often? The good stuff, anyway?"

"Yes. I can do that. There's plenty to tell. By the way, she was an artist. You do have memories after all. You just didn't know that's what they were."

"I'd like to hang around for just a bit, and then I have an errand or two to run. If that's ok with you. And also, I think I wanna go home."

"Yes. And, ok. I've already booked you a flight for the day after tomorrow. I'm staying here though. There's some loose ends to tend to before we bring in some help."

"You know, Pop. There's something you need to see. I don't know how we missed it. But, you're gonna like it."

"Alright."

Karla rummaged around within her bag, careful not to expose Ruth's diary. She pulled out a document typed on an old typewriter. Handing it to him she stood quiet as he read it. She could tell by his facial expression when he got to the good part. He glanced up at her. "Betsy wasn't a drug dealer. And she wasn't a hard user, either, just like everyone said. Of course, it's been right there the whole time. Betsy was an informant. She was doing the right thing."

Karla shook her head in agreement, with a smile. "And Ruth was helping her."

Ramone looked at it again, and this time, he read it out loud. As he read, Karla imagined Betsy's voice speaking as if in real time.

"The Sheriff's Dept. has been after me to go back to work with the MEG team, but I keep saying no. Even though I'm against hard drugs, I learned to hate that job. (I always believed in punishing the pusher and treating the user. The law believes in punishing both). The only thing I liked about it is that it brought me to you...."

Ramone gave a thoughtful gaze out into the distance. "So when was this written? And to whom?"

"It's right there, in the top right corner. But, there's only a first name. May be hard to track down."

"Hard, but not impossible. And, oh yes, here it is, March that same year. So, they were wanting her to go *back* to the job, meaning she had already done work with law enforcement before. I wonder what MEG stands for?"

"Well, I have a hunch that it means 'Metropolitan Enforcement Group'. Just a hunch." Karla grinned.

"Hmmm. A hunch, huh? What have you been up to? Do I ask where you get these hunches of yours?"

"Not right now. Another day maybe."

"But Mesa County wasn't metropolitan, especially not in those days. And that's not the same thing as that MCNET program we came across. Makes me wonder if they were different programs or just a reorganization of programming. The DEA was still really young in those years. So much was changing."

"True. I'm thinking it wasn't necessarily a local thing she was sharing information about. Maybe something on a bigger scale? There was that report that said someone thought she may have been planning a trip to Salt Lake City. We know for sure she had plans to go to Los Angeles. Salt Lake City could be on the way. And Salt Lake City is where the DEA had done restructuring in '73 and all. They were funding all sorts of operations that were looking more for bigger fish than small time users or dealers, not that small-time action didn't bring in its share of the money. It's just that the way I see everything, the users weren't who Betsy was concerned with. The people she wanted to see go down? They

363

were the big shots, the abusers of authority. That's who she was after. The hard-core money was in cocaine. Yeah, there was all kinds of other stuff, weed, LSD, heroin, even Methamphetamines was cropping up back then. But we know she had information regarding someone or some event in Aspen. That speaks of something high-end. Somebody with money or power, or both."

"You're right. There was that report that said there were three train tickets scheduled for Salt Lake City that had never been used. I didn't follow up on that because there was no way to verify who purchased the tickets. So, I brushed it off."

"Yes, but it doesn't mean that someone else didn't buy them for her, on her behalf."

"Alright. But why Salt Lake City? Wouldn't she go to Denver? The DEA's regional office for this area was in Denver."

"That's a question that I can't answer. But I do remember that the train tickets were for one adult and two children. Investigators thought it was relevant, or they wouldn't have taken pictures of the tickets. We know she was planning to leave sometime soon and was willing to do anything to get the money to go. She said in her letter to Derek that she had a plan to get the money, but that Trevor wouldn't like it. Not to mention, she had that friend, the one who played in that band. He had a gig in Salt Lake City within just a few weeks after the murders. Maybe that's who she was working with?"

"What was his name again?"

"Dwaine. I think it was Dwaine."

"So, maybe she was headed to Salt Lake with this Dwaine? But who was she reporting to? A musician wouldn't be her contact person. He didn't even live in town. Just in town on military leave."

"Well, that I don't know. Something tells me that it might be good to keep looking into that lawsuit in Pitkin County by that Pete, you know, Suzanne Denison's brother-in-law? Maybe focus on things or people from Grand Junction that may have had ties to Aspen in those years? I know they got that rapist for Suzanne's murder, but something tells me it's not wrapped up in a neat little bow, like they presented it. Like people want it to be. I just can't help but ask questions like, 'Who could have been in Aspen the night that Jennifer died? Who really knows how she died, or who could have been with her and what were the circumstances'? Nobody knows, 'cause there's no public record that anyone looked into it. Law enforcement may claim to have dug into every lead, but they had this investigation wrapped up in less than two months, from the time that the bodies were found until they arrested Curtis. That's not even remotely enough time to investigate all the leads that cropped up. Betsy had too many people in her life to have a valid suspect nailed down in that short period of time. The simple fact is, they wanted a conviction. A quick one. An easy one. They didn't want the truth, Pop. The truth was too complicated."

"Well, you pose some really good thoughts, Karla. Maybe Suzanne's husband really did have a legitimate reason for the lawsuit against Pitkin County. Good Stuff, Karla. Good Stuff." Ramone grinned in her direction, knowing somehow that she wasn't finished giving her input. He let her talk. Proud to hear what she had to say.

Karla seemed just as proud that she had something to give. "And think about what mattered to them. Those women. They both needed money to get away. Money was a means to an end for them, to find a place of solitude for them and their children. Unfortunately, there were those who used women to get money, simply for money's sake. What's the motive to kill women and children? In this case, I can assure you money was involved. Money and power. Not just getting it, but keeping it. And even more important, not just the money and power, but the secrets behind it all. Keeping secrets. It's not rocket science to know that people kill to protect their secrets."

"Not everyone." He glanced up to the sky.

She smiled back. "So, I guess your next step is to enlist someone to help you tighten up this whole tangled mess? Someone with the means to begin legal proceedings?"

With his eyebrow raised like it always did when he was contemplating something, Ramone stopped and thought for a minute. He put his hands into his pants' pocket and leaned onto one leg. "You do have a real knack for this kind of work."

Karla grinned, delighted that he was proud of her. Proud to be like him. "Which reminds me, I've been thinking." She paused to take a breath. "I wanted to ask you. Is there some kind of job position or something that you can do in law enforcement that works directly with crime victims? I mean, I've been thinking that if I got a degree in sociology and criminology, I could do something that works directly with the victims. Like in victim's assistance, or something like that."

Ramone nodded in her direction, glowing from the inside out. "What about being a chef? And writing music?"

"Well, I can always cook. Don't need a degree to do that. And I don't have to make my money doing it. You like to eat after all. Who says I can't do both? And Pop, even I know writing music for a living isn't my calling. I like it, but it's just for fun." Karla stopped and realized Ramone's mind had wandered. She studied his face as he looked past her out to the river. He was deep in thought. *He still has so many questions. We still don't know who killed them. He wants to know who actually did it.*

Ramone finally spoke up. "Do you think it will be ok if we never figure this whole thing out? Of course, we don't stop trying, but what if we never solve it? It is a possibility. We have to be realistic."

"Never say never. There's always the afterlife. Right?"

"Boy, will I want to talk to some people." He grinned, then looked around. "God, it's amazing out here. I could settle down in this area. You?"

"No. I like it here. But I like it at home better."

Karla turned to lean up against the bridge's structure, looking down at the river again.

"Why them? Why my mother? I just don't get it. The why of it all? It doesn't seem fair."

"It's not. This life is flawed with good and evil and everything in between. It's unpredictable, and we can't control the choices and actions of others. It isn't fair."

"Why would God allow it?"

"You're asking the wrong person, kiddo. I'm no scholar about God. Ah, shit, I'm not even sure I know anything at all about God. But I've been told that his love is the kind of love that gives choice. A will. Doesn't force us, shows us, if we're willing, willing to know. At least that's what I've been told. Bill's got it. He tried to explain some things to me just the other day. Funny that you are thinking about it too."

"I guess God doesn't want a bunch of robots that are programmed to just follow commands. He wants us to choose. To want what's right and go after it, I guess."

"Yeah, like little kids with their parents. I've never wanted you to be a part of my life because you have to and because you have no choice. I want you to want to. I want you to want to have me in your life."

367

"So, he lets us choose to love, or not?"

"Yeah, I guess. That's what it sounds like, anyway."

He lets us choose love. God is love. He lets us choose him. Karla had read that somewhere once. Now, she actually believed it.

"So, what if people choose to hate? Choose to hurt."

"People get hurt. People suffer. And it's not fair. But then again, those who love rise above it. And then when they do, there's no power in hate anymore. Hurt is overcome. It's like it never existed. It cancels it out. Do I sound like a wise old Pop?"

"Yeah, Pop. You're a wise ass, alright."

Ramone put his arm around her, and they both stood at the railing looking down river for a few minutes in silence, until a breeze fluttered past them, flipping a loose piece of paper that had slid away out of her bag. It was folded in two, and she thought she had tucked it away into a safe place. Clearly, she hadn't. *That must've slipped out when I put the diary away. I can't lose that.*

"What was that?"

"Oh, just a list of things to do before I leave." She folded it another time and placed it into the pocket of her jeans.

They walked back to their rental cars in silence. Neither had much of anything to say. They strolled at a lazy pace, taking in the scenery. Karla knew this might be her last time to see this place. Or maybe not.

The leaves rustled the brush near the river's edge, breaking the silence.

Karla allowed Ramone to walk ahead, turning back to the river, away from him a bit. Taking the folded paper from her pocket and unfolding it, she read it, hoping he wouldn't notice. He did. But he only turned slightly to watch, as he had a few dwindling tears still visible. "You coming?"

"Yeah, in a minute." Karla started walking into the shrubbery, toward the river's edge. "I just wanna pick some of these flowers down here, to dry them."

"Alright. Don't go wandering off too far." Ramone turned back around and loaded into his car. Karla stood near the water's edge and read the scribbles on the piece of loose notebook paper. She smiled out toward the river, took in a deep breath, then folded it back up and placed it back into the diary, where she found it in the first place.

When she reached the parking lot, Karla climbed into her rental car, waving him away. She still had a couple of stops to make before meeting him back at the hotel for dinner. Traveling back into town, she eventually pulled into a parking space with a long stretch of well-manicured grass in the distance. Karla had been here before, twice, so the location was easy to find. Several trees lined the park-like scenery amidst the scattered headstones.

Karla kneeled in front of the final resting place of Betsy Kendall and her two young boys. She took out a nail file from her bag to dig a hole in the grass, exposing the dirt underneath. Then, she took out the loose piece of paper from the diary that she had almost lost at the river and unfolded it. "I believe this is yours. It's really good, by the way. You had so much to say. I wish I could write what I wanted to say, so beautiful like this." Karla read it out loud into the silent air, holding back the tears:

Lurking, crawling, creeping so close

Hovering, never quite there

They're just out of reach these echoes of light

Linger so quiet by day or by night

They trick, they tease, they shift then fade

Mimicking fear, then disappear

Illusions of death, reflections of life

Why do we fear them? Why live in strife?

Simple shadows made from light

They cannot harm, nor do they dare

Instead they reach out to give us rest

Reflections of God, covered, caressed

Like wings of eagles high above

Rest in the shadows, shades of love

Where is the victory in death? We cry.

Swallowed in peace, by God the Most High.

Shadows, By Betsy Kendall

At the bottom of the page hastily scribbled was this side note:

Peace is not the absence of evil, but the presence of God.

Karla didn't read that part out loud. She just sat still, allowing the tears to escape and roll down her face to freedom. "Thank you for sharing it. I'm sure you're able to share your way with words wherever you are now. Heaven must be quite grateful to have you. Your boys are lucky to have you." Karla gently placed it in the hole that she had dug, and covered it the best that she could, although not deep enough to completely cover it forever. *That'll do. It's not going anywhere. Maybe someday, someone will find it. Lucky them.*

The cemetery that Ruth was buried in was much larger, and Karla had to walk further into the grass to get to her grave site. The trees hovered above, whistling in the soft breeze. Karla stood for several seconds before bending down into a cross-legged sitting position. She took out the diary and held it in her hands. "And this would belong to you, now doesn't it? I know. There's a lot of good stuff in here. But you've been at rest for a lot of years now, and I suppose it's time for us to do the same. He'll get the job done without it, in due time. My father is like that, you know. I hope you don't mind, but I gave Betsy back the poem she wrote for you. I figured you'd want her to have it. I wanted her to have it. Or at least if someone came to visit her, they would have it, you know. As far as this goes, well, I'll make sure it's deep enough that no one can get to it, no one. It's yours, and there's nothing in it that we don't already know. They can't use it in court anyway. I used to think it was a shame for you. But now, I know it was only a shame for those who knew you, those who loved you and those who never got the chance."

Karla bent over and dug a deeper hole, one that spanned at least a foot on all sides and nearly as deep. She pulled away the grass and dug at the soil with not only the nail file but both hands until it was deep enough to be secure. *This kind of healing has to be deep.* She then placed Ruth's diary inside its final resting place once and for all, and covered it completely, first with dirt, then with the block of grass, then with a flat stone she had picked up and carried back from the river. Karla pounded the section as hard as she could, making sure it was secure and wouldn't break loose.

371

It took more than a few minutes, which was ok. These things should take time. Things that matter do. Walking away, Karla brushed the dirt from off of her hands in a few simple slaps and then wiped them across her bare legs. She picked up her pace, almost to a jog. A bounce of sorts. She didn't turn around. She didn't need to.

Oh grave where is thy victory? Death where is thy sting?

Death is swallowed in the victory of the Cross,

In everlasting life there is peace, where there is loss.

Afterword

Long term residents of Grand Junction, Colorado report that the years from 1973-1976 were some of the most violent years the community has endured. The homicide rate was high for a population of less than 50,000 (the "Grand Valley" of Mesa County). In 1975, eleven murders were reported, some of which remain unsolved. One notable case was the quadruple homicide of Patricia Botham, Linda Miracle and her two boys, Troy and Chad Miracle. Patricia's husband, Ken Botham, was convicted for all four murders. A trial had been held in Mesa County in 1976, which was determined to have had procedural errors and judicial prejudice resulting in a second trial by a Colorado Supreme Court ruling, which provided a change of venue. In 1981, Mr. Botham was convicted in Golden, Colorado and continues to serve his life sentence in a Colorado State Prison.

Two other books address Grand Junction's homicides in the summer of 1975--Marti Talbott's Suspects and Alex French's The Killing Season. Both books shed light on a dark time that most Mesa County residents have forgotten. Some residents have not forgotten, however. Without doubt, there has been no shortage of rumors and speculations creeping up over the years, inevitably resulting in controversy, especially concerning the Miracle-Botham case. Most native residents have no problem maintaining there was no miscarriage of justice in convicting Ken Botham. There are some, however, who disagree with this outcome, doubting Mr. Botham's guilt. Among those who question the validity of the conviction are former businessmen, former law enforcement officers, family and friends of the victims, and even a former editor of the Grand Junction Daily Sentinel, who is reported to have stated that he suspected the case was related to drugs.

The two Botham children, Thayer and Thad Botham, have not been quiet about their own doubts. In 2003, the website www.kenbotham.com was created by Thayer Botham that details the case and advances concerns about the investigation and the trial. Journalist Blake Higgins launched on i-Tunes a free and compelling pilot episode of a podcast called 'Junction.' His podcast critically examines the evidence, including evidence not presented at either trial. The continuation of this podcast has been interrupted due both to a lack of financial resources as well as to an inability to locate and interview witnesses still alive and who were not called to testify at either trial.

Dr. Thad Botham's doubts go well beyond a simple love for his father and a hope for innocence. He has found compelling evidence, evidence never presented at either trial, that Ken Botham is innocent. Some of this evidence includes original law enforcement reports, documented interviews, and testimonials from living witnesses. More important, authoritative documents show that there were many biological samples secured in 1975. There are strong reasons to think that these samples would result in an exoneration if they were tested by today's DNA standards.

374

Made in the USA
Coppell, TX
07 December 2020

43049399R00210